ENOUGH ON MY PLATE

DeJuan Kight

ISBN: 979-8-9882698-0-9 (Paperback)

ISBN: 979-8-9882698-1-6 (eBook)

Library of Congress Control Number: 2023909041

Front cover image by Thomas Strickland.

Book design by D. Kight Publishing Company.

Printed by D. Kight Publishing Company, in the United States of America.

First printing edition 2023.

DEDICATION

To My Butta'flies, & My Grandbabies,
My Inspiration for Everything.

TABLE OF CONTENTS

ACKNOWLEDGMENTS

**MOST HIGH, GREAT SPIRIT,
(THE PAINTER, POET, & SCULPTOR OF ALL THINGS)
GREAT ANCESTORS, GREAT GUARDIANS,
MY ENTIRE DIVINE TEAM
I'M SO THANKFUL FOR YOU
& CAN DO NOTHING WITHOUT YOU!**

My Butta'flies, My Grandbabies, My Mama, My Mike-Mike, Fannie
Magnolia Turner, Michael-V, Lexxus, My Brothers & Sisters (by Blood &
by Love), My Nieces & Nephews, Shalle', Aunt Dot, Auntie Ree Brand,
Verdie Bady & The Bady Family, Lena Mae Bohannon, LeAndrew,
Queenie, Mookie, Claudia, Goldie, My Cousins, My Family, ALL of The
Northside Manor Mamas, Northside Manor Family, TVA4LIFE, Tonya
Dyson, The Word Family, El Hakim, Juju Bushman, Reap, TamE, Artistik
Lounge Family, Virghost, YZA, P.B.E, At-Chill, Middle Eye, AZ-Truly,
CCDE, Paragon, Dutchess, Artistik Approach, Thomas Strickland, Cequita,
Gary & Precious Cargo, Richie Domino, Wolfian, House of Mtenzi Family,
DJ Redeye, Cool Demeanor, My Entire Poetry Family both Near & Far,
GranGran & BaBa, Angela Beverly, Mama Gloria,
Avenging Wind, Bonton, Petty, Meridith C. Conyers,
All of My Memphis, Musician Friends, & Entertainers,
Frayser, Ridgecrest, Andre Woods, My DT Family,
& The City that's like no other…Memphis, Tennessee,
THANK YOU!!!
& A SPECIAL THANK YOU to those who were there for me when no
one knew how close I was to leaving this realm, you were there for me,
crying for & with me, cheering for me to keep going even when I didn't
want to, & encouraging me more than I could ever say, I am eternally
grateful for you… & there are so many MORE that I could name, but there
is simply not enough ink & paper in this world…
please know that I love & appreciate all who helped me
at my highest & my lowest, & whatever you did for me, please know that
IT WILL NEVER BE FORGOTTEN!
(I'm so fortunate to know a lot of Really Good People…)
I'M SO THANKFUL FOR YOU &
KNOW THAT YOUR PRESENCE IS GREATLY APPRECIATED.

i

1 TRUST ISSUES

It was the year 2000, and the sound of Bill Clinton's voice on the television forced Maya's eyes open, she instinctively glanced over at her Powertel Nokia phone that rested on the nightstand and let out a long lazy yawn when it revealed that it was already three o'clock in the afternoon,

"Fuck!" she mumbled after releasing another long yawn. It was a hot and humid Saturday afternoon in Memphis, Tennessee and Maya still had a million and one things to do before her boyfriend, Tony-B came home. Maya rolled over onto her stomach and snuggled deep beneath her plush, chocolate and turquoise king-sized comforter. She knew it was time to get up but for some reason she was simply exhausted. Tony-B had already called and cussed her out twice because she was still in bed, but for some reason she just couldn't get herself together. She had been going nonstop for the past few months with minimal sleep, but today, her body, mind and soul had simply shut down, forcing her into bed in the middle of the day. Maya groaned as she turned onto her back and stared at the whooshing ceiling fan as it sent cool breezes across the room. She looked on intently as one of the breezes became entangled in the window treatment and caused the matching turquoise and chocolate brown sheers to dance seductively. Her eyes followed the slow movements of the free-flowing fabric as it glided from side to side with rhythmic purpose. Maya enjoyed the peacefulness filling the room as she lay sluggishly on the bed. That nap was way too short, but it was exactly what she needed to ease her adrenaline-soaked bones. Her eyelids felt like they weighed a thousand pounds, and she could feel them closing with the promise of another sweet nap, even if it was just a quick one. Maya forgot all about the tedious afternoon ahead, her only priority at this moment was to surrender to the slumber taking over her body one cell at a time, she drifted off quickly and when she opened her eyes again, the entire bedroom had morphed into a secluded beach with crystal blue waters splashing across her freshly pedicured feet. It felt so real that Maya could smell the salty ocean water and feel the warm sun as it kissed her shoulders. Maya was so elated that it was her birthday, and for once, she had nowhere to go, nothing to do, and no-one calling her name as she began to doze off once again...

"Ain't this a bitch!" Tony-B mumbled under his breath after walking into the bedroom and finding Maya snoring and snuggled deep beneath the covers. He had given her strict instructions to have everything ready by three o'clock. The guests were due to arrive by five, but Maya was still in bed. Tony-B let out a long sigh and rolled his eyes to the ceiling, his patience with Maya was long gone,

"MAYA!!!" Tony-B yelled at the top of his lungs, he stormed over to the bed and shook it as hard as he could,

"I'm up! I'm up! I'm up!" Maya said as she jumped to her feet, with the covers still draped around her shoulders,

"I thought I told your ass to be ready by three o'clock Maya, three o'clock! It's almost four and you're still in the bed like you ain't got shit to do! Why can't you just do what I ask you to do, Maya?" Tony-B asked as he snatched the comforter from her shoulders with one smooth motion and tossed it back on the bed,

"Everything is done, all l have to do is get dressed and fix my hair," Maya said as she ran to the closet and grabbed her outfit and laid it on the bed,

"What's the damn holdup Maya? You should've been ready hours ago!" Tony-B said as Maya noticed the

2

deep red creases meeting in the middle of his forehead, he glared at her as she scrambled from one side of the bedroom to another,

"I don't know why you're so angry, all I wanted to do was just lay here for a few more minutes," Maya said sluggishly,

"Hell naw! You got too much shit to do, I told you, I wanted everything perfect for the party, and you were supposed to already have your ass up and ready!" Tony-B snapped,

"But it's my birthday! This party is supposed to be for me," Maya reasoned,

"I don't give a fuck! You know these people expect my parties to be banging, and they expect them to start on time, they always have and always will, and that's not going to change, not for you, and especially not today!"

"Why couldn't you just hire somebody to cater it, I mean, just this one time," Maya grumbled, as she rolled her eyes at him and let out a long sigh,

"A caterer! Have you lost your damn mind!" Tony-B yelled in disbelief which startled Maya and caused her heart to thump, "I'm Tony-B, The Motherfucking Bar-B-Q King! What the fuck do I look like hiring a damn caterer?!? And you already know they love your cooking almost as much as they like my Bar-B-Q! You are tripping... talking about a damn caterer, now come on here, and I'm not gonna say this shit again!" he demanded,

"Okay! Okay!" Maya said, out of breath as she sat on the side of the bed struggling to tie her left shoe,

"Did you do everything that I asked you to do?" Tony-B asked,

"Yes, I did everything, you know I was up all night cooking,"

"So fucking what! Hell, I was up all morning making sure we had enough liquor and making sure that the ice machine that I just bought is working like it's supposed to," Tony-B said, "And plus me and Earl was out making sure that we had everything we need to get this thang poppin! Now hurry the hell up!" Tony-B said before he stormed out of the bedroom, but a few seconds later Maya could hear him calling her name as loud as he could, "MAAAAAAAYA!" Tony-B yelled,

"I'm coming Tony! I'm coming, I just have to put on my other shoe," Maya said with all the energy she could muster, *"I'm*

3

so sick of him and his damn ice-machine," she mumbled as she tied her other shoe,

"You need to hurry your ass up! Earl just called and said he'll be here in a few minutes!" Tony-B said peeking out of the dining room window,

"Okay! Okay! Just give me a few more minutes!" Maya said as she rushed into the bathroom, she quickly brushed her teeth and washed her face, afterwards she moisturized her face with cocoa-butter, which really highlighted her almond shaped eyes and strong Cherokee cheekbones, her caramel colored skin glowed as she outlined her full lips with a dark brown lip liner and filled the inside with a golden lip-gloss, she then picked up her wooden boar bristle hairbrush, and began to brush her long, thick, black coarse hair. Maya heard a noise behind her and glanced into the mirror as Tony-B stood anxiously behind her in the doorway, constantly checking his watch and tapping his foot, Maya rolled her eyes at his reflection and continued to brush her thick hair into place,

"You ain't got time for all this shit, Maya!" Tony-B barked as he snatched the brush from her hand and tossed it in the sink,

"I'm not going out there with my hair all over my head!" Maya said as she grabbed the brush from the sink and continued to smooth her hair into a side ponytail that hung over her shoulder,

"I don't know why you're doing all of this shit anyway, we're wearing hats, remember? And speaking of hats…" Tony-B said as he scanned the bathroom with his eyes, "Where's your hat, Maya?" he asked with a sigh so heavy, that it filled the bathroom,

"It's right here!" Maya said as she rushed past him and into the bedroom and grabbed the hat from the top of her closet and walked back into the bathroom holding it with one finger like it was contaminated, "Do I really have to wear this?" she asked as she stood to the side and rested one hand on her thick bow hip,

"Don't start that shit with me, Maya!" Tony-B said, in disbelief, "I've already told everybody that we were

4

reppin' Green Bay and that's exactly what the hell we're gonna do!" Tony-B said glaring at her so hard that his beautiful hazel eyes transformed into two tiny slits, Maya could always tell how mad Tony-B was by the color of his neck, and the bright crimson color that it had just turned, told her that he was furious,

"But it's my birthday, and I don't want to walk around all evening with a wedge of cheese on my head, Tony, it just looks foolish!" Maya tried to reason,

"Maya, you're wearing the damn hat, and that's all to it!" Tony said adamantly,

Maya rolled her eyes even harder at him before tossing the wedge-shaped hat on her head, she tried to push past him and rush down the hall, but he caught up to her and spun her around by her left arm,

"I've never seen anybody who can't do nothing right!" he said as he arranged then rearranged her hat, turning it backwards, then forwards, then to the side, then forwards and backwards again before he was satisfied, and afterwards, he snapped at her with a quick, "And keep it just like that!" as Maya stood there with her arms folded, rolling her eyes at him over and over again,

"You can stop rolling your damn eyes at me too, Ms. Lady, you know you love you some Tony-B…don't you?" Tony-B said, as he gently stroked her cheek with his knuckle, her heart melting as his face suddenly softened with a sexy grin,

"Whatever…" Maya said with a slight blush, she couldn't stand Tony-B at times, but he still had the power to make her moist between the thighs at will,

"You know you love me, with that big ass booty!" Tony-B said as he playfully slapped Maya on her plump rear end as she walked past him, she squealed and tried to act mad, but he knew better, "Baby listen, I know I've been hard on you lately," Tony-B said as he pulled her close and stared into her eyes, "I just wanted this party to be right, these parties not only represent me, but they represent *US*, you know they want to be us so bad and they wish they had all of this right here," Tony-B said eluding to his gigantic home, "but they don't, and they can't, it can only be one King and Queen in this thang, you feel me?" Tony-B asked as he stared deep into Maya's eyes, his hazel eyes mesmerizing her with each word, he flashed her another one of his million-dollar smiles, armed with

5

the sexiest dimples, especially the one sinking deep into his left cheek. Maya's heart began to race as he leaned in and laid one, and then another one of those mind blowing kisses on her cheek, soft kisses, making a trail down her neck, the kind of kisses that made her knees tremble, that made her heart thump hard, the kind that sent that same thumping down to the pit of her stomach, intensifying until it rested deep between her thighs, the kind of kisses loaded with passionate fire and anticipation of a good and nasty time later, when all the guests had left, and Maya couldn't wait! Every part of her being tingled and blushed as she parted her lips readying herself for one of his tongue kisses that lasted forever, the kind that turned her blood into lava and liquified her insides, but as soon as his lips were in reach, the moment was suddenly interrupted,

"Damn it!" Maya thought as the doorbell chimed, stopping one of their rare, intimate moments dead in its tracks,

"Showtime!" Tony-B said as he smacked Maya on the butt again and led her down the hall by the hand, she glided behind him down the hall feeling just like royalty,

"Do I look okay?" she asked smoothing down her jersey as she stood behind him in the foyer,

"You look alright," Tony-B answered with his back to her, "Are you ready to do this shit?" he asked over his shoulder,

"I'm ready…" Maya answered as confidently as she could, continuing to smooth her clothes with her free hand, she wasn't used to dressing like this, her jeans were extra snug, fitting like a second skin, the sneakers she wore were clunky and uncomfortable, and that big, heavy football jersey was already getting on her nerves because it did nothing for her 5 foot 3 inch height, she was trying her best to be just as confident as Tony-B was as he stood proudly beside her in his matching outfit, his clothes fitting his 6 foot-2 inch athletic frame perfectly, without the cheese hat of course, because he said that it would mess up his fresh haircut,

"Oh wait!" Maya said as she quickly rubbed the lip gloss from Tony-B's cheek with her thumb,

"Good lookin' out Baby!" he said with a smile, "I don't know why you put all that shit on your lips anyway, is it all off?" he asked as he rubbed his cheek in a circular motion with his fingertips to make sure,

"Yes, it's off," Maya said, still swooning,

They stood proudly, and right before opening the doors to greet their guests, Tony-B glanced over his shoulder and gave Maya a wink and a quick nod of approval,

"What up my guy!" Tony-B said as Earl, one of his closest friends, walked through the door with a woman that Maya had never seen before,

"What's up Tony-B!" Earl said, as he and Tony-B slapped hands in the air, Maya rolled her eyes subtly, thinking to herself how Earl's greedy ass was always the first one to arrive at Tony-B's parties, "And how are you, Ms. Lady?" Earl asked as he looked over at Maya and gave her a fake smile, Maya knew he was just being cordial, she knew he didn't really care for her and she was okay with that because she didn't really care for him either,

"I'm good, Earl, and how are—" Maya began, but as usual, before she could finish her sentence, Earl cut her off,

"Ms. Lady! I don't know why you keep letting Tony-B send you out! You don't even wear shit like this! How you gonna let this dude put you in a throwback jersey, a Green Bay one at that, and a damned cheese hat!" Earl teased, but Maya wasn't in the mood for Earl or his non-stop jokes at her expense, today, she rolled her eyes hard at him and gave him instant attitude, but Tony-B's friends were used to Maya's trigger-happy moods and attitudes by now, which is how she got the nickname, 'Ms. Lady',

"Why are you hating on the Packers Earl!" Tony-B chimed in, "You know they're off the chain!"

"Mane, ain't nobody hating on your old sorry ass team!" Earl said as he fanned Tony-B off, "But if you're gonna do something Ms. Lady, at least do it right!" Earl said as he rubbed the Navy-Blue Star on the front of his white t-shirt, "Mane, you know it's Dem Boys all the way, Baby!" Earl said proudly, "And you might as well go on and pay me now Tony-B, cause you already know Them damn Cheese Heads gonna lose!" Earl said with his hand out,

"This game is sold…not told, Earl! And even if they don't win, I'm still gonna make a killin' on the point spread!" Tony-B boasted,

"You ain't talking about nothing!" Earl said fanning Tony-B off once again,

"We'll see…and anyway, why are you being so rude?" Tony-B asked with a sly grin,

"Rude? What are you talking about?" Earl asked with a confused look on his face,

"I'm talking about your lady friend right here, you haven't even introduced her, she's just standing there all quiet," Tony-B said as he stared at the woman dressed in white low-rise jeans hugging her hips like a second skin, and a Navy-Blue and white sheer oversized jersey style shirt, Maya frowned because you could clearly see the woman's perky, round plum-shaped breasts, with matching silver star Pasties covering her nipples. The woman smiled as she leaned to the side with her hand on her hip as Maya eyed her long slender torso and white toenails with a Navy-Blue star painted on her big toe, with Silver strappy wedge sandals. Maya couldn't help but to think that the woman was a bit overdressed for a simple football party with those gigantic silver hoop earrings and long white fingernails with matching Navy-Blue stars. Maya noticed the tiny diagonal braids in the front of her head with wild, bushy waist length curly hair hanging down her back. She was beautiful, and Maya wanted to like her, but for some reason she could feel that something wasn't right about her, Maya frowned as the woman gushed when Tony-B scolded Earl about being rude…and if looks could kill, Tony-B would have dropped dead right there in the doorway as Maya's laser hot stare buried deep into the left side of his temple,

"My fault Tony-B! Everybody, this is my cousin Torya, she just moved down here from Seattle." Earl said, and while everyone else was busy laughing and smiling, Maya noticed how Earl's eyes kind of darted back and forth between Tony-B and his cousin, Torya as he spoke,

"Nice to meet you Torya, I really hope you're enjoying your visit in M-Town," Tony-B said as he stared deep into Torya's eyes, "May I?" He asked as he gently lifted her hand up to his lips, and kissed it slowly and affectionately while still staring into her eyes,

"Hello, I'm Maya," Maya said as she stepped in front of Tony-B and snatched Torya's hand, shaking it roughly, which stopped Torya's blushing in mid-flight, Maya looked Torya eye-to-eye and gave her a phony smile which was the best she could do at the moment,

"Hello…" Torya said, returning Maya's fake smile, as she politely jerked her hand from Maya's and pretended to search her oversized silver designer bag for an imaginary item,

"Is this your first time in Memphis?" Maya asked,

"No…it's not," Torya said as she rolled her eyes to the ceiling. Maya couldn't help but to notice that the woman's eyes were darting towards Tony-B the same way Earl's eyes had, Earl noticed it also, which is why he quickly interrupted,

"She's gonna be down here for a while, so I had to bring her over here to show her how we do thangs in M-Town!" Earl said with his chest poked out,

"Shit, you know how we get down, it's 2-K in this bitch!" Tony-B said before nodding at Earl, before he and Earl began to chant,

"Ain't no party like a Tony-B party, cause a Tony-B Party don't stop! What! Ain't no party like a Tony-B party, cause a Tony-B Party don't quit! Ain't no party like a Tony-B party, cause a Tony-B Party runnin' shit!" Tony-B and Earl chanted repeatedly, swinging their hands back and forth in the air, Gangsta-Walking in a circle, as the other guests who had just arrived, clapped and cheered them on,

"Don't pay any attention to them," Maya said to Torya as she laughed at Tony-B and Earl, "they act like this all the time…and how long did you say you were gonna be in town?" Maya asked for clarification,

"I didn't say, and why?" Earl's cousin snapped, while glaring at Maya up and down, before flinging her long bouncy curls, and flipping her hair with her free hand,

9

"Excuse me?" Maya asked as she placed her hands on her hips and did a double take, Tony-B stepped in front of Maya, and gently pulled her behind him, holding on to her wrists with both of his hands behind his back,

"She didn't mean no harm Lil' Mama," Tony-B assured Earl's cousin, "Maya can be a lil' nosey at times, but since she asked…how long are you planning on being here in M-Town?" Tony-B asked with a flirt in his voice as Maya stood behind him fuming,

"Don't play with me!" Torya spat, her tone as venomous as a deadly snake,

"Damn, Lil' Mama, you ain't gotta act like that! I just asked you a simple question," Tony-B said, pretending to be offended,

"Whatever!" Torya said, as she fanned her hand in the air, dismissing them both like mere peasants as she walked off,

"Hey Earl, why don't you take her over to the bar and get Larry to fix y'all a drink, and it's plenty of food out there in the sunroom!" Tony-B said as Maya continued to stare at the side of his head,

"Alright, Tony-B," Earl said, and out of the corner of her eye, Maya caught Earl as he pointed at Tony-B and snickered under his breath before he walked off, Maya opened her mouth to question Tony-B when he stopped her short,

"You're something else with yourself Maya," Tony-B said, his mood suddenly shifting,

"What are you talking about?" Maya asked,

"You just can't act right for shit, can you?" Tony-B asked with disappointment dripping from his voice,

"What did I do?" Maya asked, still trying to figure out why he was standing there scolding her like a little puppy who had just urinated on the floor,

"These people came all the way over here to have a good time, not to be interrogated by your wanna-be private-eye ass!" Tony-B hissed,

"What? I only asked her a question!" Maya snapped back,

"But why? Why in the hell are you questioning her anyway, Agent Maya! Who are you the F.B.I. or some shit?" Tony-B asked, still glaring at her,

"Are you serious?!?" Maya asked in disbelief,

"Hell yeah, I'm serious! You were getting ready to go off on old girl, and for what, because I was being nice to her?" Tony-B asked, as the frustration in his voice stabbed at her chest,

"No, I wasn't!" Maya lied,

"Yes, the fuck you were...I could tell! That nasty ass attitude of yours has got to go!" he said adamantly,

"She was the one with the nasty ass attitude! I was just trying to be nice to her! But I guess you were too busy grinning all up in her damn face and kissing hands to see that!" Maya said with her hands on her hips,

"Why in the hell would she have an attitude with you Maya? She doesn't even know you! But I tell you what, you just keep on with that insecure ass shit that you're pulling, and you're going to end up all by your damn self, am I understood?" Tony-B asked with a look on his face so serious that Maya knew he meant business,

"What? I didn't even...all I said was..." Maya was so shaken that her sentences began to jumble together,

"Look!" Tony-B said, with a deep frown blanketing his face, "This shit stops now! These people are guests in my house, and you will treat them with respect, or you can roll the hell on, you feel me?"

"But I didn't do anything!" Maya said still trying to comprehend what just happened,

"Am I fucking understood?" Tony-B asked as he leaned in and growled through gritted teeth,

"Yeah, you're understood," Maya answered, lowering her head like that same little scolded puppy, her feelings were hurt, but still she attempted to reason with him, "I don't understand why you're so upset with me Tony...it's my birthday, and I didn't even do anything." Maya waited patiently for a response from Tony-B, but she noticed that something over her right shoulder had his undivided attention, and when Maya turned around, she noticed that the same lady, Earl's cousin, was in the corner winding and bouncing her hips seductively to Juvenile's *'Back that Thang Up'*, and her butt, which was shaped like an incursive capital W, was jiggling and bouncing up and down in a complete circle, and all of that jiggling had Tony-B completely mesmerized,

"Tony, Tony…TONY!!!" Maya said after being totally ignored, "What the hell are you staring at? I know you hear me talking to you!" Maya said with her hands still on her hips,

"What are you talking about?" Tony-B answered, never taking his attention off of the jiggling incursive capital W,

"I said, what in the hell are you staring at?" Maya asked calmly, giving Tony-B the most intense death-glare once again,

"Huh?" Tony-B asked, not really paying attention to Maya, to him she sounded like the teacher on a Charlie Brown cartoon,

"Wonk, wonk, wonk, wonk, wonk!" Maya said as Torya turned to face them, still winding her hips slowly to the music, and biting down on her bottom lip seductively, her breasts, bouncing like little water balloons and those silver Pasties were going wild,

"I said what in the hell are you staring at!" Maya asked moving her head from side to side trying to block Tony-B's view,

"Damn, I'm just looking!" Tony-B said, irritated because Maya was blocking his view,

"Just looking, huh?" Maya asked, her already tight eyes narrowing in anger,

"Yeah! *JUST LOOKING!* I can look, can't I?" He asked sarcastically,

"You know what! You're gonna try me one time too damn many!" Maya said as she placed her finger on the side of his face and turned his head, so that he was eye to eye with her, "You got me fucked up, you do know that, right?" she said glaring into his eyes,

"Maaaaane…I ain't got time for this shit," Tony-B said as he fanned Maya's hand from his face, "I'm gonna go over here and holler at Earl, you always tripping and for nothing!" Tony-B said as he walked off,

"Yeah okay," Maya said rolling her eyes at him,

"Damn!" Tony-B mumbled under his breath as he bit down on his bottom lip, still staring at the jiggling woman, as her slithering hips slowly put him deeper into a trance,

"What the hell did you just say?" Maya asked, as she caught up to him and spun him around by his shoulder,

"Huh…?" Tony-B asked puzzled, "Why are you constantly trying to start shit with me Maya?" Tony-B asked still preoccupied with the slithering girl in the silver leggings and matching Pasties,

"Don't even worry about it!" Maya said throwing her hands in the air and walking off, but Tony-B knew better, she'd said those words before, and he later regretted it. Maya could be as lowdown as a rattlesnake when she wanted to be, so Tony-B quickly came to his senses and ran up behind her,

"Maya, Maya…Baby! You're making more out of this than it is, I was just watching the girl dance, that's all!" Tony-B said as he caught up to her,

"It doesn't even matter at this point, Tony…" Maya said trying to walk off from him again, but he grabbed her by the hand,

"What, so now you mad?" he asked while glaring into Maya's eyes,

"Nope… not at all," Maya answered as cool as a cucumber, but Tony-B knew better,

"Yes, you are, you're mad because I got on you about questioning people, aren't you?" he asked as he searched her eyes,

"No, I'm not…it's nothing, really it's not," Maya said through clinched teeth as she snatched away from him,

"If it's nothing, then why are you acting like this…I know you ain't mad because I was watching Lil' Mama dance, are you?" Tony-B asked sarcastically,

"No, I'm not mad, like I said, go ahead, do you!" Maya said rolling her eyes at him again,

"Do me? Shit, I don't need your motherfucking permission to do me! Hell, I'm gonna always *do me*!" Tony-B snapped back,

"And everybody else too, apparently…" Maya mumbled under her breath, rolling her eyes to the ceiling,

"Don't mumble Maya, speak the fuck up…what was that smart-ass shit you just said? Better yet, let's get all of this shit out in the open…you're jealous of her, aren't you? Damn Maya, I thought you were better than that…" Tony-B said as he shook his head in pity,

"Please! I don't have any reason to be jealous of her or any woman for that matter!" Maya said with her hands on her hips,

"Just because you don't have a reason to be jealous, doesn't mean you aren't jealous…but at least I'm just looking at the woman…any other man would be over there trying to get up on her, at least I'm *TRYING* to show my woman a lil' respect,"

"Respect? Do you even know what the fuck that word means? Do you?!?" Maya asked, not believing the words coming out of his mouth,

"I'm just saying Maya, I didn't realize you were such a hater," Tony-B said as he shook his head again in pity,

"I can't even deal with you right now!" Maya said as she threw her hands in the air and walked away from him,

"It's plenty of women out here who would love to take your place Maya, and you're making it real easy for them, you just remember that!" Tony-B said as she walked away,

"Yeah, well they can have this shit…" Maya mumbled under her breath as she went into the kitchen and grabbed a wine cooler from the fridge and downed it in three gulps, before grabbing another one and pulling her cell from her back pocket to call her best friend Tricia,

"What up Maya-Maya?" Tricia answered with a song in her voice,

"Hey Lady, what are you up to?" Maya whispered,

"Getting ready to come over there to get my party on, why are you whispering?" Tricia asked puzzled,

"You wouldn't believe me if I told you…" Maya said in the middle of a sigh as she sat at the kitchen table and stared out the window,

"Uh-oh! I can hear it in your voice, what did Tony-B this time?" Tricia asked, as she swiveled around in her leather office chair, marveling at the beautiful view of the Mississippi River from her downtown office,

"Girl, I just needed somebody to talk to right quick," Maya said after letting out another long sigh,

"Okay, I'm listening, so what did he do now?" Tricia asked, rolling her eyes to the ceiling,

"I just… Girl, I don't even know where to start…" Maya said, her voice trembling as tears threatened to fall from her waterlogged eyes,

"Calm down Maya, just calm down, let me go ahead and wrap up and I'll be on my way, just hold on until I get there," Tricia said comfortingly,

"I'll be alright, it's just that I work like a dog all during the week, I barely get any rest as it is, and when the weekend finally does come, MY BIRTHDAY WEEKEND! And I still don't get a chance to rest or have any peace and quiet because Tony cares more about his parties and what his friends think than he does me! It's my party supposedly, but even then, I'm the one who always ends up doing all of the cooking and the cleaning, not to mention all of the decorating, all he does is man the damn grill and the liquor, I take care of everything else, but does he appreciate that or me? Hell no!" Maya ranted as Tricia listened,

"Girl you already know how Tony-B is…" Tricia finally said, scrambling for a thimble full of pity for her best friend's ongoing situation,

"Yeah, I know…" Maya sighed, "But don't mind me, I guess I'm just tired..." Maya said, letting out another long sigh,

"Oh, I feel you!" Tricia said, as she began to think about how busy her own life had been lately,

"So how are you feeling today?" Maya asked, as she wiped her eyes, suddenly feeling the urge to change the conversation,

"I'm good, just ready to get up out of this damn office!" Tricia said,

"What are you doing there anyway Tricia, it's Saturday!"

"I know, but I had to finish going over these files before Monday, but I just finished and I'm on my way over there right now, I just have to stop by the liquor store and pick up a bottle of

Smirnoff before I come, cause I know Tony-B's flodging ass didn't buy any…" Tricia said as she rolled her eyes,

"Uggggh! I don't see how you drink that nasty stuff! You know Tony always keeps plenty of liquor around here,"

"Exactly, but I don't like that stuff Tony-B buys, and besides, I don't say anything about those nasty ass coolers you're always sipping on!" Tricia teased,

"Whatever Tricia, get off my phone and I'll see you in a little bit," Maya said forcing a smile,

"Alright then Maya, it's your birthday, so don't you let Tony-B stress you out, do you hear me?"

"Yeah, I hear you…" Maya said through sighs, she sat at the table in deep thought and was still sitting at the kitchen table nursing her third wine cooler when Tony-B's friend Chris walked in with his girlfriend Linda,

"Hey Maya, girl what's going on?" Linda asked as she greeted Maya with a hug,

"Girl I'm good, and how are you two doing?" Maya asked, trying to muster up a smile,

"Shit, we're good, Ms. Lady! Where's that dude of yours at?" Chris rudely interrupted,

"I think he's out there taking the last of the ribs off of the grill." Maya answered, her smile suddenly disappearing,

"Let me go on out there and help him get that meat together," Chris said,

"Go ahead, he's out there…" Maya said pointing at the back door, she was trying to be polite, but she really couldn't stand Chris either,

"Hey Linda, go over there and tell Larry to fix me some gin and pineapple juice," Chris said over his shoulder,

"Don't you have to go past the bar to get to the grill?" Linda asked with an attitude,

"Damn Linda! It ain't like I'm asking you to go buy the damn drink, I'm just asking you to go over there and get it for me!" Chris said as he walked out the back door,

"Ooooh! He makes me sooo sick!" Linda said after Chris walked outside, "He thinks I'm his damn maid or something, the bar is right over there! Right there! He's so stupid!" Linda fumed. Maya laughed out loud as Linda fussed and cussed, "I'll be right back girl, let me go over here and get his drink before I have to hear his damn mouth all night!" Linda said,

Maya smiled as Linda went outside, but a little while later Linda walked back into the kitchen with a frown on her face,

"He didn't want it?" Maya asked, referring to the drink that Linda was holding in her hand,

"Oh no, girl, this one's mine, come outside with me right quick, I need you to see something, you ain't gonna believe this shit!" Linda said with a strange look on her face,

"What's going on?" Maya asked as she grabbed another cooler and followed Linda outside, when they walked outside, Chris was holding his drink up in the air and slow winding with Earl's cousin Torya, and she was working him with everything she had, moving her curvy hips in every imaginable direction possible,

"What?" Maya asked, trying to ignore Chris and Torya's little sultry show,

"I know damn well you see that bastard over there grinding all over that bitch like I'm not even standing here!" Linda snapped, "Why does he always have to show out every time we go somewhere, and who in the hell is that bitch, anyway? Whoever she is, she needs to go back to wherever in the hell she came from! I know what I need to do, I need to go over there and kick her ass, don't I Maya?"

Maya knew better than to answer, because even though Linda was only 4 feet, 11 inches tall and ninety pounds soaking wet, she had a temper like a Tasmanian devil, and once she got riled up, it was almost impossible to calm her down, Maya stood there stone faced as Linda continued to rant,

"Ooh, he makes me so sick! He acts like he doesn't even see me standing over here! But I bet if I go over there and slap the hell out of him, he'll see me then, won't he?" Linda asked with her hands on her hips,

"They're just dancing Linda," Maya said trying to comfort Linda, but secretly she was just glad that it was Chris over there

17

grinding and winding with Earl's wiggling and jiggling cousin, and not Tony-B,

"We must not be looking at the same thing, because it doesn't look like they're just dancing to me! They may as well go and get a fucking room! You know what, fuck this shit, I'm gonna go over there and kick her ass!" Linda said glaring at Torya,

"Linda, why would you do that? They're just dancing," Maya said trying her best to play down this potentially violent situation,

"Maya! You may take that kind of shit off of Tony-B, but I don't play that shit!" Linda snapped,

"Linda! This has nothing to do with me or Tony-B! But if it did, and if I was gonna say anything to anybody, I would be saying it to him, and not her!" Maya said with an attitude, and Linda regretted instantly that she had hurt her friend's feelings,

"Ooh Maya, girl! I am so sorry, I didn't mean no harm, I'm just mad, and this vodka and cranberry juice right here, ain't helping!" Linda said apologetically, "And you already know how my mouth gets sometimes, but I promise that I didn't mean no harm," Linda said sincerely,

"It's okay Linda," Maya said trying to hide her hurt feelings, "I understand..."

Maya knew that Linda didn't really mean any harm, but the truth was the truth, and everybody knew that Linda was one of those people who were just born without a filter, and whatever came up her throat, also came flying out of her mouth. Maya had always admired Linda for her fiery spirit, and sometimes she wished that she could be as bold and forward as Linda was, but Maya was quite the opposite, she accepted Linda for the firecracker that she was a long time ago, Linda was another one of Maya's closest friends. Maya met Linda when she first began dating Tony-B. Chris and Linda had been in a relationship on and off for years, long before Tony-B and Maya got together, they argued constantly, and have been known on occasion to have a rumble or two, and after getting caught up in one of their notorious whirlwinds last year, which ended up with Chris getting drunk, swinging at Linda, who side stepped him and attacked him like a scalded cat, and while Maya and Tony-B were trying to break them apart, Maya ended up getting accidentally punched in the stomach by Chris, so after that, Maya knew to stay out their spats altogether,

Everybody at the party was busy laughing and enjoying themselves but for Maya's birthday, she would've rather been anywhere but there. It was her birthday weekend and she'd spent most of her time decorating and cooking, frying what seemed like a million hot wings, preparing several different kinds of dips, cooking various dishes, arranging meat and fruit trays, and everything else imaginable under the sun except for the Bar-B-Q, she left that to The Self-Proclaimed, 'Bar-B-Q King' himself, and to hear Tony-B talk, you'd swear he was an A-List celebrity with his infamous parties, often bragging that he made the best Bar-B-Q in Memphis, Tennessee, and whether it was hot or cold outside, you could always find Tony-B in front of the grill, he threw parties every chance that he could for his friends and even his friend's friends and every year it was the same thing, parties for the Super-Bowl, New Year's Eve, Fourth of July, Labor Day, Memorial Day, a costume party for Halloween, a party for Thanksgiving, and a huge party for Christmas. He had 70's, 80's, and 90's parties for no reason, he threw birthday parties for Chris, Earl, Larry, Maurice and Ricky every single year, and a bachelor's party for Earl that was held once a year that Maya had to cook for, but she wasn't invited to. Tony-B threw boxing parties, football, basketball, and any other kind of party that you could possibly think of, not to mention the dreaded pay-per-view parties, and Maya rarely, if ever, had the chance to experience a quiet weekend, which is one of the reasons she planned to go on vacation with her best friend Tricia this year instead of going with Tony-B, the other reason was because she had such a horrible time for the past two years while on vacation with him, but last year was the worst year when he took her to The Florida Keys, because he spent half of his time bikini watching, and the other half of his time disappearing, and Maya ended up spending most of her vacation stuck in a hotel room alone...

***

"MAAAAAAYA!" Tony-B called from across the yard,

"WHAT!" Maya yelled back,

"Don't say what! Come and see what I want!" Tony-B yelled back,

"I'm coming..." Maya yelled before telling Linda she'd be right back, Maya rushed across the backyard, "What is it Tony?" Maya asked,

"Baby I need you to go into the shed and get us some more ice, we're almost out!" Tony-B said over his shoulder from the card table,

"Alright," Maya said through clinched teeth, she, along with everyone else knew that *more ice* meant he wanted everybody to know he'd had a brand-new ice machine installed out in the storage shed that he'd been bragging about,

It was a well-known fact that Tony-B was a compulsive bragger, always trying to one-up the next person, Maya fumed as she went into the shed and filled four bags with ice, two bags for the gigantic beer cooler, one bag for the soda cooler, and one bag for the wine coolers and loaded them on to the matching ice-cart, and as usual, Larry just had to ask her for two more bags of ice to go behind the bar. Maya pushed the cart back into the shed and loaded two more bags and was just about to take them out to Larry when she heard somebody yell,

"What up, Iron-Man! When did you get back in town?"

"I've been here for a good lil' minute," Maya heard him answer,

"Oh my God! Oh my God! Oh my God! Oh my God!" Maya said in a panic, she could hear him walking towards the shed, so she turned her back to the shed's entrance and quickly grabbed another empty ice bag and began to load it feverishly, her fingers were almost frozen solid but she kept loading the ice, pretending to be too busy to notice as Iron-Man walked by the shed, she let out a huge sigh of relief once he passed, but then he stopped dead in his tracks and sniffed the air and turned around instantly, not stopping until he sought her out, his eyes locked onto hers and wouldn't let go,

"Maya?" Iron-Man asked as he poked his head into the shed,

"Yeah, it's me," Maya said, disappointed that he found her,

"I knew that was you, I'd know that scent anywhere! Damn girl, how have you been?" he said rushing to give her a gracious hug,

"I'm good Irony, how are you?" Maya said with a giant smile, and Iron-Man smiled wide when she called him the same nickname she did when they were kids, he opened his arms and she slid her arms around him and rested her chin on his shoulder,

"Irony...Mane! It's been a long time since I've heard that name!" he whispered in her ear, "Those were some good times," he said as he buried his head in the side of her neck and rubbed her back in a circle, and if Maya didn't know any better, she could've sworn that he was inhaling her,

"It has been a long time," Maya said as she nervously pulled back,

"Dang Maya! I'm just hugging all on you..." Iron-Man smiled, "I see you're still wearing that same old body oil, huh?" he asked with a smile painted across his face,

"Yeah, I am..." Maya said as she looked away and bit down on her bottom lip, doing everything in her power to avoid his piercing eye contact,

"I tried to get in touch with you when I first got back," he said studying her with his eyes,

"Really?" Maya said with a violent blush,

"Yeah, I asked Chris if he had seen you and he told me that you and Tony-B had gotten together, and I couldn't believe it!" Iron-Man said as he shook his head,

"I know," Maya smiled,

"How in the hell did that happen? I know you couldn't stand his ass when we were kids," Iron-Man asked,

"It's a long, long, long, long story Irony..." Maya said as she closed her eyes and shook her head back and forth slowly,

"I hear you...Damn girl! You sure are looking good!" Iron-Man said as he looked her up and down,

"Thanks." Maya said nervously staring at the ground,

"How long has it been anyway?" he asked,

"Years!" Maya said with more emotion than she anticipated,

"I know…I sure hate we lost touch like that," Irony said still staring into her eyes,

"Me too," Maya said and found herself blushing again,

"Wow, it's been a long time…" Iron-Man said again, shaking his head slowly,

"Iron, is that you?" Tony-B said as he walked into the shed and gave Iron-Man a firm handshake,

"What's up Tony-B! This sure is a nice place you got here," Iron-Man said patting Tony-B on the back,

"It's alright for now, but I'm thinking about getting a bigger place built from the ground in a few years," Tony-B bragged as Maya rolled her eyes to the ceiling, "How long have you been back?" Tony-B asked with a smirk,

"I've been back for about a week now," Iron-Man said cordially,

"Aw mane! Chris didn't even tell me! You know I would have thrown you the biggest welcome home party! Why didn't you hit me up?" Tony-B asked,

"Well…my job transferred me down here and well, you know… I've just been kind of busy," Iron-Man said,

"Oh okay, I see…well it's good to see you anyway, I know you remember my fiancée Maya, what the hell am I saying, of course you do…y'all were kind of tight back in the day, huh?" Tony-B asked as he stood behind Maya and placed his arms around her waist, resting his chin on her shoulder,

"Yeah, me and Maya go back like fat pencils and coloring books…" Iron-Man said trying to search Maya's eyes with his, but Maya bit down on her bottom lip and looked away, she tried her best not to smile, but she was in full grin-mode, until she looked over her shoulder and noticed that Tony-B was standing there with his chest stuck out like a mighty hunter, leaving her to feel like a prized animal head, mounted on his wall,

"Show him the ring Baby! Shit, I spent some chedda' on that damn thing!" Tony-B said as he grabbed Maya's hand and held it up in the air so that Iron-Man could get a clear view of her 2.5 carat, Marquee cut, diamond engagement ring,

"That's nice Tony-B, real nice…well it was good catching up with you guys, I'm gonna go on out here and get my drank on… congrats again, you guys!" Iron-Man said, as he exited the shed quickly, Maya gasped softly as he walked away,

"What was all of that about, Maya?" Tony-B asked after Iron-Man left the shed,

"What do you mean?"

"I mean, what's up with you and dude all hugged up in here and shit?"

"Who Irony? Nah, he was just speaking," Maya said casually,

"Irony, who the fuck is Irony?"

"That's what I used to call him back in the day…" Maya answered, mashing her lips together to get rid of that smile that was fighting hard to dance its way across her lips again,

"Well, this ain't back in the day, and you speak with your mouth, and not with your damn hands, Maya," Tony-B fumed,

"What? It was nothing, me and Irony used to be real good friends back in the day, but you already knew that," Maya said,

"Real good friends, huh? Got your own lil' nick-name for him and everything, I see…" Tony-B said as he eyed Maya up and down,

"It's not even like that Tony, and at least I didn't kiss his hand like you did old girl out there," Maya said rolling her eyes at him,

"You think that shit you're saying is real jazzy, but don't let me catch you slipping, Maya…it's not gonna be pretty if I do, I promise you!" Tony-B said calmly before walking out of the shed, Maya fanned him off and shook her head before letting out another big smile,

Maya was still deep in thought when Tricia sashayed into the shed,

"Girl, have you seen Iron-Man!" Tricia loud whispered,

"Yeah, I saw him…" Maya said, acting nonchalant,

"Uh-huh... You can cut that shit out Maya!" Tricia said as she twisted her lips and placed her hands on her hips,

"What are you talking about Tricia, I said I saw him..." Maya shrugged,

"Girl please! You may be able to fool all these other folks around here, but you forget...I know your ass... just like the back of my hand!"

"I know I can't fool you, Tricia!" Maya said through giggles and sighs, "Oh my goodness, I can't believe he's back!" Maya said as she bopped down in the chair beside the ice-machine,

"Me neither, and he was a skinny lil' old something when we were growing up, but now that dude is thicker than a forty-dollar egg sandwich!" Tricia joked, fanning her face,

"Girl you are so crazy!" Maya laughed, "I'm so glad you're here!"

"I started to stay at home, you know I've been putting in lots of overtime at the office, but I couldn't miss my girl's b-day party, and you sounded so sad on the phone earlier," Tricia said,

"Yeah...I was feeling kind of down, but I'm alright now, plus we only have one more week, and then Trinidad here we come!" Maya said as she rested her head back on the wall and closed her eyes,

"I can't wait either," Tricia said smiling, then she suddenly looked worried, "Maya you're looking kind of funny around the eyes, are you feeling okay?" Tricia asked,

"Yeah, I'm all right Trish, just a lil' tired, I just get sick of Tony-B and his damn get-togethers, it's burning up out here and he wants me to wear shit like this!" Maya said pulling the sleeve of her football jersey,

"I was wondering what was up with that ridiculous outfit, I figured it was something he had picked out...and he got you wearing a cheese hat too, Maya...his ass ain't even wearing that shit, that's crazy!" Tricia said as she shook her head,

"Well, I can deal with wearing all of these crazy costumes better than I can deal with his ass!" Maya sighed,

"I know Maya, but until you put your foot down, he's just gonna keep doing what he does,"

"I already know Tricia, I already know…" Maya said after taking a big breath and staring at the ground,

"Maya?" Tricia asked,

"Yeah?" Maya said with a sad tone to her voice,

"Have you ever thought about what your life would've been like had you just told Iron-Man how you felt about him before he left?"

"Girl that was a long, long time ago!" Maya said through a forced smile,

"Yeah, but you still like him, I can tell!"

"Hush Trish! I'm not trying to think about that right now," Maya said trying to hold back a wide smile, "but you can help me finish loading this ice, so we can go up in my room and talk bad about these folks!" Maya joked,

"Do you see this outfit, Maya?" Tricia asked as she rested her hands on her slender hips, showing off her shiny Navy-blue hip-hugger jeans and shiny Navy shirt with a big silver shimmery star on the front with shiny silver heels and matching silver hoops and a big gaudy silver necklace and bangles on her wrists clanking every time she moved, "I am way too cute to be doing manual labor! And anyway, there are way too many men out there for you to be in here lugging all of these heavy ass bags of ice!"

"Don't make me hit you Trish! And for your information, I don't have to lug the ice, all I have to do is put these heavy ass bags of ice on this handy-dandy ice-cart that Tony-B got me for my birthday!" Maya said sarcastically, smoothing her hands over the ice cart like one of the *'Price is Right'* girls,

"You're fucking kidding me! Child, he'd better be glad it's you instead of me Maya, because if it was me, he'd be doing all of this shit by his handy-dandy damn self!" Tricia said as-a-matter-of-factly,

"Forget you Tricia, and where's Phillip, I thought he said he was coming?"

"Nah, Phillip had to work, but he told me to tell you to send him a plate, and he also told me to tell you not to put none of

Tony-B's nasty ass Bar-B- Q on his plate either! He said the last time the ribs were dry as hell and tough as leather!" Tricia giggled,

"Ooh he's wrong for that, but you know I got him," Maya laughed,

"I had to take Lil' Man over to his grandmama's house, that's why I'm so late." Tricia added, just as Tony-B, Earl, Ricky and Larry walked into the shed, Maya could tell that they were all irritated,

"Dang Maya! What we gotta do to get some damn ice around here?" Larry asked,

"I'm moving as fast as I can!" Maya answered with an attitude,

"No, you're not! You're in here running your damn mouth instead of doing what I asked you to do!" Tony-B said as he looked at Tricia with a disgusted look on his face,

"Well since I'm not moving fast enough, then you can get your own damn ice!" Maya said as she rammed the ice-shovel into Tony-B's hand, and walked out of the shed,

Tricia sniggled under her breath as she trailed behind Maya,

"Hey Tricia, you lookin' real good in them jeans, can a brotha get some of that?" Larry asked,

"Hell naw!" Tricia said without looking back,

"Dang Tricia, why you gotta be so hard on a brotha?" Larry asked, but Tricia and Maya both kept walking,

"I see Ms. Lady trying to show out in front of her lil' company," Ricky said after Maya and Tricia walked out of the shed,

"Yeah, she did get a little sassy, didn't she? But don't worry, I'll handle that a lil' later," Tony-B said,

"Seems to me like she's the one running shit around here! If my gal would've pulled that shit, she would've been too scared to come up out this shed by the time I got through with her ass!" Larry said,

"I ain't even trying to hear that shit you're talking about Larry, hell you gotta get a woman first! Or at least keep your hands off of one long enough to keep her, when you do get her, hell Tricia just dissed you and left you standing here looking stupid as hell, but you gone try to tell me how to handle my shit!" Tony-B teased,

"I just be playing with Tricia, I ain't really trying to get with her!" Larry reasoned,

"Naw, what you really mean to say is she ain't really trying to get with your ass!" Tony-B said laughing at Larry,

"Mane, whatever!" Larry said as he snatched four bags of ice, two in each hand, from the cart, and stormed out of the shed,

"Hey Larry, you forgot to get this cart!" Tony-B yelled out pointing to the fancy pink cart as Larry stormed away,

"Mane fuck you! I ain't about to push that old girly ass cart!" Larry barked over his shoulder as Earl, Ricky and Tony-B burst into laughter,

***

"I never thought I would live to see the day you stood up to Tony-B!" Tricia said as she and Maya walked from the shed into the kitchen,

"Girl, I'm not thinking about that fool!" Maya said as she fanned her hand at the whole situation, "Now let's go up to my room, and get tipsy and talk about these folks!"

"I'm right behind you girl," Tricia said as she tucked the brown paper bag under her arm and grabbed a bowl of ice from the freezer and two plastic cups and followed Maya down the hall,

Maurice, Larry's brother, stopped them in the hall and asked if they could pose for some pictures, Maya and Tricia did silly poses and flashed their brightest smiles before finally making it to the bedroom to gossip as usual, Tricia sat on the bed as Maya went into the bathroom and changed into a pair of khaki Capri pants and a red, yellow and beige summer blouse and some cute, strappy red sandals, Maya and Tricia laughed as they made her bed from this morning and Maya repeated her Iron-Man stories that Tricia had heard a thousand times, but she listened to them over and over again because she loved Maya's energy whenever she told them,

***

BYRON "IRON-MAN" GARRETT

Byron and Chris Garrett were brothers who lived across the street from Maya when they were children. Byron got the nick name Iron-Man because he would tie a towel around his neck with a clothespin and pretend to fly everywhere he went, calling himself "The Mighty Iron-Man" but with every long nickname in the neighborhood, it was eventually shortened, and everybody just started calling him Iron-Man, but his closest friends just called him Iron. He was a scrawny little boy with coal black skin, big marble eyes and a huge curly afro, and Maya was a chubby lil' girl with tight eyes, fat cheeks, smooth dark caramel skin and thick puffy ponytails that were at least a foot and a half long. Maya still remembered the first day of kindergarten when Iron-Man snuck up behind her and pushed her out of the swing, dirtying up her brand new green and pink sundress, Maya got so mad that she chased him around the playground and punched him in the eye, sending him crying to the teacher, but later that afternoon over snacks and Fred Flintstone Activity Pads, they became the best of friends, and she nicknamed him Irony. They were inseparable over the years, and in the sixth grade the teacher seated them in rows according to their last name, and Maya ended up in the seat on the row right next to him. She would help him with his work and would even let him cheat off her paper if he wanted to. In high school Iron-Man developed into a tall, lanky young man, with dark chocolate skin, big, dreamy eyes, snow white teeth and a smile that would light up a room. He would come over to Maya's house often and she would braid his hair and listen to his endless tirades about this girl and that girl, even offering him advice when necessary. She didn't go to her Senior Prom because Iron-Man asked Laura Morgan, the most popular girl in school at the time, instead of her, but he offered to let Maya ride in the limo with them when he found out that she didn't have a date even though Laura protested, but Maya lied and told him she didn't feel well, and she wouldn't be going. Maya stayed in the bed all day, but at eight o'clock that night, Iron-Man showed up at her door with a pot of home-made chicken soup that he begged his Mama to make, and a bag full of VCR tapes,

"It just wasn't no fun there without you Maya," he said when she opened the door,

They remained close friends even after they graduated high school. Iron-Man spent endless nights at Maya's apartment and even had a key, sometimes she would wake up to find him lying in the bed next to her. He would lie on top of her covers, and she hated it, but when she woke up and saw him lying there it just felt right. Maya worked as a receptionist and went to The University of Memphis, majoring in Marketing and Business Administration, and Iron-Man went to Tennessee Technical School to be a Surgical Technician during the day and worked nights cleaning office buildings. Maya would wake up around six in the morning, anticipating when the sun would light the room, so she could watch him as he slept, she would watch him until it was time for her to get ready for work, but there were days when she would wake up looking for him, and then she would go back to bed assuming he decided to go home for the night, but when she got ready for work and headed downstairs, there he'd be, bunked out on her couch. Maya would tip-toe out of the house and close the door gently so that she wouldn't wake him, but by the time she got to work he'd be calling her and asking why she didn't wake him up before she left. The day after he got his certification to be a Surgical Technician, Irony told Maya that his uncle had gotten him a job at a new hospital in Florida, and Maya was devastated, but she hid it well as she helped him pack, drove him to the airport, and even sat there with him for three and a half hours when his flight was delayed, but Maya never told him how she felt about him, in fact, the only person she ever told about her feelings was her best friend Tricia, and Maya knew Tricia would never tell him or anyone else for that matter...

After Iron-Man left town, Maya buckled down with her schoolwork and threw herself into her work, which paid off in a major way, she was recently promoted to Director of Marketing for a huge Pharmaceutical Company in Memphis, Tennessee, with a beautiful corner office, and a lucrative salary. Maya was doing very well as far as her career was concerned, but she always considered Iron-Man as the one who got away, especially after they lost touch,

***

"Tricia, Guess what?" Maya said before telling her what happened between her and Earl's cousin Torya,

"Girl, we would have been straight thumping, do you hear me? I would've slapped the taste out of her mouth and his too for playing with me!" Tricia said,

"Well, I ain't worried about either one of them Tricia, he can do what he wants to do, I don't even care anymore,"

"I don't see how you do it Maya," Tricia said pursing her lips and shaking her head,

"Tricia, don't start with me, okay," Maya pleaded,

"I'm just saying…" Tricia said as she poured herself another glass of wine,

Meanwhile, downstairs...

"Let's go!" A drunken Chris slurred as he stood over Linda, who sat on the couch, rolling her eyes and deliberately ignoring him, "You heard me, I said get the fuck up and let's go!"

"I ain't going no damn where!" a tipsy Linda said as she continued to sip on her drink,

"I ain't got time for this shit Linda, are you coming home with me or not?"

"Nah, you go ahead, I'm good." Linda said as she stood to her feet only to walk across the room and sit down in another random chair and cross her legs,

"How in the hell am I supposed to get home then, Linda?" Chris asked, following up behind her, his words slurring,

"I don't know, and I really don't care, better yet, I have an idea, why don't you go and ask that lil' stripper bitch over there to take you home, I'm sure she would be more than happy to!" Linda said pointing in Torya's direction,

Torya rolled her eyes at Linda and looked away,

"You better look away, cause I ain't but two inches off of your skanky ass anyway!" Linda yelled across the room,

"Mane forget this! Fuck you!" Chris said storming off,

"Fuck you too!" Linda yelled back while he was still in earshot...

Tricia and Maya were involved in a deep conversation. Tricia was still sipping on her Smirnoff and Maya was still nursing her wine cooler that she had poured some of Tricia's Smirnoff into when Linda came bursting into the bedroom,

"What are you two in here gossiping about?" a tipsy Linda asked, leaning against the doorpost,

"Nothing Linda, we're just in here running our mouths, what's going on out there?" Maya asked, she could tell that something wasn't right by the look on Linda's face,

"I just came up here to tell you again how sorry I am about what I said earlier, I was just mad at Chris, and I shouldn't have taken it out on you Maya," Linda slurred,

"I understand Linda, Tony-B gets on my nerves too sometimes,"

"Yeah...well I'm about to take my drunk ass on home, them fools out there clowning and shit," Linda said fanning her face, trying to stop her drunken yawns,

"What are you talking about Linda, who's out there clowning?" Tricia asked, looking just as puzzled as Maya,

"Girl...Chris and Tony-B are out there acting a fool! All up in each other's faces, pushing on each other and shit, like they really gonna fight, but I think they're just wolfing, don't worry Maya, because Earl, Iron-Man, Ricky and Larry are already out there trying to break them up!" Linda said between yawns,

"What the hell?" Maya yelled as she struggled to put on her sandals and go downstairs,

"What happened?" Tricia asked as Maya strapped up her sandal and headed toward the door,

"Well..." Linda said as she swayed to one side with her hand on her hip, "Tony-B told Chris to get out of his house because Chris was trying to start a fight with me, so Chris got mad and tried to pull me out the door by my arm, but I snatched away from him cause I wasn't ready to go, and I wasn't gonna go nowhere with his drunk ass anyway, so he starts clowning with me, but you know I wasn't going for that! But like I said, he was ready to go, hollering at me and shit, but I was like, hell naw! I told him, to go home with that whore in them stanky ass silver leggings and that see through shirt that he was grinding all over, then she had the nerve to stand up, put her hands on her hips and roll her eyes at me like she was a bad bitch, so I walked over there and got all up in her face, and I cussed her weak ass plum out! That bitch don't know nothing about me, I will smack the hell out of her and won't think nothing about it! So, I was just about to beat the breaks off the shaky ass whore when Tony-B snatched me from behind, talking about it ain't gonna be none of that in his house! Then Chris got mad and pushed Tony-B for snatching me... and after that all hell broke loose!" Linda said still fanning her face in between yawns,

"I don't understand! Why in the hell would Tony-B put his hands on Linda?" Tricia asked as Maya stood there dumbfounded,

"I don't know, maybe he just didn't want them to fight in the house again," Maya said trying to defend Tony-B, but inside her mind was raging,

"I don't know either, and to be honest I really wasn't paying any attention, I was too busy trying to get at that bitch, he just grabbed me, he didn't hurt me or anything, hell I thought it was Chris who snatched me until I turned around," Linda said with a shrug,

Maya and Tricia were both as lost as ever, but they invited Linda to stay up there with them and let the guys sort it out for themselves until they heard the rumbling and loud yelling from outside, they hurried downstairs to see what was going on, and when they got outside, Tony-B was drunk, mad, and cursing loudly, Maya was shocked because she had never seen him like that, she stepped in front of him and tried to calm him down,

"Tony-B what are you doing! Come back in the house, you're embarrassing me!" She said as she grabbed him by the hand, trying to pull him back inside,

"Naw Baby, this fool thinks he can punk me like he did when we were kids, but I'm gonna show his ass today, now move out of my way so I can whoop his ass," Tony-B slurred as he jerked away from her,

"Don't worry about him," Maya reasoned, "Chris is just drunk that's all, you both are, now let's just go back in the house, I don't want the neighbors to call the police, come on back inside," Maya reasoned, purposely speaking with calmness so that Tony-B would calm down as well, and it seemed to work, he was following Maya back inside, when Chris yelled out,

"Yeah Maya, take his lil' weak ass on in the house, he was always a lil' bitch anyway!"

"Bitch? I got your bitch!" Tony-B yelled as he shoved Maya aside and ran towards Chris, Maya's sandal got entangled in the extension cord connecting to the hanging lights, she lost her footing, stumbling wildly, trying to catch her balance, she tried her best to grab anything in her path, but there was nothing to grab, everything was happening in slow motion as she headed straight for the glass patio door. Maya closed her eyes tightly, crossing her forearms over her face and bracing herself for the impact, when out of nowhere Tricia dived and shoved Maya to the side with all of her might, and both she and Maya landed on the lawn with a hard thud,

"What the hell!" Tricia yelled as she jumped up and then helped Maya who was in tears to her feet. Tricia was still cursing under her breath as she walked over to the spot where her shoes were and held them in her hands. It was so much chaos and people yelling, running, and screaming back and forth as Tony-B ran up to Chris and punched him in the jaw, Chris stumbled back, grabbed a liquor bottle out of the trash, broke it on the brick wall, and began swinging it wildly, Tony-B ducked and dodged Chris' wild jabs until he was backed into the wall, Chris swung as hard as he could, trying to slice at Tony-B's face with the broken bottle when Chris' brother Iron-Man tackled him from behind and wrestled the broken bottle from his hand, Tony-B was so enraged that he started stomping and kicking Chris from behind as Chris and Iron-Man were struggling on the ground,

"Old jealous ass bitch, trying to fuck up my face! Just mad cause these bitches be all over me and not your ugly ass!" Tony-B yelled as he kicked and stomped Chris repeatedly, Iron-Man sat there in shock, but after seeing his baby brother ball up in a knot trying to shield himself from Tony-B's thunderous kicks and stomps, Iron-Man leaped to his feet and grabbed Tony-B and threw him hard into the brick wall,

"I ain't scared of your ass either Iron-Man, I'll fight both of you motherfuckers!" Tony-B yelled as he shoved Iron-Man, who instantly took on a fighting stance,

"Nobody's gonna stomp my brother while he's down, that was a bitch move Tony-B!" Iron-Man said, he was breathing so hard that his chest was heaving up and down, he could just imagine stomping and kicking Tony-B the same way that Tony-B had just stomped and kicked his younger brother,

"You weren't saying that shit when he just tried to cut my motherfucking face up with that damn bottle!" Tony-B said as he stood toe-to-toe with Iron-Man,

"Mane fuck that! Kick him again and see what I do to you!" Iron-Man said as he shoved Tony-B so hard that his feet left the ground, causing Tony-B to bounce off the brick wall again,

Tony-B tried to swing at Iron-Man but Larry grabbed him and put him in a tight bear hug, and when Tony-B stopped struggling, Larry let him go and stood in-between them, everybody knew Iron-Man was the boxing champ on his high school team, and they also knew that he could snap Tony-B in two if he wanted to, Larry actually wanted to see Iron-Man pummel Tony-B and had no intention of breaking up their fight, because he was still salty about Tony-B teasing him in the shed earlier, but Earl persuaded him to go over there and get Tony-B before Iron-Man could hurt him.

"Mane, y'all need to chill out before somebody calls them folks on y'all crazy asses," Larry said as he stood between them,

"Mane, fuck this!" Iron-Man said as he walked over to Chris and pulled him to his feet and dragged him over to the passenger side of his car and shoved him inside, and while everybody else was paying attention to the drama, Linda quietly snuck around Earl and shoved his cousin Torya in the back as hard as she possibly could, Torya's neck snapped back as she stumbled forward before her wedge sandals buckled beneath her and she spilled onto the ground. With lightning speed Torya snatched off her shoes, jumped to her bare feet and ran towards Linda with her shoe high in the air, but when she saw the wicked smile on Linda's face, she stopped dead in her tracks and just stood there with a shocked look on her face,

"Go ahead bitch, hit me with that shoe if you bad!" Linda said as she marched up to Torya and mushed her in the face with the palm of her hand, Torya's eyes got big and she dropped her shoe when she caught the glare of the razor in Linda's right hand,

Linda smirked when she saw the fear on Torya's face, "Old scary ass bitch, I don't even need this razor for your shaky ass," Linda said as she threw her razor to the ground and mushed Torya's face again, Torya slapped Linda's hand to the side and Linda drew back to hit her with all of her might when Earl jumped in front of his cousin Torya and gently pulled her behind him,

"Naw, Linda, I can't let you do that, whatever y'all got going, you need to take that up with your dude, and not my cousin," Earl said adamantly,

"Earl, this ain't got nothing to do with you, now move!" Linda said, trying her best to reach over him to get to Torya,

Torya stood frozen in place, still stunned by Linda's surprise attack,

"Linda, you need to calm your lil' ass down!" Earl said as he gripped Linda's shoulders and shook her firmly,

"Let me go Earl! I don't give a fuck! You ain't gonna be able to protect her forever, I might not get her today, but best believe I'm gonna get her, and when she least expects it!" Linda said as she struggled to get away from Earl, "I'm gonna beat that bitch if it's the last thing I do!" Linda said as she swung wildly, the moment she broke free from Earl's grip, Torya didn't realize how crazy Chris' girlfriend was and she wasn't about to fight her over a guy that she didn't even like, a guy that she only danced with once, Linda aimed, swinging as hard as she could, but Earl jumped in the way and Linda landed a punch, busting Earl's lip, he grabbed Linda again before he knew it and began shaking her violently,

"You need to take your lil' crazy ass home Linda, I'm not telling you again!" Earl said before shoving Linda and touching his lip, but when he saw that his lip was in fact bleeding, he grabbed

35

Linda again and shook her even harder, Linda flew back
and forth like a rag doll, but she had Earl by the neck,
digging into his flesh with her left hand and her right fist
was flailing wildly, popping him repeatedly anywhere she
could, when Larry stepped in,

"Earl, let that crazy ass girl go, Tony-B is over there
waiting on y'all!" Larry said as he grabbed Earl from
behind and swung him free from Linda's grip,

"Mane, I ain't about to let that crazy ass girl jump
on my cousin, especially not over no damn dude! And her
crazy ass bust my damn lip and scratched my fuckin' neck
up! You see this shit!" Earl said as he pulled his shirt down
exposing the deep pink scratches on his neck, "I ain't never
wanted to hit no girl so bad in my life! But I swear I wanna
knock her lil' ass out! Ooooh I almost hurt her lil'ass, I
almost hurt her, Larry!" Earl said punching his right fist
into his left hand as he paced back and forth,

Linda's adrenaline level was over the top and her
wheels were spinning, Larry was still wrestling with Earl,
and Linda figured that she could run past them and at least
get a few licks in on Torya before they could grab her, but
Larry knew Linda well, so he stood in front of Torya to
block Linda's path,

"It's over with Linda, I'm not gonna let you jump
on this gal either, now go on home and calm your damn
nerves, go on now!" Larry told Linda, but when Linda
hesitated, Larry got irritated, "I ain't playing with you
Linda, you think you bad, sprangin' on men and shit, but I
bet you won't try that shit with me, cause I promise, I'ma
lay your lil' ass out! Now go on home, before I get on your
ass!" Larry said, his voice thundering, Linda was still
focusing on a way to get past Larry to get to Torya, but
when she saw the look on Larry's face she changed her
mind quickly, Earl wasn't the type to hit a woman, and
Linda was surprised that he had even grabbed her when she
mashed his cousin in the face, Earl was always cool as a
cucumber, but she had scratched up his neck and bust his
lip, so she could understand why he was a little upset, but
Larry on the other hand, he was notorious for fighting

women, and as bad as Linda wanted to fight, she didn't want to chance being slugged by a 6 foot 4 inch, two hundred and eighty pound, angry Larry,

"It's cool...it's real cool," Linda said calmly with a smile on her face as she picked up her shoes and her razor, "I'll get up with you soon, real soon," Linda said nodding her head slowly before turning on her heels and walking away, Torya was in shock, she stood in place watching Linda as she walked over and began talking to Tricia and Maya,

"That bitch is bat shit crazy!" Earl said as Linda walked away,

"I know, I don't see how Chris does it, but I was about to knock her lil' ass clean across the yard if she hadn't walked away, she knew I wasn't playing with her ass," Larry said with a frown,

***

2 IT'S JUST A DREAM...

While Tricia helped Maya into the house, Earl and Torya jumped into Earl's car with Tony-B and sped off, and Larry got into his car and sped off behind them. Linda was too mad and too tipsy to drive, she crawled into the back seat of her minivan and stretched out, but that was typical Linda, she fell asleep in the back of her minivan so much that she kept a blanket and a pillow back there for that purpose.

Maya wasn't sure if it was the wine or the excitement of the day that made her head spin, in her mind, she just knew that she was about to crash through that glass patio door. but thankfully her friend Tricia had saved the day, Maya was so exhausted that she had to go and lay down, and she fell asleep almost as soon as her head hit the pillow and the next morning she woke up with a throbbing headache,

"Whoa!" Maya whispered after getting up too fast,

"You awake?" Tricia said as she sat up in the recliner beside the bed,

"Yeah, I'm awake, but I was hoping last night was just a bad dream,"

"I know what you mean, last night was all kinds of crazy!" Tricia said as she closed her eyes, massaged her temples and shook her head,

"Where's Tony?" Maya asked looking around,

"I don't know Maya, last night he left with Earl, and everybody else left shortly after he did, so I locked the house up and decided to stay here to make sure you were okay,"

"Thanks Tricia," Maya said, "Is Linda still outside?"

"No, she left around three this morning, she woke up and had to pee, so I let her crazy ass in and we talked for a while, she was the one who helped me clean most of the house, but she had to leave and go get the girls from the babysitter's house, did you know that crazy ass girl tried to fight Earl's cousin and ended up busting his lip last night?"

"You are lying!" Maya said as she tried to laugh but her head was really spinning,

"Yeah, I was cracking up," Tricia said, but then she noticed Maya's eyes again,

"I was scared to leave you here by yourself, Maya you don't look so good, maybe you need to go to the doctor,"

"I have an appointment first thing in the morning," Maya said with her eyes still closed, she massaged her throbbing temples with the balls of her fingers, "Tricia if you don't mind, I'm about to take a long shower," Maya said as she stood and walked into the bathroom,

"Girl go ahead, I'll still be here tidying up, I don't have much left to do," Tricia said,

"Girl, y'all didn't have to clean up, I got it," Maya said,

"Whatever, that's what friends are for, shoot every time I have something at my house, you're always the first one to help me clean, washing dishes even before the guests leave," Tricia laughed,

After Maya showered, she came downstairs to join Tricia in the kitchen, they were still laughing and talking when Maya heard Tony-B's keys rattling at the door, she frowned when she glanced over at the clock and it read 6:47AM,

"Maya, I need to holler at you," Tony-B said as he walked into the kitchen, where she and Tricia were sitting at the table,

"What were you saying Tricia?" Maya asked, deliberately ignoring Tony-B,

"I'll talk to you later Maya, I have to go and get ready for church, I bet Darrion is already up driving Phillip crazy by now, you know he's still waking up in the middle of the night because his spoiled self wants somebody to hold him," Tricia rambled on as she grabbed her purse and walked toward the door, Maya followed silently behind Tricia, still dressed in her pajamas and a satin cap, "Remember what I said Maya, take your tale to the doctor!" Tricia said over her shoulder as she walked down the front steps to her parked car,

"I will." Maya said as she waved goodbye, she could tell that Tricia was really worried about her, Tony-B had already walked down the hall into the Master bedroom, before Maya could even close the front door,

Maya rolled her eyes hard at him, *"At seven in the morning, he can talk to his damn self!"* Maya mumbled as she sat her mug on the coffee table and bopped down on the couch, she was still sitting on the couch wrapped in a blanket with her feet propped up, watching the Sunday Morning News when Tony-B finally came out of the bedroom,

"I thought I told you that we needed to talk, Maya!" Tony-B said as he stood over her, blocking her view of the television,

"Ain't shit to talk about!" She wanted to say, even yell, but thought it better if she kept quiet, to at least give him a chance to explain,

"Look, I just wanted to apologize to you for last night, I embarrassed myself and I know I embarrassed the hell out of you. And honestly, I really didn't mean to shove you, Maya, you know I have never put my hands on you, and I never will again, I know I do a lot of stuff, but I would never ever put my hands on you, ever!" Tony said sincerely, but Maya rolled her eyes at him and kept sipping on her coffee,

"What's with the attitude? I just poured my damn heart out to you and nothing!" He asked, but Maya didn't answer, she just stared at him, "Maya, I know you hear me talking to you!" He said with a big sigh,

"Where were you last night?" Maya asked calmly,"

"Is that what you're tripping about? I'm sitting here trying to talk to you and all you can think about is where I was last night! Mane, I was drunk as fuck! I went over to Larry's house and passed the fuck out on his couch, that's where I was," Tony-B said and Maya could tell that he was aggravated,

"Well why didn't you call me? I would've drove over there and picked you up," Maya said as she stared him up and down,

"Baby I was too drunk to call anybody, and plus last night was all kinds of fucked up, did you see when Chris tried to cut my face up with that damn beer bottle? That shit fucked with me real bad, I haven't been that mad in a long, long time... I really had to go somewhere and clear my head before I did something stupid to that dude!" Tony-B said between deep breaths.

"What happened between you two, and why did you snatch Linda in the first place? I'm still kind of confused about the whole thing," Maya asked, her anger slowly subsiding,

"That crazy ass girl right there..." Tony-B said as he let

out a long sigh and shook his head, "I told Linda that I didn't want her and Chris fighting in my house no damn more, especially after what happened with you the last time, and I meant just that! I get sick of that shit, and if they break something neither one of their broke asses can afford to replace it! Linda had been picking with folks all night, and Chris told me that they had already been arguing before they even got here, he told me about it while we were outside by the grill, and they had been saying lil' slick shit to each other all evening and frankly I was just over it and was really ready for both of them to go! But I don't feel like talking about those crazy ass folks or nothing else right now, I got a hangover out of this world, I'm tired as hell, and all I wanna do is take a hot shower and lay up with my Big Baby for a little while, is that alright with you?" Tony-B asked with an exasperated tone to his voice,

"Yeah," Maya whispered,

"Good! I'm gonna go in here and take a hot shower, go on in there and lay down and I'll be in there in a minute," Tony-B said as he walked down the hall,

Maya was lying in the bed with her back to the bathroom door when Tony-B came out of the shower, he slid beneath the covers and wrapped his arm around her waist, pulling her closer to him until her back was up against his chest, he then drifted off instantly, snoring softly in Maya's ear as she laid wide-awake, her mind asking a million and one blaring questions, but soon, her eyes began to get heavier and heavier and before she knew it... *a combination of sandy beaches, blue waters, and swaying palm trees filled her head, as she drifted deeper and deeper into a dream filled with shirtless, sun-kissed men with chiseled bodies who catered to her every whim as she rested beneath a gigantic tent, like something out of an Egyptian movie, Maya smiled wide while a servant with huge muscles and waist length dreadlocks kneeled in front of her offering her an exotic beverage of some sort,*

"Will there be anything else, My Queen?" he asked,

"No, that will be all, thank you," Maya answered with a regal tone as she sipped on her beverage,

"Are you sure I can't get you anything else, My Queen?" The waiter asked with a sly smile,

"Well, there is one thing..." Maya said with a smile,

"I bet I know what that is..." he said with a nod, still kneeling in front of her,

"Do you, now?" Maya asked, still smiling,

"I know exactly what you need," he said as he placed the serving tray on the table beside her and lifted her foot gently and rested it on his lap, he grabbed a bottle of fragrant oil from the sand and

41

poured a generous amount in the palm of his hand before rubbing his hands together to warm the oil, he then slathered the oil all over her foot and began to knead into the fleshy parts of her foot with his firm, warm hands,

"Oh, my word!" Maya mumbled as his roaming hands began to move up her calves, tiny moans escaped her lips, she closed her eyes and suddenly they began to float high into the sky on a big fluffy cloud while Mr. Coco-Brownskin massaged her tired feet and legs. Maya's heart raced as his eyes met hers, he smiled as he moved in closer... and closer...so close that she could smell his pineapple scented breath, she welcomed him as he covered her, the weight of his body pressed down on her, but she didn't mind, she could feel him growing the length of her thigh as she explored the deep crevice in the center of his back with her fingertips. He showered her face and neck with tender kisses as tingles danced up and down her spine, his lips brushed softly over hers, as he moved in even closer, Maya stared deep into his eyes and opened her mouth slightly to welcome his sweet, sweet kiss... a kiss that would never come because Tony-B's cell phone rang, and Maya suddenly found herself lying on the bed staring at Tony-B's back as he sat on the side of the bed. Reality rained down on her like hailstones as she realized that Mr. Coco-Brownskin, his warm hands, his heavy body, his tender kisses, warm oil and fluffy clouds were gone forever...Maya frowned and instinctually tuned her well trained ears to Tony-B's coded conversation,

"Hello?" Tony-B whispered as Maya laid still behind him, "Hey what's up... oh, no it's straight... yeah, she's still knocked out... she sleeps like a brick... no, it's nothing like that... I got this over here, you just handle that over there..." Tony-B whispered, "Yeah, we'll get up later... I have to go, bye!" Tony-B said, quickly ending the phone call once he felt movement behind him, he glanced back at Maya who was now sitting up in the bed, staring a hole into the back of his head with her arms folded, Tony-B could sense Maya's attitude and he didn't feel like dealing with it or her today, the weekend had already evaporated into thin air, it was Monday morning already, and he'd had a crappy weekend, he let out a sigh as he stood to his feet and stretched his arms to the ceiling, "Good morning to you, too," he said over his shoulder before heading into the bathroom,

"Who was that?" Maya asked, stopping him in his

tracks,

"Huh?"

"You heard me," Maya said still glaring at him from behind,

"Don't start that shit with me Maya, it's too damn early in the morning! I can't even get a good morning or nothing, just starting in on a brotha!"

"Okay… good morning, Tony, now who the hell was that?" Maya asked through clinched teeth,

"It was Earl, damn! Why do I have to be bombarded with a million fucking questions about everything I do, day in and day out?" Tony-B asked, Maya could tell he was frustrated, and that he was lying,

"Earl, huh?" Maya asked with a look of disbelief painted on her face,

"Yeah, we're supposed to go play ball this afternoon, but my head is still banging," he said, trying unsuccessfully to change the subject,

"If that was Earl, then why did you hang up the phone so fast?" Maya asked with her lips twisted in disbelief,

"Because! I don't need you ear-hustling all up in my damn conversation, Maya, that's why!"

"You lie so fucking much! But, don't even worry about it!" Maya said as she rolled her eyes hard at him as she struggled to get out of bed, then she purposely shoved past him,

"It's too early in the damn morning Maya, and you just tripping for nothing! Hell I'm the one who should be mad, you all over there moaning in your sleep and shit, hell, you don't even moan like that with me!" Tony said as he followed her down the hall, he was right on her heels,

"Whatever!" Maya yelled as she stepped into the bathroom and slammed the door in his face,

"Don't be slamming no damn doors around here, damn it!" Tony-B said as he hit the door hard with the side of his fist,

Maya fanned him off as she ran the bathwater on full blast and set the whirlpool jets on full force to drown out his voice, then she put on her favorite Syleena Johnson cd and turned it up as loud as it would go. She sank into the scalding hot water and closed her eyes tight, praying that Mr. Coco-Brownskin would be kind and generous enough to come and visit her again, but no such luck. Maya's mind began to drift towards her job, she had a major presentation with a huge deadline that was fast approaching. She was behind on her research and would have to put in long hours to catch up before she went on vacation and then she would have to come back from her vacation ready to present. Maya soaked for a

long, long time, hoping that by the time she finally came out of
the bathroom Tony-B would have already left for work, but
when she walked into the kitchen, he was sitting at the table
sipping his coffee and reading the newspaper,

"Baby, can we talk? I don't wanna argue, I just want to
talk," Tony-B said,

"Talk about what!" Maya snapped,

"Well, you've been acting real funny towards me, and I
know things were kind of messed up at your birthday party
Saturday, but I'm trying to make it right, you do know that I love
you, don't you?" he asked,

"That's what you keep saying…" Maya said rolling her
eyes to the ceiling,

"You know you my Big Baby, come here." Tony-B said
as he stood slowly, grabbing her by the hand and pulling her
towards him, Maya melted like she always did when she looked
deep into his hazel eyes, Tony-B leaned in and kissed her
passionately, so passionately that she almost forgot why she was
mad at him, and Tony-B, knowing full well the power of his
kiss, flashed her a sexy smile and kissed her again making her
feel woozy, he then led her by the hand back into the bedroom.
Maya laid back on the bed and Tony-B laid his head on her soft
stomach, "This is daddy's big old playground right here!" he
said as he rubbed her belly in a circular motion, Maya gave him
a half smile and turned her head in the opposite direction, she
was trying hard to stay in the mood and ignore his little repetitive
fat jokes,

"You know I'm about to tear that ass up, don't you?"
Tony-B asked with a smile,

Maya smiled back at him and looked away again,

"I don't know why you're always tripping with me,"
Tony-B joked,

Maya just smiled again, still trying hard not to ruin the
mood,

"I have a doctor's appointment this morning!" Maya
suddenly remembered,

"And…what does that have to do with me?" Tony-B
frowned,

"Nothing…it's just that I don't want you to…you
know!" Maya whispered,

Tony-B raised his head, "I hope you're not saying that
you not gonna give me none before you go!"

"No, it's not that, I just don't want the doctor to find any surprises while he's examining me," Maya said, forcing a smile,

"I was just about to say, I ain't had no lovin' from you in days!!!" Tony-B said as he leaned in and laid another kiss on her. Tony-B's hands began to wander and before Maya could even think about objecting, his right hand found itself fingering her right nipple, and his left hand found itself deep in between her thighs. Maya tried to arch her back and moan but Tony-B covered her mouth with his as he mounted her, he slid in deliberately slow and rocked her, Maya was surprised, she thought that it would be another wham-bam session, but this time he was attentive to her body, more attentive than he'd been in a while, he made love to every part of her being, even her toes, Maya was very pleased, assuming that since he was *really* sorry this time, he might even cuddle with her afterwards, she wanted to be held badly, but she soon realized that was out of the question when he rolled over and hopped out of the bed and went into the bathroom. Maya let out a loud sigh and pulled the covers over her head after she heard the shower running, frustrated and tired, she began to doze off, but when Tony-B nudged her, she opened her eyes slowly and stared at his back as he sat on the side of the bed and towel dried his body, she narrowed her eyes, blinking them constantly at what looked like four long red scratches that ran diagonally from his right shoulder blade all the way down to the center of his back,

"Hey Baby, what time is your doctor's appointment?" Tony-B asked over his shoulder,

"At ten, why?" Maya said sluggishly,

"Good, that means you've got plenty of time to fix your man some breakfast, since I'm off today," Tony-B said, still towel drying his body,

"I don't feel like cooking…" Maya said, still staring at the mysterious scratches on his back,

"Since when?" Tony-B asked with a confused look on his face,

"Since now!" Maya said with attitude,

"Oh, so I guess I can't get a home cooked meal, even though I just hooked you up big time!"

Maya ignored him, as she threw the covers over her head and rolled over, turning her back to him,

"Come on Maya! After all that work, I just put in… I know I can get a good breakfast out of that!"

"Not from me…" Maya mumbled under the covers,

"Maya this is the second day in a fucking row that you haven't cooked for me, you didn't even cook for me and the Fellas when they came over to watch football last night, you know how embarrassing that

45

shit was? It's plenty of women out here who would love to take your damn place, Maya, and I bet they'd be glad to stay in this big old expensive ass house rent-free and cook for their man and his friends!"

Maya snatched the covers from her head and glared at Tony-B, "I didn't cook for you yesterday because I didn't feel like cooking then, and I don't feel like cooking now! Why don't you ask whoever put all those damn scratches on your back to cook for you CAUSE I AIN'T COOKING SHIT!!!" Maya said, and with that being said, she threw the covers back over her head and turned her back to him again,

"Scratches? Is that why you're acting a damn fool... hell, I knew it was something! But for your information, Chris scratched me the other day when we got into it! Now what do you have to say, with your smart-ass mouth?" Tony-B said with an arrogant smile on his face,

"Yeah right..." Maya said rolling her eyes to the ceiling,

"He did, and you could've just asked me about it instead of always assuming shit, Maya!"

"Whatever! I'm still not cooking," Maya said as she rolled her eyes to the ceiling,

"Why the fuck not?" Tony-B barked, "I work hard as hell to make sure all of these damn bills are paid around here, I even let you keep your lil' money in your pocket, and I make sure that I keep you weak in the knees when I give you this good lovin', and all I asked for was a home cooked meal, and I can't even get that! You starting to turn into one of those trifling ass women, the kind that dudes like me, fuck off on, then you wonder why I look at other women, but if you took care of business you wouldn't have to worry about where I go and what the fuck I do!"

"Whatever Tony, because I work like a damn dog, and then I come home and I make sure I do everything you want me to do, including cooking and cleaning up behind you and your worthless ass friends, so that you don't have to lift a finger, as a matter of fact, yesterday afternoon was the first time I had never *NOT* cooked or cleaned up behind you and your friends, but despite all that I do, you still had the nerve to bring your ass in here yesterday at seven in the fucking morning with scratches all over your damn back, and you expect *me* to get up and cook for you? And for the record, I don't need you to take care of me, or your damn money, I make my own!"

"I just asked you to cook me some breakfast, and you wanna throw all that independent woman shit up in my face, I knew you were still mad yesterday when you barely said anything to me the whole day, hell I was surprised that you even let me hold you when I got out the shower! But I know you and I knew that it was only a matter of time before you got back at me for coming in late, that's why I didn't say anything when you left and went over Tricia's house when the game was getting ready to start, and I didn't say shit when you came back and stomped all around the house, throwing shit and yelling, making the Fellas feel so uncomfortable that they left early! And then you didn't even want me touching you at all last night, so okay, I get it! And that won't ever happen again, I won't stay out all night, so you ain't gotta worry about that no more, but that was yesterday, then this morning you acted like everything was cool and we just finished making love, damn good love at that! And now you're telling me that you can't get up and cook me breakfast like you usually do every morning before you go to work...damn, for real Maya, is this how things are going to be between us now?" Tony-B asked, his voice softening, almost cracking like a disappointed child,

"Okay, Okay! I'll go cook, just shut the hell up talking to me!" Maya said as she threw the covers to the side and stormed past him into the kitchen,

"I still don't understand why I have to jump through all kinds of hoops just to get my woman to cook me breakfast!" Tony-B yelled down the hall,

"Say one more word and you'll be cooking this shit yourself!" Maya yelled as she marched into the kitchen,

Maya was at the stove scrambling eggs and frying bacon when Tony-B walked into the kitchen, Maya could feel him staring at her from behind and it was making her feel uncomfortable, Maya knew that he was staring because he didn't like her sized eighteen frame, but it wasn't like she was skinny when they first met, she had only gained fifteen pounds since they started dating almost three years ago. Maya turned around and sure enough, Tony-B was standing there staring at her big round behind and wide hips with a frown on his face,

"What?" Maya asked, smoothing down her nightshirt,

"Nothing...I was just looking at you," Tony-B said, still frowning,

"Looking at what?" Maya said staring down at her feet,

"I was looking at that nightshirt, you don't need to wear that anymore, it makes you look even bigger than you already are," Tony-B said with a look of disgust,

47

"Does it really make me look that big?" Maya asked, looking down at her thighs, and rubbing her belly,

"Yeah, it does, and look at your breasts, you really don't need to walk around here without a bra either," Tony-B frowned, "I thought you said that you and Trish were going on a diet,"

"We are, I've already lost five pounds!" Maya reasoned,

"Shit, I can't tell!" Tony-B said sarcastically,

Maya continued to hold in her belly and smooth down her nightshirt, hoping that somehow it would make her appear smaller, she fought back tears as she turned her back to him, trying to concentrate more on his bacon and eggs than her hurt feelings, but whether Tony-B knew it or not, he'd be dining on a few of Maya's tears with his meal,

"Could you bring my food out to the sunroom once you finish, Maya, and can you cut me up two of those mangoes while you're at it?" Tony-B asked as he grabbed his coffee mug and the morning's paper and rose from the kitchen table,

"Okay," Maya said, her tears timing themselves perfectly, racing down her cheeks and sizzling in the skillet along with his bacon and eggs, the moment he left the kitchen,

Tony-B thought about what he had just said to Maya and chuckled as he pulled out his phone and called Earl,

"What's up Tony-B, you are calling me this early in the morning, you must still be in the doghouse?" Earl joked,

"Nah, I straightened that shit up as soon as y'all left after the game last night," Tony-B bragged,

"Yeah, I was shocked as hell that Ms. Lady didn't cook for the game, I hadn't eaten all day, and was starvin' like Marvin!" Earl laughed,

"Yeah, I was surprised too, when she jumped up and left right before the game started, and then she came home stomping around and throwing shit, like she pays the damn bills around here! I was like what the hell!" Tony-B laughed,

"Mane, that fucked me up, for real, I ain't never seen Ms. Lady act like that for as long as I've known her!"

"Shit, me neither, but then again, I ain't never came in the house at seven o'clock in the damn morning either..." Tony-B laughed.

"Yeah, I'm surprised she didn't cut your ass, I know my gal would've clowned with my ass if I pulled that shit!" Earl said, still laughing,

"She was alright when I came in, she just asked me a

few questions and then we went to bed, I even held her and everything! And you know I don't even do no shit like that!" Tony-B reasoned,

"Yeah, I know," Earl laughed,

"But then after we woke up Sunday morning, she started being grumpy as hell, I think she dreamed about the shit or something, I was trying to joke with her and shit, but Mane! She wasn't having it! So, I just left her grumpy ass alone and went on about my business, but it started getting close to game time and I didn't smell no food cooking, and then I noticed that she got up and started putting on her clothes and shit, and I thought she was getting ready to go in there and start cooking, until she put her shoes on and grabbed her keys and marched her big ass right out the damn door!" Tony-B said,

"For real? She did it like that?" Earl asked in disbelief,

"Maaaane! She balled up out of here so fast! But I didn't sweat it though, hell at first, I thought she had forgotten something and had gone to the store to get it, but then it was getting closer and closer to game time, and I was like, this bitch done jetted on my ass!" Tony-B said as he and Earl erupted in non-stop laughter,

"I know that fucked you up, cause it sure as hell fucked our hungry asses up!" Earl joked,

"Shit, I'm just glad that we still had a lot of food left over from that party, or else we would've been starving up in here! And you know I don't like fast food," Tony-B said,

"Yeah, but her ass pitched a real fit when she came back and saw what we did to that damn kitchen! You know Ms. Lady can't stand no nasty ass house, shit, she can't stand for nothing to be out of place up in there!" Earl joked,

"Shit, I know," Tony-B agreed, "I thought her crazy ass was gonna break all of them damn dishes in there, she was slanging and banging them so hard! I saw a lot of broken plates and shit in the garbage when I emptied it this morning, but even if she breaks all of them, I just would've went out and brought her ass some more, you know I ain't fucked up about nothing like that!" Tony-B bragged,

"Yeah, I know," Earl agreed, "but that's what she gets for leaving us there by ourselves, she know we don't clean up and shit! We men, hell, that's what we do! And she got us spoiled and shit, and then gonna run off cause she got a damn attitude," Earl joked, "Boy, I bet she was up all-night cleaning that shit up after we finished!" Earl said, still laughing,

"Hell yeah, she was up all night, cleaning, and slinging shit and cussing and fussing…but, I bet her ass won't make us cook for ourselves no more!" Tony-B joked,

"Mane, you a fool!" Earl said, he could hardly get his words out and had tears in his eyes because he was laughing so hard,

"Shit, I felt sorry for her, so this morning I went ahead and dicked her down real good, and had her smiling from ear to ear, but then she fucked around and saw them damn scratches on my back and shit started all over again!"

"Damn Tony-B, you gone have to be more careful!" Earl said,

"Shit, I thought I was, but to be honest, I don't know if Chris' weak ass scratched me when we were tussling or what the hell happened!" Tony-B paused in deep thought, then he noticed that Earl was quiet too, "but anyway..." he continued, "I had to damn near beg her ass to cook for me this morning!"

"So, she still mad, huh?" Earl asked,

"Well, she was, until I broke her ass down a few minutes ago," Tony-B bragged,

"What did you do Tony-B?" Earl asked, already trying to hold back his laughter,

"Shiiiiiiit...I had to remind her who Daddy was, she forgot for a minute, but she got the game all fucked up! Hell, it's plenty of women out here waiting in line to take her place, and one in particular who ain't bullshitting at all about coming for that number one spot!" Tony-B said with a smile,

"You're right about that!" Earl added,

"I told her it's an honor for her to even be with a brotha like me! Hell, I pay the bills around here, I make plenty of money and she don't want for nothing! I may fuck around every now and then, but I take care of my business, you know? So, she better keep cooking and cleaning around this bitch cause what she don't know is that it's her cooking and cleaning that got her ass up in here in the first place, and it's her cooking and cleaning that keeps her ass up in here! If it wasn't for that shit, she would've been gone!" Tony-B said,

"Man, you such a damn fool! But I feel you though!" Earl laughed, but then he suddenly got serious, "But on a serious tip, speaking of Chris, have you talked to him since all that shit happened?" Earl asked,

"Naw, I ain't talked to that motherfucker!" Tony-B said, his fun mood turning serious, "When he grabbed that bottle and tried to fuck my face up, it kinda did something to me, you know?" Tony-B said, and Earl could feel the hurt in his voice,

"Yeah, I know, the whole thing went way too far, and it got real crazy and real quick!" Earl said,

"Yeah… I thought about doing something real treacherous to his ass, it took me all night to calm down, and I still get mad as hell every time I think about that shit!" Tony-B admitted,

"Yeah, I understand that, but we go back way too far to let something like that break up The Fellas, it felt really strange not having him there for the game Sunday…you know we like family, we been thick as thieves since we were little, and me and that dude go back since we were three years old playing together in the damn sandbox," Earl said,

"Yeah, I know… but still, it would've been cool if we would've just boxed, shit we would've just thrown them thangs, cussed each other out and called it a day, and tomorrow we would've been back cool as hell…it wouldn't have been the first time any of us boxed with each other, but dude really tried to fuck me up that time! It made me think about some shit, for real, like dude must hate me or something, he must have some real animosity for me, cause that was some real fucked up shit!" Tony said, his eyes misting,

"C'mon now, you know him better than that! I talked to him yesterday, and he said that night he was already heated because Linda had been fucking with him all day, you know she can be full of hell when she wanna be, I almost knocked the shit out of her lil' crazy ass myself, for trying to jump on my cousin, you know that crazy ass gal was swinging so hard and wild that she fucked around and hit me in my damn lip, so I snatched her lil' ass up, then she gonna scratch my damn neck up! She better be glad I ain't got no damn sisters, cause I would've got them to fuck her lil' ass off! You should see this shit" Earl said, as he stood in the mirror and pulled down the front of his t-shirt examining the scratches on his neck, Tony could tell that Earl was still mad about that,

"Yeah, I know, Larry told me," Tony-B said,

"Yeah, so as I was saying, Chris was already heated, then he was funky drunk, he said he didn't even remember the shit that happened, he said that Linda had to tell him everything he did, hell she called me early this morning apologizing, and she said that she went to sleep in her van and the next morning when she got to the house he started trying to fight her, she said she was trying to make him lay his ass down but he kept breaking shit and trying to swing on her, all in front of the kids, so she whooped his ass, took his keys and kicked him out of the house and locked the door, but then she had to go outside and get his drunk ass, cause she said he was out there naked as a jaybird, sitting on the steps crying like a baby! She said all of his clothes were in a pile on the porch, and he had pissed on himself and everything!" Earl chuckled, then immediately went back into serious mode, "He said that he didn't remember shit, the next thing he knew he woke up buck naked and sore as hell on the couch! I asked him what the fuck was he drinking at the party, and his crazy ass told me that he had mixed some tequila, vodka, gin and Hennessy together with some damn orange juice and he had been drinking on them shits the whole time at the party!"

"That's crazy! Why in the fuck would he do something like that?" Tony-B asked in disbelief,

"That's what I said, and I got on Larry's ass because he shouldn't have even fixed him no shit like that, that's asking for trouble, and not only that, that shit could've killed him! And shit, everybody knows that Chris can't hold his damn liquor! And normally he don't even drink like that, maybe one or two drinks at the most, he normally drinks that nasty ass vodka with cranberry juice in it, but Larry said he only gave him one drink with alcohol in it, and that was when they first got there, he said all the other times Chris just kept asking for orange juice, and ice, Larry said he got so tired of Chris asking for orange juice that he just gave him a jug with a cup of ice and sent him on his way, but Larry said he did notice that Chris was acting drunk as hell,"

"So where did he get it from if Larry didn't give it to him?" Tony-B asked trying to figure out exactly what happened,

"That's what I wanted to know, but then guess what the damn fool told me, Tony-B..." Earl said with a sigh,

"What?" Tony-B asked,

"He said that he went into one of The Bone Rooms to get away from Linda and he saw the liquor in there and just started making his own damn drinks,"

"I was wondering what happened to all that liquor we had in there! Remember, we had to go out there and get some bottles out of the shed for the game, I couldn't figure that shit out for nothing! That's crazy! He'd better be glad that he didn't get alcohol poisoning!" Tony-B said, shaking his head,

"I think he did," Earl said, "Linda called me right before you did and said that she had to take him to the emergency room this morning, I'm waiting for them to call me back to see if I need to go up there, and he asked about you when I talked to him," Earl added,

"He did?" Tony-B asked relieved,

"Yeah, he said he wanted to call you yesterday, and he

said he wanted to come and see you, but he didn't know, you know…what to say, especially now that he knows how fucked up shit got," Earl said,

"Well tell him not to worry about it, we go back too far to let some shit like that stop us, we're straight and it's squashed! Just tell him to get better and to holler at me when he gets home and rested, let him know, it's all good! But tell that dude from now on he can't have shit else to drink over here, not even water! I'd hate to have to fuck his lil' drunk ass up over some dumb shit!" Tony-B said with a relieved laughter,

"I'll tell him…wait, hold up! Linda just text me and said that the doctors say that it is alcohol poisoning and they're keeping him, I'm gonna head to the hospital and check on him before I go to work, and I'll call you and tell you what's going on once I know something!" Earl said,

"Tell him to call me if he needs anything or if he wants me to come down there!" Tony-B said,

"Alright, be easy Tony-B!" Earl said before hanging up, and even though Tony-B was still mad about what happened between he and Chris, he was glad that they had squashed it and he was hoping that his friend was okay,

It was in the middle of September, and the sun was still in its infant stage, Tony-B smiled wide as his cell phone began to vibrate, he pulled it out of his pocket and pressed the ignore button and then checked the text message that he had just gotten from Earl. The text said that they were going to keep Chris in the hospital for a few days, Earl also said that he would be by later to give Tony-B the money that he owed him from the football game, Tony-B laughed as he responded to his text, teasing Earl about the lost bet, and he texted that he was going to come to the hospital to see Chris later this afternoon. Tony-B made sure that his phone was still on silent before he put it back into his pajama pocket. At exactly eight o'clock on the dot, the high-tech irrigation system that Tony-B had installed began to mist the grass, he smiled as small fountains of water combined with the rising sun creating tiny prisms all over his huge lawn. Tony-B's seven bedroom, four-bathroom, home was his pride and joy, he had it built from the ground after he made C.F.O. at Mertle, Forman and Wolfe Financial Group, he was the youngest to ever make Chief Financial Officer at the company. He started as an intern during his senior year of college and after he graduated, he was offered an assistant's position, it was perfect for Tony-B because he was a whiz when it came to numbers, and very competitive by nature, meaning, he had to be the best in whatever he did. He worked his way up the corporate ladder and now at thirty-three years old, he could honestly say that he was where he wanted to be in life, and with his investments and his dream job, he had plenty of money in the bank. The sun began to warm the air and the prisms were in full bloom, the sound of the water softly falling on the grass relaxed him, but it was quiet, too quiet, so he grabbed the remote to his Bose Music System, and pushed the power button, filling the room with soft jazz, he stared out into the lawn and instantly began to think back to his childhood…

***

ANTHONY "TONY-B" BRADFORD

The average person would think that Tony-B had an easy childhood, his grandfather, James Elbert Bradford, who everybody affectionately called Daddy Tank, was a six-foot, nine inch tall, giant of a man born from a Cherokee Mother and an Ethiopian Father, he was born with a deep yellow tone to his skin, wavy hair, high-cheekbones and hazel eyes. He had big broad shoulders, wore a size fifteen shoe, that he had to have custom made, and he was so tall and muscular that he almost blocked out the sun when he stood. His presence was intimidating because his bite was in fact, ten times worse than his bark, he demanded respect, and had a deep baritone voice that boomed like speakers. He was a hardworking, fair-minded man who wore expensive clothes and cologne and his number one rule in life was that a man was supposed to take care of home and that you should look a man square in the eye and if that man couldn't look you back in the eye, he definitely had something to hide and was not to be trusted, and for those type of people Daddy Tank had zero-tolerance.

Daddy Tank was not one for a lot of arguing, but he was well known for those one hitter-quitters and knock down drag out brawls that he'd had, and most of the time there would be two or more on one and not in his favor, but he liked it that way because whenever he lost his temper, he would whirl out of control like a tornado, and it would be hard for anyone to calm him down, Everybody scattered when he lost his temper, well almost everybody, the only person in the whole world who was capable of calming that raging tornado was a petite lil' old four foot-eleven inch Cherokee firecracker named Emogene, her voice was as squeaky as a little mouse but she could say one word to him and reduce that giant of a man almost to tears. From the moment he first laid eyes on her as she sat at his Aunt Ree's dinner table, he was mesmerized, she was his first cousin's Anna-Mae's best friend and they were at the dinner table laughing and giggling when he walked in, she had the biggest, doe eyes that he had ever seen, her skin was smooth and dark like chocolate, she had her hair pulled back into one thick braid that was so long that she almost sat on it, and when he heard her lil' squeaky voice, his heart just melted, he tried his best to catch her eye but she paid him no mind, he asked his cousin on several occasions to fix them up but Emogene wasn't having it, in fact it took him two years to convince Emogene to let him take her out to the movies and she refused to go unless he took his cousin Anna-Mae with them, at the movie theater Emogene even insisted that his cousin Anna-Mae sit between them. No one would guess that a year later they would be married with a baby on the way. He loved her with his whole heart, and they were happy, but soon the stress of his new job, and the new baby at home was beginning to push James out into the streets. He had begun to frequent this little hole in the wall in the heart of South Memphis, at first he would only go on the weekends, and then he started going during the week as well, but Emogene never made a fuss about it, she would simply have his dinner ready and a hot bath waiting for him whenever he came home, but one particular night he had met a young lady at the club and decided to take her out to breakfast afterwards, but before he could even order coffee, Emogene showed up at the diner in her pajamas, cussing and swinging a hook blade machete and he'd worn that scar in the shape of that machete blade that she had buried deep in his shoulder until the day he died. He never spoke to that woman again and every time the woman saw Emogene she would cross the street and run the other way. Whenever Emogene told the story she would say, "He thought he was gonna get away with giving his honey and his money to that sleazy trollop while I was stuck at home tending to a house and a hollering baby! Oh no! I'd send him to meet his maker first!" Daddy Tank always wondered how Emogene found out where he was that night, and one day when they were old and gray, he finally had the nerve to ask her, and she told him that it came to her in a dream, she saw clearly where he was, who he was with, and even what the woman looked like and what she was wearing in her dream. Daddy Tank let out a hearty laughter and rubbed his shoulder, before saying, "Baby, I never told you this, but when you came in there with those eyes blazing, those braids flapping everywhere and that machete in your hand, I knew I was in trouble! I didn't know who was more scared, me or her! But I 'clare fo Lawd, I learned my lesson that night, and I told God if he would just let me live, I wasn't never EVER gonna do that no more! I tell you the truth! That old gal almost tore the door off the hinges getting out of that diner! Whew-weee! I ain't never seen nobody run so fast!" he said, as he and Emogene sat on the porch in rocking chairs, talking and laughing about old times.

Emogene wore braids that hung down to her waist when she was younger, but as she got older, she wore her salt and peppered hair pinned tightly in a bun. Daddy Tank's hard work had paid off and he now owned one of the largest construction companies in Memphis, Tennessee, and the first thing he did was to send his Emogene to college. He said that if something were to ever happen to him, he wanted her to be well educated and able to run the business. They were married for over fifty years and had two sons, James Jr., the oldest and Anthony the youngest. James Jr. never wanted the responsibility of running the business, so he joined the Navy right out of high school, so they turned the company over to their youngest son Anthony and gave him their house and moved out into a small cottage in the country to live out their Golden Years. They also gave him the money to send his young wife, Natasia, to college the same way that Daddy Tank had sent Emogene, Natasia did so well in school that she got her bachelor's in nursing and began teaching Nursing Classes at a local college. Emogene and Natasia became close, especially after Daddy Tank passed away, Emogene always treated Natasia like one of her own even though Natasia was the youngest of nine children.

Anthony Bradford and Natasia had a daughter, Karen, who was almost ten years old when she began to beg her parents to give her a little brother or sister. She was elated when Natasia finally became pregnant, but there were difficult times ahead for the Bradford Family. Emogene passed away peacefully in her sleep when Natasia was four months pregnant and Anthony Bradford, who everyone affectionately called 'Big Tony' because he was 6 foot, 3 inches tall, and two hundred and fifty pounds of muscle, with deep golden skin, wavy hair, and high cheek bones just like his daddy, went into a deep depression, and to make matters worse, Natasia Bradford tripped and fell at work, and went into labor three months early, and Anthony Bradford, Jr. was born weighing only two pounds and-two ounces, and very jaundiced. The doctors didn't think that he was going to make it, but little did the doctors know, Natasia Bradford was a praying woman, and little Anthony Bradford, Jr. pulled through after spending almost four months in the hospital. When Big Tony saw his son, who was also born with his father's yellow-caramel skin and hazel eyes, and a head full of wavy hair, he smiled for the first time since his mother had passed away and he promised right then and there that his son would never need or want for anything.

Big Tony kept his word and ever since Tony-B could remember, on every single Christmas and on every single birthday, his parents would throw him a huge party with presents piled high to the ceiling. Tony-B didn't necessarily like the parties, because as a child he had no friends, and he didn't get along well with any of his cousins on his mother's side, because they were jealous of him and he hated the fact that they would always go into his room and try to break his toys whenever they came over, and he would end up locked in his room with his toys, and to make matters worse, at nine o'clock, the liquor was brought out, and his kiddie-party would turn into a full-out adult party that continued all night long. Yes, Tony-B had everything that money could possibly buy but he was a lonely, unhappy child.

Big Tony was a strict disciplinarian who insisted that Tony-B went to a private school and while the other children were outside playing and having fun, he wasn't allowed to step foot outside the house until he finished his homework and practiced his violin, but things were even worse once he got outside, because he was constantly picked on and beat up by the neighborhood kids because he wore thick glasses and had braces, and when they found out about his violin lessons, they teased him relentlessly, and nicknamed him 'Tony-Beethoven', which he thought was dumb because he had learned in class that Beethoven played the piano instead of the violin, and during an argument with one of the neighborhood bullies he brought that up, but it backfired and they ended up laughing in his face and pushing him around and teasing him even more. Chris Garrett and his younger brother Byron, who everyone called Iron-Man, were the most popular kids in the neighborhood, Tony couldn't stand Chris because he teased him more than anybody else, but Chris and Iron-Man were the Captain and Co-Captain of a club called The Fellas which consisted of Chris, Iron-Man, Maurice and his brother Larry, Earl and Ricky. Even though Tony couldn't stand them, he would've given anything to be in that club. He tried constantly to befriend them, but they only teased and embarrassed him in front of the girls in the neighborhood. Things finally changed when Tony convinced his parents to let him invite The Fellas over for a sleepover for his twelfth birthday. Iron-Man really didn't want to go, but Chris, who was always a quick thinker and an opportunistic soul, convinced Iron-Man and the others to go to Tony's party by reminding them that Tony's parents had a lot of money and would probably buy Tony whatever he wanted, which meant that they could also get whatever they wanted if they played their cards right, so they agreed, and actually ended up having a decent time. The boys stayed up all night playing video games, laughing, wrestling, and talking. They were in the middle of a deep discussion about who was still a virgin and who wasn't, (a conversation led by Chris who bragged that he had sex all the time, even though they all knew he was lying), when the new Nike commercial that showed Michael Jordan flowing through the air with his tongue hanging out, came on the television and everybody went crazy! Everybody except Tony, he could not believe how excited they were about something as silly as sneakers. Tony's uncle James

Jr. had served his time in the military and was now a supervisor at the Nike Factory, and every year for Christmas his uncle gave him five pairs of Nike sneakers, Nike jackets, Nike socks, Nike underwear, Nike t-shirts, even Nike sweat bands and wristbands, and on his birthday, he'd get even more Nike gear from his uncle. Tony never wore the stuff and in fact the same shoes that everyone was going crazy over were sitting in his closet collecting dust. Tony hated sports gear and he believed that the only reason his uncle even gave him all that stuff was because he could get it for little or nothing at the Nike plant. Everybody knew that Tony's favorite thing to wear were Sebago Loafers with a pair of Levi 501 Jeans and a nice crisp buttoned-down shirt. Tony's parents didn't mind the gifts from his uncle because they would usually give them away as Christmas presents to their employee's children. The day after the sleepover, Tony went into his closet and pulled out all the stuff that he had just gotten for his birthday. He examined them closely and still couldn't figure out why the other boys were so crazy about those sneakers, he thought about giving the sneakers to The Fellas when he saw them the next day, but then he had an even better idea. He was so excited that he stayed up all night! The very next day he came outside dressed in a Navy-blue Nike warm-up suit, a Navy-blue and white Nike T-shirt, and a pair of Navy-blue and white Nike Air Jordan's, and the matching Navy-blue and white Nike wrist and headband, and when The Fellas saw him, they went wild!

"Tony-Beethoven! Where did you get all of this from? Mane! You Nike all the way down to your toes!" Chris teased,

"Mane! He even got on Nike socks!" Iron-Man said as he pulled up Tony's pant leg revealing Tony's Navy-blue and white Nike socks., Tony's confidence and popularity skyrocketed as they begged him to let them see his collection of Nike gear, but he would never let them in his closets and kept them intoxicated with wonder and intrigue. Tony was amazed when they began to argue over who was his best friend and who met him first and from that moment on, they treated him like a celebrity, and when he got contacts instead of glasses and his braces removed, even the girls in the neighborhood began to notice him, The Fellas even shortened his nickname and started calling him Tony-B instead of Tony-Beethoven, as Tony-B's interest in sports increased, he rarely got to see his friends during the week because he attended a private school, and most afternoons he either had basketball, baseball, or violin lessons. Usually by the time he came home from practice, he would be so tired that he would drift off as soon as he finished his homework. Tony-B would usually see The Fellas on the weekend if he didn't have a game or a recital to attend and in a short time Tony-B became The Saturday Superstar, which meant that every Saturday Morning his friends would sit on his front porch and eagerly wait to see what kind of Nike gear he would have on when he came outside. When his dad told his brother James, Jr. about Tony-B's newfound fame, his uncle made sure that he had even more Nike gear, in fact he had so much Nike gear that he never wore the same outfit or shoes more than twice, and The Fellas would usually argue and fight over the clothes and shoes that he would give away. Tony-B loved the attention and praise that he got from his friends, as a matter of fact, he craved it, spending the whole week thinking about what he was going to wear on Saturdays. Every Friday afternoon, after school, Big Tony would take his son to the barbershop owned by his best friend Blue. Blue and Big Tony had been friends ever since Tony-B could remember and he was the only one that Big Tony would let cut their wild curly hair, and they would usually get the same haircut, a plain college cut with a small part on the side. But one Friday while Blue was busy cutting Big Tony's hair, Tony-B wandered around the shop and noticed Blue's Son, BJ (Blue, Jr.), who had a station on the other side of the barbershop, he was busy cutting a Nike symbol into the back of a boy's head and Tony-B just had to have that! He begged and begged his dad to let him get it, but Big Tony wasn't having it, until Blue stepped in,

"Come on Big Tony, the boy makes straight A's! It's just a Nike sign, I could see if it was a gang sign or something like that, but a Nike sign, man that's harmless! Besides, as fast as that boy's hair grows, it'll be gone in a week!" Blue reasoned,

However, Tony-B had no intention of letting his Nike design grow out, and week after week he had BJ to cut a different Nike design in his head. Big Tony hated it, and he even had to make a large donation to the private school that Tony-B attended in order for them to allow him to continue to wear the haircut in their strict school, but Big Tony had to admit that he loved the fact that his son was not only finally fitting in with other neighborhood kids, but he was now the most popular kid on the block, and as long as Tony-B kept his grades up, he would continue to let him get his designs. Then came the girls, they started calling the house nonstop and Big Tony eventually ended up letting Tony-B have his own phone line, which rang off the hook. But truth be told, Tony-B was never really interested in having a girlfriend, he would much rather have The Fellas around than those screaming, annoying, silly little girls that never said anything to him when he walked by, but always played on his phone and giggled and left sugar sweet notes on his doorstep. In fact, Tony-B liked girls even less than he liked those dumb tennis shoes and all those stupid designs that he let Blue's son cut into his head every Friday afternoon, but for all the attention he received, he felt it was well worth it.

One day when The Fellas were over, the conversation shifted from Tony-B and his shoe collection to Kenya, who according to them, was the finest girl in the neighborhood at that time, she was a red girl with freckles, sandy brown hair, bow hips, and perfectly round breasts that looked like two orange halves beneath her shirt,

"Mane, check out these Nike's that I got last night!" Tony-B said as he pulled his new shoes out of the box,

"Mane, forget that!" Chris said, "We're talking about fine ass Kenya right now!"

"Why we gotta talk about her, she ugly!" Tony-B said in disbelief, his uncle had gone through a lot of trouble to get him a pair of Nike shoes that weren't even in the stores yet, and all that these dudes wanted to talk about were girls,

"Tony-B... I worry about you sometimes, you act like you don't even like girls, you must be funny or something?" Chris said with a frown,

"Who you calling funny!" Tony-B said as he jumped up and stood in Chris' face,

"Mane, sit down somewhere!" Larry said, as he grabbed Tony-B from the back and slung him down on the bed, "He didn't even mean it like that! Stop taking stuff so serious!"

Tony-B calmed down instantly, he didn't really want to fight Chris, and he was glad that somebody had grabbed him. Larry was always big and tall for his age, and he would've been attractive if it wasn't for his huge front teeth that pushed his top lip up and out, and his thick glasses that made his eyes look almost three times their normal size,

"Yeah mane, I didn't mean it like that!" Chris apologized, "But for real...if Kenya was my girlfriend, Maaaaane! I'd be boning her EVERY single night!" Chris said as he dived onto Tony-B's bed and dry-humped the mattress, "But she likes You Tony-B, I don't know why she likes your ugly ass, but you need to talk to her!" he said once he stopped dry-humping the bed,

"Me?" Tony-B said surprised, "Man I already got a girlfriend, her name is Rebecca, and she goes to my school!" Tony-B said, really hoping that they would stop talking about girls and get back to his new shoes,

61

"REBECCA?!? Awwwww Mane!" The Fellas yelled at the same time acting like they were falling out on the couch and the floor,

"I bet she's white too, ain't she?" Earl asked, already knowing the answer, Earl was the shortest of the group, his skin was the color of black coffee, he had a round baby face with deep dimples in his cheek, and naturally wavy hair that he kept cut in a low fade, Earl was very popular with the girls because they thought he was so cute and adorable,

"So! What's wrong with that?" Tony-B asked,

"Aw Mane! I see we gone have to school this dude!" Ricky said,

"Mane everybody at our school wants to get with Kenya, I would have boned her myself if I wasn't going with her sister, but she fine too! And yesterday in gym class Kenya was asking me all kinds of questions about you, she told me to give you her phone number, they stay three houses down from me!" Chris said excited,

"And??? I don't want her number, and anyway, my girlfriend Rebecca is the finest girl at my school!" Tony-B said aggravated,

"AAAAANNNND??? What do you mean, and??? And... that means that you can spend the night over my house and after it gets dark, we can sneak out my window and go over there and bone them together!" Chris said even more annoyed,

"I don't wanna bone her! I don't even know her!" Tony-B said with a frown,

"This boy right here so dumb!" Iron-Man said pointing at Tony-B with his thumb,

"Who are you calling dumb, Iron-Man? At least I don't like fat girls! Maya is even uglier than Kenya!" Tony-B snapped,

"Me and Maya are just friends, and why are you changing the subject anyway, I ain't never even seen you with no girl... fat or skinny!" Iron-Man shot back,

"Yeah, why you change the subject, Tony-B?" Chris asked,

"Cause I don't like that girl! Anyway... check out these new Nike's, these bad boys ain't even in the stores yet!" Tony-B said holding up his new shoes again,

"Mane we ain't thinking about no damn shoes!" Larry said smacking the shoes out of Tony-B's hand, "We're talking about fine ass Kenya, with the brown eyes, the long hair, the big titties, and the big ole' booty!" Larry said as he made an O shape with his hands,

"So! She still ugly, with all of them freckles in her face!" Tony-B said as he picked his shoes up off the floor and dusted them off,

"Y'all, I think Tony-B likes them shoes more than he like girls, I told y'all something was wrong with this dude!" Maurice said with a frown on his face,

"I'm with you Chris, I think Tony-B might be kinda...u know!" Larry said as he twisted his wrist, swinging his hand back and forth,

"I ain't gay!!!" Tony-B said as he jumped up in Larry's face, Larry balled up his fist and drew back,

"Mane sit down, he's just playing!" Chris said as he stood in between Tony-B and Larry, "Dang, Tony-B! You can't even take a joke!" Chris said as he pushed Tony-B down on the couch that was in his bedroom,

"He always trying to get serious about everything!" Larry said,

"Yeah, and always getting up in people's face and stuff, like somebody's scared of him," Chris said,

"Mane, let's go!" Maurice said,

"Yeah, let's go!" Earl agreed,

"Y'all are the ones who can't take a joke, I was just playing!" Tony-B said as he jumped off the couch and ran to the door and blocked the doorway,

"So, you gonna call her or what?" Earl asked,

"Yeah, I'll call her later on tonight," Tony-B said,

"Mane, he's lying!" Earl said to the group,

"I'm for real, I'm gonna call her!" Tony-B said, but he really hadn't planned on it,

"Call her right now then!" Chris said,

"Man, y'all just wanna hear me get my mack on so y'all can try and steal my lines!" Tony-B said,

"What lines? You ain't got no lines!" Chris said,

"I bet his lines sorry as hell, I bet he don't even know how to talk to no girl!" Iron-Man said,

"I got plenty of lines, and anyway, you ain't never heard me talk to no girl, remember!" Tony-B yelled,

"Well call her right now then and put her on speaker phone so we can hear your so-called lines!" Chris said,

Tony-B was backed into a corner, so he did the only thing he knew how... he put on his game face and called Kenya and put her on the speaker phone, Kenya dissed him at first, and The Fellas covered their mouths and laughed, but by the end of the conversation, he had Kenya eating out of the palm of his hand. Tony-B was amazed at how easy it was to break a girl down, and he was eager to get her off the phone so that he could see what The Fellas had to say,

"Kenya, I have to go, but I'll call you a lil' later, alright baby?" Tony-B said with his chest poked out,

"Okaaaay…" Kenya said as she blushed and giggled,

"Man! I didn't know my boy had it in him!" Chris said as he patted Tony-B on the back,

"I told y'all! Don't be doubting my macking skills, now go on and give me my props, gone on and admit that Tony-B is the Mack of the year!" Tony-B said with his arms folded like an 80's rapper,

"I don't know about all that, but you do got a few skills though, just a tiny little bit," Chris said pinching his pointer finger and thumb together,

"We'll see…I bet I bone her, watch!" Tony-B bragged, and the next weekend he convinced his parents to let him spend the night over Chris' house and he did just that, he snuck out of Chris' back window and into the girl's bedroom and laid in Kenya's bed while Chris and her sister were in the other bed on the other side of the room. Tony-B had no idea what he was doing but he figured how hard could it be to kiss her, feel on her breast, put his weenie inside her hole and hump up and down. Chris was nervous until he saw Tony-B getting at it, then he put his nervousness aside because he didn't want Tony-B to steal his bragging rights.

For Tony-B's sixteenth birthday, Big-Tony got him a shiny red Chevy Camaro, which Chris totaled six weeks later, but Tony-B lied and said that he was the one driving. His parents were upset, but since he kept up his good grades and stayed out of trouble, they bought him another one identical to the first one. Tony-B's fondest memories were when his dad would gather The Fellas and surprise Tony-B at his high school games. He loved that because even though he was popular at the private school that he attended, there were only a few black students there, but he blended in with his fair skin, in fact all the boys at school and in his neighborhood wanted to be just like him. However, things took a dramatic turn after Tony-B graduated high school and went off to a prestigious college up north. He was so excited about college, ready to shine like he did in the neighborhood and in high school, but when he got there, no one cared about his Nikes or his macking skills. He tried his best, but no matter what he did, Tony-B could not fit in. He made good grades, wore expensive clothes and he let his hair grow out curly and wild like everybody else's, but the white students thought he was too black, the black students thought he was too white, and the girls, they were totally out of the equation altogether. It had been three months since Tony-B had gone off to college, but it seemed like three years. Tony-B couldn't wait until Christmas break, he spent weeks thinking of stories to tell The Fellas when he got back home, he was even anxious to see Kenya even though he had only called her twice since he left for college.

Tony-B couldn't wait to get home, couldn't wait for the big party they would throw for his visit, and being back in celebrity status, but he hadn't counted on how easily the Saturday Superstar would be forgotten and that life in Memphis, Tennessee had somehow managed to go on without him, and so did Kenya. She had moved on with Paul, another guy from the neighborhood, and was two months pregnant with his child. Tony-B wasn't that bothered about Kenya, but The Fellas totally surprised him, they were all too busy with their own lives and the goings on of the neighborhood to hang out with him. He spent most of his time trying to chase them down and toward the end, it appeared that they were all trying to avoid him.

Tony-B was so depressed that he stayed in his room most of the time and couldn't wait to get back to school, and to top it off, he almost missed his flight, because Chris promised that he would take him to the airport, but he never showed up. Once he got back to school, Tony-B threw himself into his work and got in good with the Intellectuals, or the nerds as everyone else called them. He even met Bernard Phillips, a Physics Major, who became his best friend, but that didn't last long because Tony-B made the mistake of believing Bernard when he told him that he knew how to cut hair, he did, but he was self-taught and had never cut anybody's hair with the same thick crawling curls that slid through the clippers and multiple swirl patterns and cowlicks like Tony-B's hair. Tony-B found out instantly why Big Tony only let Blue or B. J. cut their hair, he almost passed out when he went into the bathroom and looked in the mirror, there were patches of hair missing, and his hairline was cut almost an inch farther back than it was supposed to be, and to make matters worse, Bernard had lined the back of Tony-B's head even with the top of his ears, no blending or anything, just a straight line, and then bald. He'd also cut an inch-thick zig-zag into the side of Tony-B's head. In a blind rage, Tony-B grabbed Bernard and slammed him into the dresser, then picked him up and held him up in the air by his neck, he drew back to punch him, but the confused and hurt look on Bernard's face snapped Tony-B back into reality. He let Bernard go and snatched a hat off his dresser and ran back to his dorm, but the next day word got out about Tony-B's botched up haircut and one of the students snuck up behind him and snatched his hat off in the middle of the crowded cafeteria. They started calling Tony-B, "Zig-Zag" after that, and every single day he was the object of ridicule. He couldn't walk down the hall without being laughed at or tripped, they snuck into his dorm and put peanut butter and cooking oil all over his room, and every five minutes somebody was snatching his hat off his head and playing keep-away with it. Something inside of Tony-B turned off, he stopped eating, stopped doing his work, and even stopped going to class. One of Tony-B's professors called his dad and told him about Tony-B's depression. Big Tony understood full well how bad depression could be, he caught a flight immediately, and when he made it to Tony-B's dorm room, he couldn't believe how miserable and skinny his son had gotten. He was like a zombie, just skin and bones. His hair had grown back, but now it was just a big curly mess that sat on top of his head. Big Tony fought back tears as he looked into his son's eyes and saw nothing, his whole soul had been emptied. He brought his son back home in the middle of the night and parked in the garage and snuck him inside. For three solid months, no-one even knew that Tony-B was back in town, he never left his room, and only got out of the bed to use the restroom. He never watched television, or listened to the radio, and he never so much as even looked out of the window. Natasia would cook for him, trying to put some meat back on his bones, and she would sit in a chair beside his bed and sing to him while rubbing his head. She would hold him in the middle of the night when he would whimper in his sleep, or when he would wake up screaming, and she would sing to him until he calmed down and she heard him snoring softly. She eventually nurtured her son back to health, and when Tony-B was ready, Big Tony enrolled him in Memphis State University. He wore the most expensive clothes and shoes and clung to dear life to the northern accent that he had acquired, but only because it drove the Southern girls wild! Soon, The Fellas began to drift back into his life and Tony-B, the Saturday Superstar was back with a vengeance and he vowed to never fall off the throne again!

***

Tony-B wiped his eyes right before Maya came in and sat his breakfast on the table, luckily for him, Maya was too busy trying to hide her own tears to pay any attention to his,

66

"This looks good Maya…you're not gonna join me for breakfast?" He asked once he noticed that there was only one plate on the table,

"No, I'm not hungry," Maya said as she walked away,

"*You're* not hungry??? I can't believe that!" Tony-B joked,

Maya ignored him as she walked out of the sunroom, and like clockwork, the moment she made it to the bedroom and got comfortable in the bed, Tony-B called her on the intercom system,

"Hey Maya!"

"Yes Tony?"

"What happened to my mangoes?"

"Oh, I forgot." Maya sighed,

"You're slipping Maya! You're really slipping!" Tony-B said as he shook his head in disappointment,

"It won't happen again." Maya said, her feelings were way too hurt to even have an attitude,

"I sure hope not, because I'm beginning to think that you've forgotten how to please your man," he responded,

Maya went into the kitchen and grabbed a few mangoes out of the refrigerator. She sliced them with a surgeon's precision and arranged them in the bowl hoping that it would lighten his foul, insulting mood. Maya hated when Tony-B behaved that way, and when she walked back into the sunroom and placed the glass bowl full of mangoes on the table she could feel his eyes on her, inspecting her, almost hunting for a new flaw that he could insult. She back peddled into the kitchen, deciding that it would be a nice gesture to bring him another glass of fresh squeezed orange juice. She walked in and gave him a defeated smile, but the disgusted look that he gave her almost sent her running out of the sunroom. She felt like she was interrupting him or something, so she hurried back into the kitchen.

Tony-B's eyes lit up when he saw the bowl of mangoes. He imagined a bronze skinned woman with long slender legs and small perky breasts lying naked on the table in front of him. He could feel himself stiffen as he bit down on a slippery slice of ripe mango. He closed his eyes and worked it around in his mouth slowly, savoring each bite. The texture and even the smell of it drove him wild. He began to devour the slippery fruit, being as messy as he possibly could. He started making slurping sounds, as he imagined the sweet juices streaming down the sides of his mouth were actually her juices. Tony-B flicked his tongue relentlessly over the fleshly parts of the mango. He was suddenly so aroused that he was about to rip through the silky material of his pajama bottoms. He imagined burying his head deeper and deeper

67

between her thighs. He inhaled deeply, flicking his tongue over the juicy piece of mango before biting down and sucking with all of his might, he sucked so hard that he actually disintegrated the flesh of the fruit until there was nothing left but the peel, and then he would start all over again with another fresh piece of mango, imagining that it was another woman, one even more beautiful than the last,

"*A threesome...,*" he thought, "*No... a foursome! Better yet, a room full of women...and all of them just for me!*" he thought,

Tony-B was delighted as he imagined being surrounded by beautiful women all waiting for him to please them with his all-powerful tongue, beautiful exotic women, way prettier than those stuck up girls from college up north who wouldn't give him the time of day, but in his mind, at that table he was King, and these women were more than happy to part their thighs for him to feast upon them, and he imagined that they held his head in place with their beautiful slender fingers, firmly pushing their juicy mangoes in his face just the way he liked it! Tony-B had a fixation with oral sex and if he could, he would both give and receive it all day, every day, but despite his obsession with both pleasing and being pleased, it was something that he didn't do with Maya often, he tried, he really tried, but her body just turned him off. Throughout their whole relationship he had only done it to her three times, once when they first started dating to turn her out, and the second time was when he proposed, and the third time was just this morning, to make her forget about him not coming home Saturday and all three times he had almost vomited right there with his head wedged deeply between her thick thighs, each time he had to play it off quick and hurry up and stick his penis inside of her before he became as soft as overcooked Ramen Noodles, but the strangest thing was that even though he hated the way her body looked, he loved the way she smelled, felt, and tasted when she was aroused, he would often stick his fingers inside of her and smell them before sucking them clean while he rammed deep inside of her from behind with his eyes closed. He loved pulling her hair and holding her shoulders while he rode her into the sunset. And strangely enough he liked when her thick legs rested on his shoulders while he plunged deep inside her and looked deep into her sexy oval shaped eyes, especially when she could barely keep them open and the wild sex sounds that she made when he went in as deep as he possibly could. He loved how tight she was on the inside and the way she throbbed wildly and continuously around his manhood as he pounded her mercilessly into submission. Maya had one of the prettiest faces that he had ever seen. He loved her full lips and her long thick hair. If only she was smaller and if only, she was as appetizing to him outside of the bedroom. Tony-B would never let Maya perform oral sex on him, one reason was because he liked experienced women, the ones who would get on their knees and let him ram their throats and choke them with his manhood, the ones who would let him call them dirty bitches in the throes of passion, and he knew Maya would never go for that, and the other reason was because it meant that he would also have to look at her naked body while she was down on her knees, because that was the only way he liked it, dominating them while watching them devour him. Tony-B liked the fact that it didn't take much for Maya to be excited by him, a few sweet words, a kiss on the neck, and a lick or two on her nipple and she was ready. When he first got with Maya, he could tell that she wasn't or hadn't been very sexually active. She was so timid and not very experienced at all. Tony-B was well-endowed, and it took him a while to get Maya as open as he wanted her, but once he finally did, he liked how she took him in, all of him, no matter how hard he pounded. She just took it like a pro, no whining or complaining like most girls did. She liked it when he went in deep, bucking like a wild horse whenever he spanked her plump behind and snatched her thick long hair. He loved it when she was close to reaching her peak, and the way she squirted everywhere when she came, but she was just way too big for his taste, not that she was sloppy and fat, or anything like that, *"Because she is rather firm to be a big girl, but she just has too much ass, if that's even possible, and her stomach is all pudgy, and we're not gonna even talk about those big old hanging titties, uggggggggh! It's a shame I have to close my damn eyes and imagine that she's somebody else just to fuck her,"* Tony-B told Earl just last weekend, Tony-B worked hard to have the body of an African Athlete, if only Maya did the same, thinking about Maya's weight made him soften instantly, and it took all he had to turn his thoughts back to his imaginary women sitting on the table again, because all of them were firm and slender, even if they were all in his mind, but nevertheless, they were all leaning back on their elbows with their legs parted wide, just waiting for him to feast upon them. He became aroused all over again when he could feel their firm thighs resting on the sides of his head and their long slender fingers caressing his head. He teased the mango with his tongue again and imagined the women one-by-one, trembling in total surrender beneath the power of his twirling tongue. Tony-B also began to tremble as his imagination ran wild, he was so preoccupied with the mangoes that he hadn't even noticed Maya staring at him from the entranceway to the sunroom.

It was strange for Maya to see Tony-B mimicking the act of oral sex with such passion when they had been together for almost three years, and this morning was only the third time he'd performed it on her. Maya didn't know whether to be jealous of the mangoes, or turned on as she watched him devour them. He was certainly in his own little world, with mango juice running like water down his chin. Maya began to thump between her legs but then it occurred to her she wasn't the one that he was fantasizing about. She slipped back into the kitchen area, her self-esteem plummeting. Maya wondered if he had been thinking about his mango-flavored inspiration when they'd had sex this morning. She could tell it was something different about it. She was surprised when he went down on her, but as soon as she began to enjoy it, he suddenly stopped and flipped her over and plunged deep inside of her, trapping her orgasm in the pit of her stomach, which was such a miserable feeling, but she never let on because she didn't want to ruin the moment. Maya suddenly felt depressed, so silly had she been to think he had developed a passion for her after three years of lukewarm, one-sided painful sex.

Maya's head hung low as she went into the bathroom at the end of the hall and stepped into the middle of the empty king-sized jacuzzi bathtub. She turned on the faucet and ran the water as hot as she could possibly stand it and poured in almost a half the bottle of her favorite Mystic Calm bubble bath. As swirls of lathering water and steam surrounded her, she laid back and closed her eyes hoping and praying that somebody's... anybody's son would care enough about her to visit her in her dreams.

Things had been very tense in their house since Tony-B's party. They were barely on speaking terms, well, Maya stopped speaking to Tony-B after he refused to tell her what the fight between him and Chris was really about. After Maya left for work, Tony-B called the office and told his assistant to reach him by email or cell if she needed him. He then went into his other favorite room in the house, the bedroom he had transformed into his own personal clothing den, with every brand name piece of clothing you could possibly imagine handpicked, and hanging on velvet covered hangers that hung from a steel conveyor belt that swung around the room by remote control, and in the center of the room stood three custom made cube shaped glass cases, almost taller than he was, with small mirrored see-through drawers on all four sides: one case was full of watches, one case full of his expensive jewelry, and the last one was full of his expensive sunglasses. He also had wooden shelves built around the four walls for his shoe collection, and a case for his expensive cologne that he had gotten from all around the world, some that were custom made just for him, and some that he had inherited from his father. Tony-B laughed when he thought about how upset Maya was when she moved in and realized that she wouldn't have her own personal office like the one he had, but he eventually bought her an Apple computer, a Mahogany desk, and an expensive Italian Leather office chair just to shut her up, but her so called home office was in the far corner of their Master Bedroom. She was lucky to have her own bathroom at the far end of the hall, even though he had four full bathrooms in the house, including the one in the Master Bedroom and a half bathroom near the kitchen. Tony-B had his house built from the ground, precisely the way he wanted it, to the very last detail. There was the Master Bedroom, the Exercise Room, the Closet Den, The Fellas' Lounge, that Maya wasn't allowed to go into unless she was cleaning or bringing refreshments for Tony-B and The Fellas on game night, then there was his Personal Office, that Maya wasn't allowed to go into at all, under no circumstances, and last but not least, he had two Bone Rooms or spare bedrooms just in case one of his friends got lucky after one of his parties, or if they wanted someplace to creep, or crash when one of their girlfriends were tripping or when they were too drunk to drive home.

Tony-B loved being surrounded by extravagant things, but Maya on the other hand, liked simplicity. She didn't mind having a regular walk-in closet in the Master Bedroom, and she didn't mind using the bathroom at the end if the hall because Tony-B had a Jacuzzi built into it, so all things considering, it was pretty nice. Tony-B allowed her to decorate the kitchen, dining room and their bedroom the way she wanted as long as she didn't fill it with flowers or make it too girly, and he never asked her for a dime for the bills or anything, he even gave her an allowance and full access to his bank accounts because she was the one who managed the bills and handled all of the errands, and he knew that he could trust her and she'd never steal from him.

***

3 TIME TO WAKE UP, MS LADY...

"Ms. Anderson…Maya Anderson...Ms. Ma-ya Ander-son...MS. ANDERSON!!!" Nurse Shelton yelled as she stood in front of Maya with her hands on her hips,

"I'm sorry, I must've dozed off," Maya said as she popped up from her unexpected nap,

"I can see that! Well come on back here! I ain't got all day to be waiting on you! You better be glad that I didn't skip over you, then you would have been sitting here all day!"

Maya stood to her feet and quickly headed toward the door behind the angry nurse. Maya was embarrassed because she had dozed off again, she found herself doing that a lot lately. She frowned and rolled her eyes at the nurse while struggling to keep up with the nurse's steady pace. Maya hated going to the doctor, but more than that, she hated his nurse's nasty attitude,

"Get undressed and put this gown on, and make sure it opens in the front this time!" Nurse Shelton barked as she grabbed a gown from a drawer beneath the bed, and tossed it on the floor at Maya's feet, Maya rolled her eyes at the nurse and walked over to the drawer and grabbed another gown before slamming the drawer shut,

"Well excuse me!" the nurse said as she shuffled towards the door,

"You're excused," Maya snapped back, "and if you wanted somebody to fetch something like a damn dog, then you should've been a nurse in an animal clinic and not in here, now if you'll excuse me..." Maya said, as she walked past the nurse and opened the room door for her to leave. Nurse Shelton was not

72

used to people talking back to her, and her blood began to boil as she stopped in her tracks and spun on her heels, so that she and Maya were almost nose to nose in the hallway,

"I hope the next time, you'll pay attention so that I won't have to call your name over and over again, next time I'm just gonna skip over you, I do have other patients to tend to, you know!" Nurse Shelton said insisting on having the last word,

"Then by all means, go tend to them!" Maya said before taking a step back and closing the door in the nurse's face. Maya giggled as she began to undress, folding her clothes and placing them in the chair with her back to the door, when suddenly the door flew wide open, Maya yelped and ran to the other side of the room,

"I forgot my charts!" The nurse said with a smirk as she held the door wide open with her foot, she snatched the charts from the counter, as Maya counted at least three people, two of them men, walking by and staring at her while she stood there with her mouth wide open trying to shield her naked body,

"Ooh I can't stand her!" Maya groaned as Nurse Shelton finally let the door close, Maya slipped into the gown and hopped onto the bed, Dr. Morris had been her doctor for years and she knew it was gonna be a while before he would come into the room.

"Man, I can't wait to get back to work, I have so much to do today," Maya thought as she laid back on the bed, she was so tired that she could hardly think straight. Maya was dreading this appointment, she knew no matter what the problem was, Dr. Morris was going to bring out the dreaded stirrups, even if you told him, you had something as simple as a headache, he would still bring out the stirrups, Maya thought as she laughed out loud and was still laughing when Dr. Morris walked into the room,

"Good morning, Maya!" Dr. Morris said as he entered the room,

"Hey Dr. Morris," Maya said,

"Are you okay, you look tired?" he asked,

"I am tired, I can barely keep my eyes open and lately I keep getting these headaches and sharp pains in the bottom of my stomach,"

"Oh, I see…well let's take a look-see down there and see what's going on," Dr. Morris said as he pushed the red button so that a female nurse could come in and assist with the examination,

"Oooh, I hate this!" Maya thought as Dr. Morris pulled out the dreaded stirrups...

"Would you like a morning, or an afternoon appointment?" The receptionist asked,

"Morning," Maya answered,

"We have an 8:30, is that okay?"

"That's fine," Maya answered, trying not to yawn,

"We'll see you then, Ms. Anderson, have a good day," the receptionist said,

"You too," Maya said as she grabbed the appointment card and headed to her car. She dropped her prescriptions off at the pharmacy and decided to stop and get a fill-in for her nails, "I may as well get a pedicure too, after the weekend I've had, hell I deserve it!" Maya thought as she sat in the whirlpool massage chair.

Maya couldn't wait to lay back in the massage chair and immerse her feet in the warmest water, full of snow-white soap suds, and as the sudsy water swooshed and swirled around her feet, her body and mind finally had a chance to relax. Maya dozed off in the massage chair and could barely keep her eyes open during the entire manicure and pedicure, when she left the nail shop, she suddenly felt energized, so she went to the supermarket to pick up a few groceries. She hadn't really cooked since Friday, so she wanted to surprise Tony-B with a nice home cooked meal. Her iron level was extremely low, which explained the faint dark circles around her eyes and the fatigue. She picked up a beef roast, some carrots, potatoes, and Brussels sprouts for dinner. Dr. Morris told her that she had also developed a urinary tract infection, which explained the pain in the bottom of her stomach, so she grabbed two jugs of Cranberry Juice and a gallon of water because she could still hear Dr. Morris saying, "You're going to have to drink more water, Maya!" She also had no idea that she was anemic, which explained her extreme fatigue. Maya couldn't wait to get home to call Tricia, she knew Tricia would be waiting for her call and even though Maya had a lot on her mind, overall, she was in a good mood. She rushed home to drop off the groceries before heading to work to put the finishing touches on her presentation which was almost finished a whole two weeks ahead of schedule. She thanked her anger for that, ignoring Tony and throwing herself into her research yesterday had really paid off.

Maya let out a long sigh as she turned the corner and saw Earl's emerald green Camaro parked in her spot in the garage beside Tony-B's Cobalt blue Jaguar instead of in the circular drive where he normally parked, Tony's Cobalt blue Jaguar and his prized-possession, his Cobalt blue Hummer was already parked in the garage, and his Cobalt blue Suzuki GSX-

R1000 bike was tucked neatly and covered in the corner which meant that Maya would have to park in the circular driveway. She was aggravated because Tony-B's friends knew better than to park in her spot, but Linda had called earlier and told her that Chris was in the hospital, so she assumed that Earl was over there trying to get Tony-B and Chris to end their feud. Maya was pissed off as she struggled to get the groceries out of the car. She thought it was strange that Tony-B had left both the garage door and the door that led from the garage to the kitchen wide open. She walked in and almost dropped the groceries when she heard them yelling, they were so loud, that they hadn't even heard her when she came in,

"I'm sick of this shit Tony-B!"

"Don't be yelling in my damn house like you crazy! And don't you pop your ass up over here without calling either!" Tony-B demanded,

"What the hell was I supposed to do, you've been dodging my calls and texts, and I've been down here for almost three months now, and you still haven't handled your damn business!"

"Baby, I haven't been ignoring your calls and I got your texts, I've just been a lil' busy lately, that's all,"

"Please! Busy doing what? Throwing parties and trying to impress bitches!"

"You know what...you can roll on up out of my house with all of that bullshit! Cause I don't have to listen to it!" Tony-B yelled,

"You're gonna put me out of your house...me, Tony?"

"If you don't stop yelling, then hell yeah...you gotta roll!" Tony-B said as he pointed to the door with his thumb,

"That's funny, just three days ago you were standing in that very same spot talking about how you were going to put her out first thing Monday morning, and now Monday rolls around and she's still here, but now you want to put me out?"

"I know what I said, but you have to understand, these things take time!" Tony-B reasoned,

"You've had all the time in the world Tony-B!"

"Just listen Baby...Listen! You keep running your mouth, but you're not listening to shit that I'm saying..." Tony-B said calmly, the tone in his voice changing from harsh to silky smooth, he reached for her hand as he continued, "I care about you, I do, a lot, shit, a whole lot, why do you think I whooped Chris' ass like I did, it was because he was disrespecting me and trying to grind all up on you! Shit got real fucked up and now he's in the hospital!"

"WHAT!!!" Maya's mind screamed out loud, so loud that she

had to grab onto the countertop to steady herself, she was almost
sure that her ears were betraying her, because she couldn't
possibly be hearing this right...

"All I did was dance with that dude, one stupid dance!
Then you started flipping out!"

"One stupid dance? The way you were grinding all over
him, you may as well have gone ahead and fucked him right
there on the floor in front of everybody!"

"Don't disrespect me Tony-B! I've never disrespected
you and you're not going to disrespect me, you're the one who's
cheating, not me!"

"Mane look! You knew what it was when you first met
me, and you think this shit is easy for me, all this lying back and
forth! Saturday night was one of the worst days of my fucking
life!"

"Really! Because it certainly didn't seem that way
Saturday night when we were at the hotel, you were just fine
then!" Torya, Earl's cousin, said as she stood there with her
hands on her hips, her outfit today was in stark contrast from her
outfit at the party last weekend, she wore fitted pink jeans, a pink
and white t-shirt with rhinestones all over the front and some
plain white Mary Jane sneakers with her hair brushed back in a
thick bushy ponytail,

"You know what the hell I mean!" Tony-B yelled,

"No, I don't know! Explain it to me...enlighten me
Tony-B!"

"You know exactly what I'm talking about, you're just
mad right now,"

"No, I'm not mad, I'm just sick of your shit, that's what
I am!"

"Baby, I know you're mad, but I just need a little more
time, and I'll make all of this up to you, I promise," Tony-B said
as he walked up to Torya and wrapped his arms around her
waist, he stared into her eyes and moved in closer with a kiss,

"That shit doesn't work for me anymore!" Torya said as
she put the palm of her hand over his lips, blocking his kiss,

"What, I can't kiss on you now?" Tony-B asked
innocently,

"Hell no!" Torya said with her hands on her hips,

"What did I do that was so bad Torya?"

"For one, you always tell me one thing and then you do
another, and I'm just tired of it!"

"Well, if that's the case, I could've just stayed my ass here with Maya after all that shit jumped off Saturday, but I spent the night with you, didn't I?"

"So! You were supposed to spend the night with me, you are supposed to spend each and every night with me, I am your woman, aren't I? Or at least that's what you tell me," Torya said smugly,

"Yeah Baby, you are, but you have to understand that things are kind of complicated right now, did you know that I got so mad Saturday night at the party that I almost pushed Maya through that glass patio door over there," Tony-B said as he pointed in the direction of the glass patio door,

"That was your damn fault! You're the one who made such a big deal out of one stupid dance, and to be honest, I don't really give a damn what you almost did to her fat ass!" Torya said with her hands still resting on her hips,

"Don't even act like that Torya, just because I'm with you, doesn't mean that I don't still care about her, and we may not be on good terms, but I still care about what happens to her!" Tony-B explained,

"And when you're finished talking, I still don't give a damn about what you almost did to that fat bitch, and you still can't have us both!" Torya said as she fanned him off,

"I'm not trying to have you both, I just need some more time to tell her, that's all, we both have a lot invested in this house and in this relationship. You just can't sort that kind of shit out overnight! It's gonna take some time,"

"I don't give a damn about that! What about us, Tony-B, when are you going to tell her about us?"

"Soon Baby, I promise, I just need a little more time, that's all,"

"You know what…it sounds like you still want to be with her, that's really what it's beginning to sound like to me!" Torya said with a bitter frown on her face,

"Ain't no love there Torya, as a matter of fact, there are no feelings there at all. I've never loved her. I got with Maya strictly for convenience, that's all! My dad had just died, and thanks to my mama's no-good ass brother, the company that my Granddad had built from the ground had just folded, and the rest of those money-hungry ass folks in my family were too busy trying to steal money from his life-insurance policies. My mama was sick and stressing and nobody else even cared, but Maya was there for us. She would cook and clean for me and my mama. She helped us through a really rough time. She's a good person, and she does whatever I need her to do. She cooks for me, and she keeps this house squeaky clean. I can't just throw that away overnight. I have to make sure that she's okay. I can't just kick her out on the streets after all she did for me and my mama," Tony-B explained,

"Fuck that goody-two shoes, Betty Crocker wanna-be ass bitch, you can afford to hire a maid, three or four maids if you wanted, so don't give me that! And I hope you don't think that I'm gonna be around here cooking and cleaning up behind you, that's not me, and you knew that when you met me!"

"Yeah, I do know that…and that's the thing…you're the most beautiful, but she's the most dutiful," Tony-B teased,

"Wait…are you comparing that bitch…to me???" Torya said almost doubling over in disgust,

"No! I was just saying that over time a man can get used to a girl like Maya," Tony-B stammered,

"So, you do love her?" Torya asked again, glaring at him,

"Torya, we've been together for almost three years…"

"That's not what I asked you, I asked you if you loved her?"

"No, I don't!" Tony-B answered after noticing the look on Torya's face, "I mean, I care about her, and I care about what happens to her, but as far as love, no, I don't love Maya…I never did," Tony-B confessed,

"Then why in the fuck is she still here, why Tony-B? Why is her shit still here, and why isn't it out there on the fucking curb where it belongs?"

"I'm not gonna be that cold to her. Torya, I've done a lot of cold-blooded shit to her over the years, but I'm not gonna put her outside. The least I can do is give her some time to find another place to stay,"

"Really? Well, I wonder if she'd still be here if I hadn't lost the baby!"

"BABY!!!" Maya was so weak that she could hardly stand, her knees buckled beneath her, and she clung to the counter for dear life …

"You're so full of shit Torya! I flew straight to Seattle the moment I found out that you had lost the baby, you said you needed me there with you and I was right there the whole time! So don't throw that shit up in my face, he was my son too!"

"Well, you sure as hell don't act like it!"

"I'm not having this conversation with you Torya! Like you said, we just lost our baby four months ago, just four months ago…and look at you…out on the dance floor shaking your ass like a damn stripper, all up in Chris' face, what was up with that shit anyway, huh Torya?" Tony-B said as he backed Torya into the wall and pointed his finger in her face,

"It wasn't even like that, Tony-B!" Torya said as she turned her head to the side, dodging his finger, "I was putting on a show for you, and you seemed to like it, until her fat ass caught an attitude!" Torya said, getting angrier by the minute, so angry that she pushed Tony-B's hand out of her face, "The only reason I even danced with that dude anyway was because his crazy ass girlfriend was picking with me from the moment they got here, so I killed two birds with one stone! I was in his face just like you were in Maya's!"

"What! I hardly said two words to Maya the whole night!"

"But you live here with her, you're *ENGAGED* to her, and contrary to what you're standing here telling me, you're probably still fucking her, as disgusting as that shit sounds!" Torya said frowning, "And you are crazy as hell if you think I'm going to just sit around and be the little jump-off while you and Maya live the good life!" Torya said as she pushed Tony-B upside his head with her finger,

"I'm not fucking her!" Tony-B yelled as he slapped her hand out of his face,

"Then why in the hell would you ask that bitch to marry you!"

"That don't mean nothing! And I know you ain't still tripping about that damn engagement ring, Torya, I offered it to you first!"

"That's right, and I told you that I wouldn't marry you until you put that bitch out, so instead of putting the bitch out, you gave that bitch my ring? My ring, Tony-B!"

"Your ring?!? You said you didn't want it!"

"Why in the hell would I accept an engagement ring from you and you're still living here with her, does that make any sense to you? I thought you were going to save it for when you put her out, when we were finally together, but then you go and pull this scandalous shit! And then I had to come to that party and see you and her dressed alike, looking like the number 10, and the fat bitch is wearing my ring on her damn finger, do you have any idea how that made me feel Tony-B?"

"I didn't tell you to come to the party, as a matter of fact, I told your ass not to come!"

"Well, I'm glad that I did! It gave me a chance to see this shit for what it really is, and not the way you want me to see it,"

"You didn't see anything, like I said, I hardly said anything to her the whole night,"

"Yeah, but you and this bitch were dressed like the fucking

Wonder Twins, it's real funny, when all you do is talk about how miserable you are with her, and how the sight of her fat ass makes you nauseous, well, it certainly didn't look that way to me!"

"Whatever it looked like, that's not the way it was, I'm gonna do what I need to do for you and I to be together, Torya. I just need some time to sort things out, okay?"

"Wait! First you say you need time for her to find a place to stay, but now you say that you need some time to sort shit out. You were the one who told me that you were going to put her out a long time ago! See, that's exactly the kind of shit I'm talking about!" Torya said, her voice was blaring by now,

"I know what the fuck I said!" Tony-B yelled back, "But there's a right and a wrong way to do shit, her name is on this damn house too, and I'm not gonna lose my house just because you want me to rush this shit!" Tony-B lied, hoping that it would get Torya off his back at least until he could figure out what he wanted to do,

"Then take her name off the house, you say she does everything that you tell her to do, right? Then tell her that you have to take her name off the house temporarily for insurance reasons, or tax reasons, hell I don't care, tell her something, tell her anything! She'll fall for it! And what do you mean, there's a right and a wrong way to do things? Was getting me pregnant before you dumped your little pet pig the right way to do things?"

"Ain't no need for all of that name calling, Torya, and it's just not that simple!"

"I'll call that fat whore whatever I want to call her," Torya said slowly, making sure to pronounce every single syllable, "You can't tell me what to say about that bitch!"

"See…that's why we're not together right now Torya, your mouth is just too damn sassy for me!"

"Oh really, okay then, if we're not together, then that means I'm single, right? Is that what you want? Okay then, let's be clear, since I'm single, I'm free to be with the next guy and you can keep on playing house with your lil' fat Suzie Homemaker! I'm over this shit! I'm gone!" Torya said in that same slow melodic tone that Tony-B hated, she tried to walk away from him, but he grabbed her by the arm and pulled her back,

"Lil' fat Suzie Homemaker? You're wrong for that

Torya!" Tony-B laughed, still holding on to her arm, "But for real...I know who I wanna be with, I just need a little more time, that's all, and I need for you to trust me, okay?"

"How do you expect me to trust you, when you gave that bitch the ring that I picked out, how could you give her my ring!" Torya said, her eyes tearing as her voice cracked,

"I'll buy you another ring baby, an even bigger one! We can go pick it out right now if you want, just don't give up on us!" Tony-B pleaded,

"I don't know, I love you, but I don't trust you, and I can tell that you still have feelings for her, you don't have to tell me, I can tell..." Torya said as tears met beneath her chin,

"If you can't trust me, then maybe you do need to go and be with the next dude, because I'm not gonna be with nobody who can't trust me! I don't need you questioning me every five minutes about where I'm going and what I'm doing once we finally do get together, I get enough of that shit from Maya!"

"How can you say that to me Tony-B, when I'm the one who's been patiently waiting on you, while you're with her!"

"I know that Baby, and I'm getting things together for us, I am...all I'm asking you to do is just be patient for a little while longer, and just trust me while I do what I got to do," Tony-B's voice softened as he grabbed Torya and pulled her close, spinning her around so that her back rested against his chest, he wrapped her in his arms and kissed her lightly on the cheek, Torya melted into his arms as he wiped her silent tears with the back of his hand, "You know you're my Baby, and we're gonna be together real soon, I promise," Torya was so emotionally wound up that she couldn't even respond, she just nodded her head up and down as Tony-B planted soft kisses on her tear soaked cheek,

"Isn't this the perfect little picture..." Maya said as she stood at the doorway, Torya didn't know whether to stand still or to run. Tony-B's eyes bucked wide open, but Maya kept her cool as she walked calmly past the two of them and had a seat on the arm of the couch. Maya wondered where she was getting all of this courage from, when her initial reaction was to just leave that now tainted engagement ring on the kitchen counter and run right back out the garage door. How easy it would've been for her to pretend that she hadn't heard what she had just heard, or seen what she had just seen, her fiancée's arms draped around another woman in such a sweet and tender, loving way, more loving than he had EVER been to her in their whole three years together. The way his lips pressed against this woman's cheek, more passionately than he had ever kissed her, and the way he affectionately nuzzled his chin inside

81

the curve of this woman's neck almost drove Maya to tears. Maya didn't even think that he was even capable of this kind of love and affection, because he'd never been that way with her, not sincerely, but that scene would forever be etched into Maya's mind, along with the words, *"Torya, you're the most beautiful, but Maya's the most dutiful..."* and *"I don't love Maya...I never did..."* those words churned deep into Maya's soul and made a thick bloody paste where her heart used to be, and on top of that, Maya's stomach began to turn when she thought about him making love to this woman the same way that he had made love to her just this morning! Maya was so devastated, pondering over and over again how she even ended up in this situation, how she became *that girl,* the kind of girl who ignored long scratches on backs and late night phone calls and hang-ups, the kind of girl who cooked and cleaned and put up with him and his rude and disrespectful ass friends, the kind who was always ignored and taken for granted, the kind who settled for a laptop in the corner, a bathroom at the end of the hall, and one stinking closet when he had the whole entire house at his disposal for him and *his* friends, the kind who stood at the door and watched as her fiancée made oral love to mangoes instead of her, and last, but certainly not least, the kind of girl who also watched quietly and patiently as her fiancée not only argued with, but explained to, and romanced another woman, right in their home, right up under her nose, *THAT GIRL!* The faithful and trusting door mat, the one who settled for a second hand engagement ring and the one who always thought about her fiancé and his friends and not herself, the one who graduated from college a whole year behind because she spent what was supposed to be her senior year in college caring for him and his mama when the whole world had turned their back on them,

Maya wondered if his mama even knew about this new girl, but it no longer mattered as Maya sat there calmly on the arm of the couch with her arms and ankles crossed while her fiancé and his new lady stared at her in silence, Maya thought about all of Tony-B's little verbal attacks on her appearance, his attacks on her love for him, on her passions, on everything about her that he didn't like. Maya thought about how he not only put her down constantly, but how he also put everything and everybody else before her, and how she dealt with all of it in stride, but this attack right here, this attack was blatant, right in front of her face, and not to be denied, so pretending and playing dumb in this moment was not even an option. Maya was not prepared for this attack, this attack that permeated her home, her own little piece of what she'd called her life. Maya's stomach began to turn as she sat there with her eyes closed to gather herself and her thoughts, this was way too much for one person to process. Maya took another long deep breath and steadied her spiraling thoughts. She could feel her heart beating in her throat and each breath was getting heavier and heavier, Maya felt faint, but she snatched herself together when Torya spoke,

"I really don't have a problem with you Maya, I'm glad that you know, in fact, the only reason I came to that tired ass party last weekend was so that I could tell you!" Torya said, interrupting Maya's thoughts,

"What!?!" Tony-B said, he couldn't believe his ears,

"Is that right?" Maya asked with a calmness that concerned Tony-B a little,

"Yeah, that's right!" Torya said brazenly with her hands on her hips,

Maya laughed slightly, then shook her head and took another deep breath,

"And you...you don't have anything to say?" Maya asked Tony-B, who stood there in dead silence,

"Maya, it's not what you think, it's a lot going on that you don't understand," Tony-B said, almost stuttering,

"Then explain it to me Tony, I'm listening..." Maya said still calm,

"I never wanted to hurt you Maya, please believe me, and I'm not trying to hurt you now, I would never hurt you on purpose, it's just that I'm kind of confused about some things,"

"CONFUSED!?! When, in the fuck, did you become confused?" Torya yelled, "You told me that it was over, and she had to leave! But now you're confused? Okay! Tell her how confused you were when you spent the night with me at the hotel after the party last Saturday! And tell her who really put those scratches on your back, the ones that you told me she was so upset about!" Torya ranted and raved as she paced back and forth around the room, flailing her arms about, but Maya hadn't moved from her spot on the arm of the couch,

"Oh...okay...I see..." Maya said as she closed her eyes and nodded her head slowly before taking another deep breath when she began to see spots,

"Torya, let me talk to Maya for a minute," Tony-B said after seeing the look on Maya's face,

"Who in the hell are you talking to?" Torya asked as she pretended to look around the room in search of some imaginary person,

"I know you're not asking me to leave because, I'M NOT BUDGING, I'M NOT GOING ANY FUCKING WHERE!!!" Torya screamed at the top of her lungs. Maya looked at Torya and then burst into laughter, Tony-B spun around and stared at her, he had never seen Maya like this, and it was beginning to freak him out. He could feel the tiny hairs standing up on the back of his neck. Tony-B decided that he'd better make it right with Maya, and quickly! He walked towards Maya and reached for her hand, but Torya was so outraged, that she stepped in between them and smacked Tony-B's hand away,

Maya still hadn't moved, for one, she was afraid that if she did, her knees would buckle, and two, she was trying with everything she had to maintain her cool, which was evaporating fast!

"Tony-B, I know you don't think that you can get rid of me that easily," Torya said as she stood there in disbelief,

"Torya, just leave! I'm asking you nicely." Tony-B pleaded,

"I don't give a flying fuck about how nice you're asking me! I'M NOT LEAVING!" Torya said and in one sentence she went from gritting her teeth to flat out screaming,

"Just let me sort this out with Maya, and I'll call you later Torya, I promise!" and as Tony-B pleaded with Torya, the only thing Maya could do is look from Torya's mouth to his, the whole thing seemed surreal to her, and it wasn't up until that point that she realized just how weak he was and how much power she had willingly given to him without question. Maya felt as if she was sitting in a movie theater watching someone else's crumbling life instead of her own, and suddenly her legs didn't feel so wobbly anymore,

"You act as if you're afraid to tell her who it is that you really want, Tony-B!"

"I'm not afraid of shit, Torya! You're just acting a damn fool, and I ain't got time for that right now! So just go ahead and leave and let me talk to Maya, okay?"

"HELL NO! I'm not leaving you here with her!" Torya yelled,

"Torya, listen, it's over! Get out! NOW!" Tony-B demanded,

"Fuck you Tony-B! If you want me to leave, then put me out!"

"Maya, I'm gonna walk her outside, then I'll be right

back so we can talk, okay? Don't go nowhere, I'll be *RIGHT* back! You hear me?" Tony-B asked as he reached for Maya with pleading eyes, but the look Maya gave him could've bent metal! The fact that this woman was in her house, with whom she thought was her fiancée, and barking orders was becoming all too real for her,

"Maya please, I'll be right back, I promise!" Tony-B said begging for her hand,

"TONY-B, FUCK THAT BITCH, AND FUCK YOU TOO, BUT I'M NOT LEAVING!!!" Torya yelled as she walked up to him with her hands on her hip,

"Torya, just go home, I'll talk to you later!" Tony-B said, changing his mind totally, about walking her out to her car,

"Well, we'll just stand here all day, because I'm not going anywhere unless you're going with me! This may as well be our house, you, me, and that bitch will just live in this house together!" Torya said as she sashayed over to the recliner and sat down with her legs crossed and her arms folded.

"Torya, I'm asking...no, I'm begging you to leave, and I will call you later, I promise!" Tony-B pleaded,

"Whatever!" Torya said as she snuggled into the recliner, making it overly obvious that she was not going anywhere,

"Maya, I'm so sorry about all of this, I'm not trying to hurt you, I never wanted to hurt you, it's just that..."

"He doesn't want your fat ass!" Torya interrupted from the recliner,

Maya was fed up, "Look...ummm...whatever your name is..." Maya finally said with an exhausted tone to her voice, "Get out of here, before I hurt you, okay?" Maya said as she pointed towards the door.

"Bitch please!" Torya said, as she stood with her hands on her hips, "If Tony-B can't make me leave, what in the hell makes you think that your fat ass can make me leave!" And speaking of leaving, Tony-B told me that he was getting ready to put you out of his house, anyway!" Torya said before walking up to Tony-B and putting her finger in his face. "And why are you standing here acting like you can't speak up for your damn self?" Torya asked, as she pushed Tony-B upside his head with her finger, Tony-B had to catch himself to keep from slapping her across the room.

"You'd better keep your hands to yourself Torya, I'm telling you!" Tony-B said, trying to calm himself,

"You're telling me? Okay, well since you're so good at telling people things, then tell this fat bitch to leave like you said you were going to do in the first place! Why don't you tell that!" Torya demanded, peering at them both,

Maya was quiet, but her blood was boiling. She looked at Tony-B in silence, but her eyes dared him to say it, because if, and when he did ask her to leave, Maya was going to claw him beyond recognition. Maya's heart sank even further when Tony-B dropped his head, Torya was still raving about, and walking back and forth swinging her arms,

"This is some straight up bullshit, Tony-B! I cannot believe that you made me quit my job and move all the way down here to this backwoods ass city for this shit! I gave up *everything* to be with you Tony-B! And now you want me to leave...WELL I'M NOT GOING ANYWHERE!" Torya screamed, "And YOU! You weak, sloppy, fat, BITCH!" Torya spat bitterly as she pointed her finger at Maya, "You may as well scoot your big ass over because we'll both be sharing that king-sized bed with him tonight! I've already fucked him in it a hundred times while your dumb ass was at work! Did you know that, Maya? He doesn't want you! If he did, he wouldn't be trying to make a family with me!" Torya said proudly,

"Torya that's enough!" Tony-B snapped, "Get the fuck out, NOW!" he said as he grabbed her by the arm,

"Oh no, I'm not finished yet," Torya said as she snatched away from him, "Did he tell you about our baby, Maya? Did he tell you about that?" Torya taunted, as she ducked over and under Tony-B's arms as he struggled to grab her arm again,

"Shit!" Tony-B mumbled under his breath, when the words came flying out of Torya's mouth,

"What baby? What baby is she talking about, Tony?" Maya asked calmly,

"She had a baby a few months ago, but it didn't make it," Tony-B said as if the baby that Torya gave birth to had nothing to do with him,

"Was it yours?" Maya asked, her eyes clouding with tears,

"Was it his? Of course, it was his! Who's else would it be?" Torya asked,

"Was it?" Maya asked Tony-B again, ignoring Torya,

"Yeah... it was mine," Tony-B said as he lowered his head,

"I just told you it was, you stupid bitch!" Torya said, she was livid that Maya had the nerve to question whether Tony-B was the father of her deceased baby,

Maya nodded her head slowly, then laughed in disbelief, she had heard them talking about it while she was in the kitchen, but to hear him say it now, it just made her want to throw up,

"Maya, I was going to tell you about it, I really was," Tony-B reasoned, but Maya raised her hand motioning for him to stop,

"And you came to the party like you had never met him, and the whole time..." Maya said more to herself than to Torya, the whole situation was finally beginning to sink in. Maya had so much anger forming inside of her that she couldn't even finish her sentence, she was thoroughly repulsed by them both, "I knew it, I knew it! For some reason, I could just feel it when you first walked through the door," Maya said to no one in particular, "And you... you... you stood there! And you acted like I was crazy and you even insulted me and scolded me like a damn dog when I asked you about it and you were screwing her the whole damn time..." Maya said trying to talk her way through the situation, she placed her hands in the praying position, then pressed her praying hands against her lips as she spoke, she was struggling hard to keep her sanity from seeping through the cracks that were forming in her mind,

"Okay then, with your psychic ass, now you know the truth, so go ahead and get your shit and leave, because we are going to be together whether you like it or not! We have a deep connection and nothing and no-one is going to come between that, not even you, Ms. Cleo!" Torya said as she flung her hand in the air,

"Ooooooooh!" Maya groaned painfully, she took a deep breath gathering in as much air as she possibly could, "Girl...you couldn't *possibly*...know how patient... I'm trying to be with you right now," Maya said between breaths,

"I'm not afraid of you Maya, you don't scare me at all with your fat ass!" Torya said as she marched up to Maya, Maya rose slowly to her feet and turned so that they were close enough for their noses to touch, things were definitely heating up, and Tony-B could tell by Maya's eyes that he'd better do something and fast!

"Come on ladies! It's no need for this, we all just need to calm down," Tony-B said as he moved in between them and stood sideways with his arms spread wide,

"Move Tony-B!" Torya screamed as she slapped his arm out of the way and leaped over his shoulder, grabbing a handful of Maya's hair, Maya's head jerked violently to the side as Tony-B tried to push Torya back, but before he could, Maya reached around him with lightning speed and grabbed Torya by the neck with her left hand, and punched her in the face with three quick right-handed jabs, Torya was so stunned that she released Maya's hair instantly, she tried to run but it was too late, Maya shoved Tony-B out of the way and knocked Torya to the ground, and before Tony-B could catch his balance, Maya was already kneeling over Torya and punching her repeatedly,

"Maya stop! You're gonna kill her! Maya stop!!!" Tony-B yelped as he tried to pull Maya off of Torya, he tried to put Maya in a bear hug, pulling her back with all of his might, which gave Torya just enough time to stumble to her feet. Tony-B noticed that the left corner of Torya's mouth was bleeding, and her left eye was beginning to swell,

"You bitch!" Torya said as she spat a mouth full of blood onto the plush beige carpet, "That's why I pulled your damn hair out!" Torya said, as she held up a handful of Maya's hair, which sent Maya into a blind rage, she elbowed Tony-B in his ribs with all of her might, causing him to double over in pain, and while he was bent over she shoved him with so much force that he went flying over the ottoman, her long hair swung from side to side as she took a boxing stance, jabbing Torya senselessly, until she fell and balled up in a knot on the floor, Maya lost it as she began to kick and stomp Torya as Tony-B sat there on the floor beside the ottoman in shock, suddenly he jumped to his feet and grabbed Maya from behind and held her tight by the waist,

"Let me go, Tony!" Maya roared as she struggled to get free,

"Maya stop please! Maya! Maya! Maya! Calm down, calm down Maya! Baby, please! Baby, calm down, calm down!" Tony-B pleaded as he wrestled to hold Maya, "C'mon Baby, she's about to leave, and we're gonna sit down and settle this, calm and sensibly like adults!" Tony-B pleaded as he swung Maya around and held her by the shoulders so that she faced him, "Calm down Baby, please! Let's be sensible!" He pleaded, but Maya was way past calm and far past sensible at this point, and before she could catch herself, she snatched away from him, then drew back, and slapped him with everything she had,

"Who in the hell do you think you are! Telling me to calm down when you got her all up in this house! And you almost shoved me into that fucking glass door because of her!" Maya yelled as she shoved Tony-B in his chest so hard that he stumbled backwards, "Calling me jealous and the whole time you were the one who was jealous because Chris was dancing with her! You could've fucking killed me because you were fucking jealous of a dance!" Maya said, and Tony-B was so stunned that he just stood there, "You think you can just do me any kind of way! You think you can just talk to me any kind of way, and you think you can have as many women as you want, and I'm just supposed to just take it! I was there for you, I was there when nobody else was and this is how you constantly treat me, like I ain't shit!" Maya screamed as she shoved Tony-B in his chest repeatedly, "You've had this woman all up in our house and in our bed, and you have the fucking nerve to tell me to be calm and sensible, and tell me to calm down? You've been screwing all of these strange ass women without protection and making babies with these nasty bitches! Making families with them and I'm just supposed to just calm my sensible ass down and just put up with this shit?" Maya asked as Tony-B stood there trying to figure out who this crazy woman was, because it surely wasn't his sweet and humble Maya, he stood there not knowing what to say, but his silence made Maya even angrier, if that was even possible, so angry, that she hauled off and slapped him again, this time leaving a crimson handprint on the side of his face, and even though it pissed him off, the only thing that he could think to do was to grab her and hold her tight until she calmed down,

"Let me go Tony!" Maya yelled as she struggled to break free, but Tony-B had already made up in his mind that there was no way in hell he was letting her go again,

Torya was still on the floor this whole time bawling with blood running from her mouth,

"Tony-B, I can't believe you let her do this to me?" Torya whimpered as she struggled to her feet,

"Girl, if you don't get your ass up out of here, the next time ain't nobody gonna be able to pull me up off of you!" Maya said still struggling to break free from Tony-B,

"Okay, I'm leaving! But can you just come outside and talk to me before I go, please?" Torya pleaded, but Tony-B was still busy trying to hold Maya back, and Maya was struggling with all of her might to break free,

Torya had plenty of time to leave, but she didn't, for some strange reason she just couldn't! She tried but her legs just wouldn't move. She had never felt like this about anybody, like her whole world would fall apart if she left him there with her, so she just stood there, begging and pleading with Tony-B as he struggled to hold Maya, "Tony-B, I'm not going anywhere without you, you know you don't want to be here with her, Tony-B come with me, please!" Torya said as tears met beneath her chin and joined the blood that stained the front of her pink t-shirt,

"Torya just go home, we'll talk later," Tony-B said out of breath, still trying to hold Maya, but his constant pleading with Torya ignited Maya's rage like gasoline to a fire, she used all of her weight to ram him back into the wall, knocking the wind from his lungs, his arms flew wide, freeing her, Torya squealed and tried to run, but she stopped dead in her tracks when Maya caught her by the hair from behind. Maya quickly entangled her fingers in Torya's hair and yanked her down as hard as she could,

"You should have left when you had the chance!" Maya growled as she tightened her grip causing Torya to fall to her knees in pain, "I'm gonna show you how it feels to pull somebody's damn hair!" Maya said through gritted teeth as she slung Torya from side to side by her hair, Tony-B watched in disbelief as Maya slung Torya over her head like a rag doll, he was still trying hard to catch his breath, but he leapt to his feet and ran over to Maya and grabbed her by the waist and spun her around, but Maya held on tight, and still had fists full of Torya's hair between her fingers when Torya finally broke loose,

"I'm gonna get you, bitch!" Torya yelled as she ran towards the door,

"Oh, you're still talking shit?" Maya asked in disbelief, not believing that Torya was still calling her names after she had just pounded her the way that she did, and before Tony-B could even think about trying to stop her, Maya reached over and grabbed a blue crystal lamp from the end table and sent it hurling towards Torya's head, Torya let out a loud yelp and ducked just as the lamp smashed against the doorpost, Maya tried to run after Torya, but Tony-B jumped in front of her and blocked the door,

"Maya…Maya! Maya! Baby! Baby! Calm down! She's gone! She left! She left!" Tony-B said, struggling to keep Maya from going after Torya,

"Move Tony!" Maya roared as she tried to push past him,

"Maya, Maya, Baby, listen, listen! Forget her! Baby, I promise, it'll never happen again, I promise Baby, I put that on everything! I promise, I'm done with her! I'm done! I'm done!" Tony-B pleaded,

"Move Tony, move!" Maya said, her voice trembling as tears flooded her eyes,

"Baby I'm not gonna let you go out there and do something you'll regret, it's over with okay, I won't talk to her ever again, I promise!" Tony-B pleaded,

"No, I'm done…I'm done…here you go…you can have this, I don't want it," Maya said calmly as she pulled the engagement ring off of her finger, and placed it in his hand, Tony-B was so shocked that he forgot all about blocking the door. Maya gently pushed him aside and ran outside to her car as Torya zoomed down the street thinking that Maya was going to chase her, but Maya had other intentions, her candy-coated anger had long since melted away exposing her deep down, excruciating pain, it was so intense that she could actually feel it clawing into her chest, Maya was delirious with it! Tears flooded Maya's eyes as she sat in her car trying to get herself together so that she could drive, she breathed a sigh of relief when she realized that she had left her purse in the front seat when she came home from the doctor's office. She was digging inside of her purse to grab her cell phone when Tony-B ran up to the driver side door and tried to open it, and when he saw that it was locked, he began to beat on the window with the palms of his hand,

"Maya, please don't leave! Let's talk, okay!" he pleaded with his palms flat on the hood of her car,

Maya rolled down her driver side window half an inch and yelled, "Move Tony! Before I run your ass over!"

"Baby please! Don't leave!" Tony-B pleaded again,

Maya shook her head in slow motion and tried to pull forward, but when Tony-B wouldn't budge, Maya put her car in reverse, as Tony-B blocked the driveway, Maya revved the engine, but he still wouldn't move,

"Maya, get out of the car so we can talk!" Tony-B yelled,

Maya shook her head slowly,

"You're being real silly, Maya!" Tony-B yelled, which pissed her off, so she floored it, and barely swerved around him, then drove all the way across his precious lawn,

"What the fuck!" Tony-B yelled, he forgot all about Maya as he jumped up and down in the air as her tires dug deep into his plush manicured grass, Maya rolled her eyes at him as he kneeled down to examine his precious lawn in her rearview mirror, she zoomed down the street even though she was unsure exactly where she was going, Maya drove around Memphis until she ended up in Harbor Town overlooking the Mississippi River. She sat in her car for hours watching the waves with her windows up, crying her heart out,

"What the hell am I going to do now???" Maya yelled out, and as if on cue lightening parted the sky with a vengeance and gigantic raindrops began to fall, she cried for what seemed like forever, until she was thoroughly empty, she looked at her reflection in the rearview mirror, through red, swollen, and puffy eyes,

"C'mon Maya, you can do this…" she said to her reflection, and after taking a few deep breaths, she pulled out of the parking lot and headed to the only place in the world where she could find peace, she was so relieved when she finally pulled into her mother's garage and quickly let the garage door down, she covered her car with one of her mother's old car covers and turned off the garage lights so that no one would know she was there. She knew her mother was out of town visiting relatives and wouldn't be home for at least another week. Maya staggered into the kitchen and looked into the fridge, but she didn't see anything she wanted, so she drug herself into her old bedroom and slid beneath the covers and dozed off, but a few minutes later she became so nauseous that she jumped up and ran into the bathroom, she vomited and gagged until she saw spots, afterwards she laid on the bathroom floor until she finally caught her breath, then she crawled down the hall and climbed back into bed to rest before the next wave of nausea crashed violently on top of her. This went on for hours and between the constant vomiting and the yelling at Tony and Torya earlier, her voice was completely gone, which is why Dwayne Reynolds, her Supervisor, fell for it when she told him that she had the flu, and since she never missed a day of work, he insisted that she stay home and get better, then go straight into her vacation which gave her a full two weeks off work to recover,

"Thank you so much Mr. Reynolds, I really appreciate this!" Maya whispered,

"You just get better Maya, and make sure to get plenty of rest. We'll see you when you get back, and with all of this time off, that presentation better be a killer!" he said,

"You got it!" Maya whispered with a smile,

After speaking with Mr. Reynolds, Maya turned her phone off and placed it on the nightstand before pulling the covers over her head. She slept like a brick for two days, and was still sluggish, but she dragged herself out of bed on the third day, wandering around her old room, looking at old pictures and journals that she kept as a teenager and listening to old 80's Slow Jam cassette tapes which made her so sad that she cried herself back to sleep. On Thursday she woke up feeling much better, the sadness was beginning to subside, but now regret and shame had taken front stage,

"Three years, down the fucking toilet! THREE DAMN YEARS!" Maya yelled as she stomped through the house, she was thoroughly ashamed of the way she'd behaved, fighting like a wild animal, and pounding Earl's cousin the way that she did, but the one thing that she did not regret, nor was she ashamed of, was the fact that she had hauled off and slapped Tony-B twice, and the fact that she had ruined his precious lawn! She replayed that scene in her head over and over as a big smile made its way across her face, "I should've made donuts in his fucking lawn! I should've spelled my name in cursive on that bitch!" Maya thought out loud, she wanted to eat, but the very thought of food made her want to vomit all over again, but she fixed a bowl of cereal and forced herself to eat it anyway, after all, she had another life to look after,

"Pregnant... how could I be pregnant? I mean I know it's possible, but now, why now?" Maya asked her reflection as she stood sideways and stared at herself in the bathroom mirror, she let out a long sigh and picked up her cell phone to call and ask her mom when she'd be home, but the moment she pushed the power button she noticed that the message icon was blinking. She listened to the messages, and rolled her eyes to the ceiling,

"Baby we need to talk, can you call me when you get this message, please!

Message deleted,

"Maya, answer the damn phone! That's why we're having problems right now, because you are always running away from shit like a lil' ass girl!"

Message deleted,

"Maya, why won't you answer the phone? If you don't wanna be with me no more, then I understand, but at least give me a chance to explain!"

Maya erased that message and the five just like them. She simply wasn't in the mood for explanations. Tricia had also left a voicemail,

"Girl, where are you? You're really beginning to worry me! I went by the house earlier and you weren't there, I even called you at work and they said that you were out sick. I don't know where you are, but you could've at least called and told me what the doctor said, and call your Mama too with your inconsiderate tale, she's worried too! Love you, bye!"

Message saved,

"Leave it to Tricia!" Maya laughed, the first laugh she'd had for what seemed like forever,

"Hey Tricia," Maya said, still smiling,

"Don't hey Tricia me, where in the hell have you been?"

"Girl, you wouldn't believe me if I told you!"

"Well try me, because I've been calling your ass for days now!" Tricia demanded,

"Okay…" Maya said with sorrow dripping from her voice, she told Tricia what happened word for word, at times fighting back tears and at other times letting them flow like rain,

"I am so sorry, Sis! Why didn't you call me, you know I would've flown over there!"

"I know, but I couldn't, I was just too messed up!" Maya confessed through sobs,

"I can't believe you're having a baby!" Tricia said in disbelief,

"I know, after all this time,"

"Well, the good thing is, my god-baby won't have to want or need for anything,"

"Yeah..." Maya said and Tricia could tell that mentally Maya was a million miles away,

"Well answer the door because I'm on my way over there, and you better open it too!"

"I will…" Maya laughed, knowing what Tricia was about to say, and within minutes Tricia was beating on the front door,

"Okay! Okay! Dang Tricia, stop beating on the door like you're the damn police!"

"I just wanted to make sure you heard me, Ms. I-Wanna-Be-All-By-Myself!" Tricia teased, and then frowned, "Ooh Maya, you ought to be ashamed of yourself…Girl, look at your damn hair!"

"Forget you, Tricia!" Maya said while trying to comb through her tangled hair with her fingers,

"I tell you what, we're going to my brother's shop and I'm getting your hair done, you've been in here for four whole days, and I refuse to let you just sit in here all sad and depressed!"

"Whatever Tricia!" Maya laughed, her eyes still swollen and puffy,

"I'm so serious," Tricia said as she pulled her cell phone out and called her brother to tell him that they would be coming,

"What up y'all?" Tricia's brother Mike said as she and Tricia walked into his barber and beauty shop,

"Hey Mike! You gonna hook me up today?" Maya asked,

"Hook you up? Hell yeah, I'll hook you up, but you know I ain't talking about no hair, right?"

"You need to quit!" Maya laughed,

"He sure does…" Tricia added as she side-eyed her brother,

"I'm serious as a heart-attack!" Mike joked, "I'll hook her thick ass up in a New York minute!"

"Shut up!" Tricia said rolling her eyes at him, "Mama told me to give you these tickets for the Church Fair,"

"Mama be peddling these damn tickets like they dope! Man, I tell you the truth…tell her not to send the goons after me, I'll be by there Friday to pay her, and anyway, how is she gonna volunteer me to rent four inflatable jump around toys and a tent!" Mike joked, "And while you're talking Tricia, I hope you don't think you gonna get your hair done for free!" he said frowning, but his frown turned into a smile when he said, "But I can always do you Maya…I mean your hair, anytime!"

"Just trifling!" Tricia huffed,

"Stop hating Sis, and before y'all leave, don't forget to check out the boutique, I got a brand-new shipment in, support a hard-working brotha!"

Mike was the ultimate comedian, he kept everyone laughing, but Maya never knew whether he was teasing or not,

"Mike you're a trip!" Maya said,

"He sure is, he's managed to trip over four children and three wives so far..." Tricia added,

"Jealousy is so ugly on you lil' sister, I wonder if Mama knows that you're this jealous of her one and only son, and besides, I take care of all of my children, and most of my ex-wives too!" Mike said brushing imaginary dust from his collar,

"I ain't thinking about you Mike! Anyway, all I want you to do is tighten up my micros around the edges and in the top, and I want them in an updo for our trip, you know we're leaving Saturday!" Tricia said looking over at Randii, Mike's Master-Braider, who nodded at the request,

"So! It still not gonna be free! Hell, messing with you is gonna put me in the poor house for real!" Mike complained,

"Come on Mike! Hook me up just this one time!" Tricia whined,

"Nope! Anyway, what are you getting today Maya…cause Tricia ain't talking about nothing," Mike said playfully pushing his little sister away,"

"I don't know, surprise me!" Maya said self-consciously combing through her hair with her fingers,

"She needs the works!" Tricia interrupted, "From her head to her toes, give her a manicure, a pedicure, and some kinda cure, any kinda cure…better yet, every kinda cure you can think of for that hair! And don't worry, I'll pay for it!" Tricia teased,

"Don't pay any attention to her," Mike whispered, "Tricia needs to thank God for them braids she got in her head! The only reason she even comes to me in the first place is because I'm the only one in Memphis who keeps enough rice in stock to roll that stuff with!"

"You know what, forget you Mike!" Tricia said rolling her eyes,

"You can't forget me, you know ain't nobody else out here brave enough to put their hands in your head!" Mike said as everybody in the Beauty Shop laughed, Tricia rolled her eyes at her brother repeatedly, "Maya, I'm getting Norma to do your hair, okay?" He said as he beckoned for her to have a seat, "and Randii is taking care of you Trish,"

Maya got her hair body wrapped, which took almost two hours drying time, and while she sat under the dryer, Valencia gave her a manicure and pedicure. Maya was so relaxed that she dozed off and her mind instantly drifted back to last Saturday's gathering, but this time, she was able to see everything in prospective. She thought about the first time she and Tony-B went out on a date, which turned out to be at a high school gym for a Jamboree, but that was typical Tony-B, sometimes he could be fun to talk to and sometimes he was touchy-feely, which was a plus, but as far as the romance department, Tony-B didn't have a romantic bone in his body, his shed, his ice machine, or even in his entire seven bedroom house, which made the relationship almost unbearable at times. Maya never expected to be with Tony-B forever, and deep down inside she knew he wasn't in love with her, and truth be told, she wasn't in love with him either. There was just so much about her that Tony-B didn't know, didn't like, or didn't care about. Maya knew almost from the beginning that Tony-B never appreciated her individuality or respected her opinions. Ever since she was a child, Maya loved to paint and she loved writing poetry, but Tony-B hated art and poetry, so she gave them up. Tony-B also hated when Maya wore her hair in a ponytail and to please him, she had to go to the beauty shop continuously to manage her long thick hair, he always tried to get Maya to change the way she dressed, the way she talked, what she ate, even what she watched on television.

Tony-B constantly teased her about her weight, especially in front of the
Fellas, but Maya accepted that it was just the way he was, one person in
front of his friends, and a whole different person when they were alone,
but as long as he took care of home, Maya was okay with it, but lately
she had begun to feel like an untapped geyser, just waiting to explode,
she felt like life was full of possibilities, and they were all passing her by,
she thought about leaving Tony-B several times, but every time she was
just about ready to leave, he would come up with something as sticky as
molasses, and just as sweet, to reel her back in, and in no time she would
be bright eyed and full of renewed hope, only to be disappointed once
again, which brings us to the infamous proposal...

***

THE PROPOSAL

Tony sounded so excited when he called Maya at work and told her that he wanted to take her to The Cabins in Hot Springs, Arkansas for the weekend, he gave her specific instructions to come straight home from work so they could leave early, but what Maya didn't know was that Rickey had gotten tickets to the game, so when Maya rushed home from work, she was surprised that Tony wasn't there, she called and called, but he didn't answer, and after a while her calls went straight to voicemail. Maya could tell because his answering machine began to pick up on the first ring. Maya waited patiently for him all night long, she refused to believe he had stood her up like this, especially since it was his idea in the first place. At around midnight, Maya rested her head on the back of the couch, still dressed, shoes and all, just in case...but as time ticked by, her eyelids began to get heavier and heavier, she fought as hard as she could to stay awake, but sleep crept in and took over. Maya was in a deep sleep, but she jumped right up, wiping the slobber from the side of her face when she heard Tony's keys jingling inside of the doorknob,

Tony staggered in smelling like a mixture of beer, stale cigarettes, marijuana, and cheap perfume,

"Where in the hell have you been?" Maya asked before he could even take his key out of the front door,

"I was at the game Baby, why?" Tony slurred,

"I thought you said we were going to The Cabins for the weekend!"

"Aw, we can do that anytime, Ricky got tickets to the game and all the Fellas pitched in for a skybox, and I was NOT about to miss that for nobody!"

"Well, you could've at least called and let me know something, you told me to come straight home after work!"

"It ain't too late Maya, if you still want to go, we can go, we can leave right now if you want!" Tony slurred, he was trying his best to appear sober, but his body was swaying back and forth,

"I ain't going nowhere with you Tony!" Maya growled as she stormed down the hall into the bedroom,

"Well, if you don't wanna go, why are you tripping and shit?" He asked,

"Because you had me waiting' for you all damn night, THAT'S WHY!" Maya yelled,

"What was I supposed to do, tell them I couldn't go to

98

the game because I was going' to go to The Cabins with you?" Tony laughed,

"I really don't give a damn what you tell them, because this shit right here is for the birds!"

"So much drama all the damn time..." Tony said exasperated, "Look Maya do you wanna go or not?"

"Hell no!" Maya said folding her arms and rolling her eyes to the ceiling,

"You get on my nerves with that spoiled shit! At least I wanna spend time with you, any other man wouldn't even wanna go nowhere with your ass!"

"You don't have to do me any favors Tony, I was doing just fine before you, and I'll do just fine after you!

"I can't tell! Wasn't nobody trying to get with you before me Maya, and if it wasn't for me, you'd still be by your damn self!"

"And I probably would've been happier!" Maya said as she rolled her eyes at him so hard that her head began to hurt,

"I could've just stayed where I was instead of coming home to this shit, but no... I rushed home to be with you, but do I ever get credit for the shit that I do? Hell no! I just get nonstop nagging, bitching, and complaining, all the damn time! Don't you think I get sick of that shit? Maya, I swear you ain't satisfied unless it's some drama around you!"

"No, I like peace just as much as anybody else, hell, it would be very peaceful around here if you would stop putting your friends and everybody else before me!"

"You're damn right The Fellas are gonna always come before you and anybody else, just like I come first with them, you knew that when you met me, and if you don't like it then let the doorknob hit you! Bye!"

"You know what... you're right. I'm done with this shit!" Maya said throwing her hands in the air, "I'll be back in the morning for my things!"

"Well don't be mad if you come back up in here and see another woman laying up in my bed! A fine ass woman, with sexy lips and long ass legs!" Tony slurred,

"Good, then you'll be her problem and not mine!" Maya said as she walked out of the front door and slammed it as hard as she possibly could,

Maya drove straight to her mama's house, she hadn't seen her mama in a while. She walked in the door to find Mama Anderson sitting at the kitchen table snapping her fingers and tapping her foot to the blues that flowed from a tiny radio on the kitchen counter, and of course *it was on her favorite station, 1070 WDIA, a local Memphis, Tennessee radio station,*

"Hey Mama!" Maya said forcing a smile,

"My word! Look what the wind blew in! I haven't seen you in a month of Sundays! What brings you over this early on a Saturday?" Mama Anderson said all smiles,

"Do I have to have a reason to come and see my beautiful Mother?" Maya said as she bent down and kissed Mama Anderson on the cheek,

"No ma'am, you most certainly do not, now come on in here and sit down with me," Mama Anderson said as she pushed a chair from the table with her foot,

"I've been sitting down all day," Maya said not wanting to face her mother, she knew that Mama Anderson could sense when something was wrong with her from a mile away,

"Well stand up then, they your legs," Mama Anderson chuckled, "I picked some collard greens before the sun came up this morning, they're over there in that stewpot, stankin' good too!" Mama Anderson said as she took a deep whiff,

"They sure are Mama, I can't wait to taste them, what else are you cooking?" Maya asked, excited about her mama's cooking,

"Chile, let's see...I got some candied-yams, some smoked neck bones, I got some regular neck bones too, I may even throw some of them in the oven and pour some bar-b-q sauce over them, I got some corn on the cob, some homemade cornbread, some boiled okra, and some black-eyed peas, you know how your brothers love them thangs!"

"Ooh Mama, I sure do miss your cooking!"

"Well you wouldn't miss it if you came by more often, you'd think my baby gal lives all the way on the other side of the world!"

"Don't say that, Mama...I'm gonna come by more often, I promise, I'm just so busy all the time,"

"Umm-hmm...well they say if the devil can't slow you down, he'll certainly speed you up!" Mama Anderson said as she studied her daughter from head to toe,

"He sure will Mama...he sure will..." Maya said as she turned to face the counter not wanting her mom to search her face, "Mama, where's your comb so I can scratch your dandruff for you?"

"You know where it is, it's where it always is, in there

on my dresser," Mama Anderson said, instantly sensing that something wasn't quite right, but she figured that her only daughter would open up to her when she was ready,

Maya spent all day spoiling her Mama rotten, fixing her hair, polishing her fingernails, and even giving her a pedicure, spending this much time with her mother was rare, especially since she got that promotion last year. It was 8 p.m. before Maya knew it, and like clockwork, Mama Anderson was ready for bed,

"Mama, do you mind if I bunk out on your couch tonight?"

"Yes, I mind...you know I don't like nobody lounging on my living room furniture, but you're always welcome to sleep in your old room," Mama Anderson said with a knowing smile, "I knew it was something, you must be mad at that old boy again, that's the only time you seem to come around here lately,"

"No Mama, I'm not mad at him, I just needed some time to myself," Maya said as she sat down on the couch,

"Uhmm-hmmm..." Mama Anderson said as she bent down and kissed Maya on the cheek, then she stood up straight and stretched her back, "...and they say they gonna fill the Mississippi River back up by peeing in it too!" Mama Anderson said as she walked down the hall to her bedroom, Maya smiled, she was always amazed at her mama's quirky little sayings, she waited until Mama Anderson went to sleep and popped some popcorn in the microwave and settled in on the couch to watch a movie when her cell phone rang, she answered it on the first ring,

"What!" Maya answered with an attitude,

"You miss me?" Tony-B asked,

"Hell no!"

"Aw Baby, don't act like that, you know you miss me!" Tony-B teased,

"Bye Tony!"

"Baby, Baby wait, don't hang upon me!"

"What do you want Tony?"

"Can you please stop tripping and come home?"

"Tony, I don't feel like this today!"

"Baby Pleeaase! I'll make it up to you, I promise! Just come home so we can talk, okay?"

"I don't know about that..."

"Pleeaase?" Tony-B whined,

"Ooh! I hate it when he does that!" Maya thought as she imagined his cute lil' hazel puppy dog eyes and his long sexy eyelashes, she thought about it over and over again in her mind, but in the end, she *just couldn't resist,*

"Okay, okay, I'll be there after a while!" she said before hanging up on him,

When Maya turned the corner, cars were parked up and down the street, and in the driveway, there were people going in and out of the house and loud music playing. Maya had to park on the street and she was pissed off, she burst through the front door to cuss him out, but to her surprise, when she walked in, Tony-B was dressed in a tuxedo, holding a dozen roses and on one knee in the middle of the kitchen, with a banner on the wall above his head that read:

"MAYA, I LOVE YOU! WILL YOU MARRY ME?"

Maya's first thought was to say, "Hell no!" and hightail it out of there, but she could feel anxious eyes all around her, and Tony-B wasn't worried, he knew Maya wouldn't dare embarrass him in public, and just as he predicted, Maya said, "Yes,"

Tony spent the whole evening telling Maya how he had planned the whole thing, how he had stayed out last night on purpose to make her mad enough to leave, so that he could set up the party, he had even gone through the lengths to invite Tricia and all of her friends to help cook and decorate, Maya couldn't believe it, she was all smiles as she showed off her big beautiful diamond ring,

Maya was flying high, elated at how thoughtful and loving Tony-B had been to go through all of those lengths to plan an engagement party for her, but then she thought back three months ago when all of the wind was let out of her sails,

Maya and Tony were getting along great since her engagement party, Maya didn't even mind all the cooking and cleaning and the extra parties Tony had afterwards, it was Chris' birthday party and Maya didn't even mind the basketball theme he had chosen, she proudly wore the matching purple and gold jersey and short set Tony had chosen for her, Maya and her girlfriends were buzzing around the kitchen, cooking and gossiping as usual, when Maurice, Larry's brother walked in. Maya was deep into a conversation with Tricia, but she could feel Maurice staring at her from behind. She smiled inside and let out soft, silent sighs. Tricia and the other women began a deep conversation about childbirth and labor pains, but Maya couldn't relate since she didn't have any children and had never been pregnant, she soon began to float off, drifting deeper and deeper into her own world, picturing Mr. CoCo-Brownskin running towards her in slow motion, she bit down on her bottom lip as she imagined beads of sweat dripping from his sun baked muscular body, her heart skipped a beat as his strong arms wrapped around her waist, pulling her close and looking deep into her eyes as his full thick lips took her mouth hostage, drowning her with sweet kisses, as her fingers made a trail down his spine—

"Maya, what are you daydreaming about?" Tricia asked, elbowing her in the ribs,

"Huh...I'm sorry, what were you saying Tricia?" Maya asked, really trying to get back into the conversation, but it was like they were speaking a foreign language, and it didn't take long before Maya began to drift off again,

Meanwhile, Maurice pretended to search the kitchen for the perfect snapshots, but what he was really trying to do is to take some off-guard pictures of Maya, he learned a long time ago that the camera loved her, and he liked to take pictures that captured her natural essence, especially the day dreamy ones. Maurice didn't look at Maya the way other people did, he entered her with his eyes, trying hard to invade her most private thoughts and dreams, sometimes he got so caught up, marveling at her beauty whenever she smiled, and feeling her sadness whenever Tony-B would go out of his way to embarrass her in front of his friends, Maurice had studied her for so long that he could tell when she was feeling alone even in a room full of people, like she was now. Maurice was a deep individual, who loved poetry, but his main passion was photography, he even printed his own photographs, it was one of the reasons Tony-B's parties were so popular, because he would walk around taking pictures at one party, and then he would print them out and pass them around at the next one and he would sell them for ten dollars a picture, but Maya and Tricia's pictures were always free. and not to be outdone in any fashion, Tony-B actually purchased an industrial printer made especially for photographs and a backdrop to make the pictures look like the ones people take at a nightclub, Maya thought the whole thing was cute, and Tony-B loved the fact people were crazy about the idea and they thought he'd engineered it himself, but he also thought Maurice took way too many pictures of Maya, though his pride would never let him admit it,

Maya rose from the table and walked towards the counter, being careful to keep her back turned to Maurice as she grabbed the platter of meatballs and carried them out to the dining room table. Tricia and the other girls followed suit by taking a bowl of this and a platter of that out to the table also, the women continued to arrange the food on the table

*while Maya headed back into the kitchen to finish cooking the
hot wings. When she walked into the kitchen, she noticed that
Maurice was sitting at the table alone, she ignored him as she
poured Ranch and Blue Cheese dressing into serving bowls.*

*"Maya..." Maurice called out to her with a tease in his
voice,*

*Maya smiled inside at the way he said her name,
Maurice didn't yell her name like Tony-B did, he sang it as if it
was the chorus to a sexy love ballad, pronouncing each and
every syllable with his thick southern accent, Maya fought the
urge to turn around, she knew better, Maurice had gotten her
picture like that many times before,*

"What Maurice?" Maya said without looking back,

"Why don't you turn around and see what I want,"

*"I can't, I have to finish cooking and taking this stuff out
to the table." Maya said excusing herself to take the bowls into
the dining room,*

*"Let me get that for you," Maurice said reaching out for
the bowls, he moved in close enough for her to smell his
peppermint scented breath, and not to mention his Sandalwood
scented body oil, the kind that would make you close your eyes,
throw your head back and go somewhere sunny... somewhere
where white waves pound hot sandy beaches, and...*

*"Maya, Maya?" Maurice said as he tapped Maya on the
shoulder, interrupting her thoughts,*

"Huh?" Maya answered, her mind still spinning,

"Are you okay?" Maurice asked,

*"Yeah, I'm okay." Maya said as she snapped out of her
daze. She was so embarrassed that she bit down hard on her
bottom lip.*

*Maurice smiled and winked his eye at her before leaving
the kitchen, his scent lingering in the air, causing her to inhale
as hard as she could. Maya drifted off again while stirring the
onion dip when Maurice crept up behind her, lightly brushing
his fingers down her bare shoulder. Maya forgot where she was
for a minute, dropping the glass serving bowl on the floor,*

*"Sorry about that!" Maurice said covering his mouth
with his hand, Maya was embarrassed and outdone as she
kneeled to the floor to pick up the glass pieces,*

"Let me help you with that Maya,"

*"No, that's alright, I got it," Maya said as she took the
piece of glass from his hand,*

"What's up Maya...Maurice?" Tony-B said as he walked into the kitchen after watching Maurice put the serving bowls on the table and go back into the kitchen where Maya was,

"Oh, hey Tony-B, I was trying to help Maya take some of this stuff out there, but I'm just in here breaking stuff," Maurice said trying to dismiss the nervous energy inside of the room,

"Oh, okay..." Tony said as he walked up behind Maya and wrapped his arms around her waist, "Baby why didn't you tell me you needed help, you know I would've helped you take that stuff out there,"

"Really?" Maya said before catching herself, because Tony-B never offered to help her with anything,

"Of course, I would, you know that!" Tony B said turning Maya around by her waist so that she faced him, Tony-B tried desperately to search Maya's eyes, but she nervously looked away, "Now tell me, what do you need for your man to carry out there for you?" Tony-B asked,

"You can...um... take this platter of wings out to the table," Maya said, trying to get herself together,

"Okay, I'll do that, and if you need anything else, be sure to let ME know, I am your Man, right?"

"Huh?" Maya said, confused by Tony-B's sudden concern,

"Dang, you act like you're deaf or something! I said...I am your Man, right?"

"Yeah...," Maya said through a forced smile,

"Maurice come on out here with us, you don't need to be in here with these women, plus, I want you to come out here and take some pictures for me in the back yard," Tony-B said, as he led Maurice out of the kitchen, Maya shook her head at the whole situation, especially when she noticed that Tony-B had left the whole platter of wings sitting right there on the kitchen counter, she took it and placed it on the dining room table over the warmers and returned to the kitchen to brown the ground beef and Italian sausage for another batch of Rotel dip, which always left fast, Maya smiled, it was times like these when it seemed as if Tony-B really cared about her, and Maurice, "What the hell was he doing?" Maya thought, he had never behaved that way before, and Maya actually felt some sort of nervous tension between the two of them, she had never felt that before, Maya was in deep thought when something hit the window snapping her out of a daze, the second one startled her, and the third one pissed her off, Maya ran outside to see what was constantly hitting the window when...

Snap! Snap! Snap! Snap! Snap! Snap! Maya saw spots as Maurice jumped from behind the bushes and snapped picture after picture of her!

"You scared the hell out of me!" Maya said holding her chest,

"You should've seen the look on your face!" He said laughing,

"You need to quit!" Maya said with an attitude, but deep down inside she was flattered by his sudden attention, "I have to finish cooking Maurice,"

"My fault, I didn't mean to disturb you," Maurice said apologetically,

"Well, you did!" Maya said as she rushed back up the stairs into the kitchen door,

"Maya wait! I...ummm...need to tell you something," Maurice said, and Maya noticed he had a sadness in his eyes for some reason,

"What is it?" Maya asked, concerned,

"Uhmmm... never mind... don't you want to pose for one last picture?"

"No!" Maya blushed,

"Please," Maurice asked with a smile,

"No!" Maya said before looking away,

"So mean...and yet so beautiful!" Maurice said shaking his head at Maya,

"Forget you Maurice..." Maya said, as she rushed inside and let the door slam behind her, she pretended to be mad, but once she made it back into the kitchen, she blushed so hard that her face hurt,

"Tony-B is going to break your damn neck!" Tricia said as Maya walked into the kitchen and she saw the huge smile on Maya's face,

"What? I didn't do anything!" Maya explained,

"Uh-huh... you and I both know that, but if you keep smiling hard like that, Tony-B's not going to see it that way,"

"Girl I'm not thinking about Tony!" Maya said before telling Tricia what happened when Tony-B came into the kitchen and caught Maurice helping her,"

"You really can't be too mad at him Maya, he's just trying to make sure Rece ain't trying to steal nothing off of his plate, you know people get real mad when you try to steal their meat off their plate, they may let you take a few vegetables, may even let you play with their bread...but they'll downright clown about their meat! People get stabbed in the hand with a fork for that kinda mess!" Tricia joked,

"Girl, Maurice is just being nice, that's all," Maya insisted,

"But what if he's not just being nice, and I don't know Maya...Rece is fine, and evidently he must think you're worth getting stabbed in the hand for!" Tricia teased,

"Girl! I am engaged!" Maya reminded Tricia,

"Shit, I know! But you ain't married yet!" Tricia said snapping her finger in the air,

"Ooh Tricia, you are so bad!" Maya laughed,

"And getting badder by the day baby, don't you ever forget it!" Tricia said as she laughed out loud,

Although Maya was flattered by Maurice's constant flirting, cheating on Tony was out of the question. She was eternally faithful, she never cheated on any of her past boyfriends, which weren't that many, and she felt guilty for even thinking about Maurice the way she did. She couldn't believe she was actually blushing again!

Maya's mind began to wonder, she wondered what it would be like to give in to all those unfulfilled thoughts, dreams, and desires she'd ignored for the past few years, though Tony-B did satisfy her sexually, or did he? He was only the second person she had been with in her whole entire life, the first person was Cory, a guy she met a year after Iron-Man left for California, he was a true gentleman, they dated for months before he even tried anything, and when she finally decided to sleep with him, she was so nervous that it was painful and un-enjoyable, she tried it a few more times with him, but it just wasn't what she thought it would be, or at least what Tricia had said it was, mind-blowing and all, Tricia's sex-capades with Phillip even back when they were in high school were all Maya had to compare her mundane sex life to, and it hadn't added up by any means, but that was until Tony-B, Maya shivered inside when she thought about the first time they had sex. Maya and Tony-B grew up in the same neighborhood, she knew him as Iron-Man's brother Chris' friend, they never really saw eye-to-eye while they were growing up, Maya always saw Tony-B as a loud-mouthed show-off, but when his dad died, she saw a sadness in him that she understood because she had also lost her dad when she was almost four years old in a motorcycle accident. Maya had always been a Daddy's girl, and she could still remember the way her stomach flipped when her dad would lift her up and sit her on his shoulders, and she could still remember laying on his chest and listening to his breathing, he was a kind man who would go out of his way to help anybody that he could, thinking of her dad always made her sad, so when Tony-B lost his dad, Maya reached out to him and his mom. She would take home-cooked meals to his mom's house and sit and talk with her, and Tony-B if he was there, they'd all sit down *and laugh and talk and reminisce for hours. Maya developed feelings for him when she really got to know him, she was amazed at how Tony-B acted when he wasn't around his friends, kind and loving like her dad, one night she went to his mom's house with dinner as she did every Saturday night, but his mom wasn't there, she was out of town visiting relatives, and Tony-B just so happened to be there checking on the house like his mom had asked him to. Maya was pleasantly surprised to see him because she hadn't seen him in a while, when she reached out to hug him, he almost collapsed in her arms and began crying like a baby, she wasn't used to seeing grown men cry, especially Tony-B who seemed so strong in front of his friends, she held him tight and stayed with him way into the wee hours of the morning listening to him talk about how much he missed his dad, she fell asleep on their couch and the next morning she woke up to a horribly cooked breakfast, of burnt toast and eggs, and crispy sausage, Maya lied and told Tony-B that her stomach was upset to keep from eating his meal, but she thought it was terribly sweet of him, and they laughed and talked for a while until Tony-B had to leave, Maya told him to go ahead and she would stay behind and clean his mama's house for him. Maya spent most of the day trying to get that burned smell out of his mama's house, scrubbing those singed pans, and scouring those cement-like eggs out of that skillet. After that he would always do sweet things for her, but all of that seemed like ancient history once Tony-B began to take her for granted, Maya remembered the very day she finally began to stop ignoring the voices in her head, especially the loudest one, the one that yelled from deep within her heart, the one that told her she loved Tony-B, but she wasn't in love with him, and he wasn't in love with her either, it started out as any other day, Tony-B threw his friend Larry a birthday party as he did every year, everyone was anticipating Larry's Birthday Speech, because he was always drunk when it was time for him to speak and it would be comical to say the least, everybody was on the edge of their seats as Larry got up to give his birthday speech...*

"I would first like to thank my partner Tony-B and his gal-I mean his fiancée Maya for throwing this bangin' ass party for me. I remember when my boy came to me a year ago crying like a baby cause she had left him AGAIN! I told him all he had to do is throw a party, put on a tux, get some roses, a ring, and beg her a little bit, and she'll come back! And it worked too,

once Ms. Lady saw that big ass rock Tony-B brought her, she came running back, and she ain't tried to leave no more either, she don't care what that mane do to her, she always come back, especially since he put that big ass rock on her finger! Show them the rock Maya! Look at her acting all shy! Well anyway, that was almost a year ago, and they're still at it! Let's give the happy couple a hand!"

Maya was so humiliated, but she played it off like she always did, Tricia grabbed Maya's hand and held it tight under the table as Maya fought back tears. Tony-B had been ranting and raving for almost a year about how long it took him to plan the engagement party, and how clever he was to stay out all night and to start an argument with her to make her leave, and if that wasn't enough, Larry went on to say, "Man, I told Tony-B, you can't get rid of Maya, who in the hell are we gonna get to cook all them damn hot wings and shit when we have these parties?"

Everyone exploded with laughter, except Maya and Tricia. Maurice didn't think it was amusing either. Maya turned to look at Tony-B, but all he could muster was a nervous smile.

***

Maya stared at the empty tan on her ring finger, she felt like crying as she sat under the dryer, this trip into the past made her feel like a fool for not listening to her inner self. She was disgusted at how she let comfort permeate her life, a comfortable job, a comfortable dwelling place, a comfortable (or so she thought) relationship, Maya realized she had been living a big old comfortable lie. She had always saved her money, and was just about to move out of her apartment and sign the final papers to her dream house when Tony suggested it wouldn't look right for them to have separate houses, she cringed because she could still hear him saying,

"Maya, we've been together for almost a year now, and we're gonna get married one day, it'll just be a waste of time and money if you get this house,"

"But this is my dream house, Tony!" Maya pleaded,

"I don't know if I could handle us being in two different houses. I had this house built from the ground up, and its way better than that lil' old house that you're trying to buy, forget about that house and move in with me, you won't have to pay any bills, all you'll have to do is just cook for me every now and then, c'mon Baby, you know I love you," Tony-B pleaded,

That was the very first time Tony had ever told Maya that he loved her, and Maya ended up giving up her dream house and settling once again...

Maya continued putting two and two together, and for the past few months she noticed that Tony-B had been especially distant, and she did think it was strange when suddenly, he started pressuring her to have a baby. Maya wasn't ready for that, so she snuck and took her birth control pills faithfully, but no one told her the antibiotics she'd gotten for a bad sinus infection last month would make the birth control pills inactive, so here she was, as pregnant as ever. She wondered what Tony-B would have to say about it now, even though she still wasn't prepared to tell him...

"Ooooh Maya, your hair is laid, look how shiny it is!" Tricia complemented,

"Huh?" Maya said after being suddenly snapped back into the present,

"I said your hair is beautiful, do you like it?" Tricia asked,

"Yeah, I do," Maya said, still half in and half out of her trip down memory lane, she stared at herself in the hand mirror, blinking her eyes and smiling at her complexion, the chestnut-blonde highlights complemented her skin-tone perfectly,

"We aim to please..." Mike said, satisfied at Norma's work,

"Mike! I still can't believe you're gonna charge your own sister!" Tricia pleaded,

"Well believe it, I got to make a living somehow!" Mike sniggled,

"How much do I owe you?" Tricia huffed,

"About a hundred and fifty greenbacks, but Maya you don't owe me anything as long as you buy something in the boutique,"

"Ain't that a blimp!" Tricia said with her hand on her hip,

"See I told you she was jealous," Mike said before snatching Tricia's money out of her hand, "Maya, I ain't gone even lie, those highlights look real good on you! Maaaane...If I didn't consider you family, then I'd have to...you know..." Maya laughed and hit Mike on the arm, "You over there laughing but I'm serious as a heart attack!" he said with a smile,

Maya bought five outfits, some jewelry and three pair of shoes from the boutique, Tricia bought six outfits, loads of jewelry and three pair of shoes,

"Mike, I just wanted to tell you I love my hair, and I will be back to your shop to let you do me...oops... I mean my hair soon!" Maya teased,

"Stop playing Maya…you are playing, right? Yeah, you're playing with me…for real though Maya…are you for real?" Mike asked as he followed them out the door, Maya and Tricia laughed, as they walked out of the salon feeling like a million bucks!

"So, what else do you have planned today, Maya?" Tricia asked after they put their bags into Tricia's trunk,

"Girl, a sausage pizza and chef salad from Exline's, and a long nap would make this day perfect!" Maya said,

"Oooooh! That sounds good!" Tricia agreed,

Maya and Tricia stopped at Exline's Best Pizza in Town and ordered two 6-inch sausage and pepperoni pizzas and they split a chef salad, Maya got up and put money in the jukebox and they talked and laughed the whole time, Tricia dropped Maya back off at Mama Anderson's house, Maya was so tired that she didn't even get her shopping bags out of the trunk, she just laid across her bed and fell straight to sleep.

***

4 THE SILVER PEACH

It was about 5 o'clock in the afternoon when Maya awakened from her nap. She picked up the phone to check her messages, but she decided to call and bug Tricia instead.

"Hey Tramp!" Maya said the moment Tricia picked up her phone,

"Girl I've been with you all day, what do you want now!" Tricia yawned,

"Don't you want to go somewhere tonight, I'm bored!" Maya whined,

"Go where Maya?" Tricia asked, and Maya could tell that she was tired,

"I don't know, let's go on Beale Street and eat, ask Phillip if he wants to come too?"

"Hold on, let me ask him... Hey, Phil, you want to go on Beale Street with me and Maya?"

"Naw, I don't want to go on Beale Street, why can't we go to Nigel's club over there on Main, where Precious Cargo used to be, Cequita and Gary came and blessed the place themselves and Nigel hired her cousin as the chef and they even gave him permission to sell their famous Jerk Wings! And on top of that, tonight is Reggae night!" Phillip yelled out in the background,

"You hear him, Maya?"

"Yeah, I hear that fool!" Maya said between chuckles,

"So, what you gone do, stew or mildew?" Phil shouted into the phone,

"Tell him I'm going, but I still want to go somewhere

and eat first,"

"Tell her Nigel's got plenty of food down there at the club, they sell all kinds of food, and they got them banging ass jerk wings!" Phillip said,

"If we do go, who's driving?" Tricia asked,

"Not me!" Maya said, "I'm just playing, I'll be there around eight-thirty to pick y'all up and be ready Tricia!" Maya joked,

"I will, I will!" Tricia said, but Maya knew better,

"And wear something classy this time, none of that hoochie stuff! You know how you do!" Maya teased,

"Forget you, Maya! I ain't got time to talk to you, I have to figure out what I want to wear!"

"Okay then…Ooh Tricia, I knew it was something' I forgot to tell you!"

"What girl! What?" Tricia said excited,

"This!" Click!

Maya laughed out loud as she hung up on Tricia, "She always falls for that!" Maya said, and she laughed even louder as her cell phone started ringing, "I'm not answering, it ain't nobody but Tricia calling back to cuss me out!"

Maya pulled up in front of Tricia's house at 8:30 on the dot and blew the horn,

"Come in!" Tricia yelled out the front door,

When Maya walked in Tricia was standing behind the door in her bra and panties, holding an outfit in each hand,

"I knew you weren't going to be ready!" Maya frowned,

"I told her to hurry up!" Phillip said as he walked into the living room, He looked handsome in his olive-green slacks with a white dress shirt, and olive-green incorporated in his paisley tie.

"Gone Phil! Show me what you workin' with!" Maya said as Phillip posed and then spun around and squatted with his hand under his chin like a model in a men's magazine, "You are that fire Phillip, can't nobody mess with you!" Maya cheered,

"Looking this good is hard Maya-Maya, I just make it look easy, you dig?" Phillip said as he spun around on his heels, popped his collar then strolled back down the hall,

"Maya, don't be boostin' his head up, he already thinks he's fine!" Tricia laughed, "Anyway, I don't know what to wear!"

"Why don't you wear your blue dress like the one I'm wearing?"

"You just want me to wear mine cause you are wearing yours!" Tricia said frustrated,

"Yeah, but you won't look as good as I do!" Maya said as she

113

swung her big hips from side to side,

"Maya, I don't feel like doing the twin-thing with you today,"

"Well, what about that olive-green summer dress you got the other day?"

"Oh yeah, I forgot about that!"

"See, you can be twins with Phil, I bet he'll like that!" Maya suggested,

"Yeah, I'll surprise him,"

"But which shoes?" Tricia said as she opened her shoe closet,

"Tricia!"

"What? You can at least help me pick out some shoes!"

"Girl, you got at least 500 pair of shoes in this closet!"

"For your information, there are only three hundred and forty-six pairs of shoes in my closet, thank you!"

"Well...I tell you what, if you don't hurry up and put your clothes on, I'm leaving you, and your damn shoes!" Maya said with her hands on her hips,

"Okay, okay...here I come!" Tricia laughed,

When they arrived at Nigel's club, The Silver Peach, it was packed full, they were standing in line to get in when Nigel spotted them, he smiled as he walked over to greet them,

"What's up, Nigel!"

"Phil! Where you been Mane?" Nigel said punching Phillip on the arm,

"I've been on the grind, you know how it is!"

"Yeah, I know...hey Doug, these are my guests, go ahead and let them in," Nigel said to the head of security, the guard nodded as Nigel led them inside to the V.I.P. section, "Y'all let me know if you need anything, it's on the house!" Nigel said before walking off from their table and moving to the next table to greet more guests,

Phillip spotted some of his work buddies and wanted to show Tricia off,

"I'm gonna go sit down for a minute, I'm feeling kind of dizzy," Maya said suddenly,

"You okay Maya?" Tricia asked with a worried look on her face,

"Girl I'm good, I just need to put something on my stomach, that's all,"

"You want me to stay here with you?" Tricia asked with

a worried look on her face,

"Nah, I'll be fine after I eat something," Maya insisted,

"Are you sure?"

"Phillip, would you tell her that I'll be okay?" Maya said, hoping Phillip would convince Tricia,

"I don't know Maya, you don't look okay to me, are you sure you're alright?" Phillip asked, looking concerned as well,

"I'm okay, I am…I just need to eat," Maya said as she tried to reassure them,

"Maya, if something's wrong tell me!" Tricia insisted,

"I'm just a little woozy that's all, but I'll be fine after I put something in my stomach,"

"Go on Phillip, I'm gonna stay here with Maya," Tricia said, not believing Maya was okay,

"No! I'm okay, now go on and enjoy yourself!" Maya said,

"You sure?" Tricia asked and Maya could tell that she was worried,

"Girl, go on, your husband is waiting on you!" Maya said as she gave Tricia a gentle shove, "Go on now! I'm good,"

Tricia reluctantly followed Phillip as he left the V.I.P. section to go meet some of his co-workers as Maya sat down at the table. The atmosphere was amazing, and Maya forgot all about being dizzy once the reggae music flowed through the air and made love to her ears, Maya closed her eyes swaying back and forth as the music took her away,

"This is the bomb right here!" Maya thought as last week's troubles began to slip from her mind,

"What can I get you?" The server asked,

"I'll have a Bahama-Mama!" Maya said without thinking, but she remembered her little bundle, and opted for a cranberry juice instead. She hadn't been out in years, mainly because Tony hated nightclubs, or at least that's what he always told her, but Maya was convinced the only reason Tony hated nightclubs was because it took all the attention away from him. She closed her eyes and danced in her seat, reggae music was her passion, but it was a passion she couldn't indulge in often because Tony hated that too!

"Forget him!" Maya thought as she sipped on her cranberry juice and rocked back and forth to the music,

"You having a good time?" Nigel asked as he pulled out a chair and sat next to her,

"Yeah, I am, Nigel, I'm really digging this atmosphere, and the music is on point!" Maya said with a smile,

"Glad you like it Maya, but hey, can I ask you a question?"

"Sure," Maya said turning her attention to Nigel,

"What are you doing in here all by yourself? You third-wheelin' around this mug?"

"No, I'm actually here because...because my Mama said that I could come outside and play," Maya said sarcastically,

"Oh okay...your Mama said you can come out to play, but what about your Daddy? From what I hear, Tony-B got that all sewed up and locked down!" Nigel asked with a smirk,

"You better stop listening to people, Nigel, that'll get you in trouble every time!"

"Well, I ain't never been one to run from a lil' trouble," Nigel said with a wink, "but anyway, what brings you to The Peach, you looking for anybody in particular?" Nigel smiled,

"Nah, I just needed to unwind, and wind these hips a lil' bit, you know?"

"I heard that Ms. Lady...did you know it was my birthday today?"

"For real?"

"Yeah, I need to be at home hugged up with my Lady, but you know, business is business!" Nigel sighed,

"Ain't that the truth! Oh yeah, tell Paula I said hello,"

"Okay, I'll tell her...and before I go, you know Iron-Man is back in town, don't you, Maya?" Nigel asked trying his best not to smirk,

"Yeah, I saw him the other day," Maya said suddenly realizing why Nigel was asking all of those questions,

"What ever happened between you two anyway?" Nigel asked,

"Nothing happened, we weren't dating, we were just good friends," Maya said with a shrug,

"Well, you should've been, you guys made a cool lil' couple, and you can't say you don't miss him!" Nigel said as he nudged Maya's shoulder,

"I do miss him Nigel, he was my FRIEND!" Maya reiterated,

"I hear ya, and I'll get on up out of your business, but I will say one more thing, then I'll be gone,"

"What Nosy-I mean Nigel," Maya teased,

"Alright, alright..." Nigel laughed. "I asked for that... and you can say what you want, but you were much happier when you were with Iron-Man!"

Maya stared at Nigel for a minute before looking down

at her half-empty glass,

"Hmmm…silence…that's what I thought! Now give me my birthday hug so I can get on up out of here and get my reggae on," Nigel laughed as he stood, and Maya laughed also, "Alright Ms. Lady, don't let this be your last time at The Peach!"

"It won't be Nigel," Maya said with a smile,

"I'm gonna hold you to that!" Nigel said as he walked away,

"Nigel is so nosy!" Maya thought, she laughed when she thought about what Tricia was going to say once she told her, *"Murder she Wrote,"* by Chaka Demus and Pliers, one of Maya's all-time favorite reggae songs began to blare through the speakers, and Maya made a beeline towards the dance floor,

"Welcome to Reggae Nite here at The Silver Peach, I'm DJ Thunda, Tha Fiyah Starter, and we about to get it crunk up in here! This one is dedicated to Tricia and Maya-Maya, these Ladies are heading to Trinidad and Tobago, everybody ain't able y'all! But we gonna send them off Silver Peach Style! Now get on the dance floor ladies and shake that thang all the way to Trinidad and back!" The DJ Shouted over music, Tricia and Phillip were already on the floor dancing when Maya joined them,

"See, I told you Phillip, she just can't be still when that song comes on!" Tricia said,

"You better know it!" Maya said as she began to wind her hips to the beat,

"Watch this Baby!" Phillip told Tricia as he moved behind Maya, "Watch me cut her head!"

"You can't do nothing with this, Phillip!" Maya said as she wound to the floor and started bouncing up and down to the reggae beat,

"Come on back over here and dance with Mommy, Sweetheart, cause Maya just cut your head to the white meat right quick!" Tricia said as she grabbed Phillip by the hand,

"Go Tricia, go Tricia!" Maya yelled as Tricia started winding her butt on Phillip,

"You better be glad you drove Maya, or we'd be going home early tonight!" Phillip yelled over the music, with his arms in the air snapping his fingers,

Maya laughed at him and kept dancing, she hadn't heard that song in a long time and she was really feeling this place, the DJ turned the lights down low, and Maya was deep into the rhythm with her eyes closed and her lighter waving back and forth in the air. The club looked like a river of lights as the people followed suit, holding their lighters high in the air as well, twirling their bodies to the rhythm. Tricia turned to face Phillip and they hugged and kissed passionately,

"Get a room!" Maya yelled,

"Maybe later," Tricia said with her lips still pressed onto Phillips',

Maya really loved Phillip and Tricia's relationship, they were in love, and had been since high school. Maya longed to have a relationship like theirs. She closed her eyes and let the music take her mind off of her own loneliness. Maya was so into the music that she didn't even mind when a stranger's arms wrapped around her waist from behind and ground up against her,

"You know, you're too pretty to be dancing all by yourself," The smooth voice said as the thick lips brushed against her ear, Maya was so taken in by it all that she thought she was dreaming, she leaned back into his chest and listened intensely as the voice called her beautiful and told her how much it missed her. Maya really didn't care who it was behind her as long as they kept holding her like that, and whispering in her ear like that, and making her feel like that, and kept brushing their lips against her neck and ears like that, and kept smelling like that, suddenly she realized that she wasn't dreaming, and jerked away from the voice, she turned around and was pleasantly surprised as she stared straight into the most beautiful eyes that she'd seen in a while, big old dark brown marble eyes, that glowed in the black light, they were hypnotizing, electrifying, and familiar all at the same time, Maya could hardly focus but she glanced over at Tricia, who smiled and winked at her,

"How long have you been here?" Maya asked with a big smile on her face,

"I just got here, and to be honest, I wasn't going to say anything to you, but I couldn't resist when I saw you over here cutting up on this dance floor," he said as he twirled Maya around again so that her back rested up against his firm chest,

"Is that right?" Maya said, blushing and lowering her head,

"Yeah, it's not often you find someone who likes the same music you do," he said as he rested his face up against hers,

"That's true," Maya said nodding her head in agreement,

"Didn't you miss me at all, Maya?" he whispered in her ear, chills danced all over Maya as she took several deep breaths,

"Yes, I missed you!" she whispered back,

"I thought about you almost every day, but you changed your number, and I couldn't remember your Mama's number for nothing!" he said,

"Yeah, it's a shame we lost touch like that,"

"It won't happen again Maya, I promise, I'm going to go get me a drink, you want to join me?" Iron-Man asked,

"Sure," Maya answered,

"Okay, let's go over to the bar," Iron-Man said as he led Maya off the dance floor with his arm around her waist,

"Hey Iron-Man! What can I get for you and the Lady?" the bartender asked,"

"You already know what I want, and get the Lady another whatever it was she was having earlier,"

"Alright, I have a Jack and Coke for you, and another cranberry juice for the Lady," the bartender snickered,

"Cranberry juice! What kind of drink is that?" Iron-Man asked,

"It's what I like, you got a problem with that?" Maya asked, trying not to laugh,

"Nah Girl! Whatever rocks your boat!" Iron-Man spoke with a mock Jamaican accent that made Maya laugh out loud,

"I take it you come here all the time?" Maya asked,

"Yeah, you know my cousin Nigel owns the place,"

"After all these years I never knew you were cousins, it's such a small world, I used to work with his wife and he's my, how can I say this...he's my best-friend's-husband's-best-friend,"

"You must mean Tricia?" Iron-Man said with a smile,

"Yeah,"

"Yeah, I remember her, she still looks exactly the same, we walked in together at your boyfriend's get-together last week," Irony said,

"I remember..." Maya said, her smile suddenly disappearing,

"That was kind of messed up, I hated that I had to clown like that in front of you, but dude was tripping," Iron-Man said as he shook his head,

"Don't remind me!" Maya said rolling her eyes,

"Well, I'm glad to see you," Iron-Man said with a smile, "I heard about all those parties y'all be having too," he said with a smirk,

"That was his thing, not mine!" Maya interrupted,

"Well anyway I decided to check it out, where is Tony-B anyway?" Iron-Man asked as he looked around,

"At his house...I guess," Maya said dryly,

"His house? You guess?" Iron-Man said perplexed,

"Yeah...It's a long, long story Irony,"

"Okay, well one day you're gonna have to tell me one of those long, long stories..." he said with a smile,

"So, you're the reason Nigel was over here being nosy, huh?" Maya asked, changing the subject,

"Yeah, that was me, I wanted to come and talk to you, but you know how dude was tripping at the get-together, so I had to make sure you were here by yourself before I approached you, respect is respect, and he is your fiancé," Iron-Man reasoned,

"Was my fiancé..." Maya said before taking a long sip from her straw,

"I noticed you weren't wearing your ring, what happened?"

"Again...it's a long-long story..." Maya said forcing a smile,

"I feel you, but you know I'm here if you ever need to talk," Iron-Man said,

"You've been here, and you didn't even try to get in touch?" Maya asked,

"I wanted to, but then I heard you were engaged, so I stayed my distance,"

"I remember you saying your job transferred you here, so how long do you plan on staying?" Maya said, changing the subject again,

"I actually just told Tony-B that, because he was trying to be all up in my damn business," Iron-Man admitted with laughter, "I really just looked on line and saw that Baptist Hospital was hiring for Surgical Technicians, so I applied online and got an interview, so I came here and I got the job, I'm not sure how long I'll be here, that will depend on how well things go for me while I'm here, and it also depends on what I'm staying for," he said with a sexy smile,

"I see..." Maya said smiling even wider than he was, "You wanna go back over there to the dance floor?" Maya asked, running from her thoughts and his conversation,

"After you..." Iron-Man said with a smile as he stood to his feet and held out his hand for Maya as she stood to her feet, Maya melted into Iron-Man as they danced, they glided across the floor anticipating each other's moves perfectly, Iron-Man's head was spinning with questions, and so was Maya's,

"I wonder what happened with her and Tony-B," Iron-Man wondered as they danced, and they danced on the floor all

night, Maya had forgotten all about being lonely, sad, mad, hungry, or being anything but in Iron-Man's embrace. Her imagination was running a hundred miles an hour and she loved every minute of it! She and Iron-Man were slow-winding when all of a sudden, she felt hot, like lava flowing through her veins, Maya fanned her face, trying to cool off, when suddenly everything began to spin, she closed her eyes slowly before she stumbled back into Iron-Man's arms,

"Hey, are you all right?" Iron-Man asked, holding her up,

"Yeah, it's hot in here," Maya mumbled, *"Not now, please!"* She told herself,

"Maya, do you need to go to the hospital?" Iron-Man asked as he held her up,

"No, I'm okay, I just need some air," Maya insisted,

Iron-Man wrapped his arm around Maya and held her up as they walked outside, Maya felt better once the fresh air hit her,

"I'm glad you got your color back, you scared me!" Iron-Man said as he kissed her forehead, his embrace was so tender, and he smelled so good, he stroked her hair and she looked up to say thank you, but those eyes! They hypnotized her as he leaned in slowly to *(could this be?)* kiss her, but before their lips could touch, Tricia came running outside,

"Girl what were you thinking, you could have hurt the baby!" Tricia said before thinking, Maya could see the look of shock as it rained across Iron-Man's face, and at that moment so could Tricia, who covered her mouth with her hands,

"I'm so sorry!" Tricia apologized as Maya turned away from Iron-Man and slowly walked towards her car, Iron-Man stood there like a statue as Tricia caught up with Maya, she looked back hoping Iron-Man would at least try to follow her, but when she saw him with his hands in his pockets, walking back inside of the club, with his head down, her heart just dropped,

Tricia apologized and apologized to Maya all the way home,

"It's not your fault Tricia." Maya said, her voice cracking as she battled tears, "I know you didn't mean any harm. I just hate this!"

"Hate what?" Phillip said in the middle of a yawn from the back seat,

"Hush Phillip!" Tricia said looking back,

"Tricia this baby is the only thing I have now," Maya said as she broke into tears, "My whole world is falling' apart, and I don't know how much more of this I can take!"

"Maya, I don't mean to be all up in your business, but you know you always got me and Trish in your corner," Phillip said as he stretched out on the back seat, Maya and Tricia looked at each other and then glanced back at him,

"What!?" He asked with a puzzled look on his face,

"Never mind…" Tricia said, before she and Maya laughed quietly,

When they pulled up in front of Tricia's house, Tricia hugged Maya, "You know you don't have to go back to your mama's house all by yourself, you're welcomed to stay here with us and get you some rest," she assured Maya,

"Are you sure?"

"Yeah, we got plenty of room,"

"Come on Maya, you know you wanna stay!" Phillip teased,

"Hush Phillip!" Maya said,

"Well, are you staying or what?" Phillip asked,

"Yes Phillip, I'm staying!" Maya laughed,

"Good! Now help me get into this house before I fall on my damn face!"

Maya and Tricia laughed as Phillip put one arm around Tricia and one arm around Maya,

"See, that's why I don't take you nowhere!" Tricia said irritated at Phillip,

"What are you talking about Baby, I ain't drunk! Hell, I'm hurtin'! I can't be dancing like that no more, shit, I'm gettin' old!"

Maya and Tricia laughed as they pushed Phillip from behind,

"Ouch! Ouch! Ouch! My Legs! Ooh my legs! Y'all are so low-down!" Phillip moaned as he limped into the house,

Tricia paid the babysitter as Maya settled into the guest bedroom,

"You know I have the best husband in the whole wide world!" Tricia said as she walked into the bedroom and hugged Phillip from behind,

"You better know it!" Philip said trying to add a little bit of humor to this otherwise depressing situation. It was about 1:30 in the morning, and the phone began to ring, which woke Lil' Man and he began to cry loudly,

"Baby you go and get the phone and I'll go get Daddy's Lil' Man!" Phillip said as he ran into Darrion's room. Tricia sat on the side of the bed and picked up the phone, but not before looking across the hall and watching Phillip hold Darrion up in the air and give him a kiss on the cheek,

"What's the matter Lil' Man?" Phillip said as he bounced a now laughing Darrion up and down,

"Hello?"

"Hey Tricia, is Maya over there?" Tony-B asked,

"It's almost two in the morning, is everything okay?" Tricia asked avoiding his question,

"My fault Trish, I didn't mean to call so late but me and Maya had a real bad misunderstanding the other day and now I don't know where she is, I've been everywhere looking for her!" Tony-B slurred,

"Wow, what happened?" Tricia asked,

"Nothing really, she kinda walked in and caught me and ...you remember Earl's cousin Torya, don't you?"

"Yeah, I remember her," Tricia said with a frown on her face,

"Well, me and Torya were having a heated conversation, and things kinda got out of hand when Maya walked in and--"

"That's messed up!" Tricia interrupted,

"I know Trish, I really messed up bad this time...but I'm trying to fix it! She's been gone for almost a week, and I don't know where in the hell she is, I just figured that you might know so I took a chance and called,"

"Well, I hope you guys can work it out," Tricia carefully added, ignoring Tony-B's plea for Maya's whereabouts,

"If you see her, could you please tell that her I love her and that I need for her to come home so we can talk, if you'll do that for me Trish, I would really appreciate it," Tony-B slurred,

"Okay, I'll tell her,"

Tricia hung up the phone before Tony-B could ask her anymore questions,

"Who is that?" Phillip asked from Darrion's room,

"That was Tony-B,"

"What the hell does he want this time of morning?" Phillip asked with a frown,

"He wanted to talk to Maya,"

"How did he know she was over here?"

"He didn't, he was just drunk and trying to see if she was,"

"Did he say what was going on?"

"Yeah, he said Maya caught him arguing with Torya,"

"Who's Torya?"

"She's Earl's cousin,"

"Oh, the light-skinned girl with the long hair?"

"Yeah, the light-skinned girl with the long hair...and how do you know that?" Tricia asked with her eyebrow raised,

"I saw her and Earl at the mall yesterday, I thought she was his new girlfriend or something, but whoever she was, somebody must've reached out and touched her, cause she was hiding a big old black eye under those fancy shades that she was wearing, and her lip was kinda bruised!"

Tricia chuckled, "Guess what Baby?" She whispered, still snickering, as she leaned over to Phillip as if to tell him a secret,

"What's up?" Phillip asked, leaning in as well,

"Maya did that to her!" Tricia said as she burst into laughter,

"Maya sprung on somebody! You kidding me???" Phillip whispered in disbelief,

"Nope, she did!" Tricia nodded,

"Whaaaaat?! I didn't think my girl had it in her!" Phillip laughed,

"Well, she does," Tricia said with a smile,

"What is she doing fighting, anyway, didn't she say she was pregnant?" Phillip asked,

"She is…" Tricia nodded,

"And why didn't you tell me?"

"I wasn't trying to hide anything from you Phillip, it's just that it's a long…complicated story!"

"Sounds real complicated to me!" Phillip said shaking his head,

"It is baby, it is…" Tricia said as she and Phillip got into bed, and snuggled beneath the covers,

"Good morning, Baby!" Phillip said stretching,

"Good morning, my Love," Tricia said with a wink,

"I know you're glad you don't have to go in this morning!" Phillip said as he kissed Tricia on the cheek,

"Yes Lord!" Tricia said trying to force herself to wake up,

"You're worried about her, aren't you?" Phillip asked, when he noticed how drained his wife looked,

"Yeah, I am, it seems like everything's coming down on her at once,"

"Maya is stronger than you think baby, and she's gonna pull through this just fine, everything is gonna be alright, you'll see! Why don't you go back to bed, and I'll get Lil' Man dressed and take him to Mama's house on my way to work,"

"No, you go ahead and get ready for work, I'll be okay, I got Darrion,"

"Are you sure?"

"Yeah, Phillip I'm sure, now go on in there and take a shower, you stink!" Tricia snickered,

"Oh really?" Phillip said as he tried to grab Tricia's head and put it under his armpit,

"Stop boy! You smell like a burger with extra onions!" Tricia said as she wrestled away from him, "Stanky tale!" Tricia said with her face frowned up,

"Hey Baby?"

"What?"

"You wanna jump in here and get stanky with me?" Phillip teased, making his pecks jump,

"We got company, Phillip!" Tricia laughed,

"How she gone know, hell she's still asleep!" Phillip reasoned,

"Nope!" Tricia said shaking her head back and forth,

"Please…"

"No, now go on and get ready for work!" Tricia laughed as she pushed Phillip toward the bathroom,

"Okay, Okay! But you owe me! I wanna get as many in as possible before you guys leave tomorrow," Phillip said,

"Tomorrow? Aw man! I forgot all about the trip, I haven't even packed yet!" Tricia said and Phillip could tell that she was exhausted,

"Well get you some rest, I'm serious. You got all day to pack, and if you want, you can take Lil' Man on over Mama's house, she's looking forward to spending the day with him anyway,"

"Okay, I'll take him over there in a little bit,"

Maya stumbled up and sat on the side of the bed, she was so tired, Tricia wasn't there, but there was hot water waiting in the coffee maker, and a box peppermint tea on the counter. Maya was sipping on peppermint tea and eating saltine crackers when Tricia walked into the kitchen,

"Hey, you're up early!" Tricia said as she sat across from Maya at the kitchen table,

"Hey Sis…" Maya said with a smile,

"Are you feeling better?" Tricia asked,

"Yeah, I am, I hope you don't mind, I made a cup of tea,"

"Girl, you know I don't mind, it's why I left it out, are you okay?" Tricia asked,

"Yeah, I am, I feel much better than I did yesterday,"

"You know we're leaving tomorrow, are you packed?"

"Yeah, but my clothes are still over at Tony's house,"

"Well, I'm nowhere near finished packing, are you gonna go over there and get your clothes, or are you just gonna buy some more? You know we can always go back to my brother's boutique,"

"Girl, I don't even know," Maya said in deep thought,

"You know he called over here looking for you last night,"

"When? We didn't get in until after midnight!" Maya asked surprised,

"He called about 1:30 this morning,"

"What did he say?" Maya asked bracing herself for the answer,

"He said you walked in on him and Torya arguing, and he'd been looking for you for almost a week, and he also told me to tell you to come home, he sounded drunk though," Tricia said with a sigh,

"I can't believe he told you that!"

"Me neither..." Tricia said as she shook her head in pity,

"And he sounded drunk?"

"Yep, real drunk!" Tricia said as she nodded her head up and down slowly,

"Damn!" Maya said as she let out a long sigh,

"So, what are you gonna do?" Tricia asked,

"Well, he's probably at work now, I'm thinking about renting a truck and getting my brothers to help me move my stuff out, I can put it in storage until we get back, but whatever happens, we're still leaving tomorrow as planned,"

"Are you sure?"

"Hell yeah, I'm sure! I've waited too long for this trip!" Maya said as she stood with her hands on her hips,

"Okay then Ms. Maya, I'll go ahead and get packed," Tricia laughed,

"But first, I think I'm gonna go back to my Mama's house and clean it up before she finds out I've been staying there,"

"Girl, you know your Mama doesn't care about you staying over there, just like I don't care about you staying over here!"

"I know Tricia, but you're married, and I have to respect that. I appreciate y'all, I really do, but I have to make my own way," Maya said,

"I understand," Tricia added, knowing once Maya made up her mind about something, there was no use in persuading her otherwise,

"When we get back from our trip, I might go rent a hotel room downtown, you know, until my place comes through, my brother Calvin's wife is a realtor, and she told me about Pacific Bay Town Homes in Germantown, and she told me a long time ago that she would hook me up whenever I got ready, since I got good credit,"

"Pacific Bay?" Tricia said pleasantly surprised,

"Yep!" Maya smiled,

"Girl, they are nice! I wanted to move over there, but Phillip liked this house, he said it was bigger and closer to his job, Maya are you still interested in buying a house?"

"Maybe later on down the line, but I plan on staying there for at least a year or two, you know how I hate moving!"

"Ooooh yeah, I hate moving too!" Tricia said as she swept the kitchen floor, "Hey Maya, do you want me to ride over to Tony-B's place with you, so you can get some of your clothes?"

"Nah, I'll be okay, you go ahead and get you some rest Tricia, you're looking as tired as me by the eyes," Maya said,

"Are you sure?"

"Girl, go on in there and get you some sleep! I'll be just fine,"

"I'm not going to sleep until I finish packing but call me if anything jumps off and I'll come over there and tear that whole damn house up!" Tricia said,

"Girl I'll be all right, you go on to sleep, and I'll call you once I make it back to mama's house,"

Maya waved to Tricia as she got into her car, she drove past the mall and then did a u-turn to do some last-minute shopping, Maya was trying on shoes when her cell phone rang,

"Hello?" she answered dryly,

"Hey Baby!" Tony-B said, relieved that Maya finally answered the phone,

"What do you want Tony?"

"Can I see you, please?"

"See me for what?"

"Baby don't be like that, can you come home so we can talk?"

"There is nothing for us to talk about,"

"Don't say that, Maya! I can make all of this up to you if you just give me a chance, just one more chance! Hey?" Tony-B said even more excited,

"What?" Maya answered with a long sigh,

"Can you come by so we can talk, I can order us some food,

anything you want, c'mon, you know you miss me!" Tony-B said, and Maya could just imagine those deep dimples in his cheeks,

Maya found herself parked on the curb in front of Tony-B's house, she just didn't feel right parking in his driveway anymore, it felt strange to be at his house, even though she had been there for the past three years, Maya's mind began to wander off again, this time in a hundred different directions at once, she knew what Tony-B had done, there was no doubt about it, but she was anxious to hear what he had to say. She just had to hear an explanation, she hoped somehow that it would close the gaping hole inside of her. She wasn't heartbroken anymore, he'd shattered her heart into a million pieces a long time ago, so the hole wasn't in her heart, it was located right in the middle of her pride. Maya felt betrayed, she couldn't believe that he would go so far as to have a baby by another woman and have a woman in their house, and in their bed, after all the time they'd spent together, she hated him for betraying her and wanted to see him aching for her, she wanted him to be heartbroken, and almost destroyed because she had left him, she wanted him to beg so she'd have the chance to turn him down cold and see the rejected look on his face when she told him off, she wanted to see him worried and bogged down like she was, she wanted to feel powerful and he feel weak for a change,

Maya felt ashamed for going back to his house, but she needed answers, and was determined to get them. Tony-B stood in the doorway waiting for her, he smiled wide when she pulled up and greeted her with a giant hug,

"You see I'm getting my front lawn repaired, don't you?" Tony-B said pointing at his lawn, "That shit was expensive too, but we ain't gonna worry about that, as long as you're back at home, it almost fucked up my chance to get Lawn of the Year for the Homeowner's Association, but it's okay," Tony-B said, staring out at his lawn, "it should be back to where it was in a few weeks,"

Maya rolled her eyes at him, she couldn't believe how good he looked, she expected him to look tired and run down, but he didn't, he looked happy and well rested, which pissed Maya off, she didn't even attempt to hug him back and even turned her head when he tried to kiss her,

"I missed you so much," he whispered softly as his lips grazed her ear,

Maya rolled her eyes at him as she walked into the house and sat on the couch, she could tell he was a little nervous,

"I have something for you," Maya said,

"What is it?" Tony-B said, excitement dancing in his eyes,

"These..." Maya said, and the excitement immediately left Tony's face when she reached in her purse and gave him back his checkbook and credit cards,

"Why are you giving me these, you can keep them Maya, just in case you need something, even though you straight tripping, I still want to make sure you got everything you need," Tony-B said,

"No, I'm good, I don't want you accusing me of anything," Maya said, and after he wouldn't take them from her hand, she placed them on the table,

"Maya, I'm not worried about those cards, if you wanted to clean me out, you could've done it a long time ago," Tony-B joked, "and besides, I trust you more than I trust anybody,"

"I wish I could say the same," Maya said as she rolled her eyes,

"Aw that's cold, Ms. Lady... real cold," Tony said as he dropped his head,

"Whatever," Maya said dismissing him,

"You wanna watch a movie?" he asked,

"No." Maya said rolling her eyes at him,

"C'mon Maya, the least you can do is watch a movie with me,"

"I'm good," Maya said with her face frowned up, she sat on the couch with her arms folded, barely touching her meal as he dug into his,

"Aren't you gonna eat your food?" he asked,

"No, I'm not hungry," Maya barked,

"I wish I had known that before I ordered all of this damn food! Why didn't you say that when I asked you?"

"Because..." Maya shrugged,

"Because? Dang Maya, why are you acting like that, and why are you so quiet?" Tony-B asked as Maya sat there looking at him as if she could kill him,

"I don't have anything to say,"

"Baby, don't be that way, you know I love you, right?" He said finally turning away from his meal,

"No, I don't..." Maya sighed, turning her head to the side, carefully avoiding his eye contact,

"Look, to be honest I just got caught up in something I couldn't get out of at the time Baby, but I'm done! I just wanna be with you and only you from now on!"

Maya wanted to slap the hell out of him again, but her pride craved the attention, she melted like butter when he told her how much he wanted to be with her instead of Torya, but in her heart of hearts, she knew they were all sugar-filled lies, but she wanted to hear them, she needed to hear them, and every time he touched her, she felt both aroused and sick to her stomach at the same time, she tried to focus her attention on the movie and avoid his sexy eyes, but Tony-B grabbed her and began kissing her passionately, his kiss sending her mind and body out of control, she wanted to fight him off, she really did, her mind hated him, but her body craved him, her mind called him every name she could possibly think of, but her body was on fire and anxious for his touch. Tony-B could feel heat generating from Maya and he teased her until she was almost ready to beg him to make love to her. He lifted her dress and kissed her breasts and then moved down to her round belly.

"I wonder what he'd say if he knew that our baby was in there?" Maya thought as he laid gentle kisses on her belly,

"By the time I get through with her, she'll never want to leave me again!" Tony-B thought, he was in a sexual frenzy, but Maya was still trying to figure out how she ended up here, making love to the man who had just betrayed her, the man she thought she hated. Her baffled mind began to wonder if he ever did to Torya what he was doing to her right now, as his head nestled between her thick thighs, Tony-B devoured her with more passion than he did with the mangoes, Maya threw her head back, overcome by orgasm, after orgasm, after orgasm, and before she could catch her breath he climbed on top of her and tried to kiss her, but she turned away, and frowned, he wasn't going to let that stop him so he kissed her on the neck instead knowing it always turned her on,

"You ain't going nowhere!" Tony-B whispered in her ear confidently as he entered deep inside of her cave, causing Maya to reach her peak continuously, "You know I can't be without you, and I can't let you be without me!" He whispered,

"Yeah, I got her now!" Tony-B thought, as Maya's body pulsated from pleasure, he was very pleased at his performance, but after it was over Maya felt dirty, violated, and used. She knew he had played on her emotions, and she felt ashamed for letting him,

"I knew you were gonna come back to me. You know you can't leave me alone!" He said confidently, but when Maya suddenly jumped up off the couch, he looked confused, "Where are you going, baby?" He asked,

"I need a bath!" Maya said, her face frowned as she hurried down the hall into the bathroom,

"Can I get in with you?" Tony-B asked ad he rushed behind her,

"Hell no!" Maya yelled as she slammed the door in his face,

"Aw man, that's messed up!" Tony-B said as he jumped back when the door almost hit him,

Maya locked the door and fell against the wall, doubling over and holding her belly. She scrambled for air as nausea pounded her mercilessly, causing the peppermint tea and saltine crackers to rush into her throat. Maya fell to her knees instantly as yesterday's dinner flooded the toilet with a vengeance! She didn't think she would ever stop vomiting, but once she did, she didn't even wait for the bathtub to fill with water before she jumped into it, scrubbing her body vigorously. Maya's mind played horrible tricks on her as a vision of Tony-B and Torya suddenly appeared at the other end of the bathtub, kissing on each other, laughing and toasting champagne. She even imagined him making love to Torya on the same couch, the same way he'd just made love to her, Maya tried to shake those images out of her head as she scrubbed herself even harder, she scrubbed and scrubbed until her skin stung, she then jumped out of the bathtub and gathered her clothes, she was just about to toss them into the dirty clothes hamper by habit when she noticed a skimpy red lingerie set laying on top of her dirty clothes. Maya didn't even have to guess who the lingerie belonged to. She crept into the bedroom leaving Tony asleep on the couch and grabbed a pair of jeans and a t-shirt out of the drawer, then she got dressed and walked out of the door without looking back,

Maya drove home in a daze, she climbed out of the car and stuck her spare key into her mother's front door and stepped into the house, she almost jumped out of her skin when she turned the corner and saw Mama Anderson sitting at the kitchen table in her housecoat and slippers, peeling sweet potatoes,

"Mama?" Maya said as she entered the kitchen,

"Hey Lil' Gal, this is a nice surprise!" Mama Anderson said as she gave Maya her cheek to kiss,

"Hey Mama, I just came by to check on the house,"

"Uhmmm-hmmm...is everything alright? You seemed surprised to see me," Mama Anderson said, as she grabbed another sweet potato off the kitchen table and began peeling it,

"Yes Ma'am, everything is okay, I just came to check on the house, I wasn't surprised to see you, I just didn't think you were coming back so soon," Maya stammered,

"I know you didn't, but every shut-eye ain't sleep, and every goodbye ain't gone!" Mama Anderson said as she glared at Maya, "And you know I can tell just as good when something ain't right with my children, which is exactly why I cut my trip short and came on back to the house, and then when I got home last night, I saw that you've been sleeping in your old room! AND I know it's got something to do with that old boy, cause he done already called twice and he came by this morning, looking for you, you better tell me what's going on with you Lil' Gal, and I ain't gonna ask you twice!" Mama Anderson said as she stopped peeling her yam just long enough to point the knife at Maya,

"Yes ma'am..." Maya answered humbly,

"What's going on, I said!" Mama Anderson raised her voice,

"Me and Tony broke up, and I left him…" Maya answered nervously,

"Well why didn't you just say that Lil' Gal, you said it was nothing, but it sure sounds like something to me, but at any rate, I wouldn't worry about it if I were you, y'all will get back together, you always do…" Mama Anderson said as she rested back in her chair and picked up a turnip green leaf and began picking the tender parts off the stem,

"I don't think I'm going back to him this time, Mama, I think I'm done," Maya said as she fought back tears,

"Well…maybe you're just a lil' mad at him right now," Mama Anderson said as she tossed the bare stem into the plastic bag hanging from the chair beside her,

"No Mama, I think I'm finished this time," Maya nodded,

"You don't have to act all tough around me, Lil' Gal… I'm your Mama, I don't care if you with him or not, as long as *you* happy!" Mama Anderson said picking up another turnip leaf,

"But I'm not happy Mama, not at all, I'm just tired…I'm real tired! Of him, and everything! I was thinking about getting Marvin and Calvin to help me move my stuff out of his house and put it in storage until I come back from my trip,"

"Naw, you not tired Baby Gal, and you know how I know you ain't tired?" Mama Anderson asked, still looking down at her turnip greens,

"How?" Maya asked,

"I know you're not tired because you still talking about

132

it, when you really tired, I'll know because you won't wanna talk to nobody, you'll just do what you have to do and be done with it!"

"No Mama, I'm really tired this time, I'm tired deep down in my bones, and I'm gonna ask Marvin and Calvin to help me move my stuff out his house as soon as I can," Maya said,

"Maybe the two of you just need to sit down and talk it out first, you know, before you bring family into it, you know how your brothers are," Mama Anderson suggested,

"Yes ma'am, I know…and I've thought about it for a long time, but I really am ready, and I just wanna get my stuff out of his house, I don't want them to do anything to him or anything like that, I just need them to help me move,"

"You sure this isn't another one of your lil' spats, y'all been together for what, three years now?"

"Yes Ma'am,"

"And now you done got engaged, are you sure you wanna end it?" Mama Anderson asked,

"No Mama, I'm not sure, but I know I don't like the way he treats me, and on top of that he doesn't even make me feel special when I'm with him, he treats me like I'm nothing!"

"Now that's not his fault Lil' Gal!" Mama Anderson said still picking her greens,

"I don't understand," Maya said with tears in her eyes,

"You can't rely on a man, or anybody else, to make you feel special, your worth has to come from you! *YOU* set the tone in a relationship, and you set that tone when y'all shacked up for two whole years before he even saw fit to ask you to marry him, and you set the tone whenever you get mad at him and you leave, then you go right back to him before he can even tell you he sorry about what he did to make you leave in the first place!" Mama Anderson said tenderly,

"You're right Mama," Maya nodded in agreement,

Mama Anderson continued, "Baby Gal when you do stuff like that, men feel like they can have the milk whenever they want it, they feel like they ain't even gotta work for it, and any man who keeps his belly full of free sweet-milk, ain't gonnna value nothing, especially not the cow who gave it to him so freely! Everybody wants something for free, but how often do you appreciate it when you get it that way?" Mama Anderson asked as her glasses slid down to the tip of her nose,

"Never," Maya answered dryly,

"Baby…a man needs to feel like a man, he needs to know that what he got, he had to work for, and he also needs to know he has to continue to work for it if he intends to keep it! Shoot! In my day, we just didn't do stuff like that! Your Daddy was a good man, a decent man! A real man, but I wasn't gonna rely on him or nobody else to determine my value! Baby, you gone have to learn, that in life, you teach people how to treat you, and when you respect yourself, you ain't gone let nobody else disrespect you! I didn't play that shackin' up stuff! If a man intended to lay down with me, he had to marry me plain and simple!" Mama Anderson said as she pushed her glasses back up with the tip of her finger, "And another thing...always know your role and act accordingly, you ain't got no business acting like you somebody's wife when you're just a girlfriend, cooking for them, cleaning up his house and his mama's house, and catering to them hand and foot...shooooot! I wish I would! That's wife stuff, but honestly, I don't know if I'd even clean his mama's house if I was married to him, you ain't nobody's doggone maid, and just look at you sittin' over there with them dark bags under your eyes, all depressed and stressed out like an old broken down horse, now when that boy came over here lookin' for you earlier today, I bet he wasn't all broken down, he looked like he ain't missed a wink of sleep or nothin' else since you been gone!" Mama Anderson said as she let out a strong puff of air and rolled her eyes to the ceiling,

"I wish I was strong like you Mama," Maya said as she wiped the tears flowing down her cheeks,

"Aww come here Lil' Gal, ain't no need for all that..." Mama Anderson said, as she stretched her arms wide, Maya fell to her knees at her Mama's feet and rested her head on her lap, Mama Anderson stroked her daughter's hair, comforting her in a way that only a mama could, Maya's shoulders shook violently as she sobbed on her mother's lap,

"I know Baby, ooh I know...and I didn't mean a bit of harm, Lawd knows I didn't, but it's my job to tell you right from wrong, but it's alright, you ain't gotta deal with none of this today, nope! You ain't gotta deal with it today..." Mama Anderson said still stroking Maya's hair, "And as long as I'm living, and even after I'm gone, you'll always have a place to lay your head Lil' Gal, and you welcome to stay here as long as you need to, you hear me?" Mama Anderson asked, Maya nodded slowly as Mama Anderson raised her up by her shoulders and looked into her eyes, "Don't you worry about nothing, the Good Lawd says, trouble may endure for a night, But JOY! Cometh... in the... morning?" Mama Anderson paused in the middle of her sentence and looked Maya up and down with a puzzled look on her face,

"What's wrong Mama?" Maya asked still rubbing her eyes,

"No, you didn't... no you did not!!!" Mama Anderson said as she leaped from her chair with a stunned look on her face,

"Mama, what's wrong?" Maya asked, confused,

"Well, I'll be!!!" Mama Anderson said as she stood with her hands on her hips,

"Mama, what's wrong, you're scaring me?" Maya asked, her heart thumping,

"I know good and well you ain't done went and...Lil' Gal I ought to slap your fo'head!" Mama Anderson said, her pitch growing higher and higher with each word, like it always did when she was excited or angry, "Oh my word!" Mama Anderson said as she paced nervously back and forth across the room, fanning her face with an oven mitt,

"What's wrong Mama?" Maya said still sniffling and wiping her eyes,

"You gone! And good and gone too! Done went and got yourself knocked up! That's what's wrong! And don't you lie to me neither, Lil' Gal cause that vein over there on the side of your neck is just thumpin' like crazy!!!" Mama Anderson shouted,

Maya's mouth dropped wide open!

"Lil' Gal I ought to slap fire from you for trying to keep something like that from me! Lawd, have mercy!" Mama Anderson said fanning her face, "I knew it! I just knew it! I been dreaming about fish all month! But I thought it was Marvin's wife, whew! Done got me all riled up, I don't know whether to whoop you or hug you!" Mama Anderson said as she let out a long sigh and sat down in the kitchen chair to gather herself,

"I'm sorry Mama, I wasn't trying to keep it from you," Maya pleaded,

"Don't you be sorry now, and when was you gone tell me?" Mama Anderson said as she stood, then sat back down in the chair and fanned her face again,

"I just found out Mama, and I was gonna tell you, I promise!" Maya said with tears in her eyes,

"When did you find out?" Mama Anderson asked,

"Last Monday,"

"Last Monday? And you couldn't call and tell me!"

"Mama you were out of town, and I didn't wanna bother you," Maya whined,

"Bother me! Lil' Gal please, you could've called and told me!

135

Now say something else and I'm gonna smack your fo'head so help me! Lawd have mercy! Done ran my pressure up!" Mama Anderson said as she stood and began pacing back and forth across the kitchen floor again, wiping and fanning her face with a drying towel,

"I'm sorry Mama, I didn't mean to upset you," Maya said, her eyes tearing,

"Oh child...ain't no need for them tears, what's done is done!" Mama Anderson said fanning the air, "Shoots! No wonder you all emotional! You are planning on keeping it, aren't you?" Mama Anderson asked,

"Yes Ma'am, but I'm so scared Mama, I don't know anything about raising a child,"

"Aw don't worry about that! It'll come to you, and plus you got me and your friends and family to help you, so don't worry, now go on over there and sit down while I fix you and that baby something to eat,"

"I'm really not that hungry Mama, I'll just eat something after I go and clean up my room,"

"I done already cleaned it, now you go on over there and sit down like I said, you need to get off your feet, they lookin' kinda swole, I noticed that when you first walked in!"

"Really?" Maya asked as she stared down at her feet,

"Yeah, they lookin' kinda swole to me," Mama Anderson said inspecting Maya's feet,

"I'll elevate them when I come back, but I can't eat right now...I have to go and get my clothes from Tony's house,"

"Not right now you don't! All you have to do right now, and all you *GONE* do right now is sit your lil' fast tale down while I fix you something to eat! This gal done went and got herself knocked up, and think she gone starve my grandbaby, oh no you ain't either! Now gone and sit down, it ain't gone take nothin' but a minute for me to whip up some breakfast," Mama Anderson said as she fussed around the kitchen, pulling out skillets and baking pans from the bottom cabinet, and grabbing a pack of thick Country Style Slab bacon and a carton of eggs from the fridge,

"Yes Ma'am," Maya said as she washed her hands in the kitchen sink and sat at the kitchen table...

Maya's brothers showed up about 4:30 that afternoon,

"Hey Mama!" Marvin and Calvin, said in unison,

"Heeey Mama's babies..." Mama Anderson said as her

sons took turns kissing her cheek,

"Y'all hungry?" Mama Anderson asked, glad to see her handsome sons,

"Yes ma'am," they answered in unison,

"Mama, you got it smellin' good up in here!" Calvin, the oldest said,

"Well go on in there and wash up, while I fix your plate,"

"What you cook Mama?" Marvin asked,

"I fixed some greens, candied-yams, a beef roast with carrots and potatoes, some neck bones, corn on the cob, boiled okra, black-eyed peas, hot-water cornbread, and I got a butter-roll warming over there in the oven," Mama Anderson said proudly,

"Move Marvin, I already got my plate!" Calvin said trying to push his older brother out of the way,

"Naw, I was here first," Marvin argued,

"Y'all stop it! It's enough food in here for everybody, grown-tale men actin' like children, and don't be fishin' all my ham-hocks out of them greens, either Marvin! They wasn't on sale this week and I couldn't buy nothing but three! I tell you the truth, acting like y'all ain't got no home-training!" Mama Anderson fussed,

"Yes ma'am." Calvin and Melvin said lowering their heads like little children, then they started elbowing each other again once Mama Anderson turned her back,

"And when y'all finish eating, I'm gone need you to go over to that boy's house and get this gal's belongings and take them to the storage for her, okay?" Mama Anderson said as she fixed both her sons a heaping plate of food,

"You movin' out?" Marvin asked, as he pulled out a chair and sat at the table beside Maya,

"Yeah," Maya answered trying to concentrate on her meal,

"What y'all do, fall out again?" Calvin asked,

"Yeah," Maya answered dryly,

"He didn't put his hands on you, did he?" Calvin, the meaner of the two, asked between bites,

"Y'all so nosy!" Mama Anderson interrupted, "Gone on and get through eating so y'all can go and get this gal's stuff like I asked you! And don't forget to take some of this food home, especially you Marvin, you know your wife works them 12 hour shifts at that hospital, and she ain't gone feel like doing no cookin' when she gets home!" Mama Anderson instructed,

"Yes ma'am!" Marvin said as he shoveled a forkful of food in his mouth,

"And Calvin make sure you take your wife a plate, that lil' old skinny gal you got needs to eat as much as she possibly can," Mama Anderson said,

"Yes, Ma'am," Calvin said as Marvin and Maya sniggled,

When Maya and her brothers pulled up to Tony-B's house, she unlocked the door and made a beeline to the bedroom to pack her clothes into giant plastic bins. She was trying to drag one of the full plastic bins back down the hall when Calvin snatched it from her hands,

"Mama said, not to let you carry nothing," Calvin said as he picked the bin up like it weighed nothing at all,

"I can carry it," Maya insisted, as she followed behind him, but Calvin ignored her, taking the bin outside and tossing it in the back of the moving truck,

"Hey Maya, why you ain't tell nobody you was finna have a baby?" Marvin, who was already in the back of the truck, asked,

"Because I just found out, that's why!" Maya said irritated,

"Then why in the hell are you moving out if you pregnant by dude?" Calvin asked, scratching his balding head,

"Because I want to, and why are y'all asking me all of these questions?" Maya whined, the way she always did when she wanted them to leave her alone,

"Okay, okay, you the boss! We'll leave you alone," Marvin said as he stood inside of the moving truck,

"But before we start loading all this shit up in this truck, are you sure you wanna do this? Cause we ain't coming back over here for no foolishness!" Calvin asked,

"Yes, I'm sure!" Maya said with an attitude,

"Alright, now go on in there and finish packing the rest of your stuff, and we'll take all the bins and put them in the truck," Marvin said, after noticing his little sister was getting upset,

"Yeah, and calm your lil' ass down, we just wanted to know what was going on with you, and stop all of that pouting, you gone have Mama getting on us cause you all emotional and shit!" Calvin added,

"I'm not pouting," Maya huffed as she sucked the tears back into her watering eyes,

Maya only took what she needed from Tony-B's house.

She only took two of the big screen televisions, even though Calvin wanted her to take all seven of them. She also took one of the Bose stereo systems, and the 32-inch TV that she had when she had her own apartment that Tony-B kept in the storage room. She left all of the pictures on the walls, except for the one that Irony had given her as a house-warming gift years ago, and all of the ones that she'd had blown up and framed that Maurice had taken of her, it just didn't feel right for her to leave those. Maya smiled when it dawned on her that out of all the pictures that Maurice had taken, there wasn't any of her and Tony-B together. Maya shrugged it off and kept packing, she left all of the furniture in both the great room and the dining room, all though she had hand-picked it herself, she didn't trust that Tony-B hadn't slept with anybody else on it, and she left all of the pots, pans, dishes, silverware, and everything else that remotely reminded her of Tony-B and his get-togethers. Her main interests were her clothes, shoes, designer bags, jewelry, expensive perfumes, body washes, and lotions. Maya let out a big sigh when she realized that a few of her expensive perfumes, lotions, body oils, and body washes were missing from the dresser,

"Is this everything?" Marvin asked as he lugged the last of the bins out of the house and onto the moving truck,

"Yep, that's it…" Maya said as she took a deep breath and laid Tony-B's keys on the stand beside the front door then locked it and pulled it shut. Calvin was sliding the door down on the moving truck and Maya was getting into her car when…

"What the hell are y'all doing in my house?" Tony-B yelled as he sped into the driveway and jumped out of his car,

"Mane, I bet you better take some of that damn bass out of your voice!" Calvin said trying to be calm, he really didn't care for Tony-B, and was itching to get at him the first chance he could, Marvin came walking around the passenger side of the truck, and stood behind Tony-B, anxiously waiting for Calvin to give him the signal to go ahead and knock him out,

"I ain't trying to start no shit," Tony-B said once he looked back and saw that Marvin was behind him, "But this ain't right, y'all ain't got no business taking shit out of my house, especially when I ain't here!" Tony-B added,

"They were just helping me, I came to get my stuff, and I left your keys in there on the table, so it won't happen again," Maya said as she walked up to the moving truck where Tony-B and her brothers stood,

"You mean to tell me you're movin' out, over that lil' shit?" Tony-B asked, he was in total disbelief,

"I really don't wanna get into this right now," Maya answered,

"Maya! How you gonna do me like this?" Tony-B asked as he grabbed Maya by the arm, but she frowned and snatched away from him instantly,

"You better keep your damn hands to yourself!" Calvin said as he shoved Tony-B in his chest,

"Yeah, all that other stuff is between y'all, and we ain't in it, but don't put your damn hands on my baby sister! I'd hate to have to fuck you up in front of all your lil' neighbors," Marvin said, as he stood behind Tony-B,

"I wasn't trying to hurt her, I'd never put my hands on her! I just wanted to talk to her," Tony-B pleaded,

"Maya, do you wanna talk to this dude?" Calvin asked,

"No, I don't," Maya said still angry that Tony-B had grabbed her by the arm,

"Then go on over there and get in your car, and we'll trail you," Calvin told her,

"Maya, don't do this!" Tony-B pleaded, but Maya ignored him and got into her car and sped off, and Marvin and Calvin left Tony-B standing in the driveway as they got into the moving truck and pulled off,

Maya followed them back to the storage company, she sat in her car still fuming and rubbing her still stinging arm as her brothers unloaded the truck, then she trailed them back to the moving company where they had left their cars and then they trailed her back to their mother's house. Maya was tired, but she felt like a big burden had been lifted off her shoulders, she laid down to take a nap, and had just begun to drift off, when her phone rang,

"What Tricia?" Maya answered with her eyes closed, she just knew it was her best friend,

"Who?"

"Who is this?" Maya asked, not recognizing the female voice,

"You know who this is, Maya and I know Tony-B is over there with you! But you can have him! Just tell him I'm tired of his shit and I'm moving back to Seattle!" Torya yelled into the phone,

"Girl you ain't got nothing else better to do than to call and bug the hell out of me?" Maya asked, not even bothering to open her eyes,

"Whatever Maya, just tell Tony-B what I said!"

"Tell him yourself, after all he is yours, you took him,

remember? So you deal with him!" Maya said before hanging up on Torya and turning over to finish her nap. Her phone kept ringing, so she turned it off, and slept peacefully and when she awakened from her nap, she felt much better, "Let me call Tricia and tell her about Torya calling me," Maya said as she turned her phone back on, but it started ringing again, it was a number Maya didn't recognize, but she was just in the right mood for the drama,

"Hello!" Maya said with an attitude,

"Damn, I have to call from a different number in order for you to answer the phone for me!" Tony-B said,

"What do you want Tony?"

"Maya, don't hang up, just hear me out, please!"

"What is it?"

"Why did you move out?"

"You know why! Maya barked,"

"We could've talked this out Maya! You had your brothers thinking I was gonna do something to you, and Calvin almost got dealt with, had all my neighbors looking out the windows and shit!"

"What do you want Tony?" Maya asked exasperated,

"Did your mama tell you that I came over there looking for you?" Tony-B asked, changing the subject,

"Yeah, she told me," Maya said as she rolled her eyes to the ceiling,

"I even went to your job, they said you were gonna be out until next month sometime, why you take off for so long, I know you ain't that messed up over what happened?" Tony-B asked,

"Why, are you worried about me and what I do Tony, and why are you constantly calling me?" Maya asked, her patience wearing thin,

"You must be sick or something, you never take off work," Tony-B said,

"Yeah, I am sick," Maya answered,

"You sure didn't act sick when I was tapping that thang earlier!"

"Well, I am sick, Tony, I'm sick of you!" Maya said angrily,

"Damn Maya, I didn't call to argue with you, I just needed to talk to you," Tony-B said, and Maya could tell he had been drinking, "I know you moved out, and you're over your mama's house and all, but is there anything that you need?"

"Yeah, I need you to tell your lil' girlfriend to stop calling me," Maya said with an attitude,

"I'm trying to talk about me and you, and you worried about some other broad!" Tony-B yelled into the phone,

"Worried no, but tickled, yes!" Maya said forcing a fake laugh,

"Okay, I see you're on some bullshit, but can we talk about us without you getting smart with me or talking to me about some other gal, can we? And can we talk about us getting back together?"

"No Tony, because we're not getting back together!"

"Why the hell not?" Tony-B asked, and Maya had to take the phone off of her ear and look at it in disbelief,

"We tried that, remember?" she said, still unsure if she was really having this conversation with him or if she was dreaming,

"Baby, we've been together too long to let something like that tear us apart,"

"Tony you should've taken your own advice because you're the one who tore us apart,"

"Maya let me take you away for the weekend, we can even go to The Cabins if you want to," Tony-B pleaded,

"We've tried that already too... remember? But honestly, I don't want to go nowhere with you, and anyway I'm leaving tomorrow, and I still haven't finished packing," Maya said with a cool tone to her voice,

"Packing? Where are you running off to?"

"To Trinidad, with Tricia, remember?" Maya said,

"Oh yeah, that," Tony-B said uninterested,

"Yeah, that!" Maya repeated, rolling her eyes to the ceiling,

"Well, when are you coming back?"

"That's none of your business," Maya said with attitude,

"Well, can we talk when you get back, maybe by then you'll be off this crazy shit that you're on, I know how you can get when people get all up in your ear, but I'll wait until you get back, then we can talk about us getting back together,"

"We're not getting back together Tony, I'm serious this time, the only thing I want you to do is take care of this baby,"

"*BABY!?!* What the fuck do you mean, baby?" Tony-B asked, confused, Maya had totally forgotten that Tony-B didn't know about the pregnancy, Maya could just feel the confusion dripping from his voice,

"Well, you may as well know, I'm pregnant," Maya admitted reluctantly,

"Are you serious?" Tony-B said suddenly overwhelmed, he rubbed the top of his head repeatedly, the way he always did when he was nervous or stressed,

"Why would I say something like that if I wasn't serious?" Maya asked,

"Damn Maya, I don't know if I'm ready for this, wait...hold up!" Tony-B paused, suddenly thinking, "Then why can't we be together for the baby? What kind of shit is this, you say you're pregnant, but now you wanna leave me... what kind of sense does that make?" Tony-B asked, his thoughts and questions running rampant through his mind,

"I don't want to be with you just because I'm pregnant!" Maya frowned,

"Maya!"

"What?"

"I got something to ask you, promise me you won't get mad…"

"I'm not promising anything!" Maya said with anger dripping from her voice,

"Well, I'm gonna ask you anyway!" Tony-B said,

"Go ahead…" Maya said, her lips cocked and ready like a 12-gauge shotgun,

"Well, you know…I've been in situations like this before, and you have been acting funny lately…I know what you said, but I really need to know for sure, and I hope you're not lying to me, because I got ways of finding out…"

"Ways of finding out what?!" Maya said with her lips curled in disgusted disbelief,

"Ways of finding out if the baby is really mine, what did you think?"

"Bye Tony!"

"Maya, hold on now! You can't blame me for wanting to know! It would explain why you're so quick to throw our three-year relationship away!"

"I didn't throw it away Tony, you did…"

"Come on Maya, we have been through worse stuff than this and you gone leave me now, now Maya?"

"Now is a good a time as any!" Maya said with absolutely no emotion in her voice,

"It must be some other man's baby, and you just trying to break up with me, so you can be with him, is that it?" Tony-B asked,

"You know what Tony... you are truly amazing! I mean really! But for your information, I am not like you, okay! I gave this sorry ass relationship all I had and look what I got for my troubles! But you know what amazes me the most?"

"I don't feel like arguing with you Maya," Tony-B said, sensing the rising anger in Maya's voice,

"I don't wanna argue with you either, but I'm gonna say what I have to say, and you're gonna listen," Maya said with confidence, more confidence than she had in their whole three-year relationship,

"Okay Maya, go ahead, finish saying what you were saying…what's amazing to you Maya?" Tony asked as sarcastically as he possibly could,

"It's amazing to me that you didn't deny or even doubt whether Torya's baby was yours or not, even though she was way across the damn country! But me…I was with you every day, *EVERY SINGLE DAY!* Faithfully! You cheated on me, had a baby with someone else, had her all up in *our* house and in *our* bed, and now you got the nerve to question me about whether or not the baby in my belly is really yours, that's amazing to me Tony, really fucking amazing!" Maya said, as her voice began to tremble,

"If it's my baby then why are we not together, I don't want my baby calling nobody daddy, but me!" Tony-B said adamantly,

"That's up to you, if you take care of your responsibilities then we shouldn't have a problem, should we?" Maya shot back,

"That's messed up Maya, real messed up…"

"Whatever!" Maya said dismissing him,

"Maya I'm just saying…I can't talk to you over this phone, I'm coming over there!"

"I don't wanna see you, and believe me, you don't wanna see me! Whether it's yours or not Tony, it's mine, and it WILL be taken care of, that I can promise you! So you and your lil' pitiful ass girlfriend can stay y'all sorry asses away from me! Cause if I ever see either one of you again, I'm not gonna be responsible for my actions!"

"Why you trying to be all violent, Ms. Lady?" Tony-B teased,

"Bye, you fuckin' bastard!" Maya spat,

"Maya wait…"

CLICK! Maya pushed the end button and threw the phone across the room,

"You have reached Maya Anderson, sorry I'm not available to answer your call but if you would please leave your name, number and a brief message, I will return your call as soon as possible," Beep!

"Maya, answer the damn phone! Maya you better answer this phone or I'm coming over there!" Tony-B yelled into the phone as loud as he could,

Message deleted,

***

"Hello?"

"Hey Phillip, is Tricia there?"

"Yeah, she's here, how you doing, Ms. Lady?" Phillip asked,

"I'm okay Phillip and thank you for being there for me last night, I really appreciated it!" Maya said,

"Anytime, anytime…hold on, let me go get Tricia,"

"Hey Maya!" Tricia said full of energy,

"Hey Girl," Maya said exhausted,

"What's wrong with you?" Tricia asked,

Maya filled Tricia in on the day's events,

"Girl you are lying, he grabbed you?"

"Girl yeah, and it tripped me out, because he had never grabbed me like that before, I thought Marvin and Calvin was gonna kill him!"

"They should have whooped him like he stole something! Wait Girl! You say he asked you what?"

"Girl, he asked me if the baby was his!"

"That dude is straight tripping…but I still can't believe you went off on him like that, and you mean to tell me old girl had the nerve to call you after the beat down you gave her?"

"Yep, I felt bad about it at first, but I don't anymore, then he wasn't even tripping about the credit cards I had, he knew I would never do anything to hurt him, even if he hurt me, I just can't deal...forget both of them!" Maya said, and Tricia could tell her friend was mentally exhausted,

"That's a lot for you to deal with in one day…" Tricia said,

"I'm tired Tricia, but nothing's gonna keep us from leaving tomorrow!"

"I hear you girl!"

"You think Phillip is gonna be able to handle Lil' Man and be without you for a whole week?"

"Phillip will be fine, I already asked my Mama to come and help out!"

"Oh yeah, he's gonna be just fine with your Mama around!"

"I know!"

"Well, have a good night Tricia, why don't you guys do something romantic, do you need for me to come and get Lil' Man?"

"Girl, Lil' Man is already gone! Phillip is picking him up from

145

his mother's house tomorrow afternoon,"

"I heard that! Well, I guess I'll go pack my last-minute things and I'll see you guys' tomorrow morning around seven,"

"Okay."

"And Tricia…"

"Yes Maya?"

"Don't hurt Phillip too bad tonight, okay?" Maya teased,

"Bye girl! You so silly!" Tricia laughed as she hung up,

***"

.

5 ONE FOR THE ROAD

Sweet, jazzy melodies floated through the air as Tricia stood at the window and stared out into the backyard. Phillip was doing all he could possibly do to set a romantic mood, but the only thing Tricia could think about is Maya and what she could do to cheer up her best friend. Phillip was tired of being ignored by Tricia and decided to take charge of the situation by sneaking up behind her, grabbing her by the hips and spinning her around in one smooth motion. Tricia laughed out loud as he two-stepped her across the floor, they glided as Phillip's warm hands worked their way beneath Tricia's pajama shirt, he gently stroked the small of her back guiding her towards the window, he stood behind her, massaging her tense shoulder blades as they stared out into the backyard, he planted soft kisses up and down the side of her face as she tilted her head forward allowing him full access to the nape of her neck, he gently bit her left earlobe while reaching around and unbuttoning her pajama top. He placed his hands beneath her shirt and slid it off of her shoulders, Tricia let out soft moans as he slowly kneeled down to the floor while placing silk-like kisses down her spine, his lips barely brushing over her soft skin, he pulled her teal green pajama shorts down to her ankles, while kissing down the back of her thighs, her body twitched anxiously every time his fiery lips seared her skin. Phillip took his sweet time to kiss, bite, and suck every area from the nape of her neck to the back of her calves, biting down on her buttocks one cheek at a time which drove Tricia wild, then suddenly he twirled her around so that she faced him, Phillip indulged himself with the scent of Tricia's skin, as he bit and sucked her thighs, her wobbly knees soon gave out and she plopped down right there on the windowsill of the bay window in plain view,

"Thank God for wood fencing!" Tricia thought as she leaned

147

back and pressed her naked back against the windowpane.
Phillip kissed and licked as close as he could to Tricia's private
stream without actually kissing it, so close was he, that she could
almost feel his breath inside of her, he bit down right there where
her left thigh began and sucked with such intensity, it made the
rest of her body feel a little left out, he kissed his way down her
leg and kissed her well-manicured toes, he then moved back up
to where her right thigh began and started all over again, the cool
window stuck to her bare back and created a steamy silhouette.
Tricia was in her own world, anticipating Phillip's every move,
she slowly opened her eyes when he stopped touching her, she
frowned when she didn't see him, but then he tapped her ankle
with the palm of his hand and when she leaned forward and
looked down he was stretched out on his back with a wicked
smile on his face, he beckoned for her with one finger and she
smiled knowing full well what he wanted, she stood over him,
facing the window with her hands on her hips, smiling as she
eased down slowly. Phillip placed his hands against her flesh in
the Delta formation spreading her lips, he flicked his tongue over
moistness and Tricia almost leaped into the air like a startled cat,
but just as he knew how to rile her up, he was well experienced
in calming her down as well,

"You're...so...fucking nasty!" Tricia moaned through
clinched teeth,

"Umm-hmmm..." Phillip mumbled without missing a
beat, he slowed his pace and licked her up and down, then
flicked his tongue across her love button and sucked with
expertise. The slurping sounds drove Tricia wild, she moaned
and groaned, jerking, jumping, and twitching as he feasted on
her super-sensitive flesh. Phillip took his time to please and tease
her until she could no longer control her herself. Tricia trembled
uncontrollably as Phillip licked and lapped her until his belly
was full of her juices. He balanced her thighs with his strong
hands until she collapsed on the windowsill. He laughed as he
suddenly snatched her to the floor causing her to let out a soft
moan as her body landed on the plush carpet. She pulled him
close and kissed him passionately, slowly sucking her essence
from his lips, it was her guilty pleasure and Phillip loved it, she
kissed him so hard and wild that she came right then and there
before he had a chance to enter her, she convulsed beneath him
and sprayed her juices on his naked thighs,

"Damn girl! That was a big one!" Phillip teased,

"Whew!" was all Tricia could say as she turned on her side and snuggled up against him,

"Don't go to sleep yet Baby, I'm not done…" Phillip said as he got on his knees and pulled her up, positioning her so that she was on all fours, "I told you, Daddy was laying it down tonight, you gonna have to beg me to stop!"

Tricia didn't bother to respond because she was too busy steadying herself for his entering. Phillip was brick hard as he teased her with his manhood, he slid the tip in slowly then slid right back out, Tricia's back arched in anticipation, as he slid in once again, but just a little deeper,

"Baby please!" She moaned,

"Please? Are you begging for this dick, Baby?" Phillip teased,

"Yes!" She moaned,

"Hmmmmm…" Phillip said as he eased inside of her once again, Tricia trembled with pleasure as he dove into her slowly, methodically, inch by wonderful inch, and he didn't stop diving until her butt was flush up against his stomach,

"Ohhhh!" Tricia whined, as Phillip slid out of her the same slow and deliberate way that he slid into her, Tricia shivered uncontrollably, she wanted him so bad that she could literally taste him, Phillip reached up and gently entwined his fingers into her braids and then squeezed his fingers together knowing it always drove her crazy, he pulled her towards him by her braids, and she arched her back until her left ear was even to his lips,

"How do you want it, Lil' Nasty ass woman?" Phillip asked through clinched teeth,

"Rough!" Tricia said as she began to buck like a horse, but Phillip pulled back,

"You think you just gone ride this dick like you want to? Naw, Baby, I'm gone slide this dick up in you slow, then I'm gonna give it to you! And you just gone take it, you hear me?" he asked, and before she could answer, Phillip plunged into her hard until her ass was flush against his stomach once again, then he pulled out slowly,

"Oh, please don't tease me…" Tricia moaned,

"What do you want, then? Tell me what you want…" Phillip teased as he bit down on her earlobe,

"Fuck me Phillip, FUCK ME DAMMIT!!!!" Tricia yelled, she was so full that she felt like she was about to explode,

"Nope!" Phillip said, his lips brushing against her neck, he slid into her slow, deliberately slow, snatching her head back by her braids and sucking on her neck hard, he stayed right there, deep inside of her as his thighs rested against her buttocks, he waited there sucking on her neck and pulling her hair until she began to tremble, and at that moment Phillip pulled out and dove into her as deep and as hard as he possibly could, pulling out slow and diving in fast and hard until Tricia whimpered like a baby, he released her hair and wrapped his right hand around her neck and squeezed slowly knowing that it drove her mad,

"Oh God!" she squealed,

"No... not God...Daddy!" He teased, "You ready for this pounding, Baby?" he asked, his lips still pressed up against her left ear,

"Yeeees!!!" She screamed, arching her back, her body begging for him,

"You sure you want it? Nah you don't want this..." he said, pretending to slide completely out of her, Tricia was so excited that she almost passed out, she tried once again to buck against him, but he pulled back again,

"No-no.." he teased, smacking her hard on her butt, Tricia was so excited that she clawed at the windowsill,

"Baby pleeeeeease!" She begged,

"What's my name Goddammit!" Phillip asked as he slid all the way inside of her, while gritting his teeth,

"Daddy...Daddy!!!" Tricia moaned and Phillip could tell that it was time for him to bring the noise, deep wrinkles formed across his forehead, and he bit down on his bottom lip, holding his brick hard Johnson in his hands, he slammed into her without mercy and rode her like the wild stallion she was, and the louder she screamed and moaned, the harder he pounded,

"You fuckin' Beast!!!" Tricia yelled, as he slapped her on the ass and snatched her by her hair repeatedly,

"Shut up woman and take this dick!" Phillip said as he bit down on his bottom lip,

Tricia thrashed in the throes of painful pleasure, she began to buck hard against him, and this time he let her, meeting her in mid-flight, he was so deep inside of her that she could feel him deep in her spine, but she was so excited that she couldn't stop bucking even if she tried,

"Awwwww shit now!" Phillip teased, as he interlocked his fingers behind his head, thrusting his pelvis forward and locking his body in place, "That's it, Baby! Give it to Daddy! Ride... this... muthafuckin'... dick!" Phillip demanded between breaths, and this time he slapped her on the ass so hard that he

150

left his handprint on her right butt-cheek, Tricia came instantly, her juices flowing down his thighs and sinking into the plush carpet, "C'mon Baby, I know that ain't all you got! I want you to flood this fucking carpet! Give it to me dammit, and I want all of it, every single drop!" Phillip said as he reached around her waist and slid his hand between her thighs, massaging her love spot, pinching, pulling, and rubbing, all the while still pounding, causing Tricia to have multiple explosive orgasms. She climaxed so hard that her eyes crossed, so hard that you could actually hear her juices splashing against his thighs and raining down on the carpet, "That's right! Drown me with that shit! Give it to me, cause I'm gonna fuck you until you run all the way out, do you understand me, Woman!" Phillip said as he drove deeper and deeper inside of her, so deep that all she could do is moan, she came so many times that she drenched the carpet beneath them, and Phillip kept his word and didn't stop until she was totally depleted, and afterwards he laid her on her back and licked and sucked her on magic spot again just to make sure,

Tricia couldn't stop shivering, she begged him to stop, but Phillip kept going, even snickering a little bit as she turned on her side and arched her back, awaiting for his entering, she knew this was his favorite position, her eyes rolled slowly to the back of her head as he eased inside her and this time he fingered her nipples as he rocked her deep and slow, he wrapped his arm around her waist and held on tight, they made love rhythmically, their bodies, no longer slamming into one another but winding together as one, he flicked his tongue on her earlobes and bit down on her neck before sliding his palm over her shoulder and pulling her down while pushing himself deeper inside of her,

"You feel so damned good Baby, and you're so fuckin hot!" Phillip moaned, and Tricia could tell he was near his peak, but she wanted to delay it for as long as possible. She reached up and entwined her fingers with his on her shoulder. They rocked slowly, and with each thrust he traveled deeper, so deep that he was not only inside of her body, but now he was in the depths of her soul. She could feel him trembling behind her, but she was so excited that she was nowhere near an orgasm, Phillip sensed she was too excited to release, so he gently moved his hand which was still entwined with hers, down between her thighs, and while he slow-stroked her, he worked his fingers, through her fingers on her love spot and massaged gently until she let out breathless moans,

"Don't leave me Baby, this time we gone do it together, okay?" he whispered in her ear, she nodded in agreement and bit down on her bottom lip, "You ready?" he asked, his voice trembling,

"No!" Tricia said,

"No?" Phillip asked, surprised by her response,

"No... I've fed you, now it's your turn to feed me," Tricia said with a sexy tease,

Phillip smiled before lying flat on his back,

"No, not like that...I want it nasty, real nasty!" Tricia said, her eyes gleaming with passion,

"Damn baby, how nasty do you want it?" Phillip asked, the anticipation was making him stiffen even harder,

"I want to bow before my King and I want to swallow him whole, I want you to grab my head and literally fuck my face... can you handle that?" Tricia asked with a serious tone,

"Shiiiiiiit!!! Can I??? Maaaaane!" Phillip said as he jumped to his feet and stood before her, brick hard, "Damn Baby, you gone make me bust before I can even get to you!" Phillip said still stroking the entire length of his throbbing manhood,

"Shut up and feed me!" Tricia demanded as she snatched him to her and took him down her throat as deep as she could, in and out slowly, over and over again while using her tongue to create circular motions around his tip which drove him wild, Phillip screamed like a girl when she took his jewels into her mouth one at a time and teased them with her tongue, she pleased him thoroughly, and the way he jerked and moaned sent her into overdrive, so much so that it drove her rapidly towards Planet Orgasmic as well, she exploded over and over again, spraying the already soaked carpet and sucking him with even more passion and intensity until she felt his legs beginning to tremble and she could tell he was close,

"Feed me, Daddy..." Tricia pleaded, speeding up the pace, and forcing Phillip to oblige, Tricia swallowed every single drop, draining him dry but not stopping until he pushed her back and fell on one knee, so that they were face to face, she smiled wickedly and bit down on her bottom lip,

"Damn Baby...what the hell are you trying to do, kill me!" Phillip joked as he collapsed on the carpet beside her and turned his back to her, "Don't touch me!" he said, slapping her hand as she tried to rub his thigh, Tricia laughed when he shook all over as she snuggled up behind him, wrapping her arm around him and burying her head into his back, Tricia laid sweet kisses on his sweaty back as her eyes weighed heavy with sleep,

"Don't you wanna go and get in the bed?" Tricia whispered, barely able to keep her eyes open,

"Hell yeah, I wanna go get in the bed! But hell...I can't

even move!" Phillip joked as he laid there still trying to catch his breath,

"Hell, I can't either!" Tricia tried to laugh, but she was too tired,

"Got me laying here on this wet ass carpet..." Phillip mumbled,

Tricia chuckled softly, she smiled wide when he intertwined his fingers into hers and snuggled back into her right before she heard him snoring and a few seconds later, she dozed off as well, and they slept right there in that same spot...

***

By eight o'clock Maya was finished packing, she took a hot bath and went straight to bed. The next morning Mama Anderson's cooking tickled her nose as she rolled out of bed, Maya was still tired because Tony-B called all night long, forcing her turn her phone off at around midnight. After washing up for breakfast she stumbled into the kitchen, Maya was shocked to see a huge spread of sausage, bacon, eggs, French toast, grits and fresh fruit on the table,

"Mama! I can't eat all of this!"

"Lil' girl, hush and eat this food! you and Tricia traveling all over the world like y'all grown, so you gone need a good meal to get you through the day, and besides, it ain't for you no way, it's for my grandbaby!" Mama Anderson said over her shoulder as she wiped the kitchen counter, "Go on and sit down at the table, I done already called Tricia and her husband, and they said they'll be here in ten minutes, Marvin and Calvin said they were coming to see you off too, so go on and eat while it's piping hot, I done already blessed the food!"

"Yes Ma'am." Maya said, knowing full well that Mama Anderson wasn't taking no for an answer,

***

As they sat in the airport waiting for their flight, tingles waltzed up and down Tricia's spine when she shifted in her seat and felt a slight sting, she could still feel Phillip inside of her. She leaned over towards him and whispered in his ear, "Thanks for last night," she said with a wide smile,

"You just remember last night when them lil' knuckle-head ass Island Boys start smiling all up in your face!" Phillip said pretending to pull his pants up by the belt loops, Tricia blushed hard as Maya frowned and pretended to gag herself with her pointer finger, "And be ready for Round Two, Three, Four and Five when you get back!" Phillip whispered back in Tricia's ear,

"I can't wait!" Tricia said as she nibbled on his earlobe.

"I can't either, I'm gone tear that ass up!" Phillip said biting down on his bottom lip, he could feel himself began to harden again,

"I don't even wanna know what y'all nasty asses are over there

153

talking about, but I'm gonna need you two to cut it out before
Tricia change her mind about getting on the plane!" Maya said
with a disgusting look on her face after overhearing Phillip,

"Maya, don't be a hater *all* your life! Sheeeesh! And get
on over here and give me a hug before y'all go!" Phillip teased,

"Oh Phillip, my Darling! I shall hugeth you tighteth and
misseth you terribly!" Maya teased, placing the back of her hand
over her face, in a true Shakespearian Fashion,

"Don't go, dear Maya, for I can't beareth to be without
you!" Phillip said as he and Maya carried on, trying their best to
make a scene and embarrass Tricia,

"I can't take y'all asses nowhere!" Tricia said, as she
hugged and kissed Phillip on the cheek and pretended to pull
Maya through the gate,

"Bye Baby!" Phillip said as Tricia walked through the
gate,

"Bye-Bye, My Love!" Tricia said with a smile, blowing
him an air kiss,

The moment Tricia and Maya walked through the gate,
Phillip jumped in the air and danced in a circle! "I'm finna go
steam clean that damn carpet and after I get through, I'm gone
strip down to my draws, eat some pork skins, and watch football
all day! Hell, I might even drank me a whole damn six-pack!
Better yet, I might even call the boys over…this right here is a
damn good night to whoop one of them dudes in some
Dominoes!" Phillip said as he pulled out his cell phone to call his
buddies, he almost dropped the phone when it suddenly rang,

"Hello?" he hesitated,

"And no playing dominoes in the house either! Love
You, Bye!" Click!

"Damn, how the hell she know!" Phillip said looking
around to see if Tricia had a secret camera or something hidden
in the airport,

"Trish, let the man have some fun, what you want him to
do, sit around horny, lonely and thinking about you the whole
damn time you gone?" Maya reasoned,

"Well yeah!" Tricia laughed selfishly,

"We're gonna be gone a whole week, are you sure you
want that?" Maya asked,

"Well, um... I don't know..." Tricia answered suddenly
unsure,

"You done already played with the boy all night, did all

kinds of freaky, nasty and probably illegal shit to him, and now you gone be out of the country... for a whole damn week, he's already not used to being away from you this long and on top of that, right before you got on the plane you got him all worked up by nibbling on his ear and shit, now he's full of energy... and he's gonna use up that energy one way or another..." Maya reasoned,

Suddenly Phillip's cell phone rang again...

"What is it this time Baby?" Phillip asked, this time knowing it was Tricia,

"Okay...you can have your friends over, but I want the house back spotless by the time I get back home, do you hear me?"

"Yes Darling, I hear you, and don't worry, I got it covered..." Phillip answered with a solemn tone,

"Are you sure you got it covered?"

"Yes Baby, I got it covered," Phillip said, and this time Tricia could tell that he was smiling through the phone,

"Okay then, love you! Bye Baby!"

"Love you too, bye Pooh!" Phillip said, he hung up the phone and did the cabbage-patch dance in a circle for about five minutes...

***

Tricia slept the whole flight from Memphis to Miami, but Maya was too excited to sleep. They stepped off the plane to board the connecting flight to Trinidad, people were running back and forth gathering luggage and greeting each other. Maya bit down on her bottom lip when she noticed the handsome men walking around the airport,

"Man Maya, I'm missing my Phillip already!" Tricia whined,

"Aw girl come on here!" Maya said dragging Tricia by the arm,

Once they were seated on the flight to Trinidad, Maya was so excited that she began to babble on about all the things she wanted to do once they landed, Maya was in mid conversation with Tricia when she looked over and noticed Tricia had fallen asleep again,

"Nasty Lil' Worms!" Maya mumbled, "I bet their nasty asses freaked each other all night long!" Maya laughed, she wanted to rest so she wouldn't be tired by the time they made it to Trinidad, but she was just too wired. This would be the first vacation without Tony-B and his antics, and she was going to enjoy every minute of it. They arrived in Trinidad hours later, and caught a taxi to the hotel from the airport, and by that time Tricia was the one who was wide awake, and Maya was the one who was sleepy,

"Tricia I'm dog tired, I think I'm gonna go upstairs and take a nap, I'll meet you in the lobby later, okay?" Maya yawned, as they stood in the elevator, the overflowing energy she had earlier was suddenly

155

zapped by the adrenaline-soaked anticipation, and the long, long flight,

"Girl, I'm too excited to sleep, this is one of the best hotels in Downtown Port of Spain, and the brochure said there was a bar with a live band playing tonight and I'm going to check it out after I get unpacked," Tricia said suddenly full of energy,

"Well, could you call my room and wake me up in about an hour and a half?" Maya asked, still yawning,

"Okay girl, I will, I think this is my room right here," Tricia said examining the numbers outside the suites to make sure it matched her card key,

"And mine is right here across the hall, don't forget to call and wake me up, Trish," Maya said still yawning,

"Oh, I won't!" Tricia said as she went into her room to unpack, but she was too wired, so she decided to check out the hotel first and unpack later,

Maya marveled at her beautiful suite, it was decorated in turquoise and deep blues, even the plush carpeting that seemed to melt beneath her bare feet, and the artwork was simply amazing, but not as amazing as the view from the balcony, she sat on the couch and rubbed her aching feet and it was so comfy that she wanted to doze right there, but that view, it was beckoning for her, and she answered willingly. The warm sun baked her skin as she stepped through the glass patio doors and sat on the patio chair with the shaded umbrella and reclined, she closed her eyes and took a few deep breaths, the past week had been one for the books and it had taken a toll on her. For the first time since everything happened, she had a chance to slow down and take everything in. Tears flooded her eyes before she could stop them, but they weren't sad tears, they were tears releasing her from Tony-B's toxic grip, tears that meant she was free now, and after this cry, Maya was determined to never cry over Tony-B or any man, ever again. When Maya finally opened her tear-filled eyes, her vision was blurry, but soon she began to see things clearly, through brand new eyes, the view of the waters were breathtaking, the colors and sounds of Trinidad seeped into her soul and gave her an overwhelming sense of peace, it relaxed her and she took a few more deep breaths and before long she was in the middle of a sweet dream right there on the patio, when she heard someone banging on the door to her suite, she was in such a deep sleep that she woke up thinking she was back in her room at her mama's house, it took her a few moments to get herself together, she wobbled to the front door still groggy,

"Maya, Maya! Open up, I got something to tell you!" Tricia said into the crack of Maya's door,

Maya stumbled to the door with her eyes half closed and opened it. Tricia's face was lit up with excitement, "What the hell Trish? With your loud, country ass! I had just started snoring, and here you come beating on my damn door...this had better be good!" Maya said, vigorously trying to wipe sleep from her eyes,

"Giiiiiiiiiirl! You will not believe who's downstairs, you just won't believe it, hell, I don't even believe it, I thought I was hallucinating at first, but I wasn't... Girl, this is gonna trip you all the way out..." Tricia rambled on, pacing back and forth across the room as she often does when she is excited,

"What the hell are you talking about?" Maya asked, still sleepy,

"You have got to sit down for this one Maya, I'm so serious!" Tricia said as she flopped down on the couch,

"I don't wanna sit down, girl just go ahead and tell me!" Maya said still rubbing her face and eyes,

"Okay, but don't say I didn't warn you!"

"What???" Maya said as she stood there with her hands on her hips,

"Okay, here it goes..." Tricia said taking in a giant gulp of air, "Okay...girl you won't believe this, I can't even believe it myself, this shit is so wild!" Tricia rambled,

"Tricia!" Maya impatiently interrupted,

"Okay, okay...it's just crazy, and you are not even going to believe this, but Giiiirl! Guess who I just saw... right here in this hotel, THIS HOTEL! Of all the places in the world!!"

"Aw shit... don't tell me Tony is here, please don't tell me..." Maya said as she plopped down on the bed with tears in her eyes,

***

6 MOONLIT COINCIDENCES

Who? Girl naw, ain't nobody thinking about his ass,"
Tricia said with a frown,

"Then who? Tell me, and I don't feel like guessing…"
Maya said as she snatched a Kleenex from the nightstand and
dabbed her eyes,

"Okay, okay, but don't say I didn't warn you…"

"Okay, who?"

"Girl, Maurice… Maurice is here…and not only is he
here, but he's right downstairs in this very hotel!"

"You're shitting me!" Maya said as she plopped down in
the recliner,

"No! I'm dead serious! He's right downstairs sitting at
the bar!"

"You're lying!" Maya yelled as she covered her mouth
with her hands,

"No, I'm not, you can go down there and see for
yourself…but go brush your teeth first girl, your breath is
kicking like a fifth degree black-belt!" Tricia teased, frowning
and fanning her nose,

"Forget you Tricia! You have to help me pick out
something to wear!" Maya said as she jumped up and went into
her bedroom and drug her suitcase back into the living room
area,

"Just pick something, Maya and hurry up before he
leaves!"

"Did he see you?" Maya asked,

"C'mon now…you know me better than that! I was

standing in the corner checking out the club when I thought I saw him walk past me, so I hid behind this huge potted plant and waited to see if was really him, and it was! I tried to see if he was with anybody, but he didn't seem to be, so I jumped on the elevator and ran up here,"

"Good looking out!" Maya said as she and Tricia slapped hands,

"What are friends for!" Tricia smiled,

"Wait! Hold the hell up!" Maya stopped suddenly in her tracks,

"What's wrong!" Tricia asked confused,

"Earlier when I talked to Tony, I told him I was coming here to Trinidad, what if this is all some trick, masterminded by the Great Tony-B, himself..." Maya pondered out loud,

"Damn, I didn't even think about that..." Tricia said as she stopped at the door, but then she thought, "But Maya, what if it's not...I mean, why would Tony-B go through all of that trouble just to send somebody else way over here when he could've just jumped on the plane himself, or even hired somebody that you didn't know to spy on you, I mean, what if Maurice just so happened to be in the same continent, and at the same hotel on the other side of the world as you, wouldn't that be an awesome coincidence?" Tricia asked, her eyes beaming,

"But what if he is here, what if they're all here, Tony-B and all of the Fellas," Maya said as she shuddered at the thought,

"But what if he's not, and even if he is, this is our damn vacation, and we are going to enjoy it whether Tony-B is here or not!" Tricia said adamantly,

"I don't know if I'm up for this," Maya said as she sat down on the bed, suddenly apprehensive,

"We don't have to go downstairs specifically to see Maurice, we can just go just to be going..." Tricia said with a slick smile, but deep down inside Maya knew better, Maya put her apprehensions aside and began searching through her luggage for the perfect outfit, because she knew Tricia was going to worry her silly if she didn't go downstairs, Maya freshened up and changed into a cute peach colored maxi dress with gigantic orange, pink, and red blossoms, with large sea-foam green leaves, she accented the orange in her dress by wearing an orange beaded necklace and earring set and orange sandals, and while Maya got dressed, Tricia decided to go change into a one-piece, lime swimsuit and a beautiful multi-colored sarong with abstract designs that draped around her slender hips, and lime green sandals,

Maya could hear the music once the elevator doors opened, "Oh, I can't wait to get on the dance floor!" she thought to herself, just the thought of being in Trinidad suddenly filled her with energy. Maurice was nowhere to be found, not that Maya was looking for him, but Tricia

was, and although she was a little disappointed, she and Maya
had a blast! It wasn't hard considering the music was live and
there were people dancing from wall to wall,

"Dang, I must be really homesick," Maurice thought as a
woman who looked exactly like Tricia caught his eye, he was
just about to order dinner and go back up to his room, but his
curiosity got the best of him, so he searched out the woman that
looked so much like Tricia that he saw earlier, "Man that woman
looked just like her, I know I'm not crazy!" he mumbled to
himself, "Wait...is that...it can't be! Hell naw, not way over
here..." Maurice thought as he almost leaped from the barstool
and rushed over to them, he was so glad to see somebody that he
knew that he almost tripped over his own feet,

"Maya, I think he spotted us!" Tricia whispered, as
Maurice walked towards them,

Maya saw Tricia's mouth moving, but because the music
was so loud, she couldn't figure out what Tricia was saying,

"Maya! He's right behind you!" Tricia mouthed, but
Maya still couldn't understand what Tricia was saying, Tricia
tried to discreetly point her finger at Maurice who was standing
directly behind Maya, but Maya just smiled back at Tricia
obliviously, and pointed her finger back at Tricia and kept
grooving to the beat, Tricia was so frustrated, that she just threw
her hands up in the air,

"Hey Kinfolks! Maurice said as he walked up to Tricia
and Maya,

"Hey Rece!" Tricia said, with excitement dancing like
fire in her eyes,

Maya rolled her eyes at him then looked away, she was
still on guard, waiting for Tony-B and the rest of the Fellas to
jump out at any minute,

"Dang Maya, you can't speak to nobody?" he said,

"Oh hey," Maya said with as little energy as she could
muster,

"What are y'all doing way over here?" Maurice asked
just as the live band took an intermission,

"We're here on vacation, you're not following us, are
you?" Tricia asked because Maya was standing there with a
disgusted look on her face and rolling her eyes,

"Following you? Nah, I was just getting away for a
minute, "What's up with her?" Maurice asked Tricia,

"I don't know, ask her..." Tricia said as she shrugged her

shoulders,

"Aw, well okay…" He said nervously, "Maya are you enjoying yourself?" he asked,

"I was…" she answered still rolling her eyes,

"Oh, is your folks here with you, Maya?" Maurice asked eying around the club,

"What folks is he talking about?" Maya asked Tricia,

"I don't know who he's talking about," Tricia laughed,

"You know who I'm talking about, Maya…" Maurice said trying to hold a straight face,

"Ummm, let's see, my mama's at home, my brothers are too… so who else could you be asking about?" Maya asked sarcastically,

"I was talking about Tony-B, is he here with you guys?" Maurice asked as he scanned the club again with his eyes,

"You would know better than I would," Maya said with as much attitude as she could,

"Really?" Maurice asked, trying to figure out what she meant by her response,

"Yes, really!" Maya answered,

"Hmmm…trouble in paradise?" Maurice asked,

"Yes, big trouble…we broke up," Maya said, "but I guess you know that already or you wouldn't be here,

"That's hard to believe," Maurice said,

"Well believe it!" Maya said adamantly,

"Wait a minute, did you say or else I wouldn't be here? What does that mean?" Maurice asked,

"It means that I'm still tripping off the fact that we came all the way over here to get away from Memphis and yet here you are, way in Trinidad, and in the same hotel… that's some coincidence!" Tricia interrupted, sensing Maya's attitude,

"I ain't gone lie, I was glad as hell to see somebody that I knew way over here! I was over there at the bar and I thought I saw Tricia, and I was like, I know that ain't Tricia over there dancing, I really thought my mind was playing tricks on me, until I saw you Maya, and I was like dang…it's really them!" Maurice said, still in disbelief,

"Well, I'm gonna go to the bar and get me a drink!" Tricia said, giggling as she walked off,

"So… Maya, where are you guys sitting?" Maurice asked,

"We're over there," Maya pointed, while making a mental reminder to cuss Tricia out later for leaving her with Maurice, Maya gave Maurice a fake smile when he pulled out her chair for her, and when he sat beside her, she looked away pretending to be preoccupied by something on the other side of the club,

"What?" Maya asked when she looked up and found Maurice staring at her,

"I'm just looking, that's all," Maurice said with a sly smile,

"You should just take a picture…it'll last longer," Maya teased, before rolling her eyes at him,

"I see you got jokes," he laughed,

"Yeah, I do,"

"I still can't believe you guys are here, all the way over here," Maurice said shaking his head,

"Well, we are…" Maya said, she was trying not to be irritated, but she was still sleepy and not in the mood for small talk or games,

"Are you okay, I mean… did I do or say something wrong?" Maurice asked, sensing her irritation with him,

"Yeah, I'm good, and why do you ask?" Maya asked curiously,

"Well, to be honest, I did hear about what happened between you and him," Maurice confessed,

"I know, I bet everybody has heard by now," Maya sighed,

"Yeah, I also heard you moved out," Maurice added,

"I did," Maya said as-a-matter-of-factly,

"Well, I'm glad,"

"Really, why?" Maya asked kind of surprised by his bluntness,

"Yeah, I mean, I never knew what you saw in him anyway," Maurice shrugged,

"I didn't either," Maya said as her smile disappeared, she was intrigued about where this conversation was going,

"But you don't seem to be too messed up about it," he added,

"I'm not…" Maya said casually,

"Well good, because you didn't need nobody like that, you're a good woman and you need a good man in your life,"

"Okay, here we go…and where would I find one of those?" Maya asked, bracing herself for his bullshit, knowing that at any moment Tony-B was going to jump out from the shadows,

"What do you mean here we go?" Maurice said with a mild but serious tone to his voice,

"What, you said it like you knew exactly where one was," Maya said sarcastically,

"Contrary to what you may think, there are still some good men out here,"

"Really, where?" Maya said while pretending to search the room with her eyes,

"There are, you just have to know where to look," Maurice said,

"Well, that's news to me," Maya said,

"As a matter of fact, there could be one closer than you think," Maurice said with a smile,

"Really..." Maya asked with a sigh, before looking down at the floor,

"Ms. Lady, I know I ain't exactly the tallest brother in the world, but I know I ain't that short!" Maurice said pointing towards the ground,

Maya blushed, and Maurice moved in closer and lifted her chin with his finger, "Let me see those big, beautiful eyes of yours," he said,

Maya shook her head and frowned before fanning his hand away,

"What's wrong?" he asked,

"Maurice, I can't do this,"

"You can't do what?" He asked, puzzled,

"I can't play this game with ya'll, so go ahead and go tell Tony-B that his plan didn't work, and he can stop the bullshit and come on out," Maya said with a sigh,

"Maya are you serious?" Maurice asked in disbelief,

"Dead serious..." Maya said, and her icy stare stabbed Maurice right in the middle of his chest,

"Wooooow....," Maurice said, he couldn't believe what he was hearing,

"I don't know what y'all got planned, but it won't work with me, so you can run back and tell him that I said--"

"Hold up!" Maurice interrupted, "You got me all wrong, you really don't know me at all, cause if you did, ain't no way in the hell you'd think that shit about me, that's what you meant when you said that if I didn't know then I wouldn't be here?" Maurice asked,

"Well, yeah..." Maya shrugged,

"Let me clear something up for you..." he said as Maya rolled her eyes to the ceiling, "Number one...I ain't nothing like dude! I don't play them type of games and ain't no way in hell I would travel clear across the country just to spy on you, Maya, I got better shit to do! And number two..." He said and Maya could feel the anger rising in his voice, "I ain't nobody's flunkie! Nobody's! I'm my own damn man and

Tony-B can't send me nowhere! And it's fucked up that you would think something like that about me, so I tell you what, since you think I'm a damned spy for somebody way on the other side of the world. then you don't have to say nothing to me while I'm here, and I don't have to say anything to you," Maurice said, and Maya was frozen in place by his seriousness, then there was a long uncomfortable silence between them before Maurice stood and nodded to excuse himself from the table with every intention of putting as much distance between he and Maya as he possibly could, when Maya stopped him by putting her hand over his,

"I didn't mean any harm," Maya said, still taken aback,

"No harm taken, I mean, I just thought we were cool…" Maurice said, and Maya could tell he was still kind of disappointed with her,

"We are cool Maurice, it's just that I've been through a lot over the past few weeks,"

"I know, but I'm not the one who took you through any of it," Maurice added,

"I understand that Maurice, but I need you to also understand I'm not looking for anything other than a friend right now,"

"You're getting ahead of yourself, I haven't asked you to be anything, all I said was that there are good men out here, that's all!" Maurice said adamantly,

"I'm sorry, I just assumed," Maya said,

"Then do me a favor and don't assume!" Maurice said with way more aggression than he intended,

"Well, excuse me!" Maya said, she wasn't used to seeing Maurice this way,

"It's all good, and we *can* be friends, we're on this beautiful island, this music is jamming, and I feel like dancing, you do dance with your friends, don't you?" Maurice asked with a smile, to try and lighten the mood,

"Yes, Maurice, I do," Maya said with a giggle, *"Lord PLEASE don't let me faint this time!"* Maya prayed silently as he led her to the dance floor,

The dance seemed to calm them and they laughed and talked for the remainder of the night, although she had known him for years, she really didn't know much about Maurice other than the fact that she thought he was cute, he was Larry's brother, and he took great pictures, but she had no idea he was actually a professional photographer as well as a Master Barber who owned his own barbershop, and she also had no idea that he also painted and wrote poetry. He showed her pictures of his paintings that he'd taken with his phone, Maya was mind-blown!

Her eyes were shining as he read her a few pieces of his poetry that were in his phone as well, one in particular titled *'Her Eyes'* was her favorite so far, it was as if someone had taken her most private thoughts and placed them in his poems, and if she didn't know any better she would've sworn that he had written it about her, but she quickly dismissed that thought as he read another one of his poems about racism and police brutality in Memphis, she was totally intrigued by him and was smiling wide when Tricia came strolling up to their table with a handsome specimen of a man, with his arm draped around her waist. Maya couldn't help but notice his hair, there were a million or so tiny locs pulled back into a thick ponytail that hung halfway down his back,

"Hey you, I was wondering where you ran off to!" Maya said to Tricia,

"Maya and Maurice, I would like for you guys to meet my new friend, Ahmar," Tricia said with a smile,

Maya gave Tricia a concerned look as Ahmar and Maurice shook hands,

"Hello Maya, I've heard so much about you," Ahmar spoke with a thick, thick Island accent, just the sound of his voice made both Maya and Tricia tingle inside,

"Whatever she told you it's a lie! It's all lies, I tell ya!" Maya laughed, which made everyone else laugh,

"Don't worry, she told me very nice things about you," Ahmar added as Maya blushed, "Tricia, would you like something to drink?" Ahmar asked, noticing Maya and Maurice's tall glasses,

"Why yes Ahmar, I'll have something strong and fruity," Tricia said with a smile,

"Strong and fruity... Okay, I will be back shortly," Ahmar said before placing a tiny kiss on Tricia's cheek, which took Maya by surprise,

"Hey, hold up," Maurice called out to Ahmar, "Maya, you want anything else to drink?" Maurice asked,

"Yeah, I'll have another cranberry juice,"

"A Cranberry juice? Maya, you are over eighteen..." Maurice teased,

"I know, but I'm really not in the mood for any alcohol today," Maya added,

"Okay then, cranberry juice it is," Maurice shrugged,

Tricia smiled at Maya as the men walked off,

"Girl, where did you find that!" Maya asked when the men were out of hearing distance,

"Ain't he fine!?!" Tricia asked,

"Yes Ma'am!" Maya said pretending to fan her face,

"But honestly, I didn't find him, he found me out on the dance floor! You know I don't chase dogs, I let the dogs chase the cat!" Tricia teased,

"Alright, you keep on playing and Phillip is gonna chase your cat!" Maya added sarcastically,

"Why, I ain't doing nothing wrong..." Tricia said defensively,

"I ain't the one you need to convince, Lil' Mama..." Maya said rolling her eyes,

"Girl, I am married not comatose!" Tricia snapped back,

"I hear ya...but I hope you know what you're doing..." Maya said, and Tricia could tell it was also dripping with sarcasm, but she chose to ignore it,

"Ooh Girl! Did you hear that accent?" Tricia said with a wide grin,

"Yeah, I heard it," Maya said with a dry tone,

"Listen Maya, you don't have to have an attitude with me, and you ain't gotta worry about me, okay? I know my limits, he can't go no farther than I let him, and I have no intentions of letting him!" Tricia said with her hands on her hips,

"Those are famous last words Tricia, these men are slick as oil, you're lonely and missing your honey, that's a dangerous combination! And he's fine too! Hell, I got excited just listening to him!" Maya said,

"Girl, I know! And speaking of listening...what was Rece over here talking about?"

"I'm really not sure...he kept going on and on about how I deserve a good man, and yada...yada...yada... and all that sweet shit, so I asked him if Tony put him up to coming here to spy on me..." Maya said, the smile suddenly leaving her face,

"For real!?!" Tricia asked, surprised,

"Yep, I sure did, because he already knew about the breakup, and it made me suspicious, but he wasn't happy at all about me asking him, he set me straight right quick," Maya said with a smirk,

"Dang! News sure does travel fast!" Tricia said with a sigh,

"Tell me about it..."

"Girl, what did he say when you asked him?" Tricia asked,

"I'll tell you later, but we smoothed it all out, or at least I think we did…hell I don't even know, but we've been talking all night and I still haven't told him about this yet," Maya said as she patted her belly, "and speaking of telling, why didn't you tell me he was behind me on the dance floor?" Maya asked with her hands now on her hips,

"I tried! But you were acting all dense, so I just said forget it!" Tricia said exasperated,

"Well next time, could you send me a damn smoke signal or something!"

"I did everything but pop you upside your head! Would you like for me to do that next time as well?" Tricia asked sarcastically,

"Ha-Ha! Very funny!" Maya frowned,

"Well, when are you planning to tell him?" Tricia asked,

"I don't know, I mean, I'm not even sure if I'm even ready to have that conversation," Maya admitted,

"Well, you're gonna have to tell him something sooner or later, it ain't like you can hide it,"

"Yeah...but I don't have to tell him right now, you saw what happened when Irony found out!"

"Well, Irony really didn't say anything, he just sorta stood there, you're the one who walked off," Tricia admitted,

"I was embarrassed, you saw him! Just standing there with his mouth hanging open like he was trying to catch a damn fly or something! What was I supposed to do?"

"Nothing I guess, but I think Maurice is different, he may even be more understanding than Iron-Man, I guess… I don't know, but if you plan on dating him, you're going to have to tell him,"

"Dating? I'm not even ready for all of that right now, but okay, if we ever start dating, then I'll tell him," Maya agreed,

"You promise?"

"Yes, I promise... Oh, guess what?" Maya asked like a giddy schoolgirl,

"What?" Tricia answered, intrigued,

"Girl, he has the softest lips in the world!"

"How do you know he got soft lips, have you kissed him already?" Tricia frowned, but Maya knew it was out of concern,

"No…I didn't kiss him, I ain't fast like you..." Maya smiled, "He pecked me on the cheek, it took me by surprise, but to be honest, I kinda liked it!" Maya said smiling,

"Maya your eyes are shining a little too bright, you'd better pump your breaks before you do something that's gonna have you at the altar confessing and repenting," Tricia teased,

"No Honey, you ain't gotta worry about me, but you do need to

167

take your own advice..."

"You ain't never lied!" Tricia said as she fanned her flustered face, "But for real Maya, whatever you decide, you know I got your back one hundred percent,"

"Yeah, I know... and you know I got yours,"

"No doubt! Tricia said with a smile, as the men came back to join them,

"Here you go, Tricia," Ahmar said as he placed her drink on the table,

"Maya it's getting late, do you wanna go up to my room and talk," Maurice whispered in her ear making her heart race,

"I don't know Maurice, Tricia and I are supposed to go sight-seeing first thing in the morning, and I don't want to stay up too late," she reasoned,

"You're just scared..." Maurice teased, "Okay, what if I promise to be the most perfect gentleman you've ever seen in your life?" Maurice asked with a wink,

"Okay, Okay... I'll go, but I can't stay long," Maya said,

"You can leave whenever you get ready," Maurice added assuredly,

"I'll see you later Tricia, and don't worry," Maya whispered in Tricia's ear then patted her on the shoulder, Tricia nodded and waved good-bye to them,

"So, how does a beautiful woman like you end up on such a beautiful island all by herself?" Ahmar asked once Maya and Maurice left the table,

"Because my husband trusts me," Tricia blushed,

"Oh, you have a husband?" Ahmar said surprised,

"Yes, I do," Tricia said proudly,

"Where is he?" Ahmar asked curiously,

"He's at home, Maya and I are on a Girl's Get-a-way,"

"Oh, interesting... do you have any children?"

"Yes, we have a son Darrion, he's a year old," Tricia smiled,

"How nice," Ahmar added,

Tricia was beginning to miss her husband and son, so she changed the subject, "Enough about me, tell me about you,"

"I was born here in Trinidad, but I moved to New York seven years ago. I work for one of the biggest record companies in The States. I have a wife and a daughter, Naima, she is four, because of my job, I travel all around the world, it pays the bills, but I do miss being at home with my family sometimes, you know?" Ahmar asked, and Tricia could sense the sadness in his voice,

"Yes, I know," Tricia added,

"What is it that you do back in The States?" Ahmar asked,

"I'm an attorney, in fact, I just made Junior Partner at my law firm," Tricia said proudly,

"An attorney! He'd better watch out!" Ahmar teased,

"No, my husband has no competition, and he knows I'm just here to have a good time,"

"I understand," Ahmar said with a gracious smile...

***

Maya took a deep-deep breath when she stepped into Maurice's suite, "Oh, his room smells just like him," she thought,

"Sit down and relax, I won't bite unless you want me to," Maurice teased as he sat on the couch and patted the spot right next to him, he laughed as Maya sat beside him nervously,

"Maurice, I thought you wanted to talk?" Maya asked to ease the nervous quiet that filled the room,

"I do want to talk," he said,

"Then talk, I'm listening..." Maya added,

"In all fairness, I did do most of the talking when we were downstairs, so now it's your turn Ms. Lady," Maurice said with a smile,

"Okay, what is it you wanna know?"

"Well... first of all, I want to know if you and Tony-B are gonna get back together?"

"Oh, that's easy...NO!" Maya said adamantly,

"Are you sure about that?" Maurice asked,

"Why would I lie?" Maya said with a slight attitude,

"It's not that I think you're lying Maya, or anything like that, I just wanted to know, so don't be gettin' no attitude with me," Maurice said with a smile,

"I don't have an attitude with you Maurice," Maya said, smiling back,

"Then why are you so quiet?"

"I'm not being quiet, it's called listening," Maya said sarcastically,

"Well don't just listen, I need some input or something! You're making me work real hard for this lil' conversation, I'm up here sweating!" Maurice joked,

Maya laughed at him and shook her head, "Maurice you're a trip!"

"No baby, I'm a full voyage!"

"You ain't never lied," Maya thought as she went into full grin

mode,

As time passed, Maya began to relax, Maurice sat on the floor beside the couch as Maya sat sideways and stretched her legs,

"Orange panties, huh?" Maurice said with a big grin on his face,

Maya closed her legs quickly and snatched her dress down,

"Not orange, peach, and why are you looking under my dress anyway, you perv?" Maya laughed,

"I wasn't looking under your dress, I just notice things," he laughed, "and you know what else I noticed?"

"I'm afraid to ask," Maya said,

"It's not a bad thing," Maurice insisted,

"Okay then, what did you notice?" Maya said hesitantly,

"I noticed that your panties matched your orange toes," Maurice said with a huge smile,

"They're not orange, they're peach!" Maya said, correcting him,

"Okay, I noticed that your peach panties matched your peach toes, is that better?"

Maya rolled her eyes at him, and they both laughed out loud,

"Hey, I'm starving, I'm gonna order something to eat, you want anything?" Maurice asked,

"Yes, I've been dying for some fresh fruit!" Maya said,

"Sounds good to me, do you want anything to drink?"

"Cranberry juice,"

"CRANBERRY JUICE?" Maurice asked surprised,

"Yep!"

"With vodka in it, I hope,"

"No, just cranberry juice," Maya insisted,

"You don't drink much, do you?"

"No, not really," Maya said,

"I noticed you didn't drink anything earlier either, Baby you're on vacation, so splurge a little!" Maurice said as he picked up the phone and ordered a sampler platter with stewed chicken, rice, oxtails, okra, cabbage, spinach, lentils, potatoes and roti for him and a tropical fruit platter for her, and when the operator asked him what he wanted to drink, Maurice ordered a bottle of rum, "Hold on," he looked at Maya, "Are you sure you don't want a wine cooler or something?" he asked,

"No, cranberry juice is fine," Maya said,

"All right, and could you send up a bottle of cranberry juice as well? Thanks," he said before hanging up the phone, "He said they'll be up in about twenty minutes," Maurice said after hanging up the phone,

"That'll work," Maya said, her mouth watered at the thought of tropical fruit,

"Come to think of it... I've seen you and Tricia at those parties, sitting over in the corner, talking about folks and downing that wine and those wine coolers, but now you wanna act all brand new in front of me," Maurice said,

"Whatever! And we don't talk about people, well...not that much," Maya laughed,

"I knew it, I knew it!" He laughed,

"Honestly, I have been known to drink a glass of wine every now and then, but I'm just not in the mood to drink tonight, is that okay with you?"

"It's okay with me, but just don't be acting funny with me,"

"I'm not actin' funny with you Maurice,"

"You sure?"

"Yes, I'm sure,"

"Maya, you seem really tense, but I know how to get you to relax, give me those feet!" Maurice said as he grabbed her feet and massaged them, Maya felt like passing out! Her mind instantly drifted back to the dream she had when Mr. Coco-Brownskin rubbed her feet the exact same way, and if someone would've told her that it could possibly happen in real life, she probably would have never believed them. Maya closed her eyes and let her mind drift into places she had long forgotten,

"You have really soft feet!" Maurice said before kissing her big toe,

"Ooooh, don't do that!" Maya said snatching her foot from him,

"Okay, maybe that was a bit forward, but why shouldn't a King kiss the foot of a Queen?" Maurice asked as he gently pulled her foot back towards him and kneaded into the soft fleshy areas of her feet once again,

"This is too good to be true!" Maya thought,

Maurice was deep into massaging her feet, and she was deep into her own relaxation when someone knocked on the door,

"Room service!" the man yelled out,

"Whew! I didn't know how much more I could take!" Maya said under her breath as Maurice got up and answered the door,

Maurice smiled at her as she dug into the tropical fruit bowl like she hadn't eaten in days, she closed her eyes and moaned as she sank her teeth into a slice of sweet pineapple, "What?" she asked bashfully when she opened her eyes and noticed Maurice had stopped eating his food and was staring at her,

"I'm just watching, you act like that's really good to you," Maurice smiled,

"Oh, it is!" Maya said biting into a juicy, ripe piece of melon,

Maurice laughed as he removed the cover from his steaming food,

"Man, I missed this! They don't have food like this back in Memphis!" Maurice said as he bit into a tender oxtail, "C'mon Maya, can't you drink one glass of rum with me," he asked as he filled his glass,

"I can't Maurice," Maya said, her smile suddenly leaving,

"You can't, or you won't?" Maurice asked,

"I can't..."

"I know you don't drink much, but it's just one glass of rum, just one Maya..." Maurice pleaded,

Maya paused, and took a deep breath, "I don't even know why I'm telling you this Maurice, but..."

"Telling me what?" Maurice said as he picked up a piece of stewed chicken,

"Well, I guess you're going to find out sooner or later... but here it goes..." Maya said after a deep sigh,

"I'm listening," Maurice said still concentrating on his meal,

"Well, it's just that... I can't drink because," Maya paused, then took a deep breath before blurting, "I'm pregnant," Maya said before she sighed again,

"You're what?" Maurice said, not even noticing that he had dropped his piece of chicken on the floor,

"I'm pregnant," Maya repeated herself slowly,

"Are you serious?" Maurice asked,

"Yes, I am..." Maya said nervously,

"For real, Maya?"

"Yeah..." Maya answered, and she could feel his disappointment,

"Damn!" Maurice said, "Damn..." he said again and stared off,

"See that's why I didn't wanna tell you!"

"No, it's cool... it's cool, does he know?" Maurice

172

asked,

"Yeah, I told him right before I left,"

"Damn!" Maya heard him say again under his breath as he sat there staring at her,

"Now do you see why I said I didn't want to rush into anything," Maya said as she stood and grabbed her shoes, she let out another long sigh when she noticed Maurice was still holding his hand up to his mouth as if he was holding the piece of chicken that he'd dropped on the floor,

"I… I'm gonna go… to my room and I…uh, guess I'll be...seeing you around," Maya said as she slipped through the door and closed it quietly behind her, she didn't even look back as she ran barefoot down the hall and pushed the elevator button in tears, by the time she made it to her suite her vision was blurred, and she had to feel around to slide her card key into the slot, once she made it into her room, she collapsed onto the bed in tears, "That's okay..." Maya said trying to console herself, "I know you'll love me, even if no-one else ever does!" She said to her belly as she rubbed it around in a circle,

It took a minute for Maurice to get himself together, he felt like he was running in slow motion, he waited impatiently as the elevator reached her floor and sprinted down the hall as fast as he could to her suite, "How could you be so stupid!" he told himself as he banged on the door to her suite, he was so glad that he'd remembered her room number from the conversation that they had earlier, "Maya! Maya!" he yelled, "Maya, it's me, open up!"

Maya was still in tears as she opened the door and leaned against the doorpost,

"I'm sorry Maya, and I know you're mad, but I just wasn't expecting you to say that..."

"Maurice, you don't have to feel sorry for me," Maya said, her strength drained, she had initially opened the door to cuss him out, but now she didn't even have it in her,

"Maya, you got me all wrong!" Maurice said with a confused look on his face,

"I still think you're a nice person, and I understand if you don't want to be around me now," Maya said with all the strength she had left,

"That's what I'm trying to tell you, I do want to be around you Maya,"

"No, you don't..." Maya said, she was in no mood to be anybody's charity case,

"Yes, I do!" Maurice insisted,

"Why?"

"I just do..." he said with a shrug,

"Whatever Maurice, but I'm kinda busy, so if you'll excuse me," Maya said, waiting patiently for him to take a step back so that she could slam the door in his face, but Maurice stepped inside the door and grabbed her hand,

"Maya, I'm sorry, I was just kinda shocked, I really wasn't expecting that, but it's cool, let's just go back to my room and finish eating, I should've known something by the way that you tore into that fruit like somebody was gonna come and snatch it from you!" Maurice said smiling,

Maya lowered her head and tried to stop her constantly flowing tears,

"Come here..." he beckoned as he wrapped her in his arms, wiping her tears with the back of his hand, they stood in that spot for what seemed like forever and ever before walking back to his room. Maya was still skeptical, but she ended up having a good time, they ended up dancing, laughing and talking all night long until the sun kissed her on the cheek letting her know it was morning. Maya fell asleep sitting up on the couch with Maurice's head resting on her lap, her fingers were still entwined in his thick locs, for some reason, she couldn't keep her hands out of his hair, and he was helpless to her soft touch, her hands had lured him to sleep almost instantly...

"Good morning, Mama," Maurice said stretching,

"Morning," Maya managed to get out before rushing to the bathroom, to vomit,

"You feelin' all right?" Maurice asked as he stood by the door,

"No, not at all..." Maya said before rinsing her mouth out in the sink,

"Is there anything I can get for you," Maurice asked, concern dripping from his voice,

"I'll be okay, but I have to go, the smell of that chicken from yesterday is about to take me out," Maya said as she covered her mouth, trying her best not to gag, "and I bet Tricia is worried sick about me," she said as she rushed to the door,

"You can tell her that you were in good hands, okay?" Maurice said over his shoulder,

"I will," Maya smiled,

"Will I see you later?" Maurice asked before Maya could even touch the doorknob,

"Maybe," Maya teased as she picked up her shoes and rushed out the door,

Maurice smiled wide and shook his head and Maya closed the door behind her, she floated down the long hallway and when she got off the elevator and turned the corner to her suite, Tricia was just about to knock on her door,

"Ain't those the same clothes you had on yesterday?" Tricia asked with a smirk,

"Shut up! I didn't ask you how long you stayed out last night, did I?" Maya said with a playful frown,

"Not as late as you, I see!" Tricia teased,

"Forget you Tricia!" Maya laughed,

"Me and Ahmar stayed at the club listening to the band until about two this morning, then we said goodnight and I came up here and went to bed!"

"I'm glad to hear that," Maya said,

"Well, I guess I don't have to ask what time you made it in!" Tricia teased,

"No, you don't! And I had a good time too!" Maya said,

"I just bet you did... I sure hope you know what you're doing Maya,"

"It's not even like that! Hey, let me go and take a shower, I'll meet you in the lobby in about an hour, then I'll tell you all about it," Maya said,

"Alright girl, I'll see you in a lil' bit," Tricia said, and Maya could tell Tricia was concerned about her,

Even though Maya didn't sleep much last night, she felt invigorated, Tricia noticed Maya's glow as she floated up to the table,

"Did you order yet?" Maya asked,

"No, I was waiting on you. Oh-wee...look at that glow!"

"Really?" Maya said touching her own face,

"You really had a good time, huh?" Tricia asked with her lips twisted,

"Girl yes! And listen to this..." Maya said as she filled Tricia in on what happened last night.

"He massaged your flat ass feet *AND* kissed your stankin' ass toe! Wow! He must really like you!" Tricia teased,

"Shut up Tricia!" Maya laughed,

Maya also told Tricia about his reaction to the pregnancy situation,

"Girl you are kidding me!"

"No, I'm serious,"

"Now that sounds like something out of one of those romance novels!" Tricia teased,

"I know!" Maya said, and they both laughed, and they were still busy laughing and talking when Maurice and Ahmar walked up,

"May we join you beautiful ladies?" Ahmar asked, and once again, his thick accent made both Tricia and Maya thump between the thighs,

"I don't see why not," Tricia answered,

"Hey Mama!" Maurice said as he sat down beside Maya and kissed her cheek, "What's up Trish, you can't speak to nobody?" Maurice teased,

"You didn't give me a chance, but good morning and how are you feeling on this beautiful day, Rece?" Tricia asked with a smile,

"I'm real good, and how about you?" Maurice smiled back,

"I'm alright, and what about you Ahmar?" Tricia asked,

"It is a good day," Ahmar said with a nod as he smiled at Tricia,

"Indeed, it is," Tricia smiled back,

Ahmar and Maurice decided to join Maya and Tricia on the sight-seeing tour, they caught a cab and took in the sights, in awe as they walked on Maracas Beach, there were booths stationed along the shore and each one held its own display of jewelry, clothes, hats, shoes, CD's, Cultural artwork, food, and souvenirs, they even had a tent set up for tourists who wanted their hair braided,

"Ooh, I have to try this!" Maya said as she passed by a tent where this tall slender woman was braiding a white woman's long blonde hair with lightning speed, the woman's hands were moving so fast that it was almost magical. Maya was mesmerized by this woman's work, her own hair was beginning to swell because of the humidity and even though she often wore her hair twisted up in the front, she'd never worn her hair braided to the scalp. Maya stopped at the jewelry counter that sold beaded jewelry and asked the vendor if she could buy some beads. The lady showed Maya the most beautiful iridescent and clear glass beads she had ever seen, Maya purchased the beads and rushed back over to the braiding woman's tent, "I want her to braid my hair!" Maya pointed,

"Greetings!" The woman said as they entered the tent,

"Hi!" Maya said with a big smile,

"Look at all of this thick hair upon your head," The

176

woman spoke with a Trinidadian accent thicker than Ahmar's, if that was even possible,

"Think you can do anything with it?"

"Think! Child, I know! Give me ten minutes with this here gal, and I'll braid you up in no time!"

"Tricia are you gonna wait with me?" Maya asked,

"Girl yeah, I have to see this with your tender headed tale!" Tricia teased,

"What about you?" The woman asked Tricia as she walked up and fingered her individual braids, "We can braid these up on your head to look like a basket!" The woman told Tricia,

"Really?"

"Yeah gal, now go on over there!"

"So, are you guys going to wait for us?" Tricia asked,

"Child, it don't take no time," the woman chimed in,

"I'll wait for her all day if I have to!" Ahmar said pulling up a chair,

"And you already know I'm staying here with you, Mama!" Maurice said winking his eye at Maya,

Braiding Maya's thick hair took almost two hours, but Maya and Tricia were finally finished. The time flew by so fast, they were busy laughing, talking, and listening to old West Indian folk stories. Maya's hair was braided into a maze of braids with abstract designs and decorated with the beads she had gotten at the jewelry table, and Tricia's individual braids were transformed to look like a real basket across the back and fastened with a beautiful wooden barrette with a waterfall of curled braids hanging down,

"Wow!" Tricia and Maya said as they looked in the mirror and then at each other,

"My uncle is throwing a fete tonight, and you are all invited," Ahmar said once they arrived back at the hotel,

"Okay, but first you have to tell us what a fete is," Tricia said smiling,

"Oh, a fete is what you would call a party, or a big feast..." Ahmar said with a wink, "I'll be here to pick you guys up at nine o'clock, if it's okay?"

"That's fine," Tricia answered,

"Ladies...Maurice, I'll see you then," Ahmar nodded,

After Ahmar left, Tricia turned to Maya,

"Girl, I need to call Phillip and see how Lil' Man is doing, then I'm gonna take a long ass nap, I am tired!" Tricia said in the middle of a yawn,

"Alright then Tricia, I'll see you later,"

"See you later Rece!" Tricia said as she turned toward the elevators,

"Bye Trish!" Maurice said as put his arm around Maya and they headed for the dining area, they'd spent most of the day sightseeing and souvenir shopping and they were all exhausted, so they decided to go back up to Maurice's room and relax.

***

7 KING ME!

Maya and Maurice lounged comfortably on the shaded patio of his hotel room while admiring the beautiful Trinidadian skies, "Is the baby hungry?" Maurice asked as he reached over and patted Maya's belly,

"Yep, and I am too!" Maya said with a smile,

"What do you have a taste for?" Maurice asked,

"I want some more fruit, and a lot of it, too!" Maya said, her mouth began to water at the thought,

"I can already see what you're gonna be craving," Maurice joked, Maya smiled and fanned him off,

Maurice ordered stewed beef and dumplings, and Maya asked for the biggest fruit bowl that they had, after eating they were still too wired to sleep, so Maurice called a cab and took them to Independence Square. Maya wandered around, amazed at the hustle and bustle in Independence Square and Maurice was anxious to get a good draughts game going, he had been practicing and couldn't wait to get into a good game. He and Maya strolled down the walk hand in hand, but then suddenly Maurice stopped short and nodded at the older gentleman who was sitting there looking as if he was waiting for someone, the man was dressed in faded brown khaki shorts, a short sleeved buttoned-down shirt, and worn brown leather sandals, and an old worn straw hat,

"Hey Old Man, remember me?" Maurice asked,

"Perhaps..." The man said as he took a swig from his bottle of rum, he then stroked his beard, pretending to be in deep thought, "Yah got de photograph?" he asked,

"How could I forget that you know how you like to cheat!" Maurice joked,

"Dis young boy, such a sore loser!" Sebastian said pointing at Maurice and laughing out loud, then he looked at Maya and smiled,

Maurice went into his backpack and pulled out a mini photo album and flipped through it quickly, he pulled the picture out of the album and handed it to the man, "Now, we're gonna set it up just like on this picture, and this time no cheating Old Man!" Maurice warned with a smile,

"Hah!" The Old man exclaimed, "Sebastian never cheats! Last time I beat de young boy here so quick, his head still spinnin'!" Sebastian joked as he stood, "Sebastian Lucien here! Not only is de boy here a poor draughts player, but he rude!" Sebastian said as he extended his hand to Maya,

"Maya Anderson here!" Maya said with a smile as she shook his hand,

"Come Young Boy! Let Old Sebastian school yah in draughts!"

"What's draughts?" Maya whispered in Maurice's ear,

"Oh, it's just like checkers," Maurice answered, still concentrating on the picture,

"Oh, okay," Maya said paying close attention to both the picture and the draughts board,

Sebastian looked at Maya and smiled again, he kept smiling at her like he knew a secret. Maya found herself in a deep blush, she smiled back then looked down, she was intrigued by this man. She knew he had to be at least fifty years old, even though he could probably go for a man in his early forties. Maya marveled at the stories Sebastian told about the people, places and things he'd experienced in his lifetime. He oozed wisdom, spoke in riddles, and told many jokes. Maya also loved Maurice's energy and the way that he and Sebastian interacted, she began to imagine how Maurice would be once he was Sebastian's age. Maya shifted her attention back to Sebastian, she admired his silver and black sideburns, his thick bushy eyebrows and chiseled facial features, his deep dark skin with golden undertones, she loved the patch of gray that rested on the sides of his beard and the way he rubbed his beard when he was in deep thought, and most of all she really like his laid back, mellow personality. She drifted into a daydream and could almost see herself and Maurice, much older, holding hands walking down this same street. She imagined Maurice stopping to play checkers on the street, but this time he would be the older

180

man playing against a younger man. Maya wondered if Maurice would be the kind of man who would tease the younger men the same way Sebastian was teasing him now, *"Yeah, it's exactly what he'd be like!"* Maya thought and laughed deep on the inside,

"Would yah look at dat! How dey say in de States…King Me, Boy!" Sebastian said laughing out loud, Maurice frowned and began to focus intently on his strategy,

"I hate that I even taught you that…but it's okay," Maurice laughed while shaking his head at Sebastian, "I was holding back on you last time, but this time, no mercy, you hear me Old Man!" Maurice said, still concentrating on the board,

"Ooohhh! Yah make Old Sebastian tremble with fear!" Sebastian teased,

"You better be scared," Maurice warned,

"Oh I am… Yah don't see me shakin?" Sebastian said sarcastically, he then smiled and looked over at Maya, "So… when dat baby due?" Sebastian asked still smiling,

"Wow! How did you know? Do I have a pregnant sticker on my forehead or something?" Maya asked with a strange look on her face,

"A pregnant sticker? I don't understand…" Sebastian said with a puzzled look on his face,"

"I'm sorry, it's just that you're the second person who could tell that I was pregnant just by looking at me," Maya explained,

"Oh? And who was de first?" Sebastian asked,

"My mama, she looked at me and could tell right off," Maya said still trying to figure out how they both knew,

"Sounds like yah come from good stock… yah mother, she has de gift, but it ain't hard to tell, if one knows what to look for," Sebastian smiled,

"And what is that? I'm only a month and a half," Maya said, her curiosity taking over,

"Yes… about a month and a half, and I think…" Sebastian squinted and rubbed his beard, "It's a boy… yeah… a *big* boy!" Sebastian said while rubbing his chin and nodding his head up and down slowly,

"A boy? You can tell all of that just by looking at me?" Maya asked, she was taken aback,

"Why of course!" Sebastian said, still smiling,

"Wooooooow…" Maya said, she was mind blown and more intrigued by this man than ever,

Maurice and Sebastian were having a ball and even though Maya liked watching as Maurice and the gray-haired gentleman played checkers, she was way too excited to stand still, and soon she began to

feel antsy, there was just so much going on around her, Maya
noticed a band setting up their instruments across the walkway
from where they were,

"What are they doing?" she asked Sebastian,

"Yah never seen nobody beat pan?" Sebastian asked,
surprised,

"No, what's pan?" Maya asked,

"Hah! It's a steel drum band, yah ears in for a real treat!"
Sebastian said with excitement in his voice,

"Baby is it all right with you if I go over there and check
out the band?" Maya asked,

"Sure, I'll be over there once I beat this Old Man again,"
Maurice said as Maya walked over and sat on a bench in front of
the band,

"Bend your ear dis way, Young Boy!" Sebastian said
once Maya walked away,

"What is it, Old Man?" Maurice teased,

"That is a good woman over there..." Sebastian said with
a wink,

"And how do you know that Old Man?" Maurice teased,

"Sebastian knows...believe me, it is true..."

"Yeah..." Maurice nodded,

"And I tell yah something else... even if yah didn't plant
dat seed, if you water it, feed it, give it sun and good discipline...
yah will harvest good fruit,"

"How did you know that I wasn't the father?" Maurice
asked, stupefied,

"Young Boy! If dat was yah seed, dat woulda been de
first thing yah tell me! Sebastian never meet a man who didn't
boast about his chirren," Sebastian winked,

"You are something else, Old Man!" Maurice smiled,

"Something else indeed! Now when is dat weddin'?"

"Whoa...slow down Old Man! We're not even together
yet!"

"True...true...but yah love her, and you have loved her
for a long, long time..." Sebastian said, almost daring Maurice to
dispute him,

"I don't even know why I'm asking you this, but how
could you possibly know that?"

"Yah eyes tell me, and I seem to remember yah sittin'
right in dat chair, going on and on about a gal by the name of
Ma-ya, Ma-ya dis... Ma-ya dat... just last year around this time,

Ma-ya, Ma-ya, Ma-ya..." Sebastian teased, pretending to focus on the draughts board,

"Aw Man...I forgot all about that!" Maurice said,

"I did not... Old Sebastian got de memory of a bull!"

"And the skills of an Old Man! Hah! Now crown my king, Sir!" Maurice said laughing,

"Don't fill yahself with so much pride, Young Boy! I let yah have dat one," Sebastian shrugged,

"Yeah right, and why would you do that?" Maurice asked,

"Because winnin' builds confidence...but losin' builds character," Sebastian said as he sucked his teeth, "Now King Me! Hah!" Sebastian said as he performed a move so intricate on the draughts board that Maurice shook his head in confusion,

"You are truly something else, Old Man," Maurice said, still shaking his head, trying to figure out how Sebastian won,

"Yah ask her to be your wife, yes?" Sebastian asked still staring down at the draughts table,

"I don't know," Maurice answered reluctantly,

"Well, yah better hurry before de farmer comes back to claim dat seed," Sebastian warned,

"I ain't worried about him," Maurice said confidently,

"Well, yah should be! Ma-ya is not a man, only a man can instruct a boy on de ways of men!" Sebastian insisted,

"I just found out that she was pregnant yesterday, so it's still kind of new to me, I plan to be there for her and the baby, but I don't know about marriage, just yet," Maurice admitted,

"A good life is best experienced on a steady road Young Boy, and at a steady pace! Yah don't want de gal insulted by yah dragging feet, do yah?"

"No but, don't you think it's a little too soon to be talking about marriage and stuff?" Maurice asked,

"Now is de perfect time!" Sebastian answered, excitedly,

"Well, what if I ask her and she says no?" Maurice laughed, he was tickled at how excited Sebastian was,

"She won't," Sebastian said still concentrating on the draughts board,

"How do you know?" Maurice asked while looking side-eyed at Sebastian,

"Sebastian knows..." he shrugged,

"But how do you know?"

"Sebastian knows..."

"But how?"

"It is in her eyes, Young Boy! Yah always know when a woman loves yah by de shine in her eyes," Sebastian said as he pointed to his own eye,

"And you can tell all of that just by looking in her eyes?"

"Young Boy! Eyes never lie! Her eyes shine bright like de sun when she look at yah, Can't yah see it, Boy?!?"

"Okay, okay! I tell you what! If the times comes and I ask her, and she accepts, I want you to come to the wedding," Maurice said, he couldn't believe he was having this conversation,

"Is dat so?" Sebastian said still rubbing his beard and concentrating on the draughts board,

"Yeah, and I'll even fly you out to The States, myself,"

"Sounds good...but..." Sebastian paused,

"But what?" Maurice asked,

"But how will Old Sebastian get back home?" Sebastian said trying not to laugh,

"Now you're on your own with that one! You're gonna have to hitchhike, ride a bike, swim or something!" Maurice said as they both laughed loudly,

"Sebastian does not care much for de busses wit' wings, just send Old Sebastian some photographs of dat wedding, I talk about yah so much, My Sweet Flora thinks Ah go mad!"

"Okay, I'll do that! And I just so happened to have extra copies of the pictures that I took of you when I was here last time,"

"Ha! My Flora says photographs rob de soul, if she knew about de photographs, I would have to pack up and leave!" Sebastian laughed, "Okay...okay, maybe I can show her just one, before she say Old Sebastian a madman and she ship me off!" Sebastian said laughing. "Now stop yah foolishness and go marry de gal!"

"Okay, if things are still good a year from now, then I'll ask her,"

"A whole year? Hmmm..." Sebastian pondered as he rubbed his beard again, "Fair enough... and when yah get home, tell her Old Sebastian said to stand back and let de sun shine in her eyes,"

"And what does that mean?" Maurice asked,

"Not for yah to know, Young Boy! Just tell her..." Sebastian laughed,

"Okay, I'll tell her...same place next year, Old Man?"

"Same place next year, Young Boy!" Sebastian smiled,

Maurice took pictures of Sebastian before placing his camera on its tripod and taking a few more of them together, then they went on their separate ways, Maurice walked over to the bench and sat beside Maya and listened to the band for a while,

"Where's Sebastian?" Maya asked,

"He had to go," Maurice said, and Maya could tell that Maurice was a little disappointed,

"That's too bad, I didn't even get a chance to tell him good-bye,"

"He liked you," Maurice said with a smile,

"He did!" Maya said excited, "What did he say?"

"He told me to tell you to stand back and let the sun shine in your eyes,"

"What does that mean?" Maya asked,

"I don't know, and he wouldn't tell me," Maurice said shrugging his shoulders, "but you can ask him next year," Maurice winked,

"Is that an invite?" Maya asked,

"Yep! Sure is..." Maurice nodded,

Maya's whole soul smiled, she had eaten so much and was full and sleepy, she'd had a ball listening to the band and walking up and down the Square sampling Trinidadian street foods like Curry Goat Roti with Potatoes, Corn Soup, Bake and Shark, Macaroni Pie and Stew Chicken, Doubles with Tamarind Chutney, plain, Chicken and Saltfish Pholourie, Saheena, Coconut Ice Cream, Guava and Blueberry-Watermelon Snow Cones, and Sugar Cake. Maya frowned when Maurice tried to get her to try Chicken Foot Souse which was one of his favorites. Maurice was still kind of wired, but he looked at his watch and noticed that it was already five o'clock, which left only a few hours before they had to get ready for the party,

"Baby Mama, are you ready to head back to the hotel?" Maurice asked,

"Yes, I'm beat!" Maya yawned,

"I'm not tired, but I know I need some sleep," Maurice sighed,

"Well Ms. Lady, I guess I'll see you in a little bit," Maurice said once they made it back to the hotel, ,

"Alright Sweetie call me when you wake up," Maya said over her shoulder,

"I will," Maurice said in between yawns,

**

(Meanwhile...back in Tricia's room...)
"Hey Baby!" Trish said after hearing Phillip's voice,

185

"Hey Sweetheart, are you having fun yet?"

"No, not really... are you holding down the castle?"

"Yeah, I got it under control."

"Where's Lil' Man?"

"He's asleep, he misses his mommy, and so do I!"

"Phillip don't do this to me now, I'm already homesick!" Tricia pleaded,

"You mean to tell me you ain't up there cuddling with some knuckle-headed island boy? I am shocked!" Phillip said laughing,

"Of course not, Darling, you know ain't nobody here as fine as you!"

"Yeah right, hey?"

"What Baby?"

"You wanna do it over the phone?"

"Stop playing Phillip!" Tricia said laughing out loud,

"You are laughing, but I'm for real!" Phillip said,

Tricia laughed so hard she had tears in her eyes, she really needed that laugh, "I love you Baby, you know that?" she said,

"You'd better! So...are we gonna do it over the phone or what?"

"Nope," Tricia teased,

"You gonna make me beg for it, ain't you?" Phillip asked knowingly,

"Yep!"

"Well I sure as hell don't mind beggin'...pleeeease?" Phillip whined,

"Nope..."

"Okay, okay...I know what you want, if you give me what I want...I'll buy you..." Phillip thought hard, "those shoes you liked so much, you know, the ones with the red bottoms..."

"I don't know Phillip," Tricia said sniggling to herself because she'd already gotten those shoes last week,

"Okay then I'll throw in three kisses wherever you want them, a big hug from Lil' Man, and when you get home we'll go to the mall and get that expensive dress to match those shoes that you went crazy over!"

"I don't know..." Tricia said laughing under her breath, because she had gotten the dress last week as well, and it was hanging in her closet back home as well as the shoes,

"You sure like making me work hard for it, don't you?"

"Yep!" Tricia teased,

"Well just tell me what you want, and I'll give it to you!"

"Now that'll work!" Tricia agreed,

"So...Baby Girl, what are you wearing?" Phillip asked,

"Nothing..." Tricia whispered in a sexy voice,

"Shit Girl! Don't do me like that, you already got me over here hurting for you!" Phillip teased,

***

The minute Maurice's alarm went off, he jumped up and grabbed the phone beside his bed and called Maya,

"Hey Mama, you woke?"

"Yeah, I'm woke," She answered slowly,

"How are you feeling?" he asked, and Maya could tell that he was concerned,

"Tired!" Maya answered with all the energy she had,

"You wanna skip the party? I'm sure he'd understand if you did..." Maurice suggested, hoping that Maya would agree,

"You know we can't do that! I sure wish we could though," Maya said,

"Me too!" Maurice agreed,

"Well let me get up and get motivated, I'll be downstairs in about an hour, okay?" Maurice said,

"Alright Baby," Maya said as she rolled out of bed and called Tricia who sounded even more worn out than she did,

"Tricia, you all right?"

"Girl yeah,"

"You sure? You sound like you're out of it," Maya asked.

"I'm okay, me and Phillip just finished doing it over the phone,"

"Uggghhh!" Maya said, with a deep frown on her face,

"When you've been together as long as we have, you have to spice it up every chance you get!" Tricia laughed, "So...how did it go with you and Rece?"

"Girl, I don't even know where to start, but I'm having a blast!" Maya laughed as she told Tricia about Sebastian and the music at The Square,

"I'm glad you enjoyed yourself, but just make sure you keep your legs closed tight, and your eyes wide open!"

"I will, don't worry Tricia! Anyway, what are you wearing to the party?"

"I'm not sure, I got this bad ass blue dress with the back out and matching sandals that I've been dying to wear!" Tricia said trying her

187

best to muster up some excitement about the big fete tonight,

"Sounds cute," Maya said,

"What are you wearing Maya?"

"I got this mustard dress that flows all the way down to my ankles with the head wrap to match," Maya said,

"Sounds nice, Maya let me get myself together and I'll call you when I'm ready," Tricia said,

"Alright, see you downstairs,"

They were waiting in the lobby when Ahmar walked up,

"Ready?" he asked looking directly at Tricia,

"Ready," Tricia answered with a flirtatious smile,

Maya and Maurice followed them out of the front entrance of the hotel,

Tricia and Maya marveled at the breathtaking view of Ahmar's uncle's extravagant nine bedroom, three-and-a-half-bathroom, two story, Cottage style mansion overlooking the ocean. The winding roads leading up to the mansion made Maya a little nauseous, but the view more than made up for her discomfort, she was simply amazed at how big and beautiful it was, they walked into the home and gasped at the ten-foot ceilings and intricately carved oak accents, and large glass windows with views capable of putting you in a trance. Maya and Tricia were admiring the window treatments while Maurice admired the grand staircase, marble flooring and the infinity pool.

"Young Boy!" Ahmar's uncle said from the staircase,

"Old Man?" Maurice said surprised,

Tricia and Ahmar looked confused when Maurice rushed up to Ahmar's uncle and hugged him,

"Hey Sebastian!" Maya said smiling,

"Uncle, yah know these people?" Ahmar asked as Maurice and Sebastian descended down the stairs,

"I've known dis here Young Boy for years!" Sebastian said winking his eye at Maurice,

"Small world!" Ahmar said as he shrugged and shook his head,

"Let Sebastian show you around Young Boy," he said as he put his arm around Maurice's shoulder and led him down the hall into the Great room,

"You got it like this Old Man?" Maurice said looking at the gigantic oil paintings and antiques decorating the place,

"Being in this big house gets lonely, so Sebastian likes

to go to De Square and hunt down victims like you, to beat in draughts!"
Sebastian said with a smile,

"I've always said you were something else Old Man!"

"Come, come! I have something to show you!" Sebastian said as
he led Maurice down a hall to a room off to the side, Maurice's face lit up
as he walked in, Sebastian had all the paintings Maurice had given him
over the years professionally mounted and placed on the walls of his
office.

"Maaan...you didn't even have to do this," Maurice said, "Ha!
You even have the first one I gave you five years ago!" Maurice said as
he pointed to a picture that he'd painted of a little boy sitting in a stroller,
his heart was full, he didn't know whether to laugh or cry,

"I kept them all over the years, you have a special talent Young
Boy! Well, not in draughts, but yah paint really well," Sebastian joked,

Maurice smiled, he was too amazed to make a snappy comeback,
Sebastian showed Maurice the rest of the house, and as it turned out,
Sebastian was an art collector who came from a wealthy family, his
home was decorated with the most beautiful artwork they'd ever seen
and the view from the house was breathtaking. There were people
everywhere and you could hear calypso music in the distance, there were
live bands, one of which was the same live band that was playing in
Independence Square earlier. The beauty of it overwhelmed them all,
especially Tricia, and Ahmar wasn't making it any better, placing his
warm hands on the small of her back, the last thing Tricia needed was to
be touched, but she still closed her eyes and enjoyed it. Maurice
marveled at the expensive artwork that graced the halls of Sebastian's
mansion. At times, he didn't know whether to stare at the artwork or
Maya, being that they were both equally as beautiful. Sebastian caught
Maya by the hand and led her to the dance floor, and Maurice followed
suit and led Flora, Sebastian's wife, Maurice was surprised that Sebastian
could really dance,

Flora laughed as she and Maurice danced, "I finally have a
chance to meet de man my husband has been talking nonstop about," she
joked,

"Has he been talking about me that much?" Maurice asked,

"Has he? I was beginning to think he was going mad," Flora
joked, "But I can certainly see why, you remind me of him when he was
your age, de resemblance is uncanny!" Flora continued, "Sebastian says,
de only difference is that you're a poor draughts player and he has to
make yah *'King'* him quite often," Flora said, trying her best to say it just
like Sebastian would, Maurice laughed out loud as he twirled Flora
across the floor,

Maya was impressed by the way Sebastian moved. She always held a secret passion for older men and this man was tops on her list. She could truly understand why his wife kept such a big smile on her face because Sebastian knew just how to touch a woman, caressing her hand and touching her lower back as if she was made of silk, he glided her across the floor and held her in his arms like fragile glass, she couldn't help but to blush all over herself,

"Sebastian?" Maya asked, smiling as they danced,

"Yes, Beautiful Flower?" Sebastian answered,

"What did you mean when you told Maurice to tell me to let the sun shine in my eyes?"

"You'll know when de time is right," he answered,

"Maurice said you would say that," Maya admitted,

"He said dat?" Sebastian asked with a giggle,

"Yeah," Maya said with a smile,

"Hah! He knows Old Sebastian too well!" Sebastian laughed,

"Damn, even his laugh is sexy," Maya thought as she giggled inside, then she remembered that he hadn't answered her question, "Sebastian!" Maya said as she pouted,

"Old Sebastian will tell yah when de time is right, Impatient Flower," he said as he twirled her around and caught her in his arms,

"So, I guess that's the best I'm going get out of you, huh?" Maya said smiling wide after that twirl,

"Yep!" Sebastian answered, saying it as just he had heard Maurice say on many occasions, after a few dances they changed partners, and everyone stood around clapping while the two couples danced the night away…

"Ahmar, how old is Sebastian anyway?" Maurice asked as Ahmar drove them back to the hotel,

"We don't know… all we know is that he is de oldest living member in the family. He is actually my great uncle, that would make him around 70 or so, but no one knows for sure, only Auntie Flora, and My Great-Auntie Marlean, who is sixty-seven, she is his youngest sister, she knows, but she won't tell, I asked my Great Grandmother once and she scolded me, so I never asked again!" Ahmar said,

"Man! I thought that he was in his forties," Maurice said,

"Uncle Sebastian looks the same way he did when I was a boy, he's always been very active, now my Auntie Flora, she is only fifty-two," Ahmar whispered as if he told a forbidden secret,

They all laughed, and Maya and Maurice exited the truck and hurried into the hotel. Tricia lagged back to thank Ahmar for an awesome night,

"I had a good time tonight, Ahmar," she said,

"So did I," Ahmar said as he stared into Tricia's eyes, forcing her to look away,

"Well, I'll see you later…" Tricia said, but as she reached for the door, Ahmar grabbed her hand,

"Don't go!" he whispered,

"I have to!" Tricia resisted,

"Tricia stay with me," Ahmar pleaded,

"I can't, I'm a married woman Ahmar…" Tricia said as she gently pulled her hands away from his,

"And I am a married man…" Ahmar never took his eyes off of Tricia as he spoke, "and I don't want to be alone tonight," Ahmar reasoned,

"I don't know what to say Ahmar," Tricia said, struggling to keep her will power intact,

"Then don't say a word, just speak to me with your kiss," Ahmar said as he leaned over to kiss Tricia,

"Whoa!" Tricia said pushing his face to the side, "I can't do this! I-I have to go!" she stuttered as she fumbled with the handle on the door and sprinted into the hotel and didn't stop running until she was safely inside her suite, Ahmar sat quietly in his car for a while before slowly driving away...

***

"So, what do you have planned for the rest of the day, Mama?" Maurice asked as he escorted Maya to her suite,

"I don't know Maurice, I really haven't spent any time with Tricia since I've been here, so I thought I would spend the day with her,"

"I understand," Maurice said with a smile,

"So, I'll see you later," Maya said as she hugged him and kissed him on the cheek,

"Sweet dreams Baby Mama, and make sure one of those dreams are about me, okay?"

"All right, I will," Maya said, blushing as she went into her suite and closed the door,

Maya wanted to spend this moment and every waking moment with Maurice, but she felt herself getting too attached to him. She knew she had to put some distance between them when he led her off to a secluded spot at Sebastian's mansion and kissed her with so much passion that her knees buckled, and if he wasn't planting kiss after kiss on her shoulders, her ears, cheek, and even on her forehead, he was rubbing her shoulders and her belly, or whispering something sweet in her ear. Maya found herself smiling uncontrollably when he stood behind her and wrapped his arms around her waist, while they basked at the view from Sebastian's mansion,

"A girl could get used to this," Maya thought, as she replayed the night's events in her head. She was getting undressed when someone knocked on her door,

"Ooh Lord please don't let this be him, I wouldn't be able to take it!" Maya mumbled under her breath,

"Maya, you in there?" Tricia said through the crack in the door,

"Lord thank you!" Maya mumbled as she opened the door quickly,

"What's up Tricia?" Maya looked concerned when she saw the look on Tricia's face,

Tricia collapsed on Maya's bed and exploded into tears,

"What's wrong with you?" Maya asked, not expecting Tricia's overwhelming flow of emotions, Maya knew Tricia never cried unless something was serious,

"I miss my Phillip, I shouldn't even be here without him, I'm such a slut!" Tricia said in between sobs,

"TRICIA, YOU DIDN'T!!!" Maya yelled,

"No, girl...I didn't, but I sure in the hell wanted to!" Tricia said as she wiped her eyes,

Maya took a deep breath and exhaled, she was so relieved, she loved both Tricia and Phillip and would never want to see either one of them hurt,

"I got the best husband in the world and now I wanna cheat on him, just because I'm lonely!"

"Wait Tricia, you're losing me here, start from the beginning," Maya said, trying to understand Tricia's meltdown,

Tricia told Maya about what happened with Ahmar in his van,

"Oh my!" Maya said,

"I know!" Tricia sobbed, "Maya I just feel so guilty,"

"Why Tricia? You didn't do anything!" Maya said,

"I just miss him so much Maya, he's all alone at home and here I am all hugged up with the next man!" Tricia said through sniffles,

"Tricia, you don't want Ahmar, he's just your surrogate Phillip! This is your first time away from your husband in ten years and you're just in withdrawal, that's all," Maya said, trying her best to comfort her hurting friend,

"Thank you, Maya, I don't know what I would do without you," Tricia said, forcing a smile,

"Are you okay now?" Maya asked,

"Yeah, I feel much better."

"You sure?" Maya teased,

"I think so...I probably just needed to cry, you know, empty out, whew..." Tricia said wiping her face with the damp washcloth Maya had given her,

"Good! Now you can help me!" Maya said,

"What's wrong with you?" Tricia asked concerned,

"That's just it, Tricia!" Maya said, "Nothing's wrong, everything's so right, as a matter of fact, everything's too right! I mean...Maurice seems like the perfect man, but I got sense enough to know there is no such thing!" Maya said, and Tricia could see the worry on her face,

"Okay...so again I ask...what's wrong?" Tricia said,

"Girl I'm falling... shit I done already fell!" Maya said,

"Maya it's way too soon, you have to stay focused!"

"I know...I mean, I don't know if I'm just lonely or love-starved, or what...but it's getting to the point where I wanna be around Maurice every single second of the day,"

"For real, Maya?" Tricia asked, she was surprised to hear that coming from Maya,

"Yeah, and I know it's too soon to have feelings for someone else by the average person's standards. I've only been away from Tony for almost two weeks, and not to mention the fact I'm pregnant by him, but Maurice! I've never met anyone like him..." Maya sighed, "I wish I had met him first! I mean all this time he's been throwing out his little harmless flirts, but I had to travel *waaay* across the globe to meet somebody I've known almost all of my life," Maya said with a sigh,

"Yeah, I see what you're saying," Tricia said understandingly,

"But realistically, Tony and I have been on two different levels for almost a year and a half now, he's never treated me right and I fell out of love with him a long time ago, and I know he doesn't love me either, but I can't lie, I always thought Maurice was fine as hell!" Maya admitted with a giggle,

"Shit he is fine, a blind person can see that, and I can tell he likes you too," Tricia said, "but Maya are you sure you don't feel anything at all for Tony-B, are you sure you're truly over him?"

"Yeah, I'm done, and not only that, I feel so free Tricia! To be honest, part of me wants to stay that way, you know, free and single, but then there's this other side of me that really wants to feel love, and a real relationship, I guess the bottom line is I've never been with anybody like Maurice and I really want a man like him in my life, but I'm scared shitless, I really don't want to go through anymore drama,"

"Well said," Tricia said with a nod,

"So, are you ever going to talk to Ahmar again?" Maya asked,

"Yeah, I have to clear the air with him, we still have a few days to be here, and I don't want him to feel uncomfortable around me, and I certainly don't want to spend my last few days on the islands dodging him," Tricia said,

"Understandable," Maya said,

"So, where's Rece?" Tricia asked,

"I told him that we needed some space and that I'd see him tomorrow when we go to Tobago,"

"That was a strong move Maya," Tricia admitted,

"I know, and I was praying you weren't him when you knocked on the door, because I don't know what I would've done," Maya laughed,

"Sounds like someone has a lil' fire that needs to be put out!" Tricia joked, frowning and fanning her nose,

"I do, but I can't! I mean, I'm supposed to wait until after the baby is born, right?" Maya asked,

"Shit, I don't know!" Tricia laughed,

"Wow...they should have a When-to-Give-Your-Coochie-Away Manual out there for us!" Maya joked,

"They do have one, it's called The Bible!" Tricia teased,

"You know what I mean Tricia! Don't get all religious on me...I mean, I want to wait until I'm married, but hell I wasn't married when I got pregnant by Tony, I was just engaged, but what if you're pregnant by somebody, is it okay to start a relationship with someone else?"

"Ooh...now that... I don't know," Tricia said, in deep thought...

"So, what am I supposed to do?" Maya asked,

"Nothing, you don't even need to be thinking about it right now, do you? I mean, you're not planning to do it tonight, are you?" Tricia asked,

"I wasn't talking about sex, silly! I was talking about being with him, I wish you knew how I feel when I'm with him, I would have never cheated on Tony, but if I knew then what I know now, Whew!" Maya confessed,

"Maya, you act like I can't see that twinkle in your eyes whenever Maurice comes around!"

"I know I can't fool you Tricia," Maya said with a sigh,

"No, you can't! And I wish I had all the answers for you Maya, but I don't, I just don't... but I will say this, you need to make sure you and Maurice are on the same page with each other before this goes any farther, I would hate to see you hurt my some superficial Island Fling, and if I were you, I would at least wait until you get back home before you do anything serious, that way you can gage for sure where it's going," Tricia said,

"I agree..." Maya said as she sat on the bed in deep thought,

***

Maurice was in the lobby enjoying his meal when Ahmar walked up,

"Can I join you?" Ahmar asked,

"Yeah, have a seat," Maurice said as he noticed the look on Ahmar's face, "Man you look like you just lost your best friend!" Maurice said after Ahmar sat down in the chair then let out a long sigh,

"I think I have," Ahmar said,

"What's going on?" Maurice asked,

"Dat woman has me going in circles!" Ahmar said with a long sigh,

"Tell me about it! I was just sitting here thinking the same thing about Maya,"

"Tricia's got my head spinnin'!" Ahmar admitted,

"Man, I already know! Maya's had me going since the first time I saw her, and even more now!"

"Do you know Tricia's husband?" Ahmar asked,

"Not really, I've seen him at a few parties, he's a cool guy, but to be honest, I ain't never seen her with nobody but her husband, they usually stuck together like glue! I was trippin' on how she was actin' with you last night,"

"I know, we were having a great time, I mean, we danced and talked until the sun came up, but then she totally flipped out on me last night!"

"What happened?" Maurice asked,

"I made the mistake of telling her how I felt about her after you

195

and Maya left, I even pulled out the *'I don't want to be alone tonight'* line...", Ahmar confessed,

"Aww naw...you didn't pull out that one, did you?" Maurice laughed,

"Yes, I did...I pulled out my best line, and she turned me down, cold!" Ahmar admitted,

"Damn..." Maurice said shaking his head,

"She shot me down like a wounded bird!" Ahmar said, mimicking a hunter shooting in the sky, "And left me sitting in my car outside!" Ahmar added,

"Aw, Man... that's messed up!" Maurice said, "So what are you gonna do, you know you can't go out like that!"

"I don't know what to do, I never have woman problems," Ahmar said with another big sigh,

"Well Tricia and Maya aren't your average women, but if I were you, I would at least try to talk to her," Maurice said,

"Yeah," Ahmar agreed,

"Man! And I thought Maya was giving me headaches!" Maurice joked,

"You too?" Ahmar asked surprised,

"Yeah, she told me she was pregnant by her ex-boyfriend, back home!" Maurice said with utter disgust dripping from his voice,

"Oh wow! She stepped out on you? That must be tough, I didn't take Maya for that type," Ahmar said,

"Oh no, that's not it, me and Maya have known each other for years, but she was with this guy back home, they just broke up, he's a real asshole though, he's slept with damn near every gal in Memphis, he's my brother's best friend, but I never liked his ass, and I was glad as hell when she finally caught him cheating on her about two weeks ago!" Maurice said with disgust,

"She caught him?" Ahmar asked,

"Yeah, they told me she walked in on him and the other girl, and she broke up with him," Maurice explained,

"And then she came here with you?" Ahmar asked, confused,

"No, no, believe it or not that was pure coincidence. I had no idea she was gonna be here, and she had no idea I was gonna be here,"

"Wow, *that* is some coincidence!" Ahmar said,

"Tell me about it! I was down in the club when they

spotted me, I'm still tripping out about Maya being here, she has no idea but I've been trying to get with her for a while, but I sure wish she wasn't pregnant though, it was bad enough when she got engaged to that punk!"

"Engaged?"

"Oh yeah, they were about to get married, like I said, he's my brother's best friend and we all grew up together, but anyway... I was even at the engagement party, and they were engaged for about a year,"

"Wow, what a complicated situation you got going," Ahmar said,

"Tell me about it...check this out, it was so fucked up how the whole thing happened,"

THE ENGAGEMENT PARTY
(Reese's View...)

Maurice remembered back to when he walked into the engagement party and spotted Tony-B sitting in the dining room flirting with a woman, Tony-B grinned like a chess cat as he kissed Cathy in the hall and shoved his hand under her short dress when he thought no one was looking. "But I saw his ass!" Maurice thought as he remembered how sick it made him. Maurice thought it would be the perfect time to let Maya know how he felt about her, but once he walked into the kitchen, Maya was cooking and chatting with her girlfriends. He took his camera into the kitchen to take pictures of her, and as usual he planned to take a few of the other girls as not to raise any suspicion. He was floored by Maya's beauty and instantly forgot about everybody else in the room. She captivated him, Maurice felt like there was a window inside of her that only he could peek into. He searched deep inside her soul often and could tell she wasn't happy. Maurice was so deep in his thoughts about her, that he didn't even notice she and the other girls were leaving the kitchen, but he was glad when she walked back into the kitchen alone, "Now's my chance!" He thought, Maurice could tell she liked him, but he also knew he had better be subtle about his advances. He was just about to make his move, walking up behind her, she smelled so good, he couldn't help but to touch her, he made a trail down her bare arm with his finger, she was so startled that she dropped the glass bowl she was holding when Tony-B strutted into the kitchen. Tony-B told Maurice to come and take pictures in the dining room. "Hell, it wasn't like he was paying me!", Maurice thought before he went into the dining room and pretended to take pictures, but minutes after they left the kitchen, Tony-B was at it again, Maurice counted at least five different times that Tony-B felt on Cathy's behind, Cathy thought it was hilarious, and of course she and her friends would laugh out loud every time Maya walked into the room. Maurice busied himself taking pictures when he noticed that Tony-B and Cathy were heading off together. Cathy's sister Candice, and her cousin Felicia played look out as Cathy and Tony-B headed into the storage shed, Maurice waited for a minute then followed them. Maurice was worried when he realized they were less than twenty feet away from the kitchen window in the storage house having sex. He'd heard about Tony-B and his Sex-capades, from his brother Larry, but he had never actually seen it for himself. He was so mad that he walked around to the kitchen window and tapped on it with his key, his intentions were to hide in the bushes and hope Maya would come outside and hear Cathy

198

moaning and go to the storage shed to investigate, but at the last minute he realized even though he wanted Maya to catch Tony-B in the act, he couldn't stand to see Maya devastated, so he jumped from behind the bushes and snapped a picture of her when she came outside to investigate his tapping on the glass. Maurice knew Tony-B had gotten careless and sooner or later Maya was gonna catch him, but she would have to catch him on her own,

***

Maurice went on to tell Ahmar how disgusted he was when his brother Larry busted Tony-B's engagement scam. Maurice knew that Larry didn't mean any harm, but he also knew his brother couldn't hold water once he got drunk. The broken look on Maya's face, made him want to just snatch her away from there and take her away from all of that madness, but the only thing he could do is stare in amazement as Cathy led the laughter and the applause when Larry humiliated Maya with his little speech, Maurice was too angry to eat although he loved Maya's cooking, but if he were to be honest, he really hated The Bar-B-Q King's infamous Bar-B-Q, and therefore never ate any,

Maurice always felt guilty for not telling Maya that day,

"I know you care for her, I can tell...but are you sure you will be able to accept a baby that belongs to a man you clearly don't like?" Ahmar asked,

"Now that's the million-dollar question right there Ahmar, that's the million dollar question..." Maurice said as he drifted into deep thought,

"Have you talked to her about it?" Ahmar asked,

"Yeah, I did earlier, but we really couldn't get deep into it, we really need to talk some more, but she told me that she wanted to spend the day with Tricia. Maybe I'll see her later tonight, or at least before we catch the ferry to Tobago tomorrow. At least that's what she said, but it sounded to me like she was trying to say she needed some space, but that's alright too!" Maurice fumed,

"You know, I've never cheated on my wife, never even wanted to! Never! But dat gal... it's just something about Tricia that makes me crazy!" Ahmar admitted,

"I think you're making her a lil' crazy too," Maurice said with a smile,

"I don't know about that...Whew...Women!" Ahmar said as he shook his head,

"Man, let's just talk about something else," Maurice said,

"I hear you...better yet, let's not talk at all...let's just drink!"

199

Ahmar said as he held up his glass of rum,

"Agreed..." Maurice said as he held up his glass of rum as well,

***

After the party, Tricia laid down and didn't wake up until noon, Maya finally rolled out of bed at around 2:00 P.M. and called Tricia,

"You woke?" Maya asked,

"Yeah, I just woke up a lil' while ago," Tricia yawned,

"I sure didn't mean to sleep this late. I haven't even packed yet, and we're supposed to be going to Tobago in the morning,"

"Don't panic Maya, we're only staying for one night,"

"I know, but I just wanna make sure I don't leave anything,"

"Girl, don't even worry about it, what do you wanna do today that won't take up too much energy, cause I'm still tired from last night?" Tricia asked,

"You already know what I wanna do!" Maya said with a smile,

"Where do you wanna go eat Maya?" Tricia asked, already knowing,

"It doesn't matter to me, we can go downstairs to the restaurant if you want to,"

"Alright, give me about twenty minutes to get cute!" Tricia said,

"Girl take forty and get real cute!" Maya teased,

"Bye Maya!" Tricia laughed before hanging up on Maya,

Tricia was anxious to see Ahmar again, and she was glad to have Maya to talk to, but truthfully, she knew deep down Ahmar was not just her surrogate Phillip, because no one could compare to Phillip. What she felt for Ahmar was pure unadulterated lust! And she hated herself for being so selfish, and for feeling so whorish, *"I can't do my husband like that!"* she thought, but the voices in her head were loud and clear, trying to persuade her to do the forbidden, *"If I did it just once, no one would ever know, not even Maya, and how would Phillip ever find out? Shut up! Shut up! Shut up!"* Tricia told herself, but her imagination ran wild, she bit down on her bottom lip, *"I just bet he'll be a champion love maker, and I bet he'd do all kinds of nasty things to me,"* Tricia thought as she imagined the two of them making love, she could feel his lips searing her flesh and instantly became angry at herself when she caught herself blushing, "I'm not even entertaining this shit, I'm getting out of here!" Tricia said aloud as she grabbed her bag and left her room quickly,

"Hey Dusty, I was wondering when you were gonna come out of that room!" Tricia said when Maya walked up and joined her at the table,

"Girl I was tired, have you seen them yet?" Maya asked,

"No, not yet, but it's just three o'clock," Tricia said looking at her watch, "You're anxious to see him aren't you?" Tricia teased,

"Does it show that much?" Maya blushed,

"Yeah girl, but I really can't say anything, I'm kind of anxious to see Ahmar and clear the air," Tricia admitted,

"Let's go listen to the band and pass time," Tricia said as she pointed over to the band as they set up,

Maya really liked this band, and the lead singer walked over to their table and gave her a rose while he sang a ballad about a man whose heart was broken by the love of his life, Tricia couldn't really concentrate on the band because she was busy looking around and checking her watch,

"Maya it's getting late, and we still haven't seen either one of them,"

"Don't worry, I know they'll be down here eventually, if not, we'll see them tomorrow before we go to Tobago," Maya said, trying to hide how bad she really wanted to see Maurice as well,

It was almost seven o'clock when Maurice walked in,

"Hey Mama!"

"Hey!" Maya blushed,

"Rece, have you seen Ahmar?"

"Nope, and he ain't in my back pocket either!" Maurice teased,

"I was just asking, but really, have you seen him?" Tricia asked anxiously,

"No, I haven't seen him," Maurice lied, Ahmar was still asleep in Maurice's room, they drank a little too much earlier and he fell asleep on Maurice's couch, Maurice didn't wake up until six, and when he left the room Ahmar was still on the couch knocked out,

"Hey Man, you finally let that couch go?" Maurice asked around nine when Ahmar walked up to the table where he and Maya were listening to the band,

"I slept longer than I planned," Ahmar said as he scanned the room for Tricia,

"You're looking for her, aren't you?" Maya asked,

"Yes, have you seen her?" Ahmar asked just as anxiously as

Tricia did earlier,

"She was down here, but I guess she left, she said she might be back down here a little later," Maurice said as he and Maya sniggled,

"Well, I guess I'll go and listen to the band," Ahmar said as he walked off, not wanting to be the third wheel,

***

Knock! Knock!

"What do you want now!" Tricia said as she snatched the door open,

"Well, hello," Ahmar said smiling,

"Hey, I thought you were Maya! I was gonna cuss her out, she and Maurice made me mad, all night long they kept looking at me and laughing!" Tricia said with a frown,

"Yeah, they just did the same thing to me!" Ahmar said,

"They got on my damn nerves!" Tricia pouted,

"Listen, I need to talk to you,"

"No, I need to talk to you first," Tricia said, changing her tone,

"Okay, go ahead," Ahmar said patiently,

"I'm sorry for running out on you last night, but I wasn't prepared for that and I'm still not," Tricia admitted,

"I can respect dat," Ahmar said,

"I've never cheated on my husband, I love him and he's a good man,"

"I feel the same way about my wife," Ahmar interrupted,

"Let me finish!" Tricia insisted, "I like you, but I just can't get involved with you like this, and I'm constantly shocking myself by the way I'm behaving with you, my husband doesn't deserve this!"

"Are you finished?" Ahmar asked, not wanting to interrupt Tricia again,

"Yeah, I guess I am," Tricia said feeling relieved about getting some things off her chest, she'd rehearsed her speech all day, and she still didn't get it right,

"Can I speak now?" Ahmar asked,

"Yes, I'm listening..." Tricia answered,

"I love my wife as well, and I don't want to hurt her, I'm sorry, I guess I just got caught up in de moment," Ahmar said,

"Yeah, you were definitely caught up," Tricia admitted,

"Well, let me make it up to you, let's go downstairs, get a table and ignore Maurice and Maya, is that a deal?"

"It's a deal!" Tricia said as she and Ahmar shook hands,

They went to the lobby and walked past Maya and Maurice's table, without looking at them. Maurice and Maya laughed as Tricia and Ahmar sat two tables down from them and ignored them,

"Can I get you a drink?" Ahmar asked Tricia,

"Yeah, surprise me," Tricia said,

Ahmar got up to get Tricia's drink, Tricia turned around to aggravate Maya and Maurice, and when they looked at her, she licked her tongue out and rolled her eyes at them,

"Hey Baby, I think they're mad at us," Maurice said still laughing,

"Well let's get on the dance floor and make them real mad!" Maya laughed,

"Alright, let's go!" Maya said as Maurice led her by the hand to the dance floor, Ahmar smiled as he walked back to the table,

"Shall we dance?"

"Yes, let's go out there and cut some heads!" Tricia said, she and Ahmar went out on the dance floor and jumped in between Maya and Maurice and started dancing wildly,

"You just mad because I dance better than you!" Maya teased,

They danced all night, and when Tricia and Ahmar finally sat back down at their table, he grabbed her hand,

"Tricia, you know I am here on business,"

"Yes, I know," Tricia said,

"Well, the main reason I'm here is to judge a music competition in two days, and the winner will win a music contract with the company that I work for, would you like to be my guest?"

"I would love to," Tricia said,

"I can pick you up here at the hotel, at about eight, is dat okay?"

"It's fine," Tricia answered, excited,

"I think we need to send them a peace offering?" Ahmar said,

"Yeah, let's do that," Tricia agreed,

The waiter placed two glasses of cranberry juice on Maya and Maurice's table,

"Complements of the couple at table sixteen," he said pointing at Ahmar and Tricia, as Tricia held a white napkin tied to a long straw swinging it back and forth,

"They are so silly!" Maya said with a smile,

"You think we need to thank them for this peace offering?" Maurice asked,

"Yeah, let's send them a note," Maya said,

Maya pulled a pen and a notepad from her purse and she and

Maurice laughed as they took turns scribbling things on the paper, they passed the note to the waiter, and he placed the piece of paper on Tricia and Ahmar's table,

"From the couple at table fourteen," the waiter said,

Tricia opened the note, which read,

"Thanks for the peace offering, we would've sent drinks but you've already had plenty Tricia, and you know how you get when you have too much to drink, Ahmar!

Peace and Love,

-M&M (Maurice and Maya)."

Maya and Maurice left the club around three in the morning, and once they made it into her room, Maurice's expression changed,

"Will you stay with me? Because I really don't want to be alone tonight," Maurice asked, as he thought about Ahmar's line to Tricia,

"I think that can be arranged," Maya said with a smile,

"Come here woman!" Maurice said as he hugged her tight then waited patiently as Maya packed an overnight bag...

Maya's eyes popped wide open, it was five-thirty in the morning and she had to use the bathroom badly, Maurice felt so good snuggled up behind her that she really didn't want to move, but she had held it for as long as she could, and now it was unbearable, she gently moved his arm from around her waist and slid out of the bed and went to the bathroom, afterwards she slid back into the covers and snuggled her back into his chest, she moaned softly as he wrapped his arm around her, his chest felt warm, moist and hard like steel, she was giddy about the fact that he had taken his shirt off before they went to bed. Maya felt so relaxed resting beside him that she dozed off instantly, but her eyes popped open when she felt him harden,

"What the...!" Maya thought when he pressed himself up against her, she could feel him stiffen through his thin boxer shorts. Maurice began to grind against her body slowly, moaning softly in his sleep, Maya's eyes opened even wider, but she was frozen in place. Maurice rubbed her thigh and then his hand wandered up to her breast, he cupped her breast with the palm of his hand and began to fondle her nipple, Maya's back arched which woke him, Maurice jerked back when he realized that he had gotten aroused,

"Maya I'm so sorry! I... I thought I was dreaming!" he said,

"It's okay, I knew you were asleep, and I would've stopped you way before things went too far," Maya said confidently, but honestly she was praying hard that he would've stopped on his own because her body was steaming hot, but she cooled down quickly when she thought about the damage he could possibly do with that thing,

"Let me turn around and you can put your arm around me," Maurice suggested,

"That's a good idea," Maya said as Maurice shifted around, Maya snuggled into his back and rested her head on him and drifted off to sleep, she woke up later that night and went to use the bathroom again and took off her bra because the pregnancy was making her nipples extra sensitive and her bra rubbing up against them were rubbing them raw, she slipped back beneath the covers and wrapped her arms around him, intertwining her fingers into his, but her soft breasts pressing up against his back was about to drive him insane! He was so aroused that the bottom of his stomach ached,

"This don't make no sense!" He moaned under his breath,

"Huh?" Maya asked,

"I didn't say anything," Maurice said,

"This is torture," she mumbled,

"Did you say something?" Maurice asked,

"No, I...I must've been talking in my sleep," Maya answered,

"Oh, I thought you were talking to me," Maurice said,

"No, I...I wasn't," Maya insisted,

"Well, I guess I'll go back to sleep then, I mean, unless you want me to stay up," Maurice asked,

"No, I was asleep, but if you want me to stay up then I'll get up," Maya said,

"Nah, go ahead and go back to sleep, goodnight, Maya," Maurice regretfully said,

"Goodnight Maurice," Maya sighed,

Maya could just see herself planting wet kisses all over his muscular back, and she was just as aroused as he was, *"Think about something else Maya!"* she commanded her wondering mind,

Maurice had made love to Maya a million times in his dreams, he imagined how gentle her kisses would be, he wanted to feel her soft body beneath his, and feel her lips pressed against his, he imagined how warm and tight she would feel inside,

"I have to go to the bathroom!" Maurice said as he leaped out of bed, he grabbed himself before he could even get the door closed, "I can't take this!" Maurice said as he tried to force himself to think about something else, anything else because he was too hard to pee, but every time he tried to think about something else, his mind drifted back to Maya and he would stiffen even more, but once he thought about his ex-girlfriend Kayla, he softened instantly, and by the time Maurice got back into the bed, Maya had drifted off and turned in the opposite direction,

"Thank God!" Maurice thought as he got back into the bed and turned his back to her, they ended up sleeping back-to-back for the remainder of the night,

***

After Maya and Maurice left, Tricia and Ahmar stayed in the hotel lobby talking until about six-thirty in the morning,

"It's late," Tricia said with a yawn,

"I can take I hint, Pretty Lady, will I see you later?" Ahmar asked with a smile,

"We'll have to see, won't we?" Tricia said flirtatiously,

"May I walk you to your room?" Ahmar asked as he stood and reached for Tricia's hand,

"That would be nice," Tricia said smiling,

When they made it to Tricia's room, Ahmar looked into Tricia's eyes then gave her a slow passionate hug,

"Good night," he said,

"Good night," Tricia said as she put the keycard into the slot. Ahmar kissed Tricia on the cheek and then walked away. Tricia closed the door, then threw herself on the bed, "This shit is getting harder and harder by the day!" She thought as she laid there on top of the covers and drifted off with her clothes still on...

The next morning Maya got up and walked to her suite, and again she turned the corner just as Tricia was about to knock on her door,

"Hey Harlot!" Tricia teased,

"Forget you! I haven't done anything yet, and speaking of Harlot, what did you two do last night?" Maya teased back,

"He walked me to my room, kissed me on the cheek, then we said goodnight," Tricia said proudly,

"Well good for you!" Maya said with a smile, she couldn't wait to tell Tricia about Maurice's wandering hands and hardening body parts,

The three and a half hour ferry ride to Tobago was adventurous to say the least, Maya and Tricia got seasick and had to take meds, Maurice and Ahmar was used to it so they were fine, but after the ride, and a nap, the ladies felt much better. Maurice shared his room with Ahmar since they invited him along at the last minute, Ahmar wanted to tag along so Tricia wouldn't be a third wheel and so that he could spend more time with her and take her around to see his favorite sights. Maurice and Maya made dinner plans to meet at a restaurant in Tobago that was right next door to her hotel that had private booths overlooking the ocean.

Maya and Tricia polished their toes to match the outfits they had chosen for the night. Maya chose a flowing ankle length lavender summer dress with a matching sheer jacket and scarf. She couldn't wait to pull out her lavender sandals, because she knew Tricia would go mad over them.

"Ooh you heifer! Where did you find those!" Tricia said once she saw them,

"I got them at the mall after I left your house last Friday, you like?"

"Yeah girl! You really are showing out with that ensemble!"

"You know I have to represent to the fullest!"

"Sister you are definitely doing that!" Tricia said with a nod,

Maya really tripped Tricia out when she showed her the silver and amethyst earrings and necklace set, she had also gotten to match the outfit,

"Check this out, Girl! I'm gonna be too cute!" Maya said showing off her silver and amethyst toe ring and ankle bracelet, "And if he thinks my orange panties were the bomb, then wait until he sees these!" Maya said as she pulled out her fancy laced lavender bra and panties.

"I heard that! But check this out!" Tricia held up a melon-colored body blouse and a butter yellow ankle-length skirt printed with huge melon flowers and mint green leaves. Tricia showed Maya a straw hat with the same silk flower on the front as her skirt and matching straw sandals, Tricia painted her toes a mint green to match the leaves in her skirt and because she had chosen this beautiful green and blue dress to wear to the club with Ahmar tomorrow night.

***

Maurice was already sitting on a bench looking at the fountain in front of the hotel when he spotted Maya, the cool ocean breezes blowing Maya's dress and sheer tunic styled jacket made her appear to float towards him,

"Hey Beautiful!" Maurice said as he stood to his feet and they greeted each other with a hug,

"Hey yourself!" Maya said with a gracious smile,

"You ready?" he asked,

207

"Yes, I am," Maya said as she and Maurice walked towards the restaurant, it was even more magnificent on the inside than the outside, they were mesmerized at the view as the hostess led them to one of the private booths,

"Maurice this is gorgeous!" Maya said dreamingly,

After the hostess left, Maurice looked at Maya, then turned his head,

"What's wrong?" Maya asked, she could tell that something was on his mind,

"Did the doctor say everything was okay with you and the baby?" Maurice asked,

"Yeah, for the most part," Maya said, "he told me my iron was a little low, so now I have to take iron pills three times a day,"

"You're anemic?" Maurice asked with a nod,

"Yes," Maya answered,

"My sister is anemic, and she's tired all the time,"

"Whew, I know the feeling!" Maya said with an exhale,

"And what will you and the Lady have to drink?" The waiter interrupted with pen and pad in hand,

"I'll have a glass of red wine," Maya said,

"C'mon now, you don't need that!" Maurice said with concern,

"Oh hush, I'm only having one glass!" Maya insisted, "And my doctor said it was good for me and the baby,"

"Okay then, you grown…but only one glass, and I guess I'll have the same," Maurice said as the waiter nodded then exited the booth, "Ms. Maya's drinking wine!" Maurice teased,

"My doctor said it's good for low iron, and I've had enough cranberry juice to last me a lifetime," Maya said,

"Okay then, I'm not a doctor, and I don't tell grown people what to do," Maurice said sarcastically,

"Oh whatever!" Maya laughed as she rolled her eyes at him,

When the food finally arrived, Maya and Maurice stuffed themselves with succulent steak and crab and fluffy coconut flavored rice and savory vegetables, the meal was excellent, but Maya was a little irritated because every time she sipped her wine, Maurice side-eyed her, she fanned him off and after they finished eating, they took a long walk, Maurice held Maya's sandals in his hands as they walked along the shore,

"Ms. Lady…Ms. Lady…," Maurice said as he stepped in

front of her and grabbed her hands, "I bet you're matching from head to toe, aren't you?" he asked with a devious smile,

"Yep!" Maya said, trying not to blush,

"Got purple toes and everything," Maurice said looking down at her feet,

"Yep!" She said, she was in full grin mode by now,

"Hey Maya?" He asked with a smile,

"Yes Maurice?" she said smiling back,

"I bet you got on purple everything, don't you?" he finally asked,

"Maybe..." Maya teased,

"C'mon tell me, I bet you do!" Maurice insisted,

"Why would I tell you, when I can just show you later." Maya said before walking off, Maurice stood there for a minute, and then gathered himself, running up to catch up with her,

"Are you sure you're ready for that?" Maurice asked,

"Ready for what?" Maya said innocently,

"You know, for what you just said?" Maurice asked, and Maya could feel the excitement in his voice,

"I don't know what you're talking about Maurice," Maya teased,

"Oh okay, I see what this is," Maurice said nodding his head,

"Really?" Maya asked with a giggle as they walked along the shore,

"So...what do you have planned tonight Ms. Maya?" Maurice asked, changing the subject,

"I'm not sure if I have anything planned tonight, what about you?" she asked,

"Well, Ahmar invited me to check out this club with him tonight,"

"Sounds nice," Maya said,

"Well, whatever you have planned, I hope you have fun, I know I am," Maurice said,

"Oh, I'm sure I'll find something to do," Maya hinted.

"Yeah, I'm sure you will," he said,

When they got back to the hotel, Maurice kissed Maya on her cheek then headed up to his room, he had actually turned down Ahmar's invitation, but he decided he needed a little time away from her to get his mind and thoughts together, he laughed out loud when he thought about the look on her face when he told her he was going out to a club tonight instead of spending more time with her, *"She sure wasn't expecting that shit,"* Maurice said to himself once he made it to his room, *"Trying to mess with my damn head with her purple panties and toenails, forget* her!" Maurice laughed to himself, "...well at least for tonight!" Maurice thought as he told Ahmar that he had changed his mind, and he would be going with him to the club after all,

"I can't believe this!" Maya said as she stormed into her room, she was simply out done, she snatched off her shoes and stormed into the bathroom and got undressed. Maya pulled off her lacy purple bra and underwear and slammed them along with her lavender dress into the hamper as hard as she could, then she put on the biggest white cotton underwear she could find and dug deep into her bag and found her old orange, yellow, maroon, and neon green polka dotted burgundy lounger then jumped into the bed and pulled the covers over her head, Tricia came in at about eight o'clock with bags hanging from her arms,

"Whew, I am so tired, I have never shopped so much in my life!" Tricia said as she bopped down in the recliner across from Maya's bed,

"Well good for you!" Maya said with an attitude,

"Uggggh! What's wrong with you?" Tricia said taken aback by Maya's tone,

"I'm mad as hell! Did you know Maurice and Ahmar were going to a club tonight!"

"Yeah, Ahmar told me about it," Tricia said laughing,

"Well, what's so damn funny?" Maya asked,

"I've already told you about pulling those power plays, Maya! He got you good, didn't he?" Tricia said pointing at Maya and laughing hysterically,

"Forget you, Tricia!" Maya was trying not to laugh, but she couldn't help it,

"Maya, you look so cute with that egg on your face!" Tricia teased,

"Girl, what am I gonna do, what if he meets somebody while he's there?"

"So, what if he does," Tricia said,

"What do you mean?" Maya asked curiously,

"Aren't you guys just friends, anyway?" Tricia asked,

"Yeah, but that don't mean that I want him to meet anybody," Maya said as she plopped down on the other recliner in a pout, "I thought you were going with Ahmar tonight?" Maya asked,

"Well I was, but then I overheard Maurice telling Ahmar that he had changed his mind about going to the club with him tonight, when I was in their room earlier today, so I made up some excuse not to go," Tricia said,

"Well, I don't wanna talk about this no more!" Maya said with an attitude,

"Oh no! Don't get mad now, you're the one who tried to play hard, and ended up putting your little flat foot in your own mouth!" Tricia said still laughing,

"FORGET YOU TRICIA!!!" Maya yelled as she hopped out of the bed and stormed into the kitchen area,

"Girl, stop tripping and go on in there and take off that ugly ass gown, I have to show you what I bought for us while I was out with Ahmar today!"

"What did you buy?" Maya said suddenly turning on her heels and following Tricia back down the hall,

"Nope! Not until you go in there and put on something else, that ugly thang ain't even allowed up in my room!" Tricia said blocking the door to the bedroom,

"This ain't your room Tricia, this is *our* room!" Maya said with her hands on her hips,

"Well, that ugly ass thang ain't allowed in our room, in any hotel that I'm in, or on any airplane that I'm flyin' on, or even back in the United States! You'd better leave that hideous thang up in this hotel! I ain't playing Maya, take that ugly ass thang off! It's giving me the heebie-jeebies!" Tricia teased,

"This is my favorite gown! It's comfortable, and I'm keeping it on!" Maya said rolling her eyes to the ceiling,

"Okay, but at least stay on your side of the room, you look like a dinosaur with measles with that thang on!"

Maya ran over to Tricia and hugged her,

"Move Maya, you are making me itch, I got, ugly-gown-itis!" Maya laughed as Tricia covered her eyes and pretended to be blinded by the gown, "Okay, keep playing, but you won't get what I bought for you until you take that ugly thang off!" Tricia said,

"Okay, okay!" Maya said as she snatched the gown off and threw it on the floor, Tricia looked at her and instantly started laughing,

"What's funny!" Maya said,

"Girl, no the fuck you didn't put on that ugly ass gown and them big old white cotton granny draws and that Mother Board church Bra!"

"Forget you Tricia, I was mad!" Maya laughed,

"I don't care how mad you get! Don't you ever, ever, ever put that shit on again! It's a sin before God for somebody's draws to come all the way up under their chin like that!" Tricia said in the middle of hysterical laughter,

"Leave my draws alone Tricia!" Maya whined,

"I didn't know they still made them thangs, you must've went downtown to A. Schwab's and got them," Tricia laughed,

"I sure did, and I got my Mama a few pair too!" Maya laughed,

"I just bet you did, I can see her wearing them, but you?" Tricia said shaking her head,

"Forget you Tricia, cause when I get back home, I'm gonna go and buy me some more!"

"Well pick me up some too!" Tricia said laughing, "Phillip is gonna trip all the way out when I come to bed with that on!"

"I wonder what Maurice and Ahmar are up to..." Maya said,

"Doesn't matter, we're not calling them, we're gonna enjoy ourselves, enjoy a good meal, then we're going to bed," Tricia said adamantly,

They spent hours trying on their new hats, jewelry, clothes, and shoes, and after dinner they were exhausted, so they turned in early,

***

Ahmar and Maurice left the hotel at around ten o'clock, when they stepped into the club, Maurice's eyes lit up, the place was packed with men and women winding and twisting their sweaty bodies to the music,

"Ooh-wee!" Maurice said as a tall slender woman glided towards him, she wore a shiny black bra shirt that showed off her round, firm voluptuous breasts, board-flat stomach and diamond pierced navel, and hip-hugging loose jeans with rips and cuts that showed her bow-hips and toned muscular thighs, she had flawless caramel brown sun-kissed skin, and long, thick golden locs that hung to her butt and swung back and forth as she wound her hips and stared at him,

"I think she likes you," Ahmar said patting Maurice on the shoulder,

"I see..." Maurice said as he noticed everything about her from the beauty mark above the right side of her full lips, the powder-blue eyeshadow and chocolate brown lip gloss that she wore, to her 4-inch spiked Stiletto heels,

"I have to go backstage, the show is getting ready to start," Ahmar said,

"Man, I don't know anybody in here!" Maurice said as

he scanned the club,

"It is okay, I think you can handle yourself," Ahmar said as he pat Maurice on the shoulder again and laughed as he walked off, Maurice felt lost as he stood there sipping on his drink and nodding his head to the beat,

"Hello Handsome," the woman said, her Island accent was as thick as cold porridge, she seductively danced around him moving like she had on no heels at all,

"Hey," Maurice said pretending to be unimpressed,

"You know Mar-mar, I see," the woman said, still winding her hips,

"Who?" Maurice said with a frown,

"Ah-mar," the woman said,

"Oh yeah," Maurice said with a cool tone,

"So, who are *you*?" the woman said as she slithered up to him, suddenly turning her back to him and winding up against him while wrapping her arm around his neck so that his chin rested on her right shoulder, "Do you have a name?" she asked,

Maurice inhaled, he loved the scent of her exotic perfume mixed with her sweat, it was a mixture of Jasmine, Gardenias, and a touch of Cinnamon, but it was the sexiest scent that he'd ever smelled,

"Yes, it's Rece," Maurice answered nervously, he wasn't used to this woman's boldness,

"Sounds sweet!" she said as she spun around so that they were face to face, still winding her hips, and moving her hips to the Soca beat, she bit down on her bottom lip and looked him up and down, Maurice felt like a piece of meat, but he kind of liked it,

"Do you have a name?" he asked,

"Yes..." the woman said as she spun around again, seductively grinding her hips up against him to the rhythm of the music, while reaching back and twirling her fingers in his locs and licking her full round lips,

"Well?" Maurice asked,

"Well, what?" the woman asked, still grinding against him,

"Well, what is it?" Maurice asked,

"What is what?" the woman asked, never missing a beat,

"Your name?" Maurice asked again, he was intrigued,

"You don't want to know my name..." she teased,

"Sure, I do, what is it?" Maurice insisted,

"It is Sexual," the woman said,

"It's who?" Maurice asked almost choking on his drink,

"Ha!" the woman said as she threw her head back and laughed,

213

"It is Cay-man, like de Islands," the woman laughed again, and even her laugh was sexy, "but you…" she continued, "You can call me Sex...u...al!" The woman said with her thick Trinidadian accent,

"Oh, okay like sex?" Maurice laughed, hoping that this woman wasn't serious,

"No! Not like sex! Dogs have sex! Cats have sex! Not the act, the Experience... the smell, the taste, the feel… not just sex... SEX-u-al!" The woman insisted aggressively, punctuating each syllable, and making her body gyrate to the beat of the music and her words,

"Oh okay…sexual," Maurice said with a smile even though he was thoroughly unimpressed,

"Well does Rece just stand there, or does he move?" Cayman asked as she stood in front of him with her hands on her hips,

"Shit, I can move," Maurice said with a smirk,

"Can you now?" Cayman asked, a smile forming across her lips,

"Yeah, I've been known to cut a rug or two," Maurice insisted,

"They say you can tell what ah man can do by the way he moves," Cayman said as she ground her full round butt into his pelvic area, then smiled,

"Is that right," Maurice said as he twirled her around and pulled her towards him, she wrapped her arms around his neck as he worked her around the dancefloor, Maurice was in another world, Cayman licked his earlobes and kissed his neck as they danced, causing Maurice to throb hard, she was a welcomed distraction from Maya. He danced with her most of the night, and when they finally had a chance to sit and talk at the bar, Cayman told him that she works as a record executive in New York, but she was in Trinidad scouting for new musical talent, she was originally from Trinidad, but she travels back and forth from the States. Normally, Maurice would've really enjoyed her company, but for some reason after his initial lust for her wore off, he just couldn't seem to get Maya out of his head, for one, other than dancing, Cayman really didn't seem interested in anything else with him other that what she could do to him sexually and after a while it began to turn him off,

"Ah see you've met Cayman?" Ahmar said as he walked up to them at the bar,

"Greetings Mar-mar," Cayman said as she stepped in between Maurice and Ahmar with her back to Maurice, and Maurice noticed that Cayman had that same seductive tone to her voice when she spoke to Ahmar,

"Cayman…" Ahmar said cordially, with a firm nod, and Maurice could tell that Ahmar really didn't want to talk to her,

"Rece tells me that you are here on business," Cayman said,

"I am," Ahmar answered, still being polite, but with a slightly bored tone to his voice,

"Find any new talent?" Cayman probed,

"Don't yah worry about what Ah I find, Cayman," Ahmar snapped,

"Always de competitor, Ah see…" Cayman laughed,

"We are about to leave, yah ready Maurice?" Ahmar asked,

"Don't spoil de party Mar-mar, Ah was just getting to know dis handsome morsel of a man," Cayman said as she leaned back into Maurice, he didn't mind that, but then she reached back and felt his crotch as he sat on the barstool,

"Hey watch out!" Maurice said as he slapped her hand and jumped back and stood to his feet,

"Nice...very, very nice," Cayman said as she bit down on her bottom lip and licked her lips, Maurice stared at her in disbelief,

"Yeah Man, I'm ready!" Maurice said as he hurried behind Ahmar, he looked back at Cayman, who already had another man in her sights and was dancing up on him before they had even made it out of the door,

"That girl is something else!" Maurice said as they drove back,

"Be careful with dat one Maurice, Cayman will eat yah alive and lick yah bones!" Ahmar said with a smile,

"Man, I believe you!" Maurice said, "I ain't never seen nothing like that in my whole damn life!" Maurice laughed,

"Oh, I know" Ahmar laughed, "Oh by the way, I have four VIP passes to de big talent showcase tomorrow, it is all work for me, but I want you guys to come as my guests," Ahmar said after he finally stopped laughing at Maurice,

"That's sounds like some real fun, I can't wait!" Maurice said,

*** .

215

8 SEX-U-ALL..

Maya woke up early, she was anxious to find out what happened with Ahmar and Maurice last night. She eagerly called him,

"Hello," Ahmar said, and Maya could tell that he was still asleep,

"I'm sorry to wake you Ahmar, is Maurice in?"

"Hold on ah minute, Maurice?" Ahmar called out,

"Yeah?"

"Maya is calling," he said slowly, and Maya shivered a tiny bit because of his accent,

"Hello?" Maurice said, and Maya could tell that unlike Ahmar, Maurice was wide awake,

"Hey," Maya said, not sure how Maurice would respond to her calling him this early in the morning,

"Hey Baby Mama, you're up early!" Maurice said, he was in a good mood, which concerned Maya a little,

"Did I wake you?" Maya asked,

"Nah, I was already up," Maurice answered,

"Are you dressed?" Maya asked,

"Yeah, I'm dressed," Maurice answered, wondering what Maya was up to,

"You wanna come downstairs and eat breakfast with me?" she asked,

"Sure, I'll meet you there in about twenty minutes," Maurice said,

"Tricia, I'm going downstairs to eat breakfast with Maurice." Maya said when she got off the phone,

216

"Yeah, yeah, yeah..." Tricia groaned, still asleep,

Maya went to sleep early last night, and rose up early full of energy, she cleaned the room, took a shower and had gotten dressed before she'd even called him, she was already seated when he walked in. He was wearing a snug black tank top with gray jogging shorts. The shirt was doing a good job at showing off his muscular arms, chest, and abs, but those jogging shorts were way too loose and were telling a story of their own,

"Good morning!" he said hugging her tight, Maya was so glad to see him that she kissed him full in the mouth, Maurice was a bit taken aback, but he liked her this way, and he liked the glow in her eyes,

"You ready to order?" she asked,

"Yes, I'm starving," Maurice said, still smiling and rubbing his hands together, "what do you want to eat, let me guess, fruit, right?" Maurice asked with a smile,

"Yep!" Maya said smiling, and when Maurice sat down, after glancing down at his shorts, she blushed and turned away because the material left nothing to the imagination,

"What are you laughing at Ms. Lady?" Maurice asked with a smirk, he had seen her roaming eyes,

"Oh nothing," Maya said, "I'm just in a good mood, that's all,"

"Well, what did you two end up doing last night?" Maurice asked,

"We had a girl's night, you know..." Maya said,

"Oh, I see..." Maurice said,

"And how was your night?" Maya asked,

"It was okay,"

"Just okay?" Maya asked,

"Actually, it was pretty straight, speaking of which, Ahmar got us some VIP passes to a club back in Trinidad tonight, he's on a talent hunt for some new music, and he invited us, that's if you wanna go,"

"Let me check my schedule and get back to you," Maya said as she reached into her bag and opened up her date book,

"Yeah, you do that," Maurice said sarcastically,

"Okay, I think I'm free tonight!" She said smiling,

"You think?" he asked with his eyebrow raised,

"Okay, I know!" Maya smiled,

"You know you're something else!" Maurice said shaking his head,

***

Tricia and Phillip had phone sex again late last night after Maya went to sleep. She had to drag herself out of bed when she heard

217

someone knocking on the door. "If Maya forgot her key card again, I'm gonna cuss her out!" Tricia said snatching open the door thinking that Maya was knocking on the door trying to aggravate her,

"So, this is what yah look like in de morning," Ahmar asked surprised,

"Oh hey..." Tricia said, as she stood at the door still groggy,

"Nice bonnet," Ahmar teased, pointing to the pink hair bonnet still on her head,

"Oh hush!" Tricia said snatching her bonnet off and tossing it over her shoulder,

"Shall I come back later," he asked,

"No, you're okay, uhmmmm...have a seat," Tricia said as she pointed to the couch. Ahmar sat down then he looked at Tricia and smiled,

"What?" She asked,

"I am not used to seeing yah in night clothes," Ahmar joked,

"Oh, you are just full of jokes this morning, aren't you?"

"I don't mean any harm," he said with a smile,

"None taken, now what brings you out this early in the morning?" Tricia asked,

"Early?" Ahmar asked puzzled,

"Yeah, what time is it?"

"Eleven o'clock," Ahmar said as he looked at his watch,

"Eleven! Oh, I can't believe it! I thought it was about seven or eight! I can't believe I overslept!"

"Don't worry, we still have some time left before we go back," Ahmar said,

"I'm not worried about that, I packed last night," Tricia said,

"Get dressed, I want to show you something," Ahmar said,

"All right, I'll meet you downstairs in the lobby, give me about 30 minutes, okay?"

"Okay," Ahmar said as Tricia opened the door to let him out,

"Got to be more careful!" Tricia said as she snapped her finger when Ahmar left, she was almost dressed when the phone rang, "Hello?"

"Hey Lil' Nasty! I heard you and Phillip last night!"

Maya teased,

"Forget you, you shouldn't have been listening!"

"I wasn't, that's why I covered my head with the pillow and tried to smother myself!" Maya joked,

"Anyway! You must be with Maurice?"

"Yeah, he's over there at the table,"

"What time are we leaving to go back to Trinidad?"

"We're leaving at four,"

"Well, I'm going to meet Ahmar, he says he has something to show me, I wonder what it is,"

"You know what it is!"

"Get your head out the gutter Maya!"

"Shut up and let me get off this phone so I can go back over there and talk to my man, I'll get up with you a lil' later!" Maya said though smiles,

"Wait, hold up! Did you say your man, so he's your man now?" Tricia teased,

"Yep! He is!" Maya said confidently,

"I heard that, claim him then with your jealous ass!" Tricia laughed, she liked Maya's energetic confidence,

"Oh, I already have," Maya insisted,

"Bye girl!" Tricia said with a wide smile,

"Bye!" Maya said with an even bigger smile,

Tricia hung up and got dressed. Ahmar ended up taking Tricia for a long walk after breakfast. He led her on a quiet path, and they ended up on top of a cliff overlooking the ocean,

"Tricia, do you realize your vacation is almost over and after tomorrow, we may never see each other again?" Ahmar asked,

"I know, I've thought a lot about that," Tricia sighed,

"I wish it was possible to forget about my wife for just one night,"

"Don't start Ahmar, I can't take this right now!" Tricia said,

"I won't sit here and pretend that I don't feel what I feel!" Ahmar said,

"Yes...I know, I mean, no...I mean, I don't know what I mean!" Tricia said as she shook her head from side to side,

"Okay, okay...calm down... Oh yes, before I forget, I invited Rece and Maya to de club tonight," Ahmar said changing the subject, he could tell Tricia was overwhelmed,

"That's cool, but I thought you only had two tickets,"

"I called in a favor,"

"What time do you want me to be ready?"

"Nine-thirty," Ahmar said,

"Cool!" Tricia said, and they walked silently along the path admiring the view,

***

Maya and Maurice went up to his room where Tricia and Ahmar were waiting,

"Hey folks, you ready to go back to Trinidad?" Maurice asked,

"We are ready," Ahmar said,

They slept most of the way back to Trinidad and were well rested by the time they made it back to the hotel, Maya and Tricia were glad to be back in their own suites and Maurice and Ahmar decided to share Maurice's suite since they were both leaving tomorrow, and Ahmar didn't want to drive all the way back to Sebastian's house,

"Maya, you have a really nice suite, I never noticed how big it was," Maurice said as he walked into Maya's suite and put her bags on the bed,

"Yeah, I know, and to be honest, I'm really not in a hurry to go back home," Maya said,

"Me neither, but I hope we can still be friends when we get back home, I mean, since you're not ready for us to be anything else,"

"Maurice!" Maya said,

"What?" Maurice asked, surprised, "I'm just saying what you said,"

"Maurice, I hope you know by now that you are way more to me than just a friend," Maya admitted,

"Oh really, then what am I?" Maurice asked with a smile,

"You're my Honey-Honey!" Maya teased,

"Your what?" Maurice laughed,

"You heard me," Maya laughed,

"I ain't never been called that before," Maurice said with a confused smile,

"I'm just kidding... right now we're way more than just friends, even though I'm not sure exactly what we are just yet," Maya said with a wide smile,

"That's sounds good and all Baby Mama, but what does it really mean?" Maurice asked, his smile fading,

"I tell you what, once we get back home, you won't have to ask," Maya said confidently,

220

"I'm holding you to that," Maurice said,

"Please do,"

"Can I ask you something Maya?" Maurice asked,

"Sure, you can ask me anything," Maya smiled, already knowing what he was about to ask,

"Yesterday, did you have on purple panties?"

Maya laughed so hard she almost choked,

"Maurice!"

"Well, did you?"

"I'm not telling, you should've peeked like you did when I had on the peach ones!" Maya teased,

"Maya, do you trust me?" Maurice asked, suddenly serious,

"Yes, I trust you," Maya answered trying to figure out where this was going,

"How much?" he asked,

"Enough, I guess…" Maya answered,

"Enough…to…let me dress you?" Maurice asked,

"Ooooh, see now that's a hard one, I don't know about that," Maya said with a slight frown on her face,

"I tell you what, I'll let you dress me if you let me dress you," Maurice offered,

"Okay, why not," Maya said apprehensively,

"Alright, now go in there and get your nail polishes," Maurice said,

"Nail polishes, for what?" Maya asked,

"I'm doing your toes too," Maurice said with a smile,

"I don't know about this Maurice!"

"I thought you said you trusted me,"

"I did say that… I don't know why I said it, but I did say it," Maya admitted,

"Okay then, and while you're at it, I want you to get your clothes and your lingerie collection too, I wanna see what I'm working with!" Maurice said, and Maya didn't know what to think,

"What have I gotten myself into!" she said as she went into the bathroom and grabbed her bag full of nail polishes,

"And grab your makeup bag, too!"

"Oh Lord, what have I done!" Maya mumbled to herself as she handed Maurice her makeup bag…

"Okay, you can look now!" Maurice said, and Maya jumped up and ran to the mirror, her jaw dropped.

"Where did you learn to do make-up like this?"

"Oh, did I forget to tell you, I'm a licensed barber and

beautician, I got my both my licenses, years ago, straight out of high school, photography is just a hobby,"

"I'm impressed, but I should've known by that pedicure," Maya said, still swooning over the foot massage he gave her earlier,

"You ain't seen nothing yet, wait until you see what I put together for you to wear, do you still wanna dress me?" he asked,

"Nah, that's okay," Maya said while looking at her makeup in the mirror, she was still amazed at how he took care of every detail, even arching her eyebrows,

"That's what I thought, well I'll see you in a little bit, Baby Mama," Maurice said as he went to his room to get dressed, and a short while later, Maya and Maurice met Tricia and Ahmar in the lobby,

"Look they match!" Tricia said to Ahmar,

Maya was dressed in a low-cut red blouse showing off her cleavage, and an ankle length wrap around skirt with swirls of orange, mustard yellow, burgundy and red, and a burgundy headwrap with the beaded braids hanging to one side, she wore gold hoop earrings and red sandals matching her red blouse and bright red polish on her toes. Maurice wore a burgundy linen short set that matched the burgundy in Maya's outfit and dark brown leather sandals, he let his shoulder length dreadlocks hang free, Maya had never seen him with them down and the sight of him made her heart thump,

"You planned this, didn't you?" Maya said pleasantly surprised,

"I did a lil' something-something," Maurice said with a smile,

"Are you wearing the red laced bra and panty set that I laid out for you?" he whispered in her ear,

"Maybe, maybe not," Maya teased,

"And you say I'm a trip!" Maurice joked,

***

The club had three separate dance floors, but the top floor was exclusively for the VIP guests, Maya and Maurice wanted to dance, but Tricia and Ahmar wanted to soak up the scene and have drinks,

"Do you like this band Tricia?" Ahmar asked,

"Yeah, they're nice," Tricia said, as she sipped her drink,"

Maya and Maurice danced up a sweat as Ahmar went to
introduce Tricia to some of the big wigs in the record industry,

"Maya, do you want anything to drink?" Maurice asked,

"I wouldn't mind having a…"

"Let me guess, a cranberry juice, right?"

"No actually, I wouldn't mind having another glass of red wine,"
Maya said with her hand on her hip,

"No wine for you tonight, Baby Mama!" Maurice said, half-
jokingly and half-serious,

"I've only had one glass of wine since we've been here!" Maya
tried to reason,

"Okay, okay… I'll make you a deal," Maurice said,

"I'm listening," Maya said,

"I won't drink any more if you won't, I'll even drink that nasty
ass cranberry juice if you want me to, deal?"

"Deal!" Maya said,

After the waiter placed two wine glasses full of cranberry juice
on the table, Maurice lifted his glass, "I wanna make a toast!" he said,
"To you, for also being my Honey-Honey," he snickered, "and also to us,
the best-looking couple in this place!"

"Now, I'll drink to that!" Maya said with a huge smile,

***

"My, my…and who might I ask, is dis lovely lady, an escort,
perhaps?" Cayman asked as she slithered up to Ahmar and Tricia as they
sat sipping on drinks and listening to the band,

"It is none of your concern, Cayman," Ahmar snapped, and
Tricia could tell instantly that he was irritated by the woman's presence,

"Don't be rude Mar-mar, introduce us!" Cayman insisted,

Ahmar rolled his eyes and sighed deeply before speaking,
"Cayman, this is Tricia, Tricia…Cayman," he said,

"Tri-cia...what an interesting name, have yah known Mar-mar
long?"

"Who?" Tricia asked, and Ahmar could tell that Tricia was
beginning to get irritated,

"Oh Ah-mar," Cayman corrected herself, "Mar-mar is what I call
him, I've known him since we were children, and ah had de biggest
crush on him, we dated for a while when we were teenagers, I can just
imagine why you have such a big smile on your face, he never
disappoints," Cayman giggled,

"Cayman, that is enough!" Ahmar said as he stood,

"I'm just being sociable to your lil' escort," Cayman teased,

"I'm not a fucking escort!" Tricia snapped,

223

"Oh my, Ahmar! Is she always dis classy?" Cayman
asked as she placed her hand over her chest, and leaned on one
hip, "Well I must be going, do tell yah lovely wife and daughter,
hello for me," she said before casually walking off,

"Who in the hell was that?" Tricia asked once Cayman
walked off,

"Dat is Cayman, she is one of de top music executives
for my company's biggest competitor,"

"Does she know your wife?" Tricia asked,

"No, she said dat for your benefit," Ahmar said with a
frustrated sigh,

"Well, I don't like her!" Tricia said,

"No one does... look, she's heading over to Maurice and
Maya," Ahmar laughed,

"Does he know her?" Tricia asked,

"They kind of met last night," Ahmar said with a sly
smile,

"Did something happen between them?" Tricia asked,
and once Ahmar told her what happened the night before, she
burst into laughter, "She actually grabbed him there?" Tricia
asked,

"She did," Ahmar said laughing,

"I bet he tripped all over you getting away from her!"
Tricia laughed,

"Yes, scuffed up my brand-new shoes!" Ahmar joked,

"What's wrong with that lady?" Tricia asked in disbelief,

"Well for one, she has a big appetite for men and an
even bigger appetite for nose candy," Ahmar said with a sigh,

"That's wild!"

"It is sad, she worked very hard to get where she is, and
she just throw it away!" Ahmar said as he shook his head,

"That's a shame!" Tricia said,
***

Maurice and Maya were about to go back to the dance
floor when a tall, slender woman dressed in a midnight blue,
glove fitting cat-suit and matching spiked stilettos slithered up to
them,

"My, aren't yah two color-coordinated!" Cayman joked,

"Hi Cayman," Maurice said under his breath,

"Rece...so we meet again," Cayman said with a blush as
Maya glared over at Maurice...
***

"I wonder what she's saying to them," Tricia said,
"Knowing Cayman, it is something rude," Ahmar answered,
"I hope she knows what she's doing," Tricia said thinking about
Maya's short fuse lately,
"You think we should go over there?" Ahmar asked,
"No, I think Maya can handle herself," Tricia insisted,
***

"Where in de world did you and Mar-Mar find these lovely lady escorts?" Cayman asked, and Maya could tell that she was deliberately being both ignored and insulted by this woman,

"She ain't no escort, this is my Lady, Maya, we're about to go dance, so if you'll excuse us," Maurice said sternly, he wasn't in the mood for Cayman's antics today,

"Oh God! Dat Southern accent is absolutely delicious! Ma-ya, you say? Where did you find such a unique name... no matter!" Cayman asked, dismissing Maya with a wave of her hand before turning her attention back to Maurice, "I was unaware that you had a *lady* friend Rece, and where was *she* last night when we danced the night away?" Cayman asked with a devilish smile, as she leaned in close and tried to whisper in his ear,

"Hold on now!" Maurice said, blocking her hand and moving his head to the side as Cayman tried to finger his locs,

"She looks...boring, I can see why you would leave her at home," Cayman said as she turned from Maurice and looked Maya up and down, twisting her lips in disapproval, "Why don't we go back to my hotel," Cayman said as she leaned in towards Maurice, Maya was in shock, but her shock was quickly transformed into anger,

"That ain't even my style, Lil' Mama," Maurice said with a deep frown on his face as he blocked her hand again as she tried to caress his chest,

"Reeeece..." Cayman sang his name, making it drip from her lips like melted chocolate, "Yah can't honestly tell me that yah have more fun... with her? Come now!" She said as she placed her hand on her hip,

"Don't you have something else better to do?" Maurice said frowning,

"Well, we can always do something *SEX-u-al*, like we did last night," Cayman said as she glanced over at Maya with a coy smile,

"Really Cayman, don't you see my Lady standing right here?" Maurice asked, aggravated,

"Hello, Lady-standing-right here..." Cayman said sarcastically, as if that was Maya's real name, she gave Maya a three second fake smile, and a four-finger wave, then just as quick, she turned her attention back to Maurice, "Soooo Rece, when are we leaving? Surely you won't refuse my offer," Cayman asked, narrowing her eyes and focusing on Maurice as if Maya was invisible,

"I'm gonna offer to smack the shit out of you if you don't move the fuck on!" Maya said as she stepped in front of Cayman,

"Oh my! She's ah sassy little one isn't she, and with such a nasty mouth!" Cayman said as she placed her hand over her chest in mock embarrassment, "How classy...pity..." Cayman shrugged, "Well, I won't waste my time," she said as she reached into her purse and took a business card from her handbag, "But if yah ever travel to The Big Apple, call me..." Cayman said with a wink as she extended her hand to give her business card to Maurice, but Maya snatched it out of her hand and crumpled it,

"Oh God! Priceless!" Cayman said as she looked Maya up and down again, then she sucked her teeth and turned on her heels and walked away,

"You forgot something!" Maya said as she threw the crumpled card and hit Cayman in the back of her head, Cayman kept walking never even acknowledging that Maya threw the card,

"And who was that?" Maya asked,

"That was Cayman, I met her last night,"

"I can't believe you..." Maya said as she shook her head and walked away from Maurice as well,

"Maya, I know you ain't gonna let her ruin our last night here! Maya! Maya!" Maurice said running up behind her,

"I don't like being disrespected Maurice!" Maya said through gritted teeth,

"I didn't disrespect you Maya, you heard the conversation!"

"Whatever!" Maya said as she fanned him away,

"Whatever! What do you mean whatever! I ain't got no reason to lie to you Maya! I wouldn't have even met her last night if you would've been straight up with me in the first place! You were the one who said you wanted to be just friends!" Maurice said,

"So now you're blaming me! You couldn't even wait one day, you slept with the first damn woman you saw and now it's my fucking fault??? Really!!!" Maya frowned as the words flew out of her mouth like venom,

"What? I didn't…" Maurice said, his words twisting in his brain so fast that he couldn't get them out,

"The Infamous Cayman Michaels strikes again!" Ahmar said as he and Tricia walked up to them,

"Mane, you should warn people about that damn woman!" Maurice said to Ahmar,

"Maya don't be mad at Maurice, she came over there and did the same thing to us," Tricia said laughing,

Ahmar was still tickled at the fact someone finally got the best of Cayman, and he was going to remind her of it every chance he got, especially after that wadded up card that Maya threw at her got tangled in her locs and was still stuck as she sashayed off,

"We're gonna go powder our noses gentlemen, we'll be right back," Tricia said as she grabbed Maya by the hand, "come on here Killer!" Tricia teased as she led Maya into the ladies' room,

"Girl, did you see that heffa!" Maya said still angry,

"Maya why are you letting that girl pull your chain?" Tricia asked with a smile,

"Forget you Tricia, she didn't disrespect you like she did me, that bitch acted like I wasn't even there!" Maya said as she stormed back and forth across the ladies' room,

"Oh, she tried it," Tricia admitted, "but I was on her ass…" Tricia laughed, but soon stopped when she noticed how angry Maya was, "I'm sorry Sis," Tricia smiled, then poked out her lip in mock-sadness,

"I knew he was gonna sleep with somebody last night, I just knew it!" Maya said as she made a trail back and forth in the bathroom,

"Sleep with her? Did Rece tell you what actually happened between him and her last night?" Tricia asked with a smirk,

"No, she said they slept together, and he didn't even deny it!" Maya said as her eyes filled with tears,

"Hold on Sister, you're gonna mess up your make-up, and for nothing…" Tricia said as she grabbed a napkin and dabbed Maya's eyes with a tissue, she hugged her and then proceeded to tell her what actually happened,

"You're lyin'!" Maya said in disbelief, she was still mad, but she had to laugh,

"No, Ahmar told me when we were at the bar," Tricia reassured her,

"What did she say to you guys?"

Tricia laughed as she told Maya what Cayman had said to them,

"Man, that lady is just an evil bitch!" Maya said,

227

"Don't be too hard on Maurice, he did right by you even though y'all were just friends," Tricia laughed,

"Whatever, Tricia..." Maya said, still pouting,

"You really need to calm down Maya, you're too pretty for all of those tears, and by the way, I meant to tell you, you are on fire tonight! You should do your make up like that more often, and where did you get that outfit?"

"I didn't do my makeup he did, and he wrapped my hair and picked out my clothes too, even my underwear," Maya said, still fighting tears,

"You are lying!" Tricia said as she checked out Maya's makeup even closer,

"He did, he even arched my eyebrows and gave me a pedicure," Maya said,

"For real?" Tricia asked,

"Yeah, did you know that he went to cosmetology school and then went back to school to become a Master Barber?" Maya asked,

"No, I mean, I knew he cut hair, but I actually thought he was a Photographer," Tricia said,

"Nah, he just does that on the side, he actually has his own Barber shop in Whitehaven," Maya said,

"Really? And you mean to tell me this man did your make-up, chose a bangin' ass outfit for you to wear tonight, he's considerate, introduces you as his Lady, did right by you even when he had a chance to do you wrong, even when you gave him the *Let's Just Be Friends* Speech, and he touched your lil' flat ass feet! Damn Maya! What else do you want the man to do, come riding in on a white horse?" Tricia teased,

"No, I'm just trying to be careful Tricia, and I do not have flat feet!" Maya said, she couldn't help but to laugh,

"You can be careful Maya, nothing's wrong with that, but for now just be nice to the man, and don't take your Tony-B frustrations out on him, that shit ain't right!" Tricia warned,

"Okay, okay...don't worry, I'll behave myself," Maya assured Tricia,

***

"You think she's still mad?" Maurice asked Ahmar after the girls left,

"Yeah, I think she is still very mad," Ahmar nodded,

"What in the hell was I supposed to do, I told Cayman to leave!" Maurice reasoned,

"When she comes out, just be cool, don't say anything, then she will know Cayman didn't mean anything to yah," Ahmar said as the girls walked up to them,

***

"Did you miss me?" Tricia asked Ahmar.

"Yah know I missed you, Pretty Lady!" Ahmar said with a smile,

"Hey," Maya mumbled, she was thoroughly embarrassed at how she had behaved,

"Hey Baby Mama," Maurice said, playing it cool as Ahmar suggested,

"Can we go somewhere and talk?" Maya asked,

"Yeah," Maurice answered still as cool as a cucumber,

Maya and Maurice found a staircase and walked halfway down,

"I'm sorry Maurice, I overreacted," Maya confessed,

"That's okay Maya, I know you've been hurt, but you have to realize I'm not Tony-B, I don't operate the way he does, and I don't do drama," Maurice said adamantly,

"I know…" Maya sighed,

"I was there Maya, I saw how he treated you, and I would never do that to you!"

"So…what do we do now?" Maya asked with a baby soft tone as she stared at the floor,

"This…" Maurice said as he lifted Maya's chin with his finger and kissed her until her eyes crossed, "and that's just a sample!" Maurice said when he saw the pleased look on Maya's face, Maya smiled wide as they walked back upstairs and joined Tricia and Ahmar. Maurice gave Ahmar the thumbs up signal when Maya wasn't looking, and the rest of the night was like a dream to both Maya and Tricia, they didn't make it back to the hotel until almost five in the morning, Maya wanted to spend the rest of the night with Maurice and Tricia wanted to spend the remaining time with Ahmar, Maya couldn't wait to get Maurice into her room, this time she was prepared, Maya had a red sexy nightie waiting in the bathroom. She went into the bathroom and changed, when she emerged, Maurice almost fell out of his chair,

"Maya! How do you expect me to lay beside you when you're dressed like that?" Maurice said, his eyes almost bulging out of his head,

"I don't," Maya said calmly,

Maurice jumped out of his chair and kneeled in front of her holding her full hips in his hands, "What are you saying Maya, what are you saying?" he asked,

"I'm saying, I don't expect you to lay beside me while I'm

dressed like this,"

"Then what do you expect me to do?" He asked,

"I expect you to respect me, to treat me right, to love me, to make love to me, to be my man, and to never let me go..." she said with a sexy smile,

"Wait, wait, wait! Say it one more time!" Maurice pleaded, he was not believing what was happening,

"No..." Maya teased,

"Maya don't do me like that!"

"You heard me the first time Maurice,"

"Are you for real, don't tease me Maya, this is serious!"

"I'm serious," Maya said with a straight face,

"Ooh Baby!" Maurice said as he held her in his arms,

"Are you gonna make love to me now?" Maya asked anxiously, more anxious than she anticipated,

"No." Maurice said shaking his head,

"No?" Maya asked baffled,

"No." Maurice repeated,

"I thought you wanted to," Maya said,

"I did-I mean I still do..." Maurice said as he drifted off, but he instantly snapped back to reality, "but I don't think we're ready for that yet," Maurice confessed,

"You don't?" Maya asked, feeling rejected,

"No Maya, I don't wanna make love to you because I'm caught up in the moment, I want our first time to completely blow your mind, I think we need to at least wait until we're back at home and we both know for sure that this is what we both want," Maurice explained,

"I understand," Maya said with a fake smile, *"Damn it!"* Maya screamed inside her head as he stood to his feet and wrapped his arms around her,

Maurice fell asleep with Maya in his arms, and every now and then he would mumble and smile in his sleep, but Maya was wide awake and on fire, and whenever he moved, she sizzled inside, hoping that he had changed his mind and was ready to snatch her up and ravage her, her mind raced in anticipation as she laid there in his arms with her eyes wide open,

***

Tricia had never been so nervous in her life, Ahmar put on a brave front, but she could tell he was nervous too.

"Don't worry Tricia, I won't hurt yah," Ahmar assured

her as she sat on the bed,

     "I'm so nervous Ahmar, I've never done anything like this before,"

     "Neither have I," Ahmar said,

     "Okay Ahmar, are you ready? It's now or never..." Tricia said,

     "I'm ready, choose one," Ahmar instructed,

     Tricia pulled out a pair of scissors and cut one of Ahmar's dreads in half,

     "Now I will always have a piece of you," she said,

     Then Ahmar took the scissors and cut one of Tricia's braids,

     "And I will have a piece of you with me always!" he said with a smile,

     "Listen Ahmar, I know we agreed to keep it as friends, right?"

     "Right,"

     "But you and I know we are much, much more,"

     "Yes... I know,"

     "And if a friend wanted to be held, or needed to be held, you'd hold them, wouldn't you?"

     "In a heartbeat..." Ahmar said through a deep sigh,

     "Well can we just lay here and hold each other, I wanna remember how your body felt up against mine," Tricia said as she snuggled up against him,

     "Indeed," Ahmar said as he wrapped his arm around her waist and they fell asleep,

     The sun shined bright on Tricia's face waking her from a peaceful sleep,

     "Greetings Angel." Ahmar said smiling,

     "Greetings Ahmar, and thanks for staying with me last night,"

     "No problem, dat is what friends are for," Ahmar smiled,

     "Yes, it is," Tricia said with a smile,

***

     When Maurice woke up Maya was staring at him,

     "What, was I snoring or something?" He asked,

     "No, I was just watching you sleep,"

     "Did you sleep well?" Maurice asked,

     "I tried, but I have been nauseous all night,"

     "Anything I can do?" Maurice asked,

     "No, I'll be okay, I'm just sick to my stomach," Maya frowned,

     "I know just the thing, I was at a restaurant here one time and this lady had morning sickness and I remember them telling her to drink some coconut water, I think they have some downstairs," Maurice went downstairs and picked up some and he bought her some crackers also,

"Lay down and rest, it's only eight-thirty, we have plenty of time, are you packed?"

"Almost," Maya said,

"Well don't worry about it, we'll do it together if you feel like it, and if not, I can do it for you," Maurice insisted,

Maya drank the coconut water and went back to bed, Maurice woke her up at ten-thirty,

"How are you feeling?" He asked,

"Much better," Maya said, she was so sleepy she could hardly keep her eyes open,

Maya got up and got dressed then they went to her room and packed, Ahmar paid the cab driver as they unloaded the luggage from the car and rushed into Piarco International Airport. During the plane ride Maya and Maurice sent notes back and forth to Ahmar and Tricia, and when they noticed the flight attendant was getting aggravated, they sent even more. When the plane landed, Tricia and Ahmar lagged so they would have a minute to talk,

"I've learned so many things from yah while on this trip Tricia," Ahmar said,

"Really, and what did you learn?" Tricia asked,

"I've learned dat if I ever meet a beautiful lady on vacation, and she's married, to run the other way!" Ahmar joked,

"I don't know if I should take that as a compliment or not," Tricia said, laughing as well,

"No, it was meant as the greatest compliment, I don't want to lose what I have, and I don't want to cost yah anything dat you have," Ahmar admitted,

"I'm glad we came to the same conclusion," Tricia said,

"I talked to my wife dis morning. She took me back to reality," Ahmar confessed,

"I know exactly what you mean, Ahmar, I talked to Phillip this morning as well,"

"Friends?" Ahmar asked, extending his hand,

"Friends." Tricia said as she placed her hand in his, Ahmar kissed her hand and placed it on his cheek, and Tricia teared up a little,

"Can we end dis journey with a hug?" Ahmar asked,

"Yes, I would really like that," Tricia said with a smile as she and Ahmar hugged and kissed each other on the cheek,

"Take care, My Sweet Angel!"

"You too, Ahmar,"

"I had better leave, while I still have de strength," Ahmar said,

"Please do," Tricia said as she wiped tears from her eyes, Ahmar walked away silently, without looking back,

"Okay Trish, get yourself together! You have a loving husband and an adorable lil' knuckle-headed son waiting for you! You made the right decision, and you don't have time for any regrets!" Tricia said as she tried to prepare herself for the ride back home,

"Where's Ahmar?" Maya asked under her breath,

"He went to catch his connecting flight to Texas, he's scouting a band over there tomorrow," Tricia said as she tried to fight tears,

"Are you okay?" Maya asked,

"Yeah, I think so," Tricia said, trying desperately to get herself together,

"We're home!" Maurice said as he walked up to them,

"Yeah..." Tricia and Maya said in unison, each having their own reasons for sounding sad about being back in Memphis,

"Baby, how are you getting home?" Maya asked Maurice,

"Larry's coming to pick me up," he said,

"Oh, okay," Maya said, not wanting this fairytale to end,

When they walked through the gate, Phillip was standing beside a bench with flowers in his hand waiting for Tricia, and Larry was leaning on the wall waiting for Maurice,

"Man, it's about time!" Larry said to Maurice before recognizing who Maya was, "Ms. Lady...is that you?" Larry asked, and Maya could tell that he was surprised to see her,

"Yeah, it's me," Maya said with a fake smile,

"Damn girl! I almost didn't recognize you! You lookin' good with them braids and shit!" Larry said as he eyed her up and down like she was a well-done steak on a platter, Maya suddenly felt queasy and her flesh crawled, she really didn't care for Larry at all,

"She sure does," Maurice said as he bit down on his bottom lip then winked his eye at her, Larry looked puzzled as Maya blushed when Maurice smiled at her,

"What the hell are y'all smiling for, what? Y'all know something I don't?" Larry asked, glaring at them both,

"No, it's just that we ended up in the same place," Maurice said, still smiling,

"Same place? Way over there in Trinidad? Straight up?!?" Larry asked,

"Yep," Maya and Maurice said in unison, then they both burst out laughing,

"Aw okay...well let's go Rece, you know I gottta go get ready for work after I drop you off," Larry said, "Hey Ms. Lady you need a ride or is Tony-B coming to pick you up?"

"No, I have a ride," Maya said rolling her eyes,

"I know he gone be glad to see you and you looking good too... I know he gone tear that ass up when you get home! Shit, if I would've known you were gonna be here, I would've had Tony-B to ride down here with me," Larry said, testing the waters to see if what he was beginning to sense was true,

"Ain't no need for that, I got this..." Maurice said as he walked up to Maya and gave her a long mind-blowing kiss, when he finally let her go, Maya blushed hard and placed her hand on her chest, and Larry stood there in shock with his mouth wide open,

"C'mon bro," Maurice said with a smirk, knowing he had given his brother something to run and tell Tony-B the first chance he got, "See ya later, Baby, and call me as soon as you get home," Maurice said to Maya as she headed back over to where Phillip and Tricia was, Maya was so outdone by the kiss, especially in a crowded airport, that she had to sit down on the nearest bench and gather herself,

"What the hell going on around here!" Larry said as Maurice loaded his bags into Larry's back seat,

"What are you tripping about?" Maurice asked,

"Don't even worry about it, just get in the damn car!" Larry snapped,

***

Tricia inhaled the sweet scent of the deep red velvety rose poking out of the top of the flower arrangement that Phillip had given her in the airport, she opened her arms and enveloped Phillip in as they stood outside the airport, she rested her chin on his shoulder and let out a long sigh, he felt so good to her, she breathed his cologne and closed her eyes to soak him into her thoughts as he inhaled her and laid sweet kisses on her neck, she was basking deep in her husband's presence, so thankful to have a man like him, she forgot about everything and everybody for a second, but something told her to open her eyes, and when she did, she noticed Ahmar was standing at the airport entrance, not even two feet away from them, staring at them through the glass doors. Tricia fought hard to keep her body from tensing as Ahmar leaned against the door and shook his head slowly. He held her braid in the air and kissed it, then mouthed the words, "I'll miss you Sweet Angel,"

Tricia opened her clenched hand and held Ahmar's loc between her pointer finger and thumb, her chin still resting on Phillip's shoulder,

Ahmar blew her a kiss, then walked off. The minute he walked away, Tricia released her two fingers and let the loc of hair fall at Phillip's feet, *"Never again!"* She thought, kissing Phillip with everything she had left inside of her. She rubbed Phillip's back with such tenderness, remembering this was the man she loved, and this was the man that she belonged to.

Ahmar walked away slowly, thinking of Tricia's face, reminiscing the way she felt in his arms, he could still smell her as he lifted his collar to his nose, he inhaled hard, after the week they shared, he couldn't stand seeing her hugged and kissed by another man, even if it was her husband, *"Never again!"* Ahmar said as he kissed her braid then tossed it into the nearest trash bin...

"That was some hug! You must've really missed Big Daddy!" Phillip said when they finally released each other,

"Yes, I did." Tricia said trying to contain her emotions,

"Baby, don't cry!" Phillip said as he wiped her eyes,

"I'll be okay," she said as she leaned in to kiss him when he suddenly jumped back,

"What the hell is that?" Phillip said as he stomped the piece of hair repeatedly, "Aw shit, it's just a piece of somebody's nappy ass hair...Whew! I thought it was a big ass worm or something! Oh well, I stomped the hell out of it, didn't I, Baby?"

"You sure did," Tricia said smiling with tears still glistening in her eyes,

"Give Daddy some more of that love. I missed the hell out of you Girl!" Phillip said as they embraced again,

"Lord PLEASE forgive me and give me strength!" Tricia prayed, as Phillip gathered her bags and they headed to the car,

***

Maurice hated the fact he hadn't driven himself to the airport, he could tell by the look on Larry's face that he was in for an exceptionally long ride,

"Man, what the hell do you call yourself doing?" Larry said as they pulled out of the airport parking lot,

"What do you mean?" Maurice asked, suddenly regretting kissing Maya in front of him,

"You know what the fuck I'm talkin' about Rece! Stop playing stupid! You know that's Tony-B's gal, why in the hell would you go on a trip with her?!?" Larry snapped,

"I didn't go on a trip with her, I saw her and Tricia in the hotel a

235

day after I got there," Maurice explained,

"So, you're telling me, that y'all ended up in the same hotel, at the same damn time, waaay over in another fucking country?" Larry asked,

"Yeah!" Maurice said,

"Maaane... I don't believe that shit!" Larry said with his lips twisted,

"I ain't gotta lie to you Larry!" Maurice said with a shrug,

"You mean to tell me that y'all both just showed up in Trinidad, out of all the fuckin' places in the world, at the same damn time?" Larry asked again,

"Yeah!" Maurice insisted,

"Mane, you on that bullshit and you know it! Y'all think y'all slick..." Larry said nodding his head real fast,

"Believe what you wanna believe, like I said, I ain't got no reason to lie to you," Maurice said shrugging his shoulders then looking out of the window,

"Tony-B told me a long time ago, that you was trying to get up on his gal, but naw! I told him you wouldn't do no crossed-out ass shit like that! But I had it wrong! Now I feel like the damn fool! Man, that's my Pat'na, and you gone do some shit like that!" Larry said shaking his head in disbelief,

"So! Fuck him, he ain't shit to me, y'all the ones who worship his sorry ass, not me!" Maurice said with a frown,

"Worship? I know you crazy now!" Larry said,

"Well, that's what it seems like to me!" Maurice said,

"You think I wouldn't be saying this same shit to him if he would've crossed you! Why you do that Rece? Don't no gal come before your damn boys!" Larry said, anger rising in his voice,

"He ain't shit to me! And you didn't say nothing when Tony-B was out there bangin' all them girls in his shed while Maya was right there in the house!"

"Banging all them gals?!? That ain't got shit to do with you, that ain't none of your motha-fuckin' business what that mane do to them bitches out there in his own damn shed, what the fuck does that have to do with you, Rece? What the hell is wrong with you?" Larry said, not believing Maurice, "You all up in that mane's business, I bet you told her too, I bet you ran your fuckin' mouth like a lil' ass gal, just to get in her draws, didn't you? I bet you did!" Larry said, his voice booming,

"Don't call me no fuckin' gal!" Maurice said, anger dripping from his voice,

"I didn't call you no gal, I said you ran your mouth like one, just to get some ass!"

"I didn't run my mouth about nothing! I told you it wasn't like that, I saw her in the hotel, and we just kicked it, his name didn't even come up," Maurice lied,

"Yeah, I just bet it didn't!" Larry said, "I wouldn't mention his name either if I knew I was violating!"

"Violating! How am I violating? They broke up weeks ago Larry, you told me that out of your own damn mouth!"

"So fuckin' what! They always break up! And then they get right back together! Mane, I thought Ms. Lady was better than that shit though! How she gone get with you, knowing you and Tony-B grew up together?" Larry questioned,

"So! Like I said, he ain't never been shit to me!"

"What is she trying to do, use my lil' brother to hurt the man? And you act like you got animosity against him or something! You a hater now?" Larry asked with a frown,

"I ain't thinking about him, he's your boy, not mine!" Maurice said,

"Aw damn, I can't believe this! Did Ms. Lady tell you that she was pregnant? What the hell am I saying? Of course, you know she's pregnant, hell, it might even be yours, the way y'all sneaking around with each other and shit!" Larry reasoned,

"Yeah, she told me," Maurice said before staring out of the window, he hoped his silence would make Larry shut up, but no such luck,

"Tell the truth, is it yours?" Larry asked,

"What? Naw Mane! I told you I didn't even know she was gonna be there!" Maurice said, he couldn't believe that Larry thought Maya was pregnant by him,

"Mane, how you gonna bang her knowing that she got Tony-B baby all up in her stomach! Mane, that's just fucked up!" Larry said with a sigh,

"That ain't got nothing to do with me!" Maurice shot back,

"Aw Mane! I know you fucking that bitch now!" Larry said,

"Man, I ain't fucking her, I mean…me and Maya ain't never had sex, we just kicked it, and she ain't no bitch!" Maurice said,

"Why are you taking up for her then?" Larry asked,

"What do you mean? That's my woman, I'm supposed to take up for her!"

"Did you just say she was your muthafuckin' woman!?!'"
Larry asked in disbelief, "Somethings wrong with you Rece, for
real! AHHHH!!! I can't believe this shit!" Larry yelled out of
frustration as he pounded the dashboard with his fist,

"Yeah, that's what I said," Maurice said, not backing
down,

"She's your woman after spending just one week
together?" Larry asked,

"Yeah!" Maurice said,

"That don't mean shit Maurice, hell she was with Tony-
B for years and she jumped from him straight to your ass with
his baby kickin' in her fuckin' stomach!" Larry said, "And you
say, you've never fucked her?" he asked Maurice again,

"Naw, but it ain't none of your business if I did or
didn't!" Maurice said,

"This is some real abracadabra ass shit right there!"
Larry said, shaking his head in pity,

"What the hell do you mean by that?" Maurice asked,

"Shit, let's see…she was with him when she left… even
came over to the house and let him run all up in her the day
before she left…bet you didn't know that shit, did ya?" Larry
asked, but before Maurice could respond, Larry continued,
"Then abra-ca-dabra! She's gone for one damn week and when
she comes back from Trinidad…Trinidad! The place you go to
every damn year, the place you been going to every fucking year
for what, four, five years now? Then, all of a sudden...
Abracadabra! She's with your ass now...Maaane! That's some
real magical ass shit right there, boy I tell ya!" Larry said,
shaking his head,

"For the last time, I didn't know she was gonna be
there!" Maurice said with all of the energy he could muster,

"Mane, even if by some strong ass coincidence, y'all
saw each other over there, you could've just spoke to her ass and
kept it movin', you didn't have to get with her, and make her
your fuckin' gal! Damn!" Larry said, shaking his head at
Maurice, "And this ain't got nothing to do with the fact that you
got animosity for Tony-B?"

"I ain't got no animosity for that dude, I ain't thinking
about him!"

"That's your problem right there, you ain't thinkin'
about nobody but your damn self! That gal loves Tony-B's dirty
draws! She's been with him all this time and he's been doggin'

her ass out, don't you think she gone be right back with him after he spits that game to her like he always does?" Larry asked trying to reason with his little brother,

"We'll just have to see, won't we?" Maurice said,

"You act like you in love with the bitch, or something!" Larry said, still in disbelief,

"Larry you can say whatever the fuck you want but if you call her a bitch again, it's gonna be a problem," Maurice warned,

"Alright, I didn't mean to disrespect your *'gal'* or whatever," Larry said sarcastically, using the quote sign with his fingers, "but can't you just take one minute out of your in-love-ass-life to see the position you're putting me in?" Larry reasoned,

"I don't give a fuck! You can run and tell him whatever you want, Larry! I don't give a damn! As a matter of fact, I want you to tell him! He ain't gone do shit to me!" Maurice said,

"That's messed up, that mane is at home right now, Bar-B-Q-ing his ass off for your surprise welcome home party and look at this shit you pullin'!" Larry said, shaking his head in pity,

"I don't give a damn about none of that! And I don't want none of his nasty ass Bar-B-Q! Fuck him and his party!" Maurice said with his face frowned,

"Mane, you so bogus! Now what in the hell am I supposed to tell him when I get back over there?"

"You can tell him whatever the hell you wanna tell him, I don't care!" Maurice snapped back,

"What about the party he's throwing for you? He cooked all that food and invited everybody over,"

"I ain't never liked his nasty ass Bar-B-Q, you ain't never seen me eat that shit! The only reason I even went to his parties anyway was to see Maya and to eat her cooking, not his!" Maurice admitted unapologetically,

"You so damn foul for that shit!" Larry said, "But you always was green when it came to gals, look at the shit Kayla did to you, and you still ran up behind her like a lil' sick ass puppy..." Larry said, he could tell that his words stung by the look on Maurice's face, but he didn't care,

"Look! I ain't never liked him, and he ain't never liked me! Fuck Kayla, and since you wanna bring her name up and you wanna choose that punk ass lil' boy over me, your own flesh and blood, then fuck you too! I don't wanna talk about this shit no more, it is what it is! You can just drop me off at home and you ain't never gotta worry about me no more!" Maurice said, he was so angry that he was beginning to see spots,

"I'm not choosin' him over you, Rece, but right is right and wrong is wrong, and you dead wrong for this shit! I don't know if you just sprung, desperate, or stupid as hell!" Larry said as he pulled up in front of Maurice's house,

"Fuck you!" Maurice said with as much force as he possibly could as he jumped out of Larry's car and snatched his bags out of the back seat,

"Like I said, you always have been real weak for broads!" Larry said shaking his head, "But don't call me when she leaves your lil' weak ass and goes back to her ex just like Kayla did!"

"Don't you worry about me, motherfucker! You better hurry up or you gonna be late for your Patna's nasty ass Bar-B-Q!"

"That's alright, I'll do that, but when she runs back to Tony-B, don't you call me crying like a lil' ass bitch!" Larry said before speeding off,

Maurice stood there for a minute before dragging his luggage into the house, once inside, he instantly went over to the CD player and popped in the CD that he'd gotten from Sebastian, he turned it up loud hoping that the music would somehow drown his own doubts, "Don't let me down Maya, don't you let me down," Maurice mumbled as he plopped down in his recliner and rested his head in his hands…

***

9 BACK TO REALITY

Phillip and Tricia pulled up in Mama Anderson's driveway. Maya put the key into the door expecting to see her mother.

"Mama?" Maya said but Mama Anderson didn't answer, "Well she must be gone," Maya said disappointed,

"Where do you want me to put this, Maya?" Phillip said holding her bags,

"You can put them over there," Maya said pointing to the corner, "Thanks Phillip," Maya said,

"No problem, Mon! Don't I sound like one of those Island Boys?" Phillip joked,

"Uh...no!" Maya said laughing,

"See you later Maya," Tricia yelled from the car,

Maya waved at her then stepped back into the house and fell back on the couch and turned on the TV. She grabbed her cell phone and turned it on for the first time since she left, the message icon lit up instantly,

"Maya, call me before you leave Baby, I know what I did was wrong, but we need to talk,"

Message deleted.

"Damn Maya, answer the phone! I'll be so glad when you get off this bullshit you on!"

Message deleted.

"Maya this is your Mama, I decided to leave you a message since you can't call nobody! I'm going to see about your Aunt Maggie, she ain't been feelin' too good, but I'll be back Monday evening. And when I get home, I'm gonna fix you and that baby a big ol' home cooked meal! I know you ain't ate right since you been gone! Love you, see you

241

soon!"

Message saved.

"This is Torya, I was just calling to let you know I've moved in with Tony-B, I guess it is our house now bitch, and I know--"

Message deleted!

"What's up Maya! Y'all didn't have to call nobody while y'all was out of town! This is Linda, call me girl, I got something to tell you!"

Message saved.

"Maya this is your man, call me as soon as you get back, I don't know why you're actin' funny, but you need to call me as soon as you get off that damn plane!"

Message deleted.

"Hey Baby Mama, this is Rece, I know we just got back and all, but I'm needing to see you! Can you meet me in front of the Summer-Twin at let's see, it's four- thirty now, how about seven, it'll give you plenty of time to get ready, I'll be waiting..."

Message repeated.

Maya was restless, she wanted to take a nap, but she was too excited about seeing Maurice to sleep, then her cell phone began to ring,

"I sure didn't miss this thing!" Maya mumbled as she answered the phone, "Hello?"

"Hey Baby, I missed you,"

"What do you want Tony?" Maya said, her skin was beginning to crawl at the mere sound of his voice,

"Damn Baby! I thought you'd be over that shit by now!"

"Well, I'm not, so what do you want?"

"How is my baby doing?"

"I don't go back to the doctor until Friday after next," Maya answered,

"I wasn't talkin' about that! I was talkin' about you," Tony-B sighed,

"Bye Tony!"

"Hey! Hey don't hang up,"

"What do you want!" Maya said with a long sigh,

"You didn't give none of my stuff away while you were gone, did you?"

"Didn't you?" Maya barked,

"Damn! You ain't never gonna let me live that down!"

"I have to go," Maya said exasperated,

"You act like I can't change!" Tony-B said,

"Look, I've moved on, so you can find you somebody else to play with,"

"Moved on…with who?" Tony-B asked with a frown,

"That's none of your damn business!"

"Maya we just broke up a lil' while ago, and you already moved on? Damn that was quick!" Tony -B said,

"At least I waited until we broke up, unlike you!" Maya said,

"I made a simple mistake Maya, you gone just throw us away because of that! You act like I can't make no mistakes around here!"

"Oh, that's right, you made a mistake and had sex with Torya, an then you tripped and fell on her and that's how she got pregnant, right?" Maya asked,

"No, I just made the wrong decision!" Tony snapped back,

"Well make the right one this time and leave me the hell alone!"

"Maya, you know you got me messed up, right?" Tony said,

"Whatever!" Maya said,

"Maya?"

"What!"

"Can't we talk about this?"

"You need to be talking to Torya, from what I hear, you made a mistake and let her move in with you, too!"

"Who told you that?" Tony-B asked,

"Things have a way of getting around, but I ain't mad at you. I'm just glad I didn't sign my name on that house like you told her I did, because then I'd have to burn that bitch to the ground with you and her in it," Maya said,

"Why are you tripping, I wanted to be with you, not her! But look at how you're acting, but straight up, all you have to do is just say the word and her ass will be out of here! For real!"

"Save it Tony! I'm surprised you're not having a get together, I'm sure you and Torya have a whole lot to celebrate,"

"You need to cut that out Maya, and for your information I am having a get together, I'm throwing Rece a Welcome Home Party, but you know it wasn't my idea, he's too damn sneaky for me, always grinning all up in your face. I know you gonna come and celebrate with your boy,"

"No, I'm not!" Maya said as her mind spiraled, she wondered if Tony-B was trying to tell her on the sly that he knew about her and Maurice,

"Come on Maya, stop acting like that. I don't give a damn who you're with, you're still my gal! Hold on Baby, I think it's them at the door now,"

Maya wanted to hang up, but she couldn't, she just had to hear Maurice's voice, "He can't be doing this to me!" She mumbled as she listened to Tony talking in the background,

"What's up Larry, where my boy at?" Maya heard Tony-B ask,

"Mane, I need to holla at you for real!" Larry said,

"What's good, everything straight?" Tony-B asked, he could tell something was wrong by the look on Larry's face,

"Who is that on the phone?" Larry asked,

"It's my baby, why are you asking?"

"You talkin' about Ms. Lady?" Larry asked before thinking,

"Yeah, who else would I be talking about?" Tony said as he did the cutthroat symbol with his free hand,

"Mane, call her back!" Larry spat,

Tony-B looked at Larry with a confused look on his face,

"Hey Baby let me call you back," Tony-B said into the phone,

"Bye!" Maya said with a mock-attitude. She was so relieved she could hardly hold it in,

"I'm gonna call you right back Maya, stay by the phone," Tony-B said,

"Whatever Tony, don't even bother!" Maya said before hanging up, "That's what I'm talking about! That's my Honey-Honey, right there! He didn't even go!" Maya said smiling as she danced around the room,

***

Maurice didn't see Maya when she pulled up at the Summer-Twin Drive-In Movie Theater, he was standing beside his truck looking at his watch,

"Hey!" Maya said as she greeted him with a hug,

"Hey Baby Mama," Maurice said as he hugged her tight,

"And how has your day been?" Maya asked between kisses on his cheek,

"It's been okay, are you feelin' alright?" Maurice asked,

"Yeah, I guess so, I just have a lot on my mind," Maya said,

"You wanna talk about it?" Maurice said, his expression suddenly serious,

"Actually, I do. I need to ask you something Maurice,"

"Go ahead," Maurice said,

"Why didn't you tell me about your party?"

"I wasn't going to that mess! That's my brother's shit! How did you know about it?" he asked,

"Because Tony called and invited me,"

"And what did you tell him?" Maurice asked, his eyebrow slightly raised,

"I told him I wasn't coming because I didn't wanna be around him!"

"That's my girl!" Maurice said with a big grin,

Maurice was very quiet during the first movie, and after the second movie Maurice walked her to her car and opened the door for her, she was all giggles because Tony-B never opened the door for her even when they first got together,

"Hey Maurice, you've been really quiet, what's wrong?" she asked after he sat in the passenger side of her car,

"Nothing Baby, I guess I got a lot of things on my mind, too," Maurice said,

"Maurice, do you trust me?" she asked,

"Of course, I do, why do you ask?"

"Just curious,"

"Maya, you asked me for a reason," Maurice said,

"Yeah, I did," she admitted,

"Well...I'm listening,"

"When Tony told me that he was throwing you a party, my wheels started turning, I thought...never mind what I thought," Maya said,

"You thought I was gonna do you wrong, didn't you?"

"Yeah, kind of," Maya confessed,

"I can't blame you for that, I was kinda thinking the same thing about you," Maurice also confessed,

"You got doubts about me?" Maya asked, kind of surprised,

"No, not just about you, I have doubts about you and Tony-B, me and my brother even got heated about it earlier,"

"You got into a fight with your brother?"

"Nah we didn't fight, we just kinda argued," Maurice said,

"About me?"

"That was part of it, he acts like he can't stand up to Tony-B, like he is his God or something!"

"I know what you mean," Maya admitted,

"So?"

"So what?" Maya asked,

"Are you thinking about going back to him?"

"What! Hell no!" Maya said with a deep frown,

"You sure?"

"Yes! Maurice, where is all this coming from?"

"Well, me and Larry were talking, and he said some things that kinda bothered me,"

"No wonder," Maya thought to herself, "Things like what?" she asked,

"For one…I thought you told me you broke up with him a week before you left," Maurice said,

"I did,"

"Then why did you sleep with him the day before?"

Maya wished she could've melted into the seats, evaporated into thin air, or anything but this! She took a deep breath before speaking, "Maurice, I was going through a lot at the time, I went over there just to talk, and it just sort of happened, but it was before I even knew anything about us, or had any idea that I was gonna run into you way on the other side of the world," Maya admitted,

"So, you still have feelings for him?" Maurice asked,

"No, I realized I had made a big mistake, and that's why I called my brothers and moved all of my stuff out of his house that very same day,"

"Why didn't you tell me?" he asked,

"What was I supposed to say?"

"I don't know Maya, I'm just trying to sort all of this out, and now you tell me that you talked to him on the phone, so now I'm wondering if that's all that's going on,"

"He called me, but I didn't wanna talk to him, and I even told him I was seeing somebody, plus I think your brother already told him about us anyway!" Maya said,

"Why do you say that?" Maurice asked,

Maya told Maurice about what she overheard on the phone,

"I'm not surprised," Maurice said,

"Me neither," Maya admitted,

"Maya, I need to know right now, do you wanna be with me?" Maurice asked, as he turned and faced her,

"You know I do," Maya said with no hesitation,

"Then say it, tell me you wanna be with me, and not that Honey-Honey stuff, either!" Maurice said with a serious expression,

"I do wanna be with you Maurice, what's wrong?"

"Maya, I'm not the kind of man who keeps things on the low, when I have a woman, I wanna show her off to the world,"

"Okay, Maurice, I don't have anything to hide, I've already told him I moved on, I just didn't tell him with who,"

"Did he say anything about the baby?"

"Yeah, he asked how his baby was doing, but when I started to talk about the baby, he said he wasn't talking about that, he was talking about me," Maya sighed,

"What!" Maurice said in total disbelief,

"Yeah…now do you really think I want somebody like him in my life?"

"You shouldn't, but stranger things have happened…and I don't want you talking to him any more Maya," Maurice said, stone faced,

"Maurice, we are going to have a child together, so we're gonna have to talk at some point in time, you're gonna have to either trust me or don't, for 3 years I let a man tell me what to do, I don't want to go through that shit again,"

"Calm down baby, I do trust you,"

"I'm just so tired of this, I'll be so glad when I have this baby," Maya said with a sigh,

"You think he'll help you take care of it?" Maurice asked,

"Knowing him as I do, he'll probably keep saying it ain't his, and after talking to your brother he might even say it's yours, just to get out of it, but either way, me and this baby will be just fine," Maya said,

"Let him say it then because I'm not going anywhere!" Maurice said adamantly,

***

"What's up Larry, you act like something's wrong!" Tony-B asked with a frown,

"Something is wrong!" Larry said as he blew out a long puff of air,

"What's going on?" Tony-B asked,

"Sit down Man, this ain't something you need to hear standin' up," Larry warned,

"Why do I have to sit down, just tell me!" Tony-B said,

"Okay…you know we been boys for forever and a day, right?"

"Right, ever since I can remember, what's up?"

"Well, I found out some shit, and you need to know!"

"Know about what! Just tell me Man!" Tony-B yelled,

"Alright, alright! Damn I didn't wanna tell you this…" Larry paused,

"Go ahead and spit it out," Tony-B insisted,

"Okay, here it goes…Maya and my brother are fucking, like…they're together," Larry mumbled,

"What the fuck you mean, together?"

"Like, they're together! And this ain't what nobody told me, I seen this shit with my own two eyes," Larry said,

"I knew it, I knew it! I told you he was trying to get up with her, didn't I? I told you!" Tony-B said as he sat down on the couch,

"Yeah, you told me, but that's not all of it," Larry said,

"Shit, what else could it be?" Tony-B asked,

"You know that trip Ms. Lady and her friend Tricia went on?"

"Yeah, what about it?"

"Well…"

"Don't tell me, don't even fuckin' tell me!" Tony-B said,

"It's true, but he gonna try to tell me it wasn't planned, like it was just some big ass coincidence that they ended up at the same place and at the same damn time!" Larry said with a frown,

"That's some bullshit!"

"That's what I said!"

"I can't believe this shit!" Tony-B said, as he rubbed his head, the waves in his head bouncing instantly back in place after each rub,

"When I picked him up at the airport, he was kissing all on her like they been together for fucking ever! I don't know what's wrong with him, Tony-B!"

"So that's who she's moved on with!" Tony-B said rubbing his chin,

"Huh?" Larry asked confused,

"When I was talking to her just now, she said that she had moved on with somebody,"

"Well, she sure in the hell didn't look far!" Larry said,

"I see," Tony-B said and Larry could tell that his wheels were turning,

"Tony-B, I tried to talk some sense into him, but he wasn't hearing shit I had to say, he's convinced that they're a couple," Larry said,

"I can't believe this shit! I just fucked that bitch a week ago! The day before she went on that damned trip!" Tony-B snapped,

"I told him about that too, but he said he didn't care!" Larry admitted,

"Well, he can forget about this fucking party!" Tony-B spat,

"Yeah…about that, I told him about the party and he said he wasn't coming anyway,"

"Oh, hell naw, he really trying to show his ass!" Tony-B said in disbelief,

"Yeah, he on some real live fuck shit!" Larry agreed,

"He better be glad he's like a brother to me!" Tony-B said,

"I told him all of that, but check this out, Nigel told me that Tricia's old man was throwing them a surprise party at The Peach, tomorrow night!" Larry said,

"Oh yeah, you best believe I'll be there! I got a surprise of my own for their asses!" Tony-B said staring into space as he sucked his teeth like he always did when he was pissed..

***.

"Lil' Man is staying with Mama tonight so that we could spend some quality time together," Phillip said as he passed the exit on the highway leading to Phillip's mother's house,

"I was really looking forward to seeing him," Tricia said disappointed, she had been quiet and withdrawn since they had dropped Maya off at her mother's house, Tricia welcomed the distraction of a beautiful, but busy baby boy to keep both her mind and her conscience cleared,

"We can go get him if you want to," Phillip offered,

"No… I can wait until tomorrow, I really want to spend some quality time with you too," Tricia said with a hearty flirt to her voice,

"I tell you what, if you give me some now, then I'll go and get him tonight," Phillip said as he loaded Tricia's luggage into the house, knowing his wife really wanted to see her son,

"You got a deal!" Tricia said, she was so excited to see her Lil' Man,

Phillip was being so tender and passionate with her, and yet, Tricia wasn't really responding to him, she seemed so distracted on what should've been a magical night,

"Baby, I know what's wrong with you," Phillip said after noticing how distant Tricia was being with him,

"You do?" Tricia said nervously,

"Yeah… you miss him, don't you?" Phillip said with a smile,

"Huh?" Tricia asked, confused,

"Let's just get dressed and go and get him now," Phillip bargained,

"No Phillip, we can get him tomorrow, I really do want to make love to you,"

"You sure don't act like it," Phillip admitted,

"Oh Baby…" Tricia said as she rolled over on top of him, kissing him on his chest, "Do you remember what I told you I was gonna do to you when I got back…" she asked,

"No…but I sure wouldn't mind if you reminded me," Phillip said with a smile,

After indulging her husband, Tricia forgot all about Ahmar, the trip, and everything else, that had nothing to do with the here and now. They made love to each other the whole night and the next morning Tricia woke up reinvigorated. She laid still and stared at him for hours as he slept,

"Good morning," Phillip said wiping his eyes, and still smiling from last night,

"Good morning, My Love…" Tricia said with a smile,

"What are you doing up so early?" Phillip asked as he yawned and stretched at the same time,

"I have to get ready to go to the office," Tricia answered,

"But you just got here!" Phillip protested,

"I know, but I promised I would go in for an early meeting, I won't be too long, I promise!"

"Whew! You wore me out last night!" Phillip said in between yawns,

"You are so silly!" Tricia laughed, it felt good to be back home with her husband,

"I'm serious! I hope I'm able to walk today, man Baby, you rode Big Daddy into the sunset last night! Wheeeew-weee!" Phillip said shaking his head, "Oh yeah, I have a surprise for you and Maya, I'm treating the two of you to lunch at The Peach today and tell Maya Iron-Man's been worrying the hell out of me for her phone number, he told me he was sorry for what happened last week, and he can't wait to see her today!" Phillip added,

"Well, he'll have to wait in line because Ms. Maya's seeing somebody now!" Tricia snickered,

"What!!! Don't tell me Maya done hooked up with one of those knuckle-headed Island Boys way over there in Trinidad?"

"Nope, she kinda hooked up with Larry's brother, Maurice, believe it or not…" Tricia said with a hearty laughter,

"Rece, that Photographer Dude?" Phillip asked with a guilty

250

smile,

"Yep!" Tricia said laughing,

"You kidding me! But you know what, I thought that was him and Larry leaving the airport when I pulled up, are you for real Baby?" Phillip asked with a hearty laugh,

"Yeah, he ended up at the same hotel, on the same island, can you believe that?" Tricia asked still trying to believe it herself,

"That is some damn coincidence right there!" Phillip said,

"I know, I couldn't believe it when I saw him at the hotel, she was still upstairs asleep, I ran up to her room and told her, she didn't even believe me, but once those two saw each other, it was over with!" Tricia said,

"Go ahead then Ms. Maya! Tony-B, Iron-Man, and now Maurice... dang, she's moving so fast I can't even keep up with her!" Phillip joked,

"Ooh! You wrong!" Tricia laughed,

"I'm just playing, I know my girl don't get down like that, but what is she gonna do about Iron-Man?" Phillip asked after he finally stopped laughing,

"I don't know, we'll just have to see," Tricia shrugged,

"Well, she sure looked happy when she got back, I hadn't seen her smile like that in years!" Phillip said,

"Didn't she look happy? That's the same thing I was thinking," Tricia agreed,

"Well don't forget to tell her we're meeting at The Peach,"

"I won't," Tricia said as she rolled out of bed to get ready for her mandatory weekend staff meeting, and after the meeting she went to her office to check her messages. She was busy rearranging her calendar when the phone buzzed,

"Ms. James?" Her assistant called over the speaker phone,

"Yes Beverly," Tricia answered,

"I have Ms. Anderson waiting on line one,"

"Go ahead and put her through," Tricia said, "McCall, Wesley, James & Associates, Patricia James speaking," Tricia said with a smile, it felt good to be back at work,

"Hey Lady, are you busy?" Maya asked,

"Nah, I'm just getting ready to go meet Phillip for lunch at The Peach, he wanted you to come too,"

"Tricia!" Maya said remembering what happened the last time she went to The Peach,

"Maya you can't keep running away from things. I wasn't sure if I should tell you about this, but now is just a good a time as any!" Tricia said as she stared outside her office window at nothing in particular,

"What?" Maya asked,

"Iron's been asking Phillip about you,"

"For real?"

"Yep, Phillip called right before you did, y'all just running my poor lil' assistant crazy!" Tricia joked,

"That heffa' was already crazy!" Maya said,

"Maya stop it!" Tricia said almost falling out of her chair laughing, "So, are you coming or not?" Tricia asked,

"I'm going...I might as well," Maya said reluctantly,

"Well, I'll meet you there in about an hour," Tricia said,

"Alright chic," Maya said before hanging up the phone and calling Maurice,

"Hey Baby!" Maya gushed,

"Hey Baby Mama, how are you feeling this morning?" Maurice asked,

"I'm doing alright, after we left the movies, I came straight home and crashed,"

"I did too, I guess that flight took more out of me than I thought," Maurice said,

"Well, if you're not too tired, Phillip and Tricia invited me to The Peach for lunch, do you wanna go?" Maya asked,

"Yeah, but I'm gonna be a little late, I'm at the shop getting my locs retwisted, I should be done by twelve-thirty, that's okay with you?"

"That's fine," Maya said, she couldn't wait to see him again,

Maya walked into The Peach around noon, she spotted Phillip and Tricia sitting at a table in the corner and she walked over in their direction,"

"Hey Ms. Lady," Iron-Man said as he walked up behind her and wrapped his arms around Maya's waist, Maya jumped and spun around,

"Irony you have to stop doing that," Maya said as she turned to face him while gently removing his arms from her waist,

"My fault Ms. Lady, I just had to come over here and talk to you for a minute... did Phillip tell you I've been asking about you?" Iron-Man asked,

"Yeah, he told me," Maya smiled, "I have to admit, it took me by surprise," Maya said as she blushed and looked away,

"Well, I really just wanted to apologize to you for the other night," Iron-Man said, "I was just shocked, you know, I had all of this shit running around in my head about what would happen once I got back to Memphis, and then I finally get here and we're cuttin' up on the dance floor and you just blacked out on me, and that scared the hell out of me, and then Tricia started yelling about hurting the baby! Maaaane…that night was just wild! I didn't know how to feel!" Iron-Man admitted,

"I know, it was a crazy night," Maya said,

"You know you'll always be my girl," Iron-Man said with a smile,

"I know…" Maya said, knowing deep inside that there was a gigantic *BUT* coming,

"And I know the last time we talked, you told me you and Tony-B broke up, but to be honest with you, I'm not sure if I'm ready to handle being with you and you're carrying another man's baby," Iron-Man confessed, and Maya could tell he had given it a lot of thought,

"I can respect that Irony, and I really appreciate you for being honest with me," Maya said,

"We are still cool right?" Iron-Man asked, unsure of how Maya really felt about what he had just told her,

"Of course, we are, Irony!" Maya said with a big smile,

"Good, can I have a hug?"

"Sure!" Maya said as she opened her arms to hug him,

"Wait," Iron-Man said suddenly stepping back,

"What's wrong?" Maya asked,

"You're not gonna fall out on me again, are you?" Iron-Man said as he rubbed her belly,

"Boy! Give me a hug before I change my damn mind!" Maya joked, she hugged him tight, and he kissed her on the cheek, just as Maurice walked in, Maya's eyes lit up when she saw him, but her face dropped when he turned on his heels and walked right back outside, he was almost at his truck when Maya came running up behind him,

"Maurice, wait!" Maya called out, causing him to stop in his tracks and turn around, "Why are you leaving?" Maya asked as she tried to catch her breath,

"You got one too many irons in the fire for me Maya, so go ahead and have your lil' fun," Maurice said as cool as a cucumber,

"I thought you said that you trusted me?" Maya asked with tears forming in her eyes,

"I do, but this time I saw the shit with my own eyes!" Maurice said,

"What exactly did you see that was so bad, I don't get it Maurice," Maya said trying to decide whether to be angry or hurt,

"Don't even try it Maya, I saw you," Maurice said as he turned to walk away,

"I can't believe this! Are you serious?" Maya asked in disbelief,

"Hell yeah, I'm serious!" Maurice answered a little louder than he intended to,

"Maurice!" Maya said, choosing hurt, over anger,

"What Maya!" Maurice said, and it was obvious that he had chosen anger,

"Irony and I are just friends! We have been friends for years, and that was just a friendly hug!" Maya explained,

"That's what you tell me," Maurice said not believing a word she just said,

"Maurice, I need you to trust me," Maya pleaded,

"I do Maya, but I don't wanna play games, I'm putting a lot on the line by even being with you and I need you to be sure and very sure who it is that you want!"

"I am sure! I knew who I wanted even before we left Trinidad!" Maya explained,

"I just can't deal with games, Maya, I just can't" Maurice said, and Maya could tell that he was dead serious,

"I'm not playing games with you Maurice, are we gonna go back in there or not?"

"Alright, let's go back in, but it better not be no shit!" Maurice said as he stormed back in the restaurant like a soldier ready for battle,

When Maya and Maurice walked back in, Iron-Man looked concerned,

"Is everything all right?" He asked Maya,

"Yeah, everything's fine, Maurice, you know Irony," Maya said hoping that her introducing them would cool Maurice down a little bit,

"What's up Rece," Iron-Man said extending his hand,

"What's up?" Maurice nodded with his hands still in his pockets, he eyed Iron-Man up and down, ignoring his handshake as he sat at the table with Tricia and Phillip,

"Me and Maya go way back, like fat crayons and Elmer's glue, you know what I'm saying, I hope I didn't start no confusion," Iron-Man said, trying to lighten the situation,

"It's nothing, you're good," Maurice said paying attention to everything and everybody except Iron-Man,

"You know we're just friends, right?" Iron-Man reiterated,

"I know, she told me, no harm done," Maurice said as Tricia and Phillip sat there with their mouths open, "I'm hungry as hell, let's eat! Iron-Man, you can pull up a chair if you want," Maurice said sarcastically,

"Nah, five's a crowd, I just came over here to congratulate my gal-I mean my friend… Uhmm… Congratulations Maya on your pregnancy, I guess I'll see you around... I mean later," Iron-Man said nervously, he was worried about Maya and he didn't want to cause any more confusion for her,

"Alright Irony, you take care," Maya said, "Maurice, you're a trip!" Maya said after Irony left,

"I was just trying to see something," Maurice said with a smirk,

"So, did you see it?" Maya asked with a smile, his jealousy turning her on,

"Yeah, I did," Maurice said with that same super cool tone to his voice,

"Well good, so can we eat now?" Maya asked,

"We sure can," Maurice said as he eyed the menu, things were quiet and tense as they ate their meal, Tricia and Maya suddenly excused themselves and went to the bathroom leaving the guys at the table,

"Girl!" Maya said when she and Tricia made it inside the bathroom,

"I know!" Tricia said,

"I thought Rece was gonna cut up!" Maya said,

"Shit, I did too!" Tricia said relieved,

"Why didn't you tell me that Irony was gonna be here?" Maya asked,

"I told you he had been asking about you! How in the hell did Rece know you were here?"

"I told him to meet us here, but he told me he was gonna be late, he was at the shop getting his locs twisted,"

"That was crazy as hell!" Tricia said,

"Too crazy! I'm so glad that me and Irony decided to be just friends!"

"I hope he still wants to be friends with your ass after today!" Tricia joked,

"I do too...but I'll smooth it over with him later," Maya said,

After the girls left, Phillip decided to break the ice and engage Maurice in conversation,

"My friend Nigel owns this restaurant, and he wants to throw the girls a surprise Welcome Home party tonight, I hope you guys hadn't made any plans," Phillip said,

"No, we hadn't made any," Maurice said,

"Cool, can I count on you to get Maya back here around eight o'clock?"

"Yeah, I can do that, hey Phillip?" Maurice asked,

"Yeah, what's up?" Phillip said,

"I didn't scare dude off, did I?" Maurice asked with a straight face,

"You know damn well you did!" Phillip said trying to hold his laughter,

"Good!" Maurice said,

"I like your style Rece, I like your style," Phillip said as they laughed,

"Hey Phil, be straight with me, are they really just friends?" Maurice asked,

"I'll tell you if you tell me who Tricia was with on that trip,"

"Tricia spent the whole time talking about you and the baby, what's his name, Darrion?" Maurice lied, he just didn't see a reason to hurt the guy, or Tricia for that matter,

"Yeah, that's his name, did she really?"

"Yep," Maurice said,

"Did she talk to any guys?" Phillip asked,

"Not that they didn't try, but she turned them all down,"

"Mane thank you! I was worried for a minute," Phillip admitted,

"Now tell me about dude and Maya,"

"Oh yeah, Maya and Iron-Man used to be best friends, he just got back in town not too long ago, she told him that she was pregnant, and he gave her a hug, and that's when you walked in,"

"So, she was telling the truth,"

"Yeah, she was, Mane I'm so glad I talked to you though, I was beginning to think my baby had stepped out on me!" Phillip said,

"Nah Man, Tricia would never do that to you," Maurice said, hoping that the ladies would hurry up and come out of the bathroom so that he wouldn't have to continue to lie to this man,

"I'm so glad to hear that," Phillip said with a relieved smile,

Maya and Tricia finally came back to the table,

"Phillip we gotta go and get Lil' Man!" Tricia said when she and Maya got back to the table,

"All right, we'll check y'all out later," Phillip said as he and Tricia left the restaurant,

Maurice and Maya sat at the restaurant and talked for a while,

"Maya I wanna take you out tonight," Maurice said,

"Where are we going?" Maya said,

"It's a surprise! I wanna take you to the mall and get us some matching outfits, something real classy,"

"Can you at least tell me where we're going?" Maya asked,

"Nope, it's a surprise," Maurice said,

***

Maya made it back to the house at about three-thirty, giving her plenty of time to take her braids down and shampoo and condition her hair. She wrapped it then put on her bonnet dryer and fell asleep. The phone rang and woke her up,

"Hello!" Maya said with an attitude,

"Hey Lil' Mama, I see you wasn't trying to call me and let me know you made it back in town,"

"Linda! What's going on My Lady Bug!" Maya said, she was glad to hear from her friend, they had a lot to catch up on,

"Girl! I'm so glad y'all are back, I got so much shit to tell you!" Linda said,

"What girl?' Maya said, excited to hear some juicy gossip,

"Well first of all, you ain't gonna believe this shit, but guess who Tony-B's punk ass was messin' with, when y'all was together!" Linda said,

"Who?" Maya asked, but she really didn't want to hear anything else about Tony and Torya,

"You know that girl he works with, the one who always comes to his parties, the tall, skinny one with the short blonde hair, what's her name?" Linda asked,

"Wait, Cathy?" Maya asked not believing what Linda was saying,

"Yep! That's her, that funky skank!" Linda said,

"Girl you are lying to me!" Maya said before she could catch herself,

"No, I'm not, I overheard Chris telling somebody on the phone that Tony-B was buck wild for bangin' them gals out there in the shed, and then bringing them back in the house like ain't shit happened," Linda said,

"Girl, you are lying!" Maya said, she was in shock,

"Naw Boo! If it's a lie, Chris told it! He said that Tony-B had Earl's cousin's nasty ass up in there right before all that drama went down between them and he knew that you and Tricia were in the house and wouldn't be coming out no time soon, and according to Chris, he had Cathy up in there at Larry's party, and some girl that you used to work with, a Sharon, a Sherry, a Shelia, or something like that, last weekend at Earl's birthday party when you were out of town! And I saw it for myself that time because I sure in the hell was looking!" Linda shamelessly admitted,

"You couldn't be talkin' about Sherry!" Maya said in disbelief,

"Ain't she the girl who used to work with you?" Linda asked,

"Yeah!"

"She got a real low haircut and bright red hair, kinda thick with big hips?" Linda asked, trying to make sure,

"Hell yeah!" Maya said,

"Then that's her!" Linda said,

"I can't believe this!"

"Girl, since you left, Tony-B been buck motherfucking wild!"

"I ain't surprised," Maya said with almost no emotion,

"They act like they straight, but Chris talks about him like a dog ever since they got into it," Linda confessed,

"I figured that," Maya said with a smirk,

"Yeah, and now, everything's coming out," Linda continued, "I just be listening whenever he thinks I ain't. Chris says that Tony-B is drinking like a fish, and I overheard Chris telling somebody that he thinks Tony-B is on that powder too!"

"Wait! Are you talking about cocaine?" Maya asked concerned,

"Yep! A dude that Chris knows said that he serves Tony-B that nose powder on the regular! I didn't want to believe it, but the way he's been acting, I don't know...and what's even more tripped out, at Earl's party, last Saturday...Oh yeah, before I forget! I think Tony-B and Rece fell out or something because he threw Rece a Welcome Home party last night, and Girl, Rece didn't even show up!" Linda added,

"Really?" Maya asked pretending not to know what actually happened,

"Yeah, and like I was saying, what tripped me out last week was, I went to Earl's party and I was in the kitchen getting me a beer, right? Guess who was in the kitchen, the same kitchen that me and Trish helped you decorate, and the bitch was just prancing around, wasn't cooking shit, just prancing around," Linda said, and Maya could just feel the disgust in her voice,

"Let me guess..." Maya said as she rolled her eyes to the ceiling,

"You ain't gotta guess, shit I'm gone tell you!" Linda said, "That stankin' ass heifer Torya, Earl's bitch ass cousin!"

"I am not surprised," Maya said, her tone was dry as the Sahara Desert,

"Girl Yeah! She was prancing around the kitchen, trying to act like you and everything!" Linda said as Maya chuckled, "Then she had the nerve to come up to me when I was sitting on the couch and ask me if she could get me anything, I told that bitch before I knew it that if she didn't *get* the hell out of my face, that I was gonna beat her ass! I don't care whose girlfriend she's supposed to be, I still don't like her!" Linda said,

"You're a fool Linda!" Maya said, she couldn't help but to laugh,

"I'm serious! I don't need her all up in my face like we cool! Ooh! And I forgot to tell you that them bitches got into it real bad last week while you were gone!"

"Who?" Maya asked, and suddenly the conversation was becoming a little more interesting,

"Girl, Torya and Cathy! But I have to admit, it was kinda my fault," Linda confessed,

"Your fault? I don't understand," Maya said, thoroughly confused,

"Well, you know I can be downright evil, when I wanna be, right?" Linda asked,

"Yeah, I know..." Maya said hesitantly,

"So, girl let me tell you what the hell I did," Linda said, trying her best to hold back a hearty laughter,

"I'm listening," Maya said, knowing her ears were in for a treat,

"Okay, so I found Torya's cell phone number in Chris' phone, right?"

"You what!?!" Maya said, thoroughly confused,

"Hold on! Let me finish before you say anything!" Linda interrupted, "Yeah, you heard me right, he had that bitch's number in his phone, they tried it, but check out what I did," Linda said, and Maya could just feel the mischief dripping from her voice,

"What did you do Linda?" Maya asked, not really sure if she was ready for the answer,

"Well for one, I star sixty-nined the bitch and played like I was Cathy, I changed my voice and everything!" Linda chuckled, "I told her that I was fucking her man, and that I fucked him in the shed and that I've been in the house several times and I made it a point to describe his bedroom in detail, and to make it even worse, I told her that I was gonna keep fucking him and that we've had sex several times in his office at work, and that I was gonna take him from her and kick her out and kick her ass on sight if she had anything to say about it!" Linda was beside herself with laughter at this point, she could barely get her words out,

"You didn't!" Maya said, this juicy gossip was making her tingle on the inside,

"Yes, the hell I did! Oh, back to what I was saying, so after that, Big Bad Torya took her ass up to Tony-B's job and cut a funky shine, Honey!" Linda sniggled,

"She did what!?!" Maya said, she was so outdone that she spoke in slow motion,

"Yeah, she took her ass up there, personally I didn't think the shaky bitch had it in her, but yeah she did," Linda said smiling,

259

"You are lying!" Maya said,

"Nope! And when Chris told me about it, I acted like I didn't know shit! And what tripped me out the most is that Chris told me that Torya went all the way down there to Tony-B's job and as soon as she saw Cathy, she just sprung on her!" Linda said, she could barely contain her laughter,

"She what!" Maya said, this gossip was way juicier than she could've ever imagined,

"Yeah, and when Torya sprung on her, Cathy grabbed that lil' bitch by the neck and beat the breaks off of her! They say Cathy mopped that whole office with her and tried to hit her over the head with a computer monitor and everything, they say that security had to come in and snatch Cathy up and drag her outside to cool off! Girl, they say she straight snapped!" Linda said, laughing so hard that she was out of breath,

"I can't believe what I'm hearing!" Maya chuckled,

"Girl believe it! And security also had to help Torya's ass up off the floor!" Linda said, her laughter hearty, "How you gonna march up to somebody's job and get your ass tore up cat raggedy, not once but twice over a dude who is supposed to be all yours, and by two different women! Girl! I laughed all day on that one! Tony-B was so heated that his voice was trembling when he was over here telling Chris about it, and I was in the back room eavesdropping and laughing my ass off! And on top of that, Cathy's dumb ass got fired!" Linda said, still laughing uncontrollably,

"She got fired?" Maya asked,

"Hell yeah! Dumb bitch!" Linda said, "And it wasn't even because of the fight, it was because after the fight they told her to go home for the day to get herself together, but no... instead of doing that, that silly ass girl snuck back into the building through some rear entrance and stormed into the conference room where Tony-B was having a meeting and cussed his ass plum out and tried to fight him in front of some important Big Wigs! Can you believe that shit?" Linda chuckled,

"Ooh that's so sad!" Maya admitted,

"Yeah, she splashed a glass of water in his face and sailed an office phone at his head and it missed him by an inch!" Linda said, she was laughing hysterically by now,

"Girl... I am just... I don't even know what to say..." Maya confessed, trying her best not to laugh,

"Hold up, let me tell you this and then I'll let you get back to whatever it is that you were doing, because this took the cake right here..." Linda said, trying to give Maya time to digest everything before telling her the juiciest part,

"Okay, I'm listening..." Maya said as she sat on the edge of her seat,

"Chris told me that Tony-B was so mad and embarrassed about Torya coming up there to his job, and starting all of that confusion, that when he got home, she got up in his face and he kicked her ass too!" Linda said,

"You are lying!" Maya said, her chest thumping,

"Naw, I'm so serious! Now when have you ever known Tony-B to put his hands on any woman?" Linda asked,

"Never!" Maya said, she couldn't believe what she was hearing,

"That's what I said, and I've known him way longer than you have! Girl, Tony-B has changed girl, and not for the better, he was always whorish, and he loves to show out, I mean we all know that...but he was never a fighter, I know we've had our differences, but even when me and Chris would get into it, he would stand in front of me and tell Chris that he better not put his hands on me," Linda said,

"This shit is way too much for me," Maya said as she fanned her face, "I'm so glad that I'm out of that shit! They can have it, I'm so glad that I moved on!" Maya said relieved,

"Wait! You said you moved on? With who? Do I know him?" Linda asked, as Maya laughed.

"You might," Maya teased,

"Who is it girl?"

"I'm not telling, you'll see soon enough," Maya teased,

"Girl I can't wait to see who it is!" Linda said,

"See you later with your messy ass!" Maya teased,

"Yep! That's me! Bye Girl!" Linda laughed before she hung up,

Maya's hair was still kind of damp, so she spent another hour under the dryer. Maurice picked the perfect matching outfits for him and Maya. He chose a wine-colored wide leg jumpsuit with a long shimmering sheer jacket for Maya to wear. He even bought the matching wine-colored shoes trimmed with silver beads. Maya accentuated her outfit with a silver beaded choker with matching silver hoop earrings, and Maya found a matching silver beaded handbag to bring everything together. Maurice chose wine-colored slacks and a plain white dress shirt. He found the perfect wine-colored tie with a hint of silver. Maya was checking herself out in the mirror when the phone rang,

"Hello?"

"Hey Baby Momma, you ready?"

"Yeah Maurice, just doing my last-minute things,"

"I'll be there in about twenty minutes," Maurice said,

"Can you at least tell me where we're going?" Maya asked,

"Okay, we're going to The Peach for Reggae Night," Maurice confessed, and Maya smiled wide,

"See you soon," Maya said, and after they hung up the phone, it rung again,

"Hello?"

"Hey Skank! What you got up for tonight?" Tricia asked,

"None of your business," Maya teased,

"That's okay, Phillip is taking me out tonight," Tricia teased her back,

"We had the same thing in mind, Maurice is taking me out too," Maya said with a smile,

"Where are y'all going?" Tricia asked,

"He's taking me to The Peach," Maya said,

"Hold on, I think that's where we going too, hold on, let me check...Phillip?" Tricia called out,

"Yeah?" Phillip answered in the background,

"Aren't you taking me to The Peach tonight?"

"Yeah, why?"

"Maya and Maurice said that they're going too,"

"Ask them what time they are going," Phillip asked,

"Tell him that Maurice is on his way to pick me up now,"

"She said Rece is on his way to get her now," Tricia repeated,

"Tell them to wait on us," Maya heard Phillip say in the background,

"How about if we come over there when he gets here, and we'll all leave together," Maya suggested,

"She said they're coming over here, and we can all leave together," Tricia yelled out to Phillip,

"All right then girl, I'll see you in a little bit," Maya said,

"Hey Maya, what are you wearing?" Tricia asked,

"It's a surprise," Maya teased before hanging up on Tricia,

***

"Ooh! Look at you!" Tricia said feeling Maya's jacket,

"We did a lil' something," Maya said smiling,

"Y'all are sharp but check us out!" Tricia bragged; she was dressed in a fitted Navy-blue thigh length shimmery dress with matching shoes. Phillip was dressed in matching Navy-blue slacks, with a crispy white button down with Navy-blue and white Stacy-Adams,

"Ya'll think ya'll are doing something!" Maya said smiling,

"Yeah, we did a lil' something-something too," Phillip said popping his collar and spinning on his heels like a male runway model,

262

"Boy c'mon here and let's go" Tricia said as everyone burst into laughter,

When they walked into the club, it was dark, but the music was playing loud,

"We must be early or something?" Phillip said. "I thought there were a lot of cars outside,"

"WELCOME HOME!!!" Everybody jumped out and yelled as the lights popped on,

Tricia and Maya put their hands over their mouths as Phillip kissed them on the cheek, he also hugged Maurice and shook his hand. Maurice was kind of confused about it until he read the banner that read: *WELCOME HOME TRICIA, MAYA, AND MAURICE!*

"Aw Man!" Maurice said, totally humbled, "Man, I was not expecting this at all," Maurice said as he shook his head,

"Man, you're a part of the family now." Philip said,

Tricia and Maya were pleasantly surprised, but Maurice was in total shock, no one had ever done anything like this for him before,

"This is love right here Mane, this is love!" Maurice kept saying,

"Hey Heffa!" Linda said as she walked up sipping on a mixed drink, "You could've told me about you and Rece!"

"I didn't want it told, I wanted it showed!" Maya teased,

"Forget you wench!" Linda said with a smile,

Everybody was dancing and having a good time, but every now and then Maya would notice that people were staring at her and Maurice, and she even noticed a few people whispering and giggling, Maurice grabbed Maya and spun her around on the dance floor, then he leaned in and kissed her with so much passion that she trembled,

"I'm letting the world know tonight, Baby!" Maurice said as Maya stared at him in amazement, she was grinning so hard when she spotted Sherry peering at her out of the corner of her eye. Maya hugged and kissed Maurice again then turned around and waved at Sherry, who gave her a fake smile and a four-finger wave,

"You know she was sleeping with Tony too! They had sex out there in the shed," Maya said to Maurice,

Sherry's heart raced as she read Maya's lips,

"Really?!?" Maurice said, "How'd you find out?"

"Someone called and told me earlier, they say Torya and Cathy got into a fight at the job and Cathy got fired because of it," Maya continued,

"Maya, I have a confession," Maurice said with a sad look on his face, "I knew about it, but I just didn't wanna hurt you like that. I saw them going in the shed and I wanted to tell you so bad! I even knocked on the window, so you'd come out and hear them, but I changed my mind, I just didn't want to see you hurt like that," Maurice confessed,

"I remember that!" Maya said, "But honestly I'm not mad at you, I can understand why you didn't tell me,"

"I sure hope so, I wasn't trying to keep anything from you, I just didn't know how to tell you," Maurice continued,

"I understand, but I'm over that, I don't care what or who he does. I'm just glad that I have a real man now and I don't have to worry about stuff like that anymore,"

"You got that right!" Maurice said with a smile,

Maya looked over to where Sherry was, and just as she anticipated, Sherry was long gone, Maya smirked as she and Maurice went back to the dance floor, and cut a rug as the DJ played Maya's favorite song,

"This song is dedicated to the Guests of Honor, Ms. Lady and Mr. Maurice! Ms. Lady shake that thang Girl!" the DJ said over the microphone, Maya was having the time of her life, and Maurice was grinning so hard that his face ached. She had no idea that he could dance like that, he was truly giving her a run for her money, they danced even harder as the crowd gathered around and began to cheer them on,

"Go Maya! Go Maurice! Go Maya! Go Maurice!" the crowd chanted,

"Uh Oh! Dance Contest!" The DJ yelled over the microphone. "This next song is dedicated to Phillip's Guest of Honor, the prettiest girl in here, Ms. Lady he made me say that! Phil and Trish, I know y'all ain't gonna let Rece and Maya cut y'all heads like that!" he joked,

Maya had never danced so hard in her life. When they finished dancing, they went to the bar to get something to drink,

"Two cranberry juices please," Maurice told the bartender,

"Look at you!" Maya said wiping Maurice's head with a napkin,

"Well would you look at the fucking Wonder Twins..." a voice behind her said, and Maya knew that voice from anywhere, "Ain't this some bullshit right here, and right up under my nose too,"

Maya and Maurice both turned around at the same time,

"What are you doing here Tony?" Maya asked, she was so disgusted by his presence that she began to feel nauseous,

"What do you mean? This is a public place...," Tony-B said with a shrug, "But actually, I just came here to see this bullshit for myself, but it's cool though, come outside and holler at me for a minute," Tony-B said gritting his teeth,

"Don't you see I'm busy!" Maya spat, remembering what Linda had told her earlier,

"I don't give a fuck how busy you are, you gone talk to me, or I'm gonna cut the fuck up in this bitch!" Tony-B said still gritting his teeth,

"Go ahead, cut up, but I ain't going no damn where, especially not with you!" Maya said fanning him off,

Tony-B reached out to snatch Maya by her arm, but Maurice stepped in front of her, "Didn't you hear her say that she was busy?" Maurice said as he stepped up to Tony-B,

"And who the hell are you supposed to be, dudes kill me trying to save a motherfucker! This ain't got shit to do with you, Rece, but what's up?" Tony-B said as he took a step forward so that he and Maurice stood toe to toe,

"Look at this killer! You tough now, huh, Tony-Beethoven?" Maurice teased,

"You better be glad you Larry's brother!" Tony-B said as he took a step back,

"You wouldn't do shit if I wasn't!" Maurice said with a smirk,

"Ain't nobody scared of you Rece," Tony-B said,

"I never said you was, but the lady *said* she was busy! No, let me correct that, *MY LADY said* she was busy!" Maurice said,

"And who you supposed to be, Captain Save'em?" Tony-B asked sarcastically,

"Yeah, that's me, bitch!" Maurice said with as much force as he could, "I'm whatever she needs me to be, just because you ain't man enough to take care of your business, don't mean I'm not gonna take care of mine!"

"I got your bitch! And fuck that, it's probably yours anyway!" Tony-B spat, his words digging into Maya's chest like a thousand daggers,

"Shit...if it ain't, it will be! Now what?" Maurice spat back,

"I ain't mad at you Rece, I didn't want it anyway, just like I don't want her ass! I got plenty of other bitches," Tony-B said with fake laughter,

"If that's the case, then why are you here?" Maya asked,

"Like I said, this is a public fucking place, I came here to have a good time, shit, and it's plenty of fine ass women up in here to keep a pimp like me entertained!" Tony-B said looking around and popping his collar,

"I guess your shed got a little too crowded for you, huh?" Maya said,

"What?" Tony-B asked with a frown,

"You heard me!" Maya said,

265

"Why in the fuck are you worried about what I do Maya, ain't you here with dude?" Tony-B asked with sarcastic laughter,

"I ain't worried, I just think it's pitiful," Maya spat,

"At least I ain't with your childhood friend!" Tony-B shot back,

"My true friends wouldn't have your ass!" Maya said,

"Well, I don't know about that!" Tony-B said looking around,

"I know about Sherry, and all the others too, but that don't make you a player, that just makes you a sorry ass excuse of a man!" Maya said,

"How you gonna call me sorry when you was fucking me and him at the same time! We doin' the same damn thing, Lil' Mama!" Tony-B reasoned,

"We were through before I went on my trip, and I started talking to him while I was on my trip, how is that doing the same thing?" Maya asked,

"You a damn lie, I bet you don't even know who the fuck your baby daddy is! Is it me, is it him, or is it him?" Tony-B asked as he pointed at some random guy who walked by,

"I'm not like you Tony-B, and I know who I'm pregnant by! And nobody in the world regrets it more than I do!" Maya said with tears moistening her eyes,

"You kill me acting like you're such a fucking victim, like you all sophisticated, like you so high-society, and so above everybody, but you wasn't shit when I met you, no better than any other bitch up in here!" Tony-B said,

"That's funny, and I wish I had the time, or that I was even interested in standing here arguing with you Tony, but I'm not, I'm having a blast, correction... me and my New Man, are having a blast and I'm not gonna let you ruin my night, Come on Baby, let's go dance!" Maya said as she grabbed Maurice by the hand and led him back to the dance floor,

"Oh, hell naw! It ain't gonna go down like that!" Tony-B said fuming as he stood there and thought about what had just happened, he suddenly made a bee-line to the dance floor,

"Come on Tony-B, you already did what you came here to do," Larry said, as he stepped in front of him and tried to pull him away, but Tony-B jerked away from him,

"Don't nobody walk the fuck away from me, I do all the hiring and firing around this bitch!" Tony-B said as he stormed up to Maya who was still on the dance floor with Maurice,

"Hey Rece, it ain't gotta be no animosity, shit, we both can have the bitch! It ain't no fun if the Fellas can't have none!" Tony-B joked,

266

"Tony-B, mane you going too far, Ms. Lady ain't never disrespected you like that! You spent three years with this woman, and you can't treat her no better than that?" Phillip asked,

"Fuck that! I know how to treat a Lady when I see one! But since she wanna fuck my Pat'nas, you might as well let us all hit!" Tony-B spat,

Maurice had enough, he ran up to Tony-B and rabbit punched him in his right jaw, sending him into the wall,

"Naw mane!" Phillip shouted and grabbed Maurice and pulled him back,

"Let me go Phil!" Maurice said calmly as he struggled to get a hold of Tony-B,

"Naw mane, I can't let you do nothing stupid, he ain't worth it!" Phillip reasoned as Maurice struggled,

"What I look like fighting over a fucking broad, you can have that fat bitch!" Tony-B said as he stood to his feet and dusted himself off,

"Keep on running your mouth!" Maurice said as he broke free and swung at Tony-B again, but Phillip and Nigel grabbed him and wouldn't let him go,

"Ya'll ain't gotta hold him, shit let him go! He hit like a lil' bitch anyway, and since he wanna act so tough, I got something for him and that ho' in my motherfuckin' trunk," Tony-B said confidently,

"Whatever you got out there, if you pull it, you better use it, with your shaky ass!" Maurice said struggling to get free,

"Naw mane, I'm not gonna let you do nothing stupid," Phillip repeated as he and Nigel held Maurice back with all their might,

"How you gone pull a pistol on a pregnant female?" Somebody in the crowd yelled out,

"And how a pimp gone come up in a club and get sprung on? Mane that shit weak as fuck!" Someone else in the crowd hollered out, and everyone began to laugh,

"I ain't fighting over no broad, it's too many of them out here! So, fuck both of them! As a matter of fact, fuck all y'all! Anybody can get it!" Tony-B said as he turned on his heels and walked toward the door, Maya could tell that he was embarrassed,

"Hey Tony-B, let me holla at you for a minute," Nigel said as he let Maurice go and patted him on the shoulder, before following Tony-B to the front entrance of the club,

"What the fuck do you want!" Tony-B snapped as Nigel caught up to him as he stood by the front entrance,

"I'm only gonna say this one time…" Nigel said as he held up one finger, his face like stone, "the next time you come up in my club with that foolishness, you bet'not leave your pistol outside in the trunk, with your bitch ass…" Nigel said calmly before he shoved Tony-B outside of the club and closed the door behind him,

As Tony-B stood outside, one of the armed security guards looked at him and shook his head in pity, "Gone and go home, and sleep that shit off, Lil' Dude, ain't no need in doing nothing stupid, cause this right here ain't what you want…" the guard said to Tony-B as he raised his shirt to reveal his service revolver,

**

"Gone out there with your boy!" Maurice said to Larry, after Tony-B left,

"Mane, fuck you! You still wrong!" Larry said before walking off, and Maurice just shook his head as he watched his brother walk out of the club behind Tony-B,

"Girl, are you okay?" Tricia said as she rushed over to Maya,

"Yeah, I'm fine," Maya said, her chest was still thumping from all of the excitement,

"I was over there dancing, I didn't even know anything was going on, until I saw people rushing over here, I knew he was an ass, but I didn't know he was like that!" Tricia said,

"Now everybody got a chance to see him for who he is," Maya said, her feelings were still hurt,

"Why didn't you tell me about him and Sherry, were they really doing it outside in the shed?" Tricia asked,

"I just found out myself, and from what I hear they were," Maya answered blankly, still trying to gather her thoughts and emotions,

"Ms. Lady!" The DJ yelled over the microphone, and Maya spun around, "What you gonna do, stew or mildew? Y'all know, ain't no standing around on my dance floor!" The DJ teased,

"Play my song again, and you'll see what I'll do!" Maya yelled back, deciding not to let Tony-B ruin her night,

"Well let's do this then!" The DJ yelled back over the microphone,

Maya's song began to blare through the speakers, and pretty soon, everyone forgot all about Tony-B and his drama, and they had a blast,

**

268

Tony-B was furious, he zoomed down the street and sped into his driveway then jumped out of his truck and slammed the door,

"She better not say shit to me!" Tony-B growled as he walked into the house,

"Tony, is that you?" Torya asked from the couch,

"Who the fuck else would it be?" Tony-B snapped, as he walked in and plopped down on the opposite end of the sofa,

"I was just trying to make sure," Torya said with an attitude,

"I just bet you were, you been having other dudes in my house?" He asked, his eyes turned into red and gray slits as he peered at her,

"Don't start that mess, if you were really worried about me being with somebody else then you wouldn't do the things that you do, and you'd stay at home sometimes!" Torya said as she rolled her eyes at him,

"Torya, I've had a real fucked up night and I ain't for this shit!" Tony-B warned as he rested his head in his hands,

"Whatever! And while you're questioning me, I need to be asking you if you had anybody else out there in that damn shed, that's what I need to be asking," she said with an attitude,

"Leave me alone Torya!" Tony-B warned once again,

"I wasn't messing with you, you came in the house talking crazy to me!" She said,

"Okay, it's over with, so shut the hell up!" Tony-B yelled as he fanned her off,

"Who are you talking to like that! You must think I'm Maya or Cathy or somebody!"

"Right now, I don't give a fuck who you are, I just want you to shut the hell up!" Tony-B yelled,

"You do this all of the time! You get mad at those hoes out there in the streets, then you come home and try to take it out on me!" Torya whined,

"You just know everything, don't you?" Tony-B asked calmly, and Torya knew what that meant so she tried to back pedal,

"I didn't say that I knew everything," she said as she lowered both her voice and her head,

"No, you think you do, you think you know every damn thing," Tony-B said as he slid closer to her on the sofa,

"No, I don't, you just want to start an argument with me," Torya reasoned,

"And what gets me is if you knew half the shit that you claim you know, then you'd know how to keep your damn man at home," Tony-B said even calmer, which got Torya's attention, she had seen him like that before and it made her nervous,

"You're gonna do what you want to do anyway, Tony-B, Maya was your little maid and you still messed off on her, that's why I'm here," Torya said before she could catch herself,

"You better shut up before I slap the hell out of you Torya!" Tony-B said, his voice was still calm,

"I'm not your fucking punching bag! You never put your hands on Maya or Cathy, and you're not gonna keep putting your hands on me!" Torya said as she stood with her hands on her hips,

"What did you say?" Tony-B asked, raising one eyebrow, and wisdom should've instructed Torya to be quiet, but for some reason she felt brave tonight,

"I said, I'm not your--" and before she could finish her sentence, Tony leapt up and slapped her so hard that she flipped over the arm of the sofa,

"I told you to shut the hell up!" Tony-B roared,

"I hate you! I hate you!" Torya said as she sat on the floor holding her face,

"You just keep on talking," Tony-B warned,

"You said that you would never put your hands on me again!" Torya blubbered as she stood to her feet,

"And you act like you don't understand it when I tell you to shut the fuck up!" Tony-B said calmly,

"You still didn't have to put your hands on me!" She reasoned,

"Are you're still talking?" Tony-B asked,

"Tony-B, I gave up everything for you and you treat me like I'm nothing, you wouldn't be doing me like this if I hadn't lost the baby!" Torya pouted as she plopped down on the recliner beside the sofa still holding her face,

"See, this is what I mean, you won't shut the fuck up!" Tony-B roared, and Torya ran into the bedroom and dived across the bed, he could hear her crying all the way in the living room. He let out a long sigh and poured himself a glass of gin and sat on the couch,

"Fuck y'all! Fuck all of y'all!" He said emptying his glass and pouring another, Tony-B wanted to sleep on the couch but he couldn't get Maya out of his mind, *"She did look good tonight,"* he thought as his body reacted, he found himself aroused with nowhere to go, *"I wonder why Cathy and Sherry aren't answering their phones, oh well, forget them too!"* he thought as he debated going out again since it was still early,

"Why in the hell am I trying to go out and find somebody to fuck on, when I got in-house ass in there! She lives in my house, and eats my damn food, she gone give me some tonight even if I have to take it!" Tony-B thought as he walked into the bedroom, Torya was laying under the covers with her back to him,

"Baby, Baby..." Tony-B said as he undressed, he was trying to be as nice as he could, but Torya ignored him and pretended to be asleep. "I'm sorry Baby, I didn't mean it, I won't ever do that again, I promise." Tony-B said as he lifted the covers gently and slid in the bed beside her. Torya laid stiff and still, "I know you hear me, I'm sorry, I just get so crazy when I think about you being with somebody else, I love you Baby, them bitches out there don't mean nothing to me," he said, trying his best to sound sincere,

"He loves me, I knew it! That's why he acts the way he do!" Torya thought, her body still stiff to his touch,

"Baby, you forgive me?" he asked as he slid his hand under her shorts, her body was still stiff to his touch, and he knew that he would have to work hard if he was to satisfy the monster that had grown in his pants and was now roaming free beneath the covers. He turned her over so that she faced him, she still had her eyes closed and was still pretending to be asleep,

"Okay, okay, I know what you want," Tony-B said as he lowered his face beneath the covers, he couldn't help but to see the smirk on her face before covering his head with the comforter,

"He must be really sorry this time!" Torya's emotions told her, right before an explosive climax forced her to arch her back and throw her head back into the pillow. Tony-B was so excited that he mounted her and thrust himself inside of her with so much force that he literally knocked the wind out of her. He pounded and pounded her insides until he finally moaned loudly and rolled off of her and turned his back to her,

"Forget Maya and Cathy, he's in love with Me, not them, and they can't have him!" Torya thought as she smiled and closed her eyes, just as she began snoring softly, Tony sat up with his back against the headboard,

"Hey!" he said as he nudged her,

"Yes?" she whispered,

"You sleep?" he asked,

"Almost, why?"

"Why!?! You know I ain't trying to let you go to sleep without taking care of me!" he said as he slid down so that he laid on his back with his arms folded behind his head,

"What are you talking about Tony-B?"

"Don't play with me, you know what I want!" Tony-B said as he grabbed her by the hair and shoved her head down to his crotch area, inserting himself inside of her mouth then forcing himself down her throat hard enough to make her gag several times,

The next morning Tony-B woke up earlier than usual, "Baby, Baby?" he said as he nudged her again,

"Uh, huh?" she stirred,

"I want you to get up and go fix me something to eat,"

"Okay," Torya said as she jumped out the bed without thinking and almost fell to her knees in pain, she was so raw, and the stabbing pain in the bottom of her stomach was almost unbearable. She winced silently as she headed into the bathroom to investigate the damages,

"Please, please, please, please, please!" She prayed silently as she turned on the bathroom light, "Oh good, it's just a little swollen, nothing a little make-up can't cover," she said as she examined the side of her face, "I'll just wear my hair down today," she reasoned,

Torya was so glad that her face wasn't bruised that she forgot, and sat down too fast to use the bathroom, she puffed her cheeks with air and breathed out slowly to keep from screaming, as she tried to calm herself but she leaped up suddenly when her pee stung like acid, "Oh shit, that hurts!" she said, the pain forcing her to remember last night after she pleased him and dozed off, Tony-B pushed her onto her stomach then proceeded to, as he called it, *'Try something new,'* Torya tried to wriggle away from him when she realized what he was trying to do, "Tony please, stop! You're hurting me!" she pleaded,

"You're gonna like it once I get it in, I promise!" he said as he held her down,

"Tony-B you're hurting me! Please stop!" She begged,

"Relax Baby, I'll go slow," he said still trying to enter her as Torya screamed and buried her face into the pillow,

"Tony-B please!" she pleaded,

"Shhhh...just relax! You love me, don't you?" he asked as he licked and kissed her spine, he shoved his fingers inside of her soaking wet vagina and then used her wetness to try and loosen her tight, dry hole with his fingers,

"Yes!" she screamed,

"Then just concentrate on that!" he instructed,

"Okay," Torya whimpered as she buried her face into the

pillow and tried to block out the excruciating pain that felt like he was literally ripping her apart, and once Tony-B finally forced himself inside of her completely, he inserted his fingers back inside of her and began massaging her love button in an attempt to try and distract her, entering her tight hole slowly at first, but then he began to jab in and out viciously becoming more and more aggressive with each thrust, she panted like a thirsty puppy as he suddenly gripped her hair and yanked her head back hard,

"Who do you belong to, bitch?" he growled into her ear,

"You Baby, you," she wept,

"And whose ass is this?" he growled,

"Yours!" she pleaded,

"Damn right!" he growled again and pounded her even harder, Torya remembered how relieved she was when he finally reached his peak. She winced as she wiped herself gently from behind, and when she looked at the tissue, she covered her mouth in shock when she saw the spots of red,

"I wonder if Maya ever had to endure this shit!" she thought as she flushed the toilet and washed her hands,

"Are you gonna spend all day in that damn bathroom or are you gonna fix me something to eat, hell I'm hungry!" Tony-B yelled from the bedroom,

"He so crazy, let me go and fix my man a big, big breakfast, before he starts clowning again," Torya said, blushing as she walked stiffly to the kitchen,

Tony-B sat up in the bed and laughed as he thought about how many times he'd almost called Torya, Maya last night, *"Man, I'll never let another woman get over on me! It's my world from now on! I can't believe that bitch let me fuck her in the ass like that, I'd always wanted to try that shit! Maya would've never let me do that to her!"* he thought as he grabbed the remote and turned on the television,

***

Maya and Maurice sat out on his screened in porch draped in a blanket, she rested her back against his chest as he wrapped his arms and legs around her and rested his chin on her shoulder as they watched the stars,

"Maya, I wanna apologize for the way I acted, I lost it, but I shouldn't have acted that way, especially not in front of my Lady," he said, and tingles waltzed up and down Maya's spine,

"I just wanna forget about the whole thing," Maya said not wanting the thought to ruin the moment,

"Okay then Baby, it's forgotten," Maurice said with a smile,

They fell asleep gazing at the sparkling stars in the sky and woke to the sound of birds and the sun gleaming on their faces. Maya came home late Sunday afternoon and spent the rest of the evening unpacking and getting ready for her first day back to work. She was just about to put her cell phone on the charger when it rang,

"Hello?"

"Hey!"

"What's up Tricia, you ready to go back to work, tomorrow?"

"Hell no, but I do miss it," Tricia confessed,

"Same here," Maya said,

"So how are you feeling?" Tricia asked,

"I'm okay, just a little tired, but that's because I stayed up late talking to Maurice,"

"I just bet you did!" Tricia teased,

"Not like that, Girl! We decided to wait. How are you and Phillip doing?"

"We're doing okay, but I just feel so guilty! I could've lost everything I had. Lil' Man was so glad to see me, he hugged me so tight, I just started crying!"

"Don't beat up on yourself Tricia, you didn't have sex with the man, you just spent time with him! Just appreciate what you have, Phillip's a good man and he really, really, loves you."

"Maya, I have to tell you something, it's been eating me up inside," Tricia's voice was trembling, and Maya could tell that she was about to cry,

"Tricia don't cry, you gonna make me cry!" Maya said, tearing up,

"I don't wanna make you cry, I just feel so bad! I haven't even prayed about it because I just feel so low!"

"Now that's just silly, Girl, God sees everything, even if I don't know, God knows it all! And still loves you, just repent and move on!"

"Maya I have to tell you this,"

"Okay Tricia, if you think that it'll make you feel better," Maya was stalling because she really didn't wanna know, she cared for Phillip almost as much as she did Tricia, and she would never wanna see him hurt,

"We kissed when we were in Trinidad, we didn't have

274

intercourse or anything, but he tried to go down on me and Lord knows I almost let him, but then I stopped and I didn't let it go any further, but it could have, I pushed him away though, I just couldn't go through with it. we ended up just lying in the bed holding each other. It was intense, and there was a lot of tension in the room, but I just couldn't do it, I hate I let it go as far as it did, and now I feel guilty as hell," Tricia said as tears met beneath her cheeks,

"When was this, the night before we left?" Maya asked,

"Yeah, I went too far Maya, I had no reason to do that! How can I say anything about Tony-B when I did the same thing?" Tricia asked through sobs,

"You and Tony-B are two entirely different people! Tricia forgive yourself and move on before your guilt costs you!" Maya warned,

"I'm trying to Maya, but it's eating me up inside! I've never done anything like this in my life! I'm so stupid!" Tricia whimpered,

"Tricia, you have to try, because I love both of you guys, and I don't wanna see either one of you hurt,"

"I love you too Maya, and thank you for being there for me, you tried to warn me, but I didn't listen," Tricia said through tears,

"What about all the times that you've been there for me!" Maya said through her own tears,

"I have to go and straighten up my face, Phillip will be home in a minute, and my eyes are all puffy and swollen," Tricia said wiping her eyes,

"Okay Tricia, call me back if you need to talk, and just think about what I said,"

"I will." Tricia hung up the phone and went to the bathroom, she was still sad, Phillip was her soul mate and she had never even thought about doing anything like that before. She splashed her face with cool water, but her tears kept flowing, her vision was blurred but she recognized the figure standing behind her in the mirror,

"Baby, what's wrong!" Phillip said as he turned her to face him and hugged her tight, "Tell me what's wrong!" he pleaded,

Tricia wanted to tell him badly, but the only thing that she could do is cry,

"Come in here and we'll sit down and talk about it, it can't be that bad," Phillip said as he held Tricia's hand and led her into the living room, he sat sideways on the couch and pulled her down in front of him so that her back rested against his chest, he wrapped his arms around her tightly, placing his chin on her collarbone as Tricia grabbed his hands and held them to her chest,

"If it'll make you feel better then cry all night, I ain't going nowhere, and when you get ready to talk Baby, then we'll talk," Phillip said,

Tricia didn't say anything, for over an hour, she couldn't, the only thing that she could do is cry,

"It's okay Baby, it's okay," Phillip said as he rubbed her shoulders and kissed her tear-stained face, "whatever it is, I'm sure we're gonna get through it," he assured her, Lil' Man started fussing in his sleep so Phillip got up and gave him his Teddy Bear and patted his back until he went back to sleep. He sat back on the couch beside Tricia, who was sitting up and wiping her tears,

"Are you ready to talk?" he asked,

"Yeah," she said,

"I'm listening,"

"I love you so much!" she said,

"I love you too Baby," Phillip said, but Tricia put her fingertips gently over his mouth and shook her head,

"I did something real stupid while I was in Trinidad," Tricia confessed,

"I'm listening,"

"I met someone, and I spent time with him," she continued,

"I know, the guy with the dreads that was in the door staring at you when I pulled up?" Phillip said,

"How did you know?" Tricia asked, she couldn't believe that he already knew,

"I got there early, and I saw you when y'all got off of the plane, you two were the last ones off, I had already went and got the car and came back by the time you saw me. I had a strange feeling that I couldn't shake," Phillip said, and Tricia could tell that this was hurting him,

"I'm so sorry!" Tricia blurted out,

"That's okay, you did say you just spent time with him, right?"

"Yeah, that's it, but I've never hid anything from you and I don't want to ever again," Tricia hesitated,

"I see..." Phillip said as he breathed out slowly, his eyes tearing, "Well, do you still love me?" he asked, bracing himself for the answer,

"Yes, with all my heart!" Tricia said,

"Is it something that I did to make you turn to him?"

Phillip asked,

"What? No! No! No!" Tricia said as she grabbed his hands and kissed them, trying her best to assure him,

"Then what was it?" he asked, his voice trembling,

"Honestly, I was so lonely and homesick over there, but please know that it was nothing that you've done, you're the perfect husband and I'm so fortunate to have a husband like you, I'm so sorry and I promise that if you forgive me, nothing like this will ever happen again,

"Just how far did it go?" Phillip asked, not really wanting to know the answer,

"Not far at all, we didn't have sex or anything like that, if that's what you're wondering," Tricia assured him,

"And if the situation was reversed, would you forgive me?" he asked, and Tricia could barely stand to look at him because she could see the hurt in his eyes,

"In a heartbeat Baby," she confessed,

"Okay then, I forgive you, and it's forgotten," he said as he kissed her hand and held it to his face,

"Just like that?" Tricia asked reluctantly,

"Baby, I've loved you since the first day I saw you, and I've been in love with you ever since, over ten years Tricia! That kind of love doesn't happen every day and you can't just throw people away because they make mistakes," Phillip said,

"I'm sorry, I'm so sorry!" Tricia said as tears flooded her eyes,

"Have you severed all ties with him?" Phillip asked,

"Yes, yes! You don't ever have to worry about that," Tricia assured him,

"Well then, it's over! Baby Girl, don't ever shut me out like that! I'm your husband and your best friend! I'll be there for you thick or thin, wrong or right! Whatever it is, no matter what, we can work it out, okay Baby?

"Okay, and I love you more now than I ever did!" Tricia said,

"You'd better! Now give Daddy his sugar!" Phillip said,

Tricia and Phillip laid on the couch and watched television until the wee hours in the morning,

"You are one in a million, you know that?" Tricia said,

"This is what I've been trying to tell ya!" Phillip said smiling, but Tricia knew her husband just as well as he knew her and no matter how he tried to hide it with smiles and laughter, she could still see the hurt in his eyes,

***

Maya woke up early, she was amazed at how quick she got ready for work, Time went so slow since she no longer had to get up early and fix Tony's breakfast and prepare his lunch,

"I wanna go out for breakfast!" Maya said to herself as she called Maurice,

"Heeey Baby Mama, you up already?"

"Yeah, up and dressed!" Maya laughed,

"Look at you, all early, what time do you have to be in?"

"Eight-thirty, I got a meeting first thing, what about you?"

"I'm off today, you know, Barber Shops are usually closed on Sundays and Mondays, I usually go to Harbor Town and take pictures by the river on my off days," he said

"That sounds interesting, Maya said,"

"Watching the sun rise and set on the Mississippi River is one of the most amazing things on the planet! What time do you get off?"

"Five, sometimes later depending on my workload,"

"Can I take you to work today?" he asked,

"Sure," Maya said smiling,

"Give me about twenty minutes. I wanna show you something," Maurice said,

Maurice and Maya went to Harbor Town and picked up two fruit salads and they fed each other fruit as they watched the sun rise, he snapped picture after picture of her in the park, he also gave Maya her first lesson on how to use his camera.

"Oh, it's almost eight o'clock, we gotta go!" Maya said after looking at her watch,

"Relax, I know a shortcut," Maurice smiled,

Maurice pulled up in front of Maya's job at exactly 8:15,

"Call me so I'll know what time to be here when you get off," he said as he kissed her on the cheek, Maya walked into work smiling, she spoke to her secretary as she handed her the day's messages. Sarah smiled back hurrying behind Maya, giving her the rundown on the day's workload. Maya grabbed the files from her desk and giggled as she thought of Maurice's smile, Sarah walked out of her office to begin her busy day as well,

"Ms. Anderson?" Sarah buzzed,

"Yes Sarah,"

"Mr. Bradford is on line two,"

"Okay, put him through, thanks," Maya said as she

rolled her eyes to the ceiling,

"Ms. Anderson speaking,"

"Hey Baby!"

"Don't you mean hey Fat Bitch?" Maya said sarcastically,

"You know I didn't mean any of that shit, I was just mad, that's all," Tony-B confessed,

"What do you want Tony, I hope you're not gonna start harassing me at my job!"

"No, I just wanted to talk to you," Tony-B said,

"Don't you think you said enough the other night?"

"I'm sorry about that, I guess I let my anger get the best of me,"

"What is it that you want Tony, it's my first day back and I have a ton of work on my desk!"

"I just wanted to tell you that I know it's my baby, and I wanna be in my baby's life and I don't want my baby calling nobody Daddy but me!"

"That's up to you Tony, I'm not trying to keep you from your child,"

"I thought you said that you regretted having my child!"

"I said that because of what kind of boyfriend and fiancée you were, I don't know what kind of Daddy you'll be, but I hope that last night was not an indication,"

"I wasn't a good boyfriend?" Tony-B asked, seemingly oblivious,

"If you were Tony, we'd still be together," Maya said with all of the energy that she could possibly muster,

"All right then, I hope dude makes you happy,"

"Believe me, he does,"

"How do you know that already Maya, y'all only been together for a week, or so you say,"

"True, but I'm happy as hell so far,"

"Well, that's good, I decided to go ahead and be with Torya since me and you ain't getting back together," Tony-B admitted,

"Congratulations, I wish you well, I have to go, I have a lot of work to do," Maya said,

"Maya, Maya before you go, I just wanna tell you something,"

"What Tony?"

"I still love you, I don't care who you with!"

"That's nice Tony, Bye!" Maya said before hanging up the phone,

***

10 HOT LIKE FIYAH!!!

It was Friday already, and the week had zoomed by, Maya was in the mirror brushing her hair, getting ready for her doctor's appointment, she smiled wide when she heard her cell phone ringing from the bedroom,

"Maya, your phone is ringing, I know it ain't nobody but that Maurice Boy, tell him I said, hey," Mama Anderson said from the kitchen,

"Yes ma'am," Maya said before answering the phone, "Hello?"

"Hey Baby Mama! How are you feeling this morning?" Maurice asked,

"I'm feeling okay, Oh, and Mama says hey,"

"Tell her I said hey, and tell her to put me a plate up," Maurice said with a smile,

"Okay, I'll tell her,"

"Hey, what time is your appointment?"

"It's at nine, I'm gonna be late for work, but I can still meet you for breakfast," Maya said,

"That's cool," Maurice said, "but I kinda wanted to go with you,"

"To the doctor, really?" Maya asked, pleasantly surprised,

"Yeah, is that okay?" Maurice asked,

"That's fine,"

"Okay, good! I'll be there in a little bit!"

"Okay Maurice, someone's buzzing in, I'll see you soon," Maya said before clicking over,

"Hello?"

"Hello, is this Maya Anderson?"

"Yes, it is,"

"Ms. Anderson, this is Ms. Tuggle, from The Pacific Bay Townhome Community,"

"Oh hello, how are you?"

"I'm doing fine, listen, I was calling to inform you that you were approved for a three-bedroom, two-bath town home, that's if you're still interested,"

"Yes, I'm still interested," Maya said, she was so excited that she could hardly contain herself,

"Good, will you be available to move in by the first of the month?"

"That's only two weeks away!"

"Is that too soon for you, Ms. Anderson?"

"No ma'am, that's fine,"

"Well, you'll need to come by for the initial walk through as soon as possible, will you be able to do that today, ma'am?"

"Yes, but it'll have to be sometime after ten, is that okay?"

"That's fine Ms. Anderson, I look forward to meeting you,"

Maya hung up the phone and screamed!

"Gal, what's wrong with you! Nearly scared me half to death!" Mama Anderson said as she rushed into Maya's room,

"I just got approved for a home in Pacific Bay!" Maya said as she leaned back and kicked her feet up in the air,

"I'm so proud of you! See what you can do if you just try!" Mama Anderson said as she hugged Maya,

Maya and Maurice sat the park before the sun rose, and she just couldn't stop smiling,

"Hey Baby Mama! You're all lit up!" Maurice said smiling back at her,

"Guess what!"

"What?"

"I just got approved for a home in Pacific Bay, and I move in the first of next month!"

"Oh Yeah!" Maurice said, and Maya could tell that he was excited, they ate fruit until it was time for Maya's doctor appointment, she and Maurice sat hand in hand in the waiting area of the doctor's office,

"Ms. Anderson?"

"Here I am," Maya answered as she kissed Maurice on the cheek, "I'll be back shortly,"

Maurice nodded and kept reading his magazine,

Maya followed the same procedure as last time, and as usual, Dr. Morris wanted to examine her, Maya didn't fall asleep this time, she was too excited,

"My own place, I can't wait to tell Tricia!"

Dr. Morris came into the room looking concerned,

"Maya, have you changed partners or anything like that lately?" he asked,

"No, as a matter of fact, that's what I wanted to talk to you about, I just started dating this new person and I was wonder-" Maya said,

"Maya, I wouldn't advise that right now," Doctor Morris said, cutting her off mid-flight,

"I wasn't talking about doing anything right now Dr. Morris, but if we did, how long do you think we should wait and could it hurt the baby?" Maya asked,

"You said that he's a new boyfriend?" Dr. Morris asked,

"Yeah," Maya answered hesitantly,

"And the two of you have never been intimate?"

"No, not at all, what's wrong, Dr. Morris?" Maya asked,

"When was the last time you were intimate, Maya?"

"Well, it's been over two weeks ago, is something wrong?"

"Are you guys still intimate?" Dr. Morris asked as he read over Maya's chart,

"No, you remember Tony, we were together for three years and engaged, but we broke up recently, what's wrong Dr. Morris, and what's with all the questions? You're scaring me!" Maya said tearing up,

"Maya, I've been your doctor since you were a teenager, and I hate telling you something like this, it's almost like talking to one of my own children," Dr. Morris face dripped with concern,

"What is it?" Maya asked, her heart was almost beating out of her chest,

"You have an infection, and it is sexually transmitted, it's called Chlamydia Trachomatis commonly known as chlamydia, it's curable, but none the less, you could be re-infected if you choose to be intimate with your ex again before he gets treated, or you could possibly infect your new boyfriend if you choose to have unprotected sexual contact with him, and this infection can harm your unborn child if it goes untreated,"

Dr. Morris said, Maya broke down as her head began to ache,

"You say I have what now?" Maya said as she placed her hand over her heart,

"Chlamydia, but Maya don't panic, it's curable! I'm going to prescribe antibiotics for you, just make sure you eat something first to keep your stomach from being upset, I'm also prescribing a vaginal cream for you, just in case you develop a yeast infection from the antibiotics, it'll be okay Maya, just take care of yourself, and other than that, you're doing just fine,"

Maya tried to get herself together, as Dr. Morris assuredly pat her on the shoulder,

"I want to see you back here in one week, make sure that you take the antibiotics as prescribed, that's very important, and take care of yourself," Dr. Morris said as he left the room so that Maya could get dressed,

Maya passed Nurse Patterson in the hallway, and she looked at Maya with a disgusted look on her face,

"It's some nasty people in this world, girl you don't know what people be spreading around nowadays!" The nurse said pretending to talk to another nurse, but she was looking directly at Maya,

Maya got her appointment card from the receptionist and left quickly, Maurice could tell instantly that something was wrong,

"Maya what happened, is the baby okay?"

"Just give me a minute to get myself together, do you know where Pacific Bay Townhomes are?" she asked,

"Yeah, I know where it is," Maurice answered,

Maya dialed a number on her cell phone, "Hello Sarah, do I have any messages?" she asked,

"Yes ma'am, Mrs. James left a message for you to call her ASAP, and Mr. Ronalds needs those files on his desk by Wednesday morning, for the presentation next Friday,"

"Okay, do I have anything scheduled for today?"

"No ma'am, nothing,"

"Okay, good, I'm gonna take the rest of the day off, I have a lot of work that I can finish from home, and I'll see you first thing Monday morning to prepare those files, I need you to get me everything that you have on the Alexander and Miles accounts,"

"Yes ma'am, I'll get right on it,"

"All right then Sarah, you have a great weekend and I'll see you first thing Monday morning," Maya said before she hung up the phone and laid her head against the window,

Maya loved the town home, it had a huge backyard that was

fenced in, and everything about it was perfect, Maya made arrangements to pick up her key in two weeks, she was quiet when she got back into the car,

"Since you're not going to work today, do you want to hang out with me at the shop?" Maurice asked,

"No, just take me back home, I have a lot of things that I have to do today," Maya said trying to keep her eyes from watering,

"Okay Maya that's enough, something happened at that doctor's office, and I wanna know what it is!" Maurice demanded,

"I just have a lot of things on my mind,"

"Maya don't act like that, tell me,"

"Maurice I wanna tell you but, I just…" Maya exploded into tears,

"Baby, what's wrong!" Maurice said as he reached over and grabbed her hand,

"It's not you, I just can't believe he did me like that!"

"Who, the doctor?"

"No, Tony!"

"Forget him, I said I would help you with the baby and I will!"

"It's not that,"

"What did he do, did he call and upset you while you were in the doctor's office?"

"No, it's worse than that!"

"What, Maya tell me!"

"Tony gave me a disease," Maya said and then she began to cry loudly,

"Oh, Baby," Maurice said, he pulled over and held her, he could tell that she was devastated, and he didn't know what else to do,

"I can't believe him, it seems like every day it's something, I was so dumb not to see all the stuff he was doing?"

"No Maya, he was just slick, that's all, when it was time for you to know, God showed you,"

"He could've hurt the baby, he doesn't even care! And oh my god, I could've given it to you if we had done anything in Trinidad," Maya said with tears meeting beneath her chin,

"Maya what exactly did the doctor say?"

"He said that I had chlamydia," Maya said in between sobs,

"Oh, okay, well that's not so bad, you could've gotten something that there's no cure for," Maurice said,

"That's what I mean, and then that stankin' ass nurse of his just had to have something to say, I can't stand her!"

"Forget her Maya, as long as you and the doctor know what's going on, Baby just calm down, let's just go to the pharmacy and get your medicine, don't let him bring you down," Maurice said as he hugged her tighter and kissed her on the forehead,

"I won't," Maya said through sniffles, "You still want to be with me?" she asked hesitantly,

"Yes, Baby Mama, and you were honest enough to tell me, that means a lot," Maurice said,

"I'm so sorry," Maya said,

"Baby Mama, you have nothing to apologize for, believe me it's okay," Maurice reassured her, "Now do you wanna go to the shop with me and see how your man be choppin' them up?"

"Yeah, but I have to go home and get my car first," Maya said,

Maurice drove back to Maya's mama's house, and he realized that he had left his phone at the doctor's office, so he had to go back and get it, Maya was trailing Maurice out of the doctor's parking lot when she saw Dr. Morris, he beckoned for her to come to him,

"Dr. Morris, what's going on, don't tell me any more bad news!" Maya said with tears in her eyes,

"No Maya, it's not bad news, I just wanted you to know that it was brought to my attention what Nurse Patterson said to you earlier, I have gotten several complaints about her and today was just the last straw! That was very unprofessional, and needless to say, you won't be having any more problems out of her again, at least not in my office! Well, I have to go and get a bite to eat, Will I see you next Friday?" he asked,

"I'll be there," Maya said,

Maya was glad that she took the day off, she and Maurice went into the shop and she sat beside Maurice's chair, she had no idea that he was so talented. His shop was decorated with his paintings and photographs. He introduced her as his Lady, and every now and then he'd walk over and kiss her on the forehead, Maya laughed so hard at him and his friends talking about each other that she almost forgot her problems, until her phone rang,

"Hello?" Maya said still laughing,

"Hey Baby, I stopped by your office today to surprise you, and your secretary told me that you wouldn't be in today, what did they say about my baby at the doctor's office?"

"Why are you concerned about it now?" Maya snapped,

"What do you mean?' Tony-B asked confused,

"Hold on," Maya said as she covered the phone, "Baby I have to take this outside, okay?" She whispered in Maurice's ear,

"Take care of your business, Baby," Maurice said as she exited the shop,

"I mean, where was your concern when you were giving us a fucking disease?" Maya said once she stepped outside,

"What in the hell are you talking about, I didn't give you nothing! You'd betta check with your boyfriend!"

"Boy please! You're the only one I've been with for the last three years, so now what!"

"I don't believe that! I don't know who you been with, and ain't nothing wrong with me!"

"Go to the doctor then Tony, because I don't owe you any lies!"

"I ain't going nowhere because I ain't got nothing! You need to find somebody else to blame that shit on!"

"And you need to stop sticking it in every woman you see!"

"Maya, I ain't got nothing!" Tony-B pleaded,

"Well, that ain't my problem no more, whatever you're infected with, you'll never get a chance to give it to me again!"

"I didn't the first time!"

"I'm not gonna go back and forth with you, I got my medicine, you ain't never gotta go to the doctor, just keep on spreading diseases until you rot the fuck off! You Bastard!" Maya said as she pressed the end button, hanging up in Tony-B's ear, then she turned her phone off and tossed it in her purse,

"Business?" Maurice asked when she came back into the shop,

"Nah, it's nothing, I'll tell ya about it later," Maya said,

"I hear ya Baby Mama!" Maurice said with a smile,

Maya spent most of the day at the shop with Maurice, it was three o'clock in the afternoon when she left the shop and decided to stop in and surprise Tricia at work,

"Mrs. James?"

"Yes?"

"Ms. Anderson is here to see you, shall I send her in?" her assistant asked,

"Yeah, go ahead," Tricia said still reading over her files,

Tricia was on the phone when Maya walked in, she held

up one finger and finished up her conversation,

"Yes, I'll need those papers signed and in my office first thing Monday morning, or I'm filing a motion to go to trial… all right… I'll see you then, first thing Monday, okay bye," Tricia said as she hung up the phone, "Hey Mommy!" Tricia said with a smile,

"Hey!" Maya said back,

"I've been trying to call you all day! Why didn't you go in today?"

"I went to the doctor and Maurice went with me,"

"You lying!"

"No, he really did,"

"What happened, you still didn't tell me why you didn't go to work,"

"Dr. Morris told me I had chlamydia," Maya spoke calmly to keep from crying,

"What the hell!" Tricia said as she shook her head in confusion,

"Yeah, but don't worry, he gave me some antibiotics, and I have a checkup appointment next Friday,"

"Are you okay?"

"Yeah, I am, Girl, and Tony had the nerve to call me and ask me how me and the baby was doing,"

"Oh, he's claiming it now?" Tricia asked sarcastically,

"Yeah, not that it means anything, I hung up on him,"

"You didn't!"

"Yes, I did!" Maya told Tricia about the conversation,

"You know, just when I think he can't sink any lower,"

"Forget him, I'm tired of letting him upset me," Maya said,

"Are you really okay, Maya?" Tricia asked again, she was worried about her friend,

"Yes, I have had enough of Anthony Bradford, Jr. to last me a lifetime!"

"I'm glad!" Tricia said relieved,

"How's the hubby and Lil' Man?"

"We are doing fine, we had a long talk,"

"You told him?"

"I had to, it was tearing me up inside!" Tricia confessed,

"You told him everything?"

"I told him as much as I could, and he surprised me, as he always does, he said that it's forgotten and he forgives me, and ever since I opened up to him, our sex life has been better than ever!"

"Ooh Girl! Too much information!" Maya laughed,

"Don't be jealous Maya!"

"After all this stuff that's happening to me, believe me
I'm not!"

"How long do you have to take your medicine?"

"It's just for three days," Maya said,

"That's not so bad,"

"Thank God! Dr. Morris is going to examine me again
Friday, and I almost forgot, I got approved for my townhouse in
Pacific Bay, and I move in on the first,"

"Girl, we have to celebrate!" Tricia said excited,

"What you got up for tonight?" Maya asked,

"I'm not sure but I really just wanna kick my feet up and
relax tonight,"

"Me too, but I have to do Mama's hair, I'll call you in
the morning if you're not busy, are we still on for tomorrow
morning?" Maya asked,

"Yeah, I almost forgot! I made us both an appointment
for nine o'clock,"

"Oh good, cause I'm long overdue!"

"Shoot look at me! I look like Iron-Man by the head!"

"Tricia you are sick! See you later!" Maya said, and she
laughed until she saw spots,

"Bye girl!"

***

Tony-B came straight home after work, Torya wanted to
surprise him with a candle-light dinner, she sat on the couch and
put on a sexy pose when she heard his car pull into the garage,
Torya was dressed in a pink silk negligée, with candles
illuminating the room and dinner was waiting on the table, she
became worried when she saw the look on his face,

"Baby, what's wrong?" She asked,

Tony-B walked up to her and grabbed her by the neck
and slammed her into the wall, Torya froze in place, too stunned
to move,

"Who the hell have you been fucking?" He asked as he
clinched his right hand into a fist with his other hand still
gripping her neck tighter and tighter,

"Nobody, Tony-B, nobody I promise!" Torya said
through gasps, she was having a hard time trying to scramble for
air,

"You a damn lie!" Tony-B roared, as he flung her across
the room like a rag doll, Torya felt her arm pop as she crashed
into the wall unit, she could feel it swelling as she coughed and

gasped for air, but before she could get her bearings, Tony-B ran over to her and picked her up again by her neck,

"I went to the doctor, and he told me that I had a fucking disease!" Tony-B gnarled through clenched teeth,

"Tony-B please, I haven't been with anyone but you!" Torya pleaded,

"You'd better tell me who you been fucking, Torya, and you'd better tell me right now!" His voice boomed,

"Nobody, I'm serious, I can't hardly handle you!" she admitted,

"That's what you say! But you better go to the doctor asap!" he demanded,

"Okay I will, please just don't hit me," Torya begged,

"You better take your ass straight to the damn doctor, do you hear me!" He said as he pulled her close so that they were nose to nose, his vice-like grip still tight around her neck,

"Okay, I'll go, I'll do anything, just don't hit me, please!" Torya said and when Tony-B released her neck, Torya heaved heavily as she fell to the ground, she didn't know whether to grab her neck, hold her arm, or to keep pleading, she was horrified, her mind flashed back to how loving and affectionate he was when they first started dating, tears began to flood her eyes, she was lost in the way that things used to be, but she was suddenly snapped to the present by the fury in Tony-B's voice,

"I can't believe you fucking burned me! I can't even stand to look at your disgusting ass! I'm going to bed!" Tony-B said as he stormed into the bedroom then slammed the door and locked it, Torya grabbed her arm and slowly stood to her feet, she was wobbly and light headed as she drug herself to the linen closet and grabbed a blanket and a pillow to spread on the couch, she trembled as she blew out the candles, she had a hard time emptying the now cold food into the trash with one hand, she was about to lie down when she noticed that her arm was triple its usual size and disfigured, Torya went into the kitchen and grabbed a pair of jogging pants and a T-shirt out of the dryer, after putting on her clothes she slipped on a pair of house shoes and grabbed Tony-B's car keys off of the table, she tipped-toed out of the door and rushed towards the car, Torya didn't know where she was going, but she was determined not to go over to Earl's house, after driving around for an hour, she was in so much pain that she ended up at the emergency room,

"Ms. Hughes, could you please tell us what happened to your arm?" The doctor asked,

"I was cleaning, and I slipped on the throw rug and fell against the entertainment center,"

"How did you get here?"

"I had to drive myself, my boyfriend is at work, I didn't want him to worry," Torya answered,

"And what about those scratches on your neck, and this bruise beneath your eye?" The doctor asked,

"My cat is always scratching me somewhere or another, and I slipped on that same rug and hit my eye on the door knob the other day, I wanted to get rid of the rug, right then, but my boyfriend likes it,"

"I think you need to get rid of that cat, that rug, and that boyfriend Ms. Hughes!" The doctor said with a frown,

"He didn't do this to me, my boyfriend doesn't hit me," Torya insisted,

"Uh, huh, that's what they all say, but most of the time it only gets worse," the doctor said rolling his eyes, "One day you'll get tired, I just hope he doesn't kill you, or you kill him before you do," The doctor said through sighs,

"I told you that he didn't do this to me!" Torya said, trying to convince the doctor,

"Whatever you say Ms. Hughes, I'm going to go and see what the x-ray says even though I can clearly tell that it's broken,"

And true enough it was, Torya pulled into the driveway about three in the morning, Tony-B was stretched out on the couch with his arms behind his head, Torya could tell that he was drunk, he had begun to drink more and more lately, and usually when he drank, he would get horny, Torya didn't even want to think about having sex with him, she was still tender from the last time,

"I guess you had to go and tell your boyfriend that he burned us, huh?" Tony-B said as he staggered to his feet, trying to brace himself for round two, Torya threw her hand in the air,

"Baby please, I've been at the hospital, that's all,"

"For what!" Tony-B barked,

"My arm is broken," Torya said as she lowered her head,

"I guess your boyfriend didn't like being burned," Tony-B said calmly as he laid back on the couch,

"It broke when I hit the entertainment center," Torya said waiting patiently for an ounce of remorse from Tony-B,

"Like I said, your boyfriend didn't like being fucking burned," Tony-B said, his tone was as cold as ice,

"I'm tired Tony, I'm going to bed now," Torya said

disappointed,

"Not before you take your ass in there and fix me something to eat, you're not!" Tony-B demanded,

"I can't, I'm in pain!" Torya pleaded,

"Then you shouldn't have burned me! I don't feel sorry for you, now take your one-armed ass in there and cook me something to eat before I break that other one for you!" Tony-B barked,

"Tony-B please, I'm tired, all I want to do is rest!" Torya begged,

"Are you still standing there running your motherfucking mouth?" Tony-B said as he leaped off the couch,

Torya found herself in the kitchen before she knew it, she fixed him a cheeseburger with some home cooked fries,

"See… it's amazing what you can do if you just put your mind to it," Tony-B said with a smug grin on his face as she placed his food on the coffee table,

"Can I get you anything to drink?" Torya asked, ignoring his snide comment,

"What the fuck do you think? I can't stand it when people ask me dumb ass questions!" Tony-B said as he sat up on the couch and pulled the coffee table closer to him,

Torya scurried to bring Tony-B a glass of soda on ice, and afterwards she undressed and got into bed, she tried to sleep but her eyes were wide open until the pain medicine kicked in, and by that time Tony-B had already entered her and was humping up and down, thrusting in and out as hard as he possibly could, but the medicine made her almost comatose, and after he finished he rolled off of her and threw her a quick, "Sorry,", before going into the bathroom to wash up, Torya turned over onto her side and let sleep consume her, but Tony-B woke her up early the next morning,

"Hey, you need to get your ass up and go to the doctor," he said,

"It's Saturday," she said, "But, let me call and see who's open today," she said before Tony-B could get upset, then she got out of bed and searched the Yellow Pages for a list of clinics and doctors who were open today,

"You'd better hope they are!" Tony-B barked, as Torya called different clinics frantically,

"We take walk-ins on Saturdays, but we close at twelve thirty," the receptionist on the phone said,

"Okay, I'm on my way," Torya said anxiously,

"Are they gonna see you today?" Tony-B asked from the dining room,

"Yes, I'm getting ready to leave now,"

"Hey, look here, see if they'll give you enough medicine for me, I don't need it, but I'll know for sure that you went if you bring back enough for me,"

"Okay, Baby I'll try," Torya said over her shoulder,

"Don't try dammit, just do it!" Tony-B yelled out as she walked out of the door,

Torya ended up at the emergency room again because the doctor's office wouldn't take her without medical insurance, but she was determined not to go back home without seeing a doctor, she just couldn't take anymore blows from Tony-B, and after numerous tests, the doctor at the emergency room informed Torya that she'd contracted, Gonorrhea, Pelvic Inflammatory Disease, Chlamydia, Trichomoniasis, and on top of everything else, a bladder infection, and hemorrhoids,

"Ms. Hughes, you really have to take better care of yourself! You were just here last night!" The doctor said as she glanced through her file,

"I will, I promise!" Torya agreed, "but can I talk to you off the record?" Torya asked,

"Sure, how can I help you?" The concerned doctor asked,

"My boyfriend doesn't want to come to the doctor, and it's going to cause problems if I don't bring enough medicine for him too," Torya confessed,

"These kinds of problems?" The doctor asked tapping Torya's turquoise cast with the ink pen that she held in her hand,

"I can't say, but will you please do this for me?" Torya pleaded, and the doctor could see the desperation in Torya's eyes,

"Alright Ms. Hughes, I'll do it this one time, but you have to take better care of yourself, fortunately, the infections and STD's that you've contracted are curable, I've also tested you for HIV, but you won't get those results until next Friday, this is a very serious matter, Ms. Hughes!" The doctor warned,

"I know! And I will take care of myself, I promise, thank you so much!" Torya said with tears in her eyes, she simply could not take another beating from Tony-B,

Dr. Cambridge wrote out the prescriptions, and she also gave Torya a prescription for vaginal cream, and a brown paper bag full of condoms,

"I mean it Ms. Hughes, you only get one body, so take

good care of it!" She insisted, "And be sure to come back for your
follow-up at the clinic in two weeks,"

"I will, and thank you so much," Torya said, and she broke out in
tears after the doctor left the room, but she couldn't focus on a HIV test
right now, she had to hurry home before Tony-B thought she was
cheating on him again,

***

Tony-B couldn't wait to call Ricky after Torya left,

"Hello?" Ricky answered, he sounded sleepy,

"Man, get off that damn gal and answer this phone!" Tony-B
joked,

"What's up Tony-B! What are you doing up so early, it's
Saturday morning! I thought you'd be knee-deep in something sweet at
this time of day," Ricky joked,

"Man, that's why I'm calling!" Tony-B reasoned,

"Why, what's going on?"

"You remember that gal we hooked up with the other day?"
Tony-B asked,

"Yeah, Uhm… Uhm… what's her name?" Ricky said,

"Donna," Tony-B said,

"Yeah, what about her?"

"Man, that bitch is hot!"

"I know, she was the bomb,"

"I ain't talking about that kinda hot! I mean she burnin'… like
for real!" Tony-B said,

"Straight up?"

"Yeah, Maya called and told me I gave her some shit, I ain't
hurting or nothing like that, but you know Maya, she ain't gonna lie
about nothing like that, and it's gotta be something to it because Cathy
and Sherry have been dodging my calls lately," Tony-B said,

"Damn, that's messed up! What about Old Girl?" Ricky asked,

"Who Torya?"

"Yeah?"

"Man don't worry about her, I beat the hell out of her and made
her think she gave it to me, she's at the clinic right now, I told her not to
come back without some medicine for me too!"

"Tony-B, you crazy ass hell! You betta stop puttin' your hands
on that damn gal, you know she little as fuck, you gonna mess around
and break her lil' ass in half!"

"Too late!" Tony-B laughed,

"No you didn't Tony-B! Alright, I bet you wouldn't have tried
that shit with Maya, she would've WWF'd your ass!" Ricky joked,

"Me and Maya didn't even get down like that! And I didn't mean to hurt her, all I did was slang her by the neck!"

"That's all, huh?" Ricky asked with a smirk,

"Yeah, and she flew across the room like a fuckin' airplane or something, I didn't even realize that I threw her that hard until she crashed into the wall unit and broke her damn arm!"

"For real Tony-B?" Ricky asked in disbelief,

"Hell yeah! She drove herself to the emergency room last night, and she came home this morning with a cast on her arm and everything!"

"Alright! You keep on damn fool, they gone lock your ass up!" Ricky warned,

"She ain't gonna tell nobody, she's too sprung! But I am gonna try and watch my temper though,"

"See that's why I'm single! I ain't got time for them kinda problems, and I told you to start wrapping it up when you mess with them random ass gals, but y'all dudes don't listen! I'll go and get checked out anyway though, make sure you call your boy back and tell me what they said,"

"I will, I have to call Chris too, we hooked up with the same bitch the day before yesterday!" Tony-B confessed,

"Yeah, please call him, cause that damn Linda is crazy as fuck! She is liable to kill him if he brings her anything!" Ricky said,

"You ain't never lied!" Tony-B said,

Tony-B picked up the phone to call Chris, but he hung it up as soon as Torya walked in,

"So… what did you burn us with?" Tony-B said with a sweet tone to his voice,

"The doctor told me that I had Gonorrhea, Chlamydia, Pelvic Inflammatory Disease, and some stuff called Trichomoniasis, she also said that I had a bladder infection and hemorrhoids, and she also gave me some medicine for a yeast infection," Torya said as she counted on her fingers, she avoided eye contact with Tony-B for fear of him fighting her again, but he never got off the couch,

"I see you've been a busy lil' slut," Tony-B said with a smirk on his face, but Torya knew better than to say anything back, she just lowered her head, "Did you get medicine for both of us, like I told you to?"

"Yeah, I got it…but I thought you told me that you

already went to the doctor?"

"Are you questioning me!" Tony-B roared as he jumped up off the couch and stood in her face with his fists balled up,

"No, I wasn't …I- I was just wondering, that-that's all," Torya said with a tremble in her voice,

"Get out of my damn face!" Tony-B said fanning his hand in the air,

"I'm sorry," Torya said as she cowered down,

"Uh-huh, and can I get you to fix me something to eat or are you just gonna keep standing there being sorry!" Tony barked,

***

Maya thought that Friday would never get here, Maurice pulled up ready to take her to the doctor, he was also very anxious to know what the doctor had to say, Wednesday night they had spent the night together and Maurice was so frustrated that he tossed and turned the whole night, and so did Maya,

Dr. Morris was glad to give Maya some good news,

"You are doing fine Maya, I personally see nothing wrong with you guys being intimate, just make sure that you protect yourself and the baby!"

"I think I'm gonna hold off until I have the baby, Dr. Morris, it's too much going on out there,"

"I agree, but before you go, I have to tell you this Maya,"

"Okay,"

"I didn't treat your old boyfriend, so you need to know that if you ever decide to be intimate with him again, there's a huge chance that you'll be re-infected," Dr. Morris said,

"I have a feeling that he'll be going to the doctor soon, I didn't tell him what I had, I just told him that he gave me something," Maya confessed,

"Like I said, if he's not treated then he can infect you all over again,"

"I don't intend to ever go down that road again, so you don't have to worry about that, Dr. Morris," Maya assured him,

"I won't worry, I just want you to protect yourself, no matter who your partner is," Doctor Morris instructed,

"I will, Dr. Morris, I will,"

Maya came into the waiting room smiling, Maurice saw her face then he smiled,

"We'll see you in four weeks Ms. Anderson, do you want a morning or evening appointment?"

"Morning,"

"Okay, let me see, we have an eight o'clock, is that okay?" The receptionist asked,

"That's fine,"

Maurice kissed Maya on the cheek as he pulled in front of her job,

"Five-thirty?" he asked,

"Five-thirty," Maya said with a smile,

Maurice got out of the truck and opened the door for her,

"See you later," Maya said as she pushed the entrance code to the building, Maya had two presentations today, and she was very pleased with how well they went, Maurice was waiting for her at exactly 5:30 P.M., Maya's boss caught up to her as she headed towards the front door,

"Maya?" he called out to her,

"Yes, Mr. Ronalds?"

"I just wanted to congratulate you on your presentations, I was knocked off of my feet!"

"Thank you," she said with a smile,

"Well, I'll see you Monday, and have a great weekend,"

Maya smiled as she got into Maurice's van,

"So, Sweet-Stuff, what do you wanna do for the weekend?" Maurice asked,

"I want to go to the furniture store and pick out some furniture, you know I move next week,"

"You want me to help you pick it out?" Maurice offered,

"Why not, if you pick furniture like you pick clothes then I'm sure I'll have nothing to worry about!" Maya joked,

"Dig that!" Maurice smiled,

Maurice and Maya spent hours picking out the furniture and then they went out to dinner, Maya wanted to go to the Summer-Twin Drive-in Movie Theater when they finished, now that they were free to be intimate, she suddenly became apprehensive, This would've been the first time in years that she would be intimate with anyone except Tony-B, Maurice had his own apprehensions to deal with, Tony giving Maya an infection brought back memories of his old girlfriend Kayla, before he met Maya, Kayla had totally succeeded in turning Maurice off of dating and he was content with being by himself forever. He was never one to rush into anything, he had been with Kayla for four years and they had a six-month-old son, things were going great, until he came home early one day and caught her in bed with her ex-boyfriend,

Maurice could still remember the way that his heart pounded when he walked into the house and heard his baby screaming, he ran upstairs to the baby's room and grabbed him then headed toward their bedroom to see if Kayla was all right when he heard her moaning, he remembered how he felt when the shock of it all almost caused him to drop the baby, Maurice held the baby tight in his arms and in a flash, he and the baby were gone, Maurice had time to go to the store and pick up milk, bottles, and diapers, and drive way to the other side of town before his cell phone rang,

"What the hell do you want?" Maurice spat when he saw that it was Kayla,

"You'd better bring me my baby! You bastard!" she yelled into the phone,

"What the hell do you mean your baby, he's my baby too!"

"Maurice I'm not about to argue with you, you need to bring me my baby and stop acting stupid!"

"Stupid! Stupid is when you leave your baby in the room screaming to the top of his lungs, just so you can have somebody ramming up in you, now that's stupid!"

"Bring me my baby Maurice, NOW!" Kayla screamed,

"You keep saying' your baby, but you are crazy as hell if you think I'm gonna let you mistreat my son!"

"Boy please! All you do is work and come home and go to sleep, you never take me nowhere, and you pay more attention to him than you do me!"

"That's my son!"

"No, he's not! You're so fuckin' stupid! Have you ever noticed that he doesn't look anything like you?" Kayla taunted,

"Kayla I swear, I've never hit a woman in my whole life, but if I find out that you played me like that, I'm gonna beat the hell out of you!"

"Whatever! You need to bring me my baby and come and get your shit out of my damn house! And don't come here trying to start anything either because the police are already here waiting on you!" Maurice swerved to keep from hitting an oncoming car, he was so distraught that he had to pull onto the side of the road, Maurice sat there in a daze, staring at Lil' Maurice, he had always wondered if he was indeed his, his Mama had even told him that it wasn't his baby, but he didn't want to believe it, he was still sitting inside his van rocking the baby to sleep when the police pulled up,

"Is there a problem?" The officer asked shining his light in Maurice's face,

"No, I'm just putting my baby to sleep,"

"Sir, we received a call that you kidnapped this baby,"

"No, up until a few minutes ago, I thought he was mine,"

"Well, I'm sure that we'll get this whole thing cleared up, but you're gonna have to give me the baby,"

"Okay officer, but can you trail me to the store, so I can get him some things before I go,"

"Sure, but the baby will have to ride with me," The officer said, he was about to handcuff Maurice, but he was so shocked by Maurice's kindness that he decided against it, this couldn't be the kidnapping monster that they spoke about on the radio,

"That's fine," Maurice went into the store and bought more diapers, cases of milk, clothes, pacifiers, toys, and bottles, he also bought a walker and a stroller. The bags filled both the back of Maurice's van and the backseat and trunk of the officer's patrol car,

"Man, you sure are a good one!" The police officer said while closing the trunk,

"I need one more thing from you," Maurice said,

"What is it?"

"I need you to stay here while I get my things from the house, all I want is my clothes, and my photography equipment, she can have the rest,"

"Believe it or not, I know how it is, I'll even help you pack!" The officer said sympathetically,

When Maurice and the police officer pulled up, there were police cars everywhere, the police officers rushed towards Maurice drawing their guns and nightsticks, when the officer stopped them,

"It's not a kidnapping, it's just a big misunderstanding, the baby is right here in my car, I have the baby right here!" The officer said,

"Oh, okay, I guess we can leave then," The other officer shrugged,

"Yeah, I got it covered," The officer insisted,

The other officers looked at each other and shrugged their shoulders, then one by one, they left the scene, Kayla snatched the baby from the officer's arms and hugged him tight, then she gave him to her ex-boyfriend,

"We want to press charges against him for stealing our baby!" Kayla said,

"No one's going to jail here ma'am, and if I were you, I would simmer down before I take you in for filing a false report, do you want that?" He asked,

"No sir," Kayla said humbly,

"He's just going to get his things out of your house and then you people can go on with your lives,"

"Don't let him take my stereos, or my TVs!" Kayla said storming up behind him,

"Ma'am I'm gonna have to ask you to step back," The officer said blocking Kayla from following Maurice into the house,

Maurice ignored Kayla as he walked into the house, He loaded his things in the garbage bags that he also picked up from the store, he grabbed his cameras, his tripods and camera cases and took them to his van, Kayla stepped in front of him just as he was walking outside,

"I bought those!" She said trying to snatch his tripods out of his hands, Maurice didn't even have the energy to fight with her, he just dropped them on the ground and kept walking,

"Ma'am, if I have to ask you to step back one more time, I'm gonna be forced to place you under arrest for disorderly conduct," the officer warned,

"He's trying to take the stuff that I bought!" Kayla yelled,

"Lady, this man just spent almost three thousand dollars on stuff for your baby! I can't believe you're acting like that,"

"What stuff?" Kayla asked,

"Ma'am could you step outside with me and assist me in unloading this stuff out of my car, so that I can go home to my wife and kids?" the officer said exasperated,

Kayla and the officer grabbed three and four bags at a time while her now new boyfriend and Lil' Maurice watched,

"Hey," Kayla's ex said walking towards the van, Maurice didn't acknowledge him, he just kept loading his things into the van, it was too much for him to see another man holding his child, so he turned away,

"Hey Man, I didn't know that she did it like that! I've been out of town for almost 6 months, and all of a sudden, she calls me up out of the blue and told me that this was my baby, she even sent me a picture, I couldn't believe how much he looked like me, I just got here early this morning, But she told me that you two had split up, we're supposed to get married next week, I got the rings and everything, that's the only reason I came back here, Man I swear I didn't know anything about this,"

"It's all right, I just need to put as much distance as possible between me and this place, I just wish she would've told me he wasn't my son!" Maurice said, still trying to make sense of it all,

"Man, you mean to tell me you just found that out?"
Orlando asked, surprised,

"Yeah," Maurice said,

"And you still bought him all of this stuff?" Orlando
asked,

"Yeah, until a few hours ago, he was mine, and he didn't
ask to be here,"

"That's messed up! She told me that you knew he wasn't
yours, and that's why you guys broke up!"

Maurice just shook his head, he fought back tears as he
loaded the last of his things into his van then closed the sliding
door to his brown minivan,

"Can I just hold him one last time?" Maurice asked
Orlando, it almost killed Maurice to have to ask another man if
he could hold his own son,

"Sure, here you go, I just can't believe that she did you
like that!" Orlando said handing the baby over to Maurice,

"By the way, I'm Orlando," he said extending his hand
to shake Maurice's, but Maurice was too preoccupied with
hugging and kissing Lil' Maurice to shake Orlando's hand,

"I love you so much!" Maurice whispered into the
baby's ear and kissed his cheek,

"Don't worry, I'll take real good care of him," Orlando
said as he reached over and rubbed the baby's back, Maurice
felt like he'd just been slapped in the face, then Lil' Maurice
placed both of his hands on the sides of Maurice's face and gave
him a big wet kiss and called him, 'Da-Da,' like he always did,
Maurice's head started pounding and his knees felt like they
were about to give out,

"Take him, go on and take him, I have to get out of
here!" He whispered pushing the baby into Orlando's arms, just
as Kayla and the officer walked back outside,

"Don't let him hold my damn baby!" Kayla barked,

"Shut the hell up, he was just saying' goodbye! We need
to talk! Bring your ass on in this damn house!" Orlando said,
causing Kayla to stop in her tracks, her mouth dropped, and she
covered her chest with her hands,

"Were gonna leave you folks to tend to that little one,"
The officer said patting Orlando on the shoulder, by that time,
Maurice had gotten into the van and started it up,

"Be strong, be strong, be strong!" Maurice told himself
over and over again, as Kayla and Orlando headed into the

house, with Orlando still holding the baby,

"Look fella, you did the right thing, and things are going to go well for you because you conducted yourself like a real man!" The officer said as Maurice nodded and wiped his tears, "And besides, I have a feeling that I'll be coming back here real soon, he'll start beating on her before long, I can already see it in him, take care of yourself son, it'll get easier over time," the officer said before walking away,

Maurice remembered that long drive home from North Carolina, he thought back to how he felt when he stopped at a service station and noticed that the baby's t-shirt and his favorite toy was still laying on the front seat next to his cameras, he remembered holding the baby's clothes tight against his chest and smelling them, Maurice had never cried so much in his life, not even at his grandmother's funeral, and to make matters worse, a week after that terrible fiasco, Maurice ended up at the clinic because Kayla had given him Gonorrhea,

"I ain't never going back there, I don't care what she says!" Maurice yelled,

"Never going back where Baby, you almost slept through the whole movie, are you okay?" Maya asked,

"I am now," Maurice said as he reached for Maya's hand,

Maurice left North Carolina, and never looked back, he calculated in his mind that Lil' Maurice would be about four now, and he still wasn't able to throw away the little T-shirt and the toy, they still sat in a box in the top of his closet, Maurice started a conversation with Maya to ease his aching mind,

"Maya, do you have any tattoos?" he asked,

"Yeah, I have one,"

"I didn't know that, where is it?"

"It's on my left shoulder blade,"

"How long have you had it?"

"For about two years now, Tricia and I have the same one,"

"I got three," Maurice said,

"Three?" Maya asked,

"Yeah, I got this one on my twentieth birthday, and I got this one…" Maurice lifted his shirt and turned around, "when I turned twenty-five, and this one…" He said as he turned back around to face her, "it's my favorite," Maurice said, referring to the tattoo on his chest, it was a man with long dreads dancing, and it read, "Give me Reggae 'til I die!"

"I like your tats," Maya said with a smile,

"Turn around so that I can see yours," he asked,

Maya turned around and pulled her shirt down, Shivers rushed up and down her spine as Maurice gently traced his fingertip over the butterfly encircled in grapes and grapevines that had her name written in gothic letters beneath it,

"This is unique, does it have a meaning, or did you just see something that you liked?"

"I designed it myself, the grapes represent growth and the butterfly represent change," Maya said,

"That's deep Maya, I like that," Maya turned to face him, but she smiled and looked down, "Maya can I ask you something?" he asked,

"I guess so," she said still blushing,

"What made you wanna be with somebody like Tony-B?" Maurice asked,

"I had a feeling you were gonna ask me that sooner or later,"

"I'm serious Maya, I wasn't gonna ask you, but I just need to know,"

"Well, believe it or not, I thought he was a nice person, of course that was before he transformed into The Bar-B-Q King!"

"I've known him all of my life and he didn't used to be like that, but he's always been a playa, or at least that's what he thought," Maurice said,

"Yeah, but I didn't know that, it's kind of hard to explain, I fell for him, but then he started to change into this thing, or maybe I just took off my rose colored glasses, and finally saw him for who he really was all along,"

"I know about those, they can be blinding sometimes," Maurice confessed,

"Tell me about it,"

"Well, enough about him, tell me about you, I wanna know what makes Ms. Maya tick,"

"I wouldn't even know where to start," Maya admitted,

"Try at the beginning," Maurice said,

Even though Maya was nervous and uneasy talking about herself, she let Maurice inside of her world, she found herself hesitating when she talked about her likes and dislikes,

"I know that you like poetry," he said,

"Yes, I even write when I have the time,"

"Why didn't you ever read any at those parties?" he asked,

"Well, one reason was because Tony hates poetry, so I

would just write them in my journals," Maya said,

"Have you ever recited in front of anyone?" he asked,

"I used to, but not in years…" Maya confessed,

"See that's what I like about you, you're so different from any woman I've ever met,"

"I feel the same way about you,"

"I'm just an average guy,"

"No, you're far from average, you are taking the time to know me, to explore me, to see what I like and dislike,"

"That's because I'm so fascinated by you, Maya, I always have been…" Maurice admitted,

"Really?"

"Yeah, but can I ask you something else?"

"Go ahead,"

"Could you tell me what made you even give me a chance?" Maurice asked,

"Well, I always liked you, but I was with him, and I didn't think it was right to talk to one of his friends,"

"I felt like that too, that's why it took me so long to say something to you,"

"What made you finally say something?"

"Well, when I saw you in the hotel, I just couldn't help myself,"

"See that's what I'm talking about, I like the way that you don't let yourself be tangled up by pride or by what people might think about you, and I like the fact that you're real, you don't try to be something you're not," Maya said,

"Okay, that's cute, you told me what you like about me, now tell me what finally made you decide to talk to me,"

"Well, okay," Maya blushed, "I decided to talk to you because… you're gonna think it's silly," Maya blushed,

"No, I won't, tell me,"

"Okay, I decided to talk to you because I always thought that you were a gentleman, and…" Maya hesitated,

"Come on, don't stop now!"

"I like the way you look at me, and the way that you…the way you say my name, there I said it!" Maya confessed,

"The way I say your name?" Maurice asked laughing,

"Yeah, you sing it almost," Maya smiled,

*****

Tony-B stepped out of the shower and wrapped his towel around his waist; he sat on the couch and looked around, his house had a dull feel to it, nothing like the vibrance that Maya had brought to it, and what made matters worse was the fact that Torya was nowhere near the housekeeper that Maya was, and he had to stay on her constantly just to keep the house cleaned,

"I wish I would've known that the bitch couldn't cook and can barely clean, before I broke up with Maya! But I guess everything tastes good when your dick is hard!" Tony-B thought, he could feel his manhood swelling, so he grabbed it and squeezed hard, "Calm down Boy! You're the main reason I'm in the fucked-up situation that I'm in now!" he said, Tony-B thought about the last time that he and Torya had sex, and she had been on the rampage ever since he'd accidentally called her Maya while she was pleasuring him, "Now I have to almost take it from the bitch just for her to give me some, imagine that!" He said out loud as he slammed his empty glass against the wall,

Tony-B opened a foil pack and snorted a few lines of cocaine, he wiped his nose with the back of his hand then laid his head back on the couch to relax, but when he closed his eyes all he could see was Maya's face, he fantasized about the first time they made love, he could still feel himself deep inside of her, he could still see the look on her face, and hear the sounds that escaped her lips whenever she was just about to climax, he smiled when he thought about the funny way she bit down on her bottom lip when pleasure took her over, and he wished a million times that Torya had the same kind of climactic explosions that Maya had, the kind that wet up the whole bed, the phone rang interrupting Tony's joyful memories,

"Yeah!" He said rudely as he snatched the phone off the hook and placed it on his ear,

"Mane, what's wrong with you?" Ricky asked,

"Aw what's up Ricky, I thought you were somebody playing on the damn phone,"

"Damn Mane, you got them kinda problems?" Ricky asked,

"Hell yeah!" Tony-B said as he took a deep breath,

"Who is it, some broken-hearted ass gal, who confused love with a good fuck?" Ricky joked,

"Mane, I don't even know, and I'm glad I don't, cause I'd probably be in jail by now, if I did!" Tony-B confessed,

"I heard that! Where's that fine ass gal of yours?" Ricky asked,

"Mane, don't even mention that crazy ass gal, she's out running errands, and I hope she stays gone all damn day!" Tony-

B said as he rested his head in his hand,

"It ain't like that is it, Tony-B?"

"Hell yeah, she gets on my damn nerves! Always nagging and bitching! Constantly trying to be all up under me and shit!"

"That's too bad, it's a lot of guys out here who'd be glad to take her off your hands," Ricky joked,

"Well, they can have her ass!" Tony-B said with everything he had,

"Aw mane! That's fucked up, oh yeah, before I forget, I went to the doctor yesterday and ya boy ain't got shit, not even a damn cold!" Ricky said,

"Straight up?" Tony-B asked, surprised,

"Hell yeah, ya boy got a clean Bill of Health, so it had to be one of them gals you and Chris tossed in the air the other day, did you get that taken care of?" Ricky asked,

"Yeah, I'm straight, I told you, I made her ass get enough medicine for me and her,"

"Did you tell Chris yet?" Ricky asked,

"Aw shit! It's been so much going on, I forgot to call and tell him!" Tony-B confessed,

"Well, y'all betta be careful out here! These gals out here now-a-days got shit to make your dick bend backwards!" Ricky said laughing,

"Mane, tell me about it! Look, let me get up off this damn phone, I just heard her nosey ass pull up and I don't feel like answering a whole bunch of who-you-talking-to-ass questions!" Tony-B said with a deep long breath,

"Mane, you need to cut that shit out!" Ricky laughed, but Tony-B couldn't find the humor in it,

"Alright Mane, I'll holla at you later," Tony-B said,

***

Linda was on a strict mission, she sped home after dropping her children off at her cousin Mookie's house for the weekend, when she walked into her apartment, Chris was lounging on the couch watching television with his feet resting on her coffee table, which Linda hated, she rolled her eyes at him and swiped his feet on the floor,

"What the fuck is wrong with you, Linda, and where the hell have you been?" he asked as he leaned forward and adjusted his jeans,

"Fuck that!" Linda said as she stood in front of him with her hands on her hips, "The question is… where the fuck have *you* been, and I do mean LITERALLY!"

"What are you talking about?" Chris asked, confused, "I been in the damn house all day, why are you trippin'?"

"I'm not talking about today, I mean period! Because I just left the damn doctor…"

"So!" Chris said with a shrug, "What does that have to do with me?"

"You'll see…" Linda said as she attempted to walk off, but Chris jumped up and grabbed her by the arm and swung her around so that she faced him,

"What do you mean, I'll see… what's going on?" he asked, but she snatched her arm from his grasp and put her hands on her hips,

"You got me so fucked up!" She said as she pointed her finger in his face,

"Get your damn finger out of my face," he said as he swiped her hand, "Why you trying to clown instead of just talking to me like a grown ass woman!"

"Clown? I'll show you a fucking clown," Linda said as she attempted to walk off again, but this time Chris snatched her by the arm and pushed her hard against the wall, as they stood nose to nose,

"I've been at home all day and you wanna come in here clowning, ain't cooked shit or nothing, just clowning, and for what? Just full of fucking drama all the damn time…" Chris said as he released her and stepped to the side,

"Okay… I'll go cook for you," Linda said calmly, as she waltzed into the kitchen, Chris' mind was spinning, he was racking his brain trying to figure out why she was so angry at him, he shrugged it off, rubbing his head and was just about to sit comfortably on the couch when,

SMASH!

The glass casserole dish exploded against the wall behind the couch, shattering into a million pieces,

"What the fuck is wrong with you!!!" Chris yelled,

"You're what's wrong with me, bastard, and you dying today!" Linda yelled back,

"Baby! Baby! Baby!" Chris pleaded, when he noticed the gigantic butcher knives that Linda held in each hand, "Baby, put them knives down!"

"Why are you running?" She asked, "Stop running around the table like you scared, you weren't running from those nasty ass bitches, so don't run from me!" Linda said as she suddenly charged towards him and plunged the knife forward, but Chris ducked and jumped over the dining room table,

"You crazy as hell if you think I'm gonna stand there and let you stab me!" Chris said, as he stood on the other side of the table breathing hard,

"You ain't gotta let me do a motherfuckin' thing! Calling me a clown, but at least if you were gonna cheat, you could've used protection! You nasty son-of-a bitch!" Linda screamed as she grabbed a drinking glass and hurled it at his head,

Chris ducked, letting out a high-pitched squeal as it shattered against the wall and a tiny shard of glass slashed his ear, "You crazy bitch!" he said before he could catch himself when he touched his ear and saw the red specks of blood on his fingertips,

"Bitch?!? I got your bitch, and you ain't seen crazy yet… but you will, I promise you that!" Linda said calmly as she stood in front of the front door with a butcher knife in each hand,

"Linda calm down, just think! Why would I need protection, when you're the only one I'm fucking!" he reasoned,

"So, I guess I just caught gonorrhea up out of the air then, right?" Linda asked,

"Hell, I don't know, crazy shit's been known to happen!" Chris reasoned, not knowing what else to say, he was too busy concentrating on those knives in Linda's hands, he knew how quick and crafty she was, and he also knew that if he slipped up, she'd be on him like a duck on a June bug,

"If that's true, then let's sit down like adults and have a real conversation, like you said," Linda said calmly, but Chris knew better, she'd gotten him like that, before,

"Put the knives down first!" Chris demanded,

"I'm gone put them down… once I get through with them," she said as she pulled hard on her cigarette with the knife still in her hand,

"I'm tired of running around this damn table Linda! You already cut my damn ear," Chris said as he touched his ear again and saw more blood on his fingers,

"Fuck that lil' bitty ass scratch on your ear, had me all at the fucking clinic, I'm gonna carve my name in your ass as soon as I catch you," Linda assured him,

"See! This is the type of shit I'm talking about…" Chris said as he stepped around the table quickly when Linda lunged at him again,

"I don't understand why you running? You didn't run from that nasty ass, disease carrying bitch that you fucked!" Linda said as she proceeded to chase him around the table,

"Maybe because she didn't have a damn knife in her hand!"

Chris joked, and regretted it instantly when Linda's eyes turned bloodshot red,

"Oh, so you think this shit is a fucking game, a big ass joke, okay, okay… you just stay right there," Linda said before grabbing a dinner platter and slinging it across the table in one swift motion, barely missing Chris' head before it shattered into the wall,

"You crazy! Just crazy!" Chris yelled,

"I'm crazy?" Linda asked in disbelief, "You burned me, but I'm the one that's crazy? Okay…" Linda said with a nod,

"That's what I said, and to be honest, I'm sick of this shit!" Chris said still running around the table,

"Oh! Now you want to be honest, after giving me a fuckin' disease, and then you want to call me crazy?"

"I didn't say all that, but…"

"But what!" Linda interrupted him, "You're calling me crazy, ME! The Mother of your kids! The one who's been putting up with you and your bullshit for all of these fucking years?"

"Why don't I just leave then, that way you won't have to deal with me or my bullshit!" Chris yelled across the table,

"Oh, you gonna leave, but not the way you came in this bitch," Linda said calmly,

"Linda, all I was trying to say was that maybe we just need to separate for a while, you know, take a break, maybe we just need some space, at least until we can get ourselves together, I don't like all of this arguing all the damn time," Chris tried to reason,

"You should've thought about all of that before you went out and fucked all of those nasty hoes," Linda said before pulling hard from her cigarette, and Chris was amazed that she didn't cut herself as she held the knife and the cigarette in the same hand, "but I tell you what…" Linda said as she took another hard pull from her cigarette and blew a huge puff of smoke into the air, "I'll make a deal with you, if you can make it to that front door before I can go and get my pistol, then you can have all the damn space you need," Linda said as she gently placed both of the knives on the table and then took off running towards the bedroom,

Chris wasn't sure if she was really going to get her gun, but to be safe he bolted towards the front door, he heard and felt the first two shots whizzing past his head right before he snatched the front door open, the booms were thunderous, sending his adrenaline level through the roof, and as quick as lightening, he jumped the first flight of stairs and leaped over the railing, Linda was dead on his heels, she jumped the stairs and leaped over the railing just as effortlessly as he did, running behind him and firing wildly, people screamed and ran for cover, but Linda was too mad to even notice them, she stopped firing only after she realized that the gun was empty, she unloaded and pulled another clip from her pocket and reloaded before she caught the lit cigarette between her first two fingers that had dangled from the corner of her mouth the whole entire time, she pulled hard on her cigarette then calmly walked back up the stairs to her apartment, constantly looking back and leaning over the railing to see if she could still see him, she held the loaded pistol in one hand, and finished her cigarette with the other one, and after she finished her cigarette, she flicked it over the railing, "Scary bitch, calling me crazy, but look who's running!" Linda grumbled as she stormed into her apartment and slammed the front door which had a huge bullet hole right in the center of it,

***

"Shit!" Chris whispered, exhaling deeply, looking down and around from the top of one of the tall trees in the thick woods located in the back of Linda's apartment complex, "This shit used to be way easier when I was younger," he said to himself as he climbed down slowly, he was kind of winded once his feet finally touched the ground, but his adrenaline level was still at an all-time high, "I need to see if they'll let me use the phone at the corner store so I can call Tony-B and tell him to come and pick my ass up!" he said as he eased quietly through the woods, he was ducking and dodging in the shadows, paranoia gripping his whole body, he was finally beginning to calm down, when he heard a strange noise behind him, he took off, running as fast as his legs would take him to the corner store which was only a few blocks away, Chris was in shock and could not believe that Linda had actually shot at him, but he was so relieved that he had lost her in the woods, by the time he made it to the store, he was so winded, that he had to lean on the back wall, he took a few deep breaths, and pushed himself to keep going, once he made it around to the front entrance, he leaned on the wall and took a deep breath, "I must've ran too fast cause I'm dizzy as hell!" Chris said, panting as he sat on the stoop in front of the store and rested his head in his hands,

"Hey Mane, you alright?" the store owner asked as he stepped outside of the store,

"Yeah, I'm straight," Chris said trying to catch his breath,

"Mane, you're bleeding!" The man said as he pointed to Chris' chest,

"What, where?" Chris said as he tried to stand to his feet, but he was too tired, he looked down, and saw that his once icy-white T-shirt was now soaked red,

"You need to go to the hospital!" the man said,

"I can't believe that crazy bitch shot me!" Chris mumbled,

"Who?" the man asked as he looked around,

"I'm so cold…" Chris said as he leaned back and rested his head on the brick wall behind him, he hugged himself as he felt a huge chill,

"Hey! Hey! Stay with me now, I'm calling the ambulance right now!" the man yelled as he placed his hand on Chris' shoulder and shook him gently,

"I'm so dizzy," Chris said weakly as he began to see spots,

"Hey, wake up Mane! C'mon! Stay with me!" the man yelled, shaking him harder, but Chris didn't respond, his body went totally limp as his eyes rolled slowly to the back of his head as everything went black…

ABOUT THE AUTHOR

 **D**eJuan **K**ight is a well-known local poet and writer who has spent decades writing and performing in the extensive, competitive, no-nonsense, and ultra-talented Open-Mike arenas in Memphis, Tennessee where she was born and raised. Her writings give a unique bird's eye view into real life circumstances. Her true-to-life characters are unapologetic, relatable and have both heroic and villain-like qualities that will pull you into her action packed, drama-filled novels as if the characters were right next to you. In addition to her writing career, she is also a Motivational Speaker, who has facilitated countless workshops that use poetry to motivate and activate the minds and voices of the youths, as well as adults to empower their minds, discover their strengths and use their voices not just on stage but in life as well. When DeJuan Kight is not creating, reading, or writing, she enjoys spending time with her friends and family.